JAYNE ANN KRENTZ

writing as Stephanie James

Worth the Risk

Silhouette Books

Published by Silhouette Books
America's Publisher of Contemporary Romance

SILHOUETTE BOOKS

WORTH THE RISK

Copyright © 2002 by Harlequin Books S.A.

ISBN 0-373-21801-X

The publisher acknowledges the copyright holder of the individual works as follows:

THE CHALLONER BRIDE
Copyright © 1987 by Jayne Ann Krentz

WIZARD
Copyright © 1985 by Jayne Ann Krentz

This edition published by arrangement with Harlequin Books S.A.

® and TM are trademarks of Harlequin Books S.A., used under license. Trademarks indicated with ® are registered in the United States Patent and Trademark Office, the Canadian Trade Marks Office and in other countries.

Visit Silhouette at www.eHarlequin.com

Printed in U.S.A.

CONTENTS

THE CHALLONER BRIDE

Chapter 1

There was undoubtedly an approved manner in which one went about hiring a professional soldier of fortune, but Angie Morgan didn't know what it was. The years she had put in after college doing personnel work hadn't provided any experience in that area. An engineer or a secretary or a new department head she could have managed with aplomb. This was a whole different matter.

At least she wasn't starting from scratch, she told herself as she watched Flynn Sangrey cross the floor of the open-air hotel lounge. She knew something about the man she was thinking of hiring. Enough, for example, to realize that she preferred the term ''soldier of fortune'' to the more realistic label of ''mercenary.''

Which was not to say that she knew him all that well. Two evenings spent sharing a couple of margaritas while listening to a combo in a Mexican hotel nightclub hardly constituted an extensive relationship, let alone a job interview. On the other hand how well did a woman really want to know a man she was paying for protection? Surely it was better to keep such acquaintances on a businesslike level. When her business in Mexico was concluded, she wasn't likely to see Sangrey again. From all indications he inhabited a much different world from her own. Two ships passing in the night.

She wasn't absolutely positive that he made his living as a mercenary. Her conclusion might simply be the result of an overactive imagination. She had, after all, very few hard facts. What convinced Angie she wasn't far off base was the fact that Sangrey had said nothing to counter her obvious assumptions, not even when she'd deliberately tried to give him an opening to do so. Actually, he'd said almost nothing concrete about himself, leaving her to draw her own conclusions.

It wasn't easy to ask him personal questions; not after knowing him for only two days. He had been gravely polite since he'd introduced himself, but somehow he'd made it clear he didn't invite detailed probing. He was on vacation.

Sangrey threaded his way through the maze of candlelit tables, moving with the kind of supple masculine grace that spoke of coordination and strength. It occurred to Angie that a mercenary's life must be a hard one, hard enough to keep the body of a man who was clearly on the far side of thirty-five in shape.

He was dressed much as he had been for the past couple of days, in khaki shirt and dark twill slacks. The leather belt that circled his waist was utilitarian looking and rather worn. The leather moccasins he wore appeared to have been around awhile.

There was something in Sangrey's dark gaze that said he'd been around awhile, too. Angie had the impression that this man had seen some aspects of life that most people would prefer to ignore or forget. Only to be expected in his line of work, Angie told herself firmly. Julian would probably find him fascinating.

The rest of Sangrey went along with the image created by the tough, functional leather belt and the austere khaki shirt. He had probably never been very good looking, even before life had etched the hardness on his features. But tonight the flickering candlelight and the pale gleam of the stars overhead seemed to emphasize the fierce line of his nose and jaw. There was an aggressive, predatory element in Flynn Sangrey but Angie had the feeling it was well controlled. Everything about the man seemed controlled.

Maybe too controlled.

He hadn't even made a pass at her during the past two days.

Not that she wanted him to, Angie told herself instantly. After all, she was here in the Mexican Caribbean on business. She was definitely not interested in picking up a tall, dark stranger for the purpose of having a vacation fling. It was just vaguely disappointing that this particular tall, dark stranger hadn't seemed interested in picking her up, either. At least not for a quick, passionate fling. From the moment he had introduced himself two evenings ago, Angie had gained the distinct impression that Flynn Sangrey was only looking for a little casual companionship.

Perhaps he wouldn't be interested in a small job, either, she thought worriedly. The man was clearly treating himself to a vacation.

"Good evening."

Sangrey's voice was heavy, rather like the dark leather belt and the moccasins. Angie had grown to like it during the past couple of days. She smiled up at him as he took the chair beside her.

"How was the diving?" she asked, knowing that he had spent the afternoon in scuba gear.

"Unbelievable. The water around here is like crystal, and the fish swim along the reefs with you as if you're one of them. Another world." Flynn broke off to give his order to a passing waiter. Then he turned back to Angie, his dark gaze moving over her with polite, controlled interest. "How about you? Get that book finished?"

Angie shook her head, telling herself wistfully that his merely polite interest was probably generated by the fact that she wasn't Sangrey's fantasy of a vacation fling. Perhaps he had been hoping for something a little more exciting—maybe a flashy blonde who tended to spill out of her bikini.

Angie knew she was reasonably attractive, but she was definitely not flashy. Her dark brown hair was parted in the middle and coiled into a neat knot at the nape of her neck. It was a vaguely old-fashioned style that highlighted the odd blue-green color of her eyes.

Angie knew for a fact she was considered intelligent, hardworking and reliable. When she'd worked in personnel, she'd had access to all the evaluation forms, including her own. Since she'd gone to work for her uncle, nothing appeared to have changed. He seemed quite satisfied with her performance on the job. Angie wondered on a note of humor if the recommendation would impress Sangrey.

Her clothes were good but not trendy. She had a preference for a certain rakish look characterized by bold colors: black and white and red. Tonight she was wearing an off-the-shoulder, gauzy white cotton dress that was quite suitable for a trip to Mexico. The belt was the most striking feature of her attire. It was wide, neatly defining her small waist, and set with real garnets and gold filigree.

The belt was a clue, although the average person wasn't aware of it, to a deeply hidden streak of passion that ran through her nature like a fissure of gold through dark marble. On the surface, the overall image was cool and reserved, and Angie preferred to keep it that way. She didn't really trust that vein of temperamental gold she sensed within herself. It seemed a little alien to her, not fully understood or integrated into what she considered her real personality. A part of her didn't quite accept that hidden fissure; didn't know what to make of it. She sensed it could be dangerous, but by and large it didn't interfere with her daily life.

"I didn't get a chance to finish the book because I had a message from Alexander Cardinal," Angie announced as she picked up her drink.

Sangrey regarded her with polite interest. "The man you've been waiting to hear from? The one who lives on the island?"

"Uh-huh." Angie sipped the margarita, preparing to make her pitch. She had decided this afternoon to ask Sangrey if he would be interested in working for her. But she found herself somewhat nervous about actually broaching the question. "He sent word here to the hotel that he would see me tomorrow evening. He's invited me to dinner on the island. The message said he'd send a boat to pick me up."

Sangrey raised his eyebrows in mock admiration. "Classy. You move in the right circles, Angie."

"I explained yesterday that the circles aren't mine," she reminded him dryly. "My employer has set up this whole thing. Uncle Julian was supposed to make this trip himself. If he hadn't gotten sick at the last minute, I wouldn't even be here."

"Sounds to me like you've lucked out. A free trip to Mexico and dinner with a man who owns an island. Every woman's dream."

For the first time since she had met him, Angie found herself a little irritated with Flynn Sangrey. She didn't care for the faint derision in his tone. "Believe it or not, I have other things I'd rather be doing than sitting here in a hotel waiting on the convenience of a man who gives me very unpleasant chills down my spine!''

Sangrey lowered his lashes slightly, narrowing his dark gaze. ''What makes him so unpleasant? From what you've told me he's wealthy, a collector of art, and he commands a fair amount of respect from the locals. A guy who owns his own island can't be all bad.''

''I don't believe I told you exactly what it was he collected,'' Angie said grimly.

''I'm listening.''

''Weapons.''

Sangrey studied her for a few seconds. ''Weapons?''

Angie's mouth curved wryly. ''Not new ones, fortunately. At least not that I know of. He apparently has a thing for antique stuff. Old knives and pistols, that sort of thing. I'm hoping I won't find any M-16s hanging on the walls when I arrive for dinner.''

''You don't approve of Cardinal's collection?'' Flynn paid for his drink as it arrived, then leaned back in his chair to sip meditatively.

Angie flushed, wondering if she'd offended him in some oblique fashion. ''I realize that for a man in your, uh, profession, weapons collecting probably doesn't seem all that odd.''

He shrugged but said nothing.

''It's not just the fact that he collects things like that,'' Angie went on earnestly, ''it's the whole situation. Why would a man live in a fortress on an island that he owns if he hadn't made some unpleasant enemies in his life? Why retire down here in Mexico? There's a lot of mystery about Alexander Cardinal's past and he makes me nervous. I'll bet he's a retired gangster or something. No wonder he likes old knives and things. He probably cut his teeth on a tommy gun.''

''Are you sure you're not letting your imagination run wild? What do you think he's going to do once he has you in his clutches? Assault you?''

''Of course not.'' Angie sighed, wondering how she was going to go about explaining her apprehension to a man who clearly didn't allow his imagination or anything else to get the best of him. ''I'm sure my uncle would never have sent me down here alone if he had any qualms about Mr. Cardinal. It's just that I feel, well, uncomfortable. Uneasy. Wary. I don't know. I don't like this job. I haven't liked it since Julian asked me to do it. Somehow I've lost my nerve.''

Flynn smiled fleetingly. ''Maybe you just need something to bolster your courage.''

Something in Angie responded to the brief dose of humor. ''Like another margarita?'' She stirred the one in front of her for a moment, thinking. ''You're right, of course. I am overreacting. Normally I'm quite efficient and businesslike about odd jobs such as this one. Heaven knows I get a lot of strange tasks from Uncle Julian. The variety is one of the reasons I've continued to work for him instead of going back into personnel. I don't know why this particular job is making me nervous.''

''Feminine intuition probably.''

''You don't sound as though you believe in intuition.'' She slanted Flynn an accusing glance.

''Oh, I believe in some forms of intuition,'' he retorted. ''God knows I ought to, It's come in handy more than once in my life. But I've never been too certain about the feminine variety.''

Angie's eyes lightened with humor. ''That's because you're a man.''

"I knew there had to be a simple explanation."

"Flynn?"

"Hmm?"

Angie cleared her throat softly, struggling to find the right words. "You said you were on vacation."

"Resting between engagements, I believe they say in the acting profession." He watched her over the rim of his glass.

"Yes, well, does that mean you have absolutely no interest in picking up a few quick bucks?" Angie questioned baldly.

There was a moment's silence from the other side of the table. When Flynn spoke his voice was so soft and dark Angie wasn't certain she'd heard him correctly.

"Is this a proposition?"

Aware of the sudden heat in her face, Angie shook her head angrily. "Don't be ridiculous. I'm offering you a temporary assignment. A job. Are you interested or not?"

"What, exactly, is the nature of the assignment?"

"Isn't it obvious?"

He made a small, dismissive gesture with his hand. "No."

"I would like an escort to Alexander Cardinal's island tomorrow evening. There, is that clear enough? You'll be well paid. My uncle never questions my expense accounts." How could he? She prepared and paid all of her own expense accounts. Then she handed them over to Julian's accountant. Julian didn't want to be bothered with petty details.

"Then this offer is in the nature of a proposition?" There was a hard edge underlying Flynn's words.

"This offer," Angie said feelingly, "is a request for your services as a bodyguard!"

He blinked, the slow, speculative blink of a large night animal. "You really are nervous, aren't you?"

"Yes." She waited, an element of challenge in her eyes.

Sangrey considered the matter for a long moment. "Will Cardinal allow you to bring a guest along tomorrow evening?"

"I don't see why not. There was nothing said about having to go alone. I'm sure if I just show up with you in tow and act as though I had understood the invitation to include my *friend,* he'll be polite about the whole thing. I've heard he prides himself on his good manners. Julian assured me Cardinal appears to be a gentleman. He's been corresponding with him for some time."

"Yet you're scared of the man?"

Angie smiled ruefully. "I know it doesn't sound rational."

"Feminine intuition?"

"I'm afraid so. Or maybe just plain old nerves." She waited a few seconds. "Are you interested?"

Flynn lifted one shoulder in casual acceptance. "Why not? It sounds like it could be an interesting evening."

Angie drew in a slow breath as something occurred to her. "I hope you and Mr. Cardinal won't have too much in common."

"Not likely. I don't have his kind of money. Or an island."

The sarcasm annoyed Angie. "I was referring to a mutual interest in weapons and related activities," she said caustically.

"If you didn't believe I had an interest in that sort of thing you wouldn't be wanting to hire me as an escort, would you?" Flynn countered with unassailable logic.

Angie winced and chose to alter the direction of the conversation. "How much?"

He looked blank. "How much what?"

"How much do you charge? Is there an hourly or daily rate? I've never hired someone like you before. I don't really know how to handle the business side of things."

"Someone like me," he repeated slowly. "How much do you know about people like me, Angie?"

"Very little," she admitted.

"Remember that."

"Look, if you're going to go all cryptic and enigmatic on me, let's just forget the whole thing. With Alexander Cardinal hovering in the background, the last thing I need is another man around who makes me nervous!"

Unexpectedly Flynn chuckled. "I'll try to avoid that."

"Then it's settled?"

"It's settled. You look very relieved."

"I am," she confirmed. "But you haven't told me how much you, er, charge yet."

"I'll have to think about it."

The practical side of Angie's nature intruded. "Don't think too hard about it. I'm planning to list your services under 'miscellaneous expenses' when it comes time to itemize the costs of this trip, so I hope you'll keep your charges reasonable."

"Miscellaneous expenses." He played with the word as he said it, his gaze full of sardonic humor. "Somehow that sounds so unimportant. So vague. Kind of uninteresting. Do you find me uninteresting and vague, Angie?"

She wasn't quite sure how to take his teasing. "Not any more uninteresting and vague than you probably find me," she assured him cheerfully.

Flynn set his glass down and leaned forward to bracket the drink with his elbows. His hands splayed wide on the polished black surface of the cocktail table. At the tips of his fingers the candle burned in its amber dish. He smiled.

"I find you fascinating, Angie. I'm looking forward to working for you and with you tomorrow night."

"You are?" Her skepticism probably showed. But she couldn't deny that his words created a pleasurable stir of excitement deep within her. Her eyes went to his hands. They were large hands with strong wrists and blunt fingers. A tiny shiver went through her as, involuntarily, she wondered what those hands would feel like on her body.

"Will you dance with me, Angie?"

She started a little, wondering if he'd just read her mind. It was the first time he'd asked her to dance. Without a word she inclined her head in aloof agreement. Flynn led her out onto the floor and took her into his arms. His big, powerful hands closed around her and Angie had the answer to her question. His hands felt good. Strong and warm and good. They felt right.

She was aware of the strength in his grasp, but she also sensed the control behind that strength. Angie relaxed into the rhythm of the dance, allowing herself to follow Flynn's smooth, controlled lead. Overhead the stars gleamed in the black velvet night, and the balmy air was scented with the sea. Around Angie the other dancers seemed totally absorbed in themselves. She felt alone with the man who held her. It gave her the courage to risk a personal question.

"Flynn?"

"Hmm?" His voice came from the region of her right ear. His mouth almost touched her hair.

"How long will you be staying here?"

"In Mexico? A few days. It depends."

Angie wondered what it depended on and didn't know how to ask. Part of her reticence was created by the fact that she didn't really want to know for certain how he made his living. She shied away from hearing the truth stated openly. It was unpleasant enough to assume that he was a mercenary; knowing for certain would be painful. Men who worked at the business of fighting other people's wars had an ancient and established calling. It was not, however, a particularly pleasant or respected calling. And it was definitely not a profession that encouraged long-range personal planning.

"I just wondered," she whispered. The scent of him was curiously intriguing, unlike anything Angie had ever experienced. She turned her nose unobtrusively into his shoulder and teased herself with the aroma of hotel soap and honest male sweat.

"Will you be leaving after you've made your deal with Cardinal?" Flynn asked into her hair.

"Yes. Unlike you, I'm not really on vacation. Besides, I don't want to be responsible for that damn dagger for too long."

"Dagger?" One large palm flexed at the base of Angie's spine. Flynn's strong fingers sank briefly into her skin and then relaxed. "That's what you're going to get from Cardinal?"

"I told you he collected weapons." Angie wondered if the movement of his hand on her back had been deliberate or only a reflexive motion. In either event it had elicited a small tremor of excitement and she half hoped he would do it again.

"Your employer collects weapons, too? Is that why you're down here negotiating for a dagger?"

She didn't really want to talk about the deal, but now that she'd involved him it seemed only fair to give Flynn some of the facts. With a small, stifled sigh of regret Angie lifted her head to meet his gaze. He was watching her intently.

"Julian doesn't collect weapons," she assured him. "Just this one particular dagger. It's very old, apparently. Dates back to the late seventeen hundreds. It once belonged to Julian's family, you see. The Torres family.''

Sangrey's fingers moved again in that flexing motion at the base of her spine. ''You said Julian is your uncle. That means the dagger was once in *your* family.''

''Well, I suppose so if you want to get technical. Frankly, I've never paid too much attention to the past. I've never had an interest in genealogy or family traditions. Life is for living in the present and the future.'' She smiled gently. ''I imagine a man in your line of work understands that.''

He looked down at her as though he were about to say something and then he changed his mind. ''Tell me more about the dagger.''

''There's not much to tell. It disappeared a long time ago. Over the years it went through a variety of hands, but several months ago Julian had it traced to the Cardinal collection. He opened negotiations with Alexander Cardinal, who, surprisingly, agreed to sell. I guess Uncle Julian appealed to him on the grounds of family tradition, and Cardinal seemed to understand my uncle's desire to have the dagger back in the family.''

Again Flynn's hand moved on her back and again Angie couldn't tell if the touch was deliberate or casual.

''And now you've come to collect the dagger and take it back to your uncle,'' Flynn observed. ''It must be valuable.''

Angie considered that. ''I suppose it is, but not extravagantly so. It's no dollar-ninety-eight pocketknife, but it's not exactly Excalibur, either. Julian tells me the blade is of Damascus steel and there is an intricately worked handle. I think the pommel is set with some semiprecious stones.'' She laughed lightly. ''The thing's not made of diamonds and gold. The real value of the dagger to Julian is sentimental.''

"You don't sound as if you approve of that sort of sentiment."

"Oh, I'm not hardhearted about it. I'm glad my uncle is finally getting his hands on the dagger. It's something he's been working on for a long time."

"When did Julian lose the thing?" Flynn sounded vaguely irritated.

"He didn't lose it. It was lost years ago by the family that was responsible for keeping track of it." Angie felt a flash of irritation, too, as she jumped to her uncle's defense. She frowned. "I've told you Julian's last name is Torres. He's the last male descendant of an old Spanish family that once held a lot of land in California. The dagger is called the Torres Dagger. It's a long story."

"I'm listening."

Angie tilted her head to one side. "You really want to hear the tale of the dagger?"

"I can't think of anything else I'd rather do than listen to it."

Thanks a lot, Angie thought grimly. She could think of several other things she'd rather be doing at the moment. A walk in the hotel gardens, a long, intimate discussion of the future, a soft kiss down on the beach. Hundreds of other things. But apparently Flynn didn't feel the same way. Firmly Angie reminded herself once again that it made more sense to keep her relationship with Flynn Sangrey on a polite, platonic level.

"Well, according to Julian the dagger originally belonged to a distant ancestress of ours, a beautiful Spanish woman named Maria Isabel. It seems that there was a feud going on between the Torres family and the Challoners, the family that owned the ranch that bordered Torres land in California. A dispute over a large chunk of property. Nothing gets landholding people more upset than an argument over who owns what, I guess. At any rate, according to the story the altercation was settled in the time-honored way.''

"All-out war?"

Angie shook her head, smiling. "Only for a while. Then the Challoners presented an alternative solution: a marriage alliance. The head of the Challoner clan offered to marry the eldest Torres daughter, poor Maria Isabel. The disputed hunk of ground would be her dowry and would descend through her to her children. Both families would be linked to the land they coveted.''

"Why do you call Maria Isabel poor? It sounds like a reasonable solution to me.''

"Typical male approach to the problem." Angie shot Flynn a disgusted glance. "Just use a convenient daughter to seal the bargain and settle the matter of land title. Never mind what the poor daughter happens to think about the situation.''

"I take it Maria Isabel objected to the solution?" Flynn asked dryly.

"Most vehemently, according to the legend. She stormed and argued for days, but her father was one of those old-style domineering patriarchs. He'd accepted the offer of marriage from his neighbor and his daughter was going to go through with the deal come hell or high water." Angie shuddered.

"I wouldn't waste too much time empathizing with Maria Isabel if I were you. She was a woman of her time, and that was the way things were done back then.''

"With that attitude I think you would have done very well yourself in those days," Angie muttered. "I can't imagine putting a woman through such anguish for the sake of settling a land dispute!''

"It seems perfectly reasonable to me. In those days the power of a family was directly proportional to the land it held. It was crucial to maintain control over as much territory as possible. What did the tantrums of a sulking daughter matter compared to forming an important alliance?''

Angie glowered up at him. ''If you want to hear the rest of the story, you'd better cease and desist offering opinions on the rights and wrongs of the situation!''

Flynn's fingers moved once more just above the curve of her hips and he smiled wryly. ''I get the message. Finish the story.''

''Well, according to Julian, who had the tale from his father, who got it handed down from his father, et cetera, et cetera, Maria Isabel finally told her parents she would surrender to the inevitable.''

''Smart woman.''

Angie ignored that. ''But she had plans of her own. On her wedding night she concealed the Torres Dagger in her gown.''

''I take it back. Not such a smart woman after all.''

Angie sighed. ''Actually, it sounds like a logical thing to do under the circumstances.''

''Bring a dagger to your wedding bed?'' Something feral gleamed for a moment in Flynn's eyes.

''It's obvious you're never going to understand the woman's side of the tale.''

''Finish it,'' Flynn instructed.

''There's not much more to tell,'' Angie admitted. ''No one really knows what happened on the wedding night.''

''Maria Isabel's new husband didn't wake up dead, did he?''

''Well, no.''

''And Maria Isabel survived, too?''

Angie nodded. ''According to the story they were both very much alive the next morning. Maria Isabel and her husband had seven children during the years that followed.''

"Then I think it's safe to assume Maria Isabel had her mind changed for her on her wedding night." Flynn's mouth curved laconically. "You want me to guess what happened?"

Angie laughed in spite of herself. "I can imagine what a man would assume happened that night. Your guess is that Maria Isabel's new husband disarmed her with mad, passionate love, right?"

"No, I have a hunch the mad, passionate love came later. My guess is he disarmed her very forcefully, without any love at all. He was probably madder than hell."

Angie's amusement faded. "It doesn't sound like an auspicious beginning for a marriage."

"Oh, I don't know." Flynn sounded suddenly philosophical. "It undoubtedly served to lay out the ground rules in no uncertain terms. Since no-fault divorce laws didn't exist back then, it was probably important to settle the critical issues early on in a marriage. And any bride who shows up on her wedding night with a dagger in her nightgown needs a firm hand right from the start."

Angie's eyes narrowed. Then she reminded herself that it was merely a legend about a very distant relation and didn't affect the present at all. There was absolutely no reason why she should feel obliged to defend Maria Isabel at this late date. "Well, whatever the real story is of what happened that night, the rest of the dagger's tale is known. Julian says that the morning after the wedding the Torres Dagger was hung in state over the fireplace in the master bedroom of Maria Isabel's new home. It remained there for several generations, during which time both families prospered. Apparently the Torreses and the Challoners began to see the dagger as a symbol of good luck for both families. But sometime in the early 1900s the dagger disappeared. And with it, apparently, the good luck of both families."

"What happened?"

Angie shrugged. "Julian says that after the dagger disappeared, the families began to dwindle and die out. The power and money faded. The land itself was lost during the 1920s. It's been divided up among a lot of different owners. Some of it's farmland and some of it's subdivisions now. Julian managed to buy back the site of the old Torres hacienda, though. He's had a new house built in the Spanish colonial style. And there's a charming little guest cottage, too. That's where I live. I got to move in a few weeks ago, but Julian isn't scheduled to move into the hacienda itself until next month."

"Are you and Julian about the last of the Torres line?" Flynn asked carefully.

"Well, there's my mother, Julian's sister, but I was her only child. She and my father divorced several years ago and she moved east. My uncle has never married. He's in his sixties now. He asked me to become his research assistant a couple of years ago. From what we can tell with genealogical research, there aren't any other Torres relations around. He and I and my mother are all that's left."

"What about the other family? The one Maria Isabel married into."

"Julian thinks there's a possibility that somewhere a descendant of the Challoners is still alive, but he has no way of knowing for certain. He's made a few attempts to trace the family, and the most he can determine is that there were two Challoner brothers in service in World War II. One didn't survive. The other returned and married and there may have been children. Julian wasn't able to trace the family any further. After all these years it doesn't much matter."

"It sounds to me like it matters a whole lot," Flynn

growled. "If one of Maria Isabel's descendants is alive, the dagger belongs to him."

Angie's brows came together in a fierce line above her nose. "You're beginning to sound as bad as Julian! For heaven's sake, we all live in the present, not the past. That dagger belongs only to whoever happens to purchase it next. In this case, that purchaser is Julian Torres."

"The dagger symbolizes something important, Angie. You told me yourself, it brought luck to two families for several generations. It represented the land and the power of those two families."

"Good grief! That's just a legend. Everyone is responsible for making his or her own luck in this world. I should think you, of all people, would understand that. You look as if you've been making your own way for some time."

"That doesn't mean I don't understand the value of traditions and legends," Flynn countered softly. "Doesn't the tale of that dagger mean anything to you?"

"Not particularly. It's an interesting story but that's all it is to me: a story."

He looked down at her searchingly. "You're connected to that dagger and its history. Don't you have any feeling for your past?"

She laughed up at him, amused by his unexpectedly serious attitude toward the subject. "Flynn, you are looking at a thoroughly modern Californian. A child of the present. Before I went to work for Uncle Julian, I couldn't name anyone farther back on my family tree than my grandparents! And the only reason I can do a little better now is because Uncle Julian has made me help him out on some of his genealogical research."

"But that research is just a job to you, isn't it?"

"You've got it. I much prefer the here and now. What good does it do to dwell on the distant past? There's nothing to be gained or changed. Tracking down family legends makes an interesting hobby for someone like my uncle, I suppose, but that's about it.''

"But in this case the family legend represents a lot more than just an amusing tale. From what you've said, the dagger was a link between two families and the land that gave them their power. Something important was lost when that dagger disappeared. If you'd spent as much time living in strange places as I have, you might have more appreciation for the importance of families and their legends. There are places in this world where the family tie is the most crucial tie there is. Families are how people become immortal, Angie.''

"I'm really not interested in building family dynasties,'' she temporized dryly. "It's probably more of a male fantasy, anyway, since lines of descent are usually through the male surname. Men sometimes have this thing about achieving immortality through their descendants.''

"I wouldn't call a man's desire to establish a strong, lasting family a fantasy!''

"I would. It was undoubtedly the old-fashioned equivalent of heading up a corporation. A form of power.''

"There's nothing wrong in a man's search for power and strength and nothing wrong in his wish to hand that power and strength down to the next generation. It's a survival instinct.

Angie smiled very brightly. "Well, I certainly don't share that instinct. As a woman, I would resent being used to cement a dynasty. I can understand exactly how Maria Isabel must have felt. But I can't quite figure out why we're arguing about the matter. You don't seem to subscribe to that sort of male fantasy. If you did you would be back in the States working day and night to build a ranch or a corporation or something. You'd be worrying about marrying a woman who could bring you a dowry and give you lots of sons, not vacationing alone in Mexico.''

Flynn's mouth curved abruptly and his gaze warmed. "I'm not vacationing alone. I'm with you.''

Angie's breath caught for a split second. "Yes," she whispered. "Yes, you are.''

Flynn stopped, his hand sliding more aggressively around her waist. "Let's go outside for a few minutes.''

"Why?" Angie felt a tremor of excitement rush through her. It was followed almost instantly by a shiver of sensual alarm when Flynn didn't answer. The two conflicting sensations confused her for a moment, and by the time she recovered she found herself out in the gardens that fronted the night-darkened sea.

They walked in silence for several minutes. The scent of the ocean air mingled with the aromas of the exotic tropical garden, creating an impression of timeless fantasy. Angie was vividly aware of the man beside her. It occurred to her that part of her had been aware of him on this sensual level since the first moment they'd met.

"Will you be going back to the States the day after tomorrow?" Flynn came to a halt beside a stone wall that had been built to separate the hotel gardens from the beach.

"I should leave as soon as possible. I told you, for me this isn't really supposed to be a vacation.'' Angie put her hand on the waist-high wall. The stones were still warm from the sun. "What about you? How long will you be 'resting between engagements'?''

His shoulders moved in the darkness, a casual shrug that told her nothing. "I haven't decided.''

There was silence between them again. There had often been silences during the past couple of days. At times Flynn was very difficult to communicate with, Angie reflected. At other times, and they were the majority, the conversation flowed between them as naturally as the tides. She leaned forward, resting her arms on the stone wall, and gazed out toward the sea. "You know, somehow you're not quite what I would have expected."

"What would you expect?" There was a thread of amusement in the words.

"I don't know. I've never met a man who made his living the way I think you make yours." The impulse toward honesty surprised her. For two days she had deliberately not pushed too hard to answers. She realized now that she'd been half afraid of the ones she might get. "But if I'd thought about it, I'd have guessed that a man in your situation might be far more, uh, aggressive with a woman than you've been. Especially when he was on vacation. A sort of live-for-the-moment syndrome. Eat, drink and be merry. Wine, women and song."

"Are you by any chance trying to tell me in a very delicate way that I've been too much of a gentleman?" Flynn sounded more amused than ever.

Concealing her chagrin, Angie straightened away from the wall and looked up at him with a serious expression. "That's not what I meant at all. I've appreciated your behavior. If you hadn't been a gentleman, I wouldn't have risked hiring you for tomorrow night's little scene."

"I know." He reached out to touch the side of her cheek, his dark eyes unreadable in the shadows. "If I hadn't been a gentleman for the past two days, you wouldn't have risked trusting me at all. And it was very important that you trust me."

"Flynn?"

"But every gentleman has his limits," Flynn went on softly. He slid his large hand behind her head and tilted her face up so that starlight illuminated the questions in her eyes. ''And I think I'm reaching mine.''

He brought his mouth down to hers before Angie could find the words to stop him.

Chapter 2

He'd seen the sensual awareness in her eyes the moment he'd introduced himself. It had pleased him. More than that, it had filled him with a curious sense of anticipation. He could and would use that awareness, Flynn had told himself. He would use whatever worked. He was too close now to let anything stand in his way.

Flynn felt Angie shiver delicately beneath his hand as his mouth found hers. The sensation sent a ripple of raw excitement through him. It had been clear for the past two days that the awareness in Angie was controlled with an ample amount of feminine caution and common sense. But he sensed that there was a well of passion to be tapped if the right man took his time and planned carefully. It was very satisfying to lure her over those high, self-imposed barriers and into the lush green fields of temptation. Flynn realized he had been waiting for this moment for the past forty-eight hours.

It had been difficult playing the casual, scrupulously polite gentleman for two days, especially here, where they were enveloped in the exotic, carefree atmosphere of the luxurious tropical resort. If he hadn't had more important goals on his mind, Flynn knew he would have made the pass Angie had expected the first night. He had found himself wanting to spend every waking moment with her, trying to impress himself on her consciousness.

But Flynn had hunted long enough to know that the cautious, careful quarry was most efficiently trapped through its own natural curiosity. Keeping his distance had netted him much faster and more useful results than he would have obtained through the direct approach. Angie's offer of a job tonight had told him that much.

It was all enough to make a man believe in fate, Flynn decided triumphantly as he ran the tip of his tongue along Angie's lower lip. Her mouth quivered and opened beneath the tantalizing caress. With a groan of mounting desire Flynn accepted the soft invitation.

He explored the warm, intimate darkness behind her lips, and his body began demanding the completion of the ancient formula. He hadn't planned on more than a kiss this evening. It was crucial not to alarm Angie at this stage. Flynn reminded himself that his ultimate goal was far more important than a night in bed with a woman. He knew his self-control was formidable, and he had great confidence in it.

But he couldn't stop himself from teasing the sensitive nape of Angie's neck, and when she sighed softly in response he found himself touching her just above the low neckline of her dress. She wasn't wearing a bra. Flynn urged her closer so that he could feel the gentle thrust of her breasts against his chest.

It was delicious. She made a tiny sound at the back of her throat and her fingertips closed over his shoulders. He was vividly aware of the firm peaks of her nipples and knew a sudden, fierce desire to test them with his palm.

She was so sweetly responsive, he thought. And he felt dazed by the elemental sense of power that was surging through him now. She was twenty-eight, and God knew he was getting perilously close to forty. At this stage both of them should be capable of choreographing their responses with far more finesse. It was unexpected and unsettling to find his sense of control threatened already.

Flynn knew matters were getting dangerous when he found himself sliding a probing finger inside the elasticized neckline of Angie's white dress. She stilled for a moment in his arms, and he told himself he'd better stop. It had gone far enough. The last thing he wanted to do tonight was push too fast or too hard. It would be far more effective to arouse her gently and leave her wanting him.

Easy does it, he told himself determinedly. *This is where it stops. Any further and you start risking her trust. There's too much of a chance she'll pull back and become cautious again.* And there was too much at stake to lose the advantage he had gained during the past two days.

But his hand seemed to move of its own volition and the gauzy white dress slipped downward.

"Flynn..." Angie's eyes were closed. Her nails bit into the fabric of the khaki shirt. "I don't think we should let this go any further...."

"I know. Believe me, honey, I know." But now that he was so close to touching the hardened tips of her breasts, he didn't want to stop. "Just let me see you for a moment. I want to know what the moonlight looks like on your skin." He took a breath and with both hands pushed the elasticized material down to her waist.

For an instant she stood trapped before him, her wrists

caught and tangled in the sleeves of the dress. Her lashes lifted and she met his eyes. Flynn found himself staring.

"Angie," he grated. His hands lifted to cup the small, rounded fullness of her breasts. She was delicately constructed, her body slender but softened with curves at breast and thigh. "Angie, you're lovely."

"So are you." She freed her hands and wrapped her arms around his neck. Then she put her lips to the tanned skin of his throat and pressed gently against him. "Oh, Flynn. So are you."

It was okay, Flynn heard a hammering voice in his veins say. It was all right. He wouldn't endanger his ultimate goal by making love to Angie tonight. No problem. She wanted him. She would come to him as easily as a bird to its nest. All he had to do was lead her back to his room, lock the door and lay her down on his bed. In his head he could see her there already.

The heat in his body seemed to be leaping out of control. Flynn grazed the tips of Angie's breasts with his palms and then slipped his hands around her to find the line of her spine.

Below on the beach the waves lapped at the sand in a primitive rhythm that echoed the heavy beat of his blood. Everything in his mind that was not directly connected with Angie began to recede into the distance. In a vague way he tried to remind himself of his purpose in being here, but he was already deciding it could wait until morning.

Everything except Angie could wait until morning.

"Come with me." His voice sounded rough to his own ears. He wished he could make it smooth and liquid. "Come with me, Angie. I want you tonight. I'll make it good for you. I swear it. I'll do whatever it takes to make it perfect. Angie, let's go back. Come with me, honey...."

He felt her shudder against him, and then she was pulling

free. Her reluctance was obvious, but so was the somewhat
dazed determination in her face. She looked up at him as
her hands slid down his chest and slowly she shook her
head.

"I'm sorry, Flynn. It's too soon. I should never have let
things go this far. Please forgive me for leading you on."
Her smile was tremulous, her eyes wide and pleading. "I'm
supposed to be here on business, not for a romantic fling. I
got a little carried away, I guess." Hastily she adjusted her
dress, turning toward the sea as she pulled the material back
up over her shoulders.

Behind her Flynn took a couple of slow breaths, aware
that his hands were in fists at his sides. His whole body felt
coiled and tense. She couldn't just call a halt like this. Could
she? He'd felt her response; knew she wanted him. Damn
it, he was the one who was supposed to be directing this
scene.

"Relax, Angie. It's all right. You don't have to be afraid
of me." It was a struggle to find the words. He wanted to
pick her up and carry her back to his room and forget words
altogether.

She glanced back at him over her shoulder. The moonlight illuminated her profile. Her eyes seemed very large and
strangely colorless in the night light. "I'm not afraid of you,
Flynn. I haven't been afraid of you since the moment we
met."

"Angie, please. I want you to trust me."

"I do trust you." She smiled again and put out a hand
to touch his sleeve. "It's myself and the situation I don't
trust. This can't go anywhere, can it, Flynn? I'll be on my
way home the day after tomorrow. And you...you'll be on
your way back to wherever men in your profession are finding work these days. That probably takes in a good portion
of the globe, doesn't it?"

"Is it what I do for a living that bothers you?" he asked starkly, knowing she had skirted the issue more than once during the past couple of days.

"It's not any of my business." Her hand fell away from his arm. "But I'm not a good candidate for a one-night stand, Flynn." Her mouth curved in wry humor. "I'd probably whine a lot the next morning. You know, throw a tantrum and hurl recriminations. That sort of thing. The last thing you need while you're on vacation is a woman who stages a major scene at the airport when you're trying to say goodbye. It would be better for both of us if we kept this relationship businesslike."

The sleek edge of anger knifed through him unexpectedly. That was supposed to be his line, Flynn thought savagely. He was the one who had been keeping things carefully poised on the brink between business and pleasure. He'd been doing it deliberately, using the resulting tension to attract his quarry. And now the quarry was using it against him. Hurriedly he sought for a way to recover his strategic position.

"Don't worry, Angie. The last thing I want to do is push you into something you don't want."

"It's not that I don't want—" she began urgently.

"I understand." He smiled as he cut off her small attempt to explain. "No problem." Then he stepped forward and took her arm to guide her back through the moonlit gardens. He was okay now. Back under control. "A kiss overlooking the beach is the perfect finishing touch to the evening, don't you think? What time are you going to breakfast in the morning?"

She looked as if she wanted to say something else but couldn't think of any way to get the conversation back on its original track. "About seven. Same time as this morning."

"Sounds good. I'll see you then."

"You're still interested in coming with me tomorrow evening?" she asked tentatively.

"How can I turn down such an easy assignment?" He grinned as they walked back into the main lobby of the hotel. "A free meal and a cruise on the bay. Sounds great."

"I really do appreciate it, Flynn. I know there's no logical reason to be nervous."

"But you are. Don't apologize. There's no need." He walked her into the elevator and down the hall to her second-floor room.

When he halted in front of her door, Angie turned to look up at him with a questioning expression. "Good night, Flynn. And thank you. For everything."

He bent his head and brushed his mouth against her lips. "My pleasure. See you in the morning."

He forced himself not to linger over the kiss. Angie hesitated as if trying to decide what to do next, but as he just stood politely, waiting, she quickly turned the key in the lock and stepped inside the room.

As soon as the door closed in his face, the politely reassuring smile Flynn had been wearing vanished. He swung around, then stalked down the hall to the elevator and punched the button.

"Stupid, stupid, stupid." Leaning against the wall, arms folded, he muttered the words in a soft, disgusted litany. He'd been on the verge of risking everything for the sake of a night in bed with Angie Morgan. It made no sense. His entire goal hinged on keeping her trust and friendship. A little sexual attraction was a bonus to be used wisely. He'd almost thrown away the trust and friendship by trying to sweep her into bed.

There was no doubt he would have taken a lot of satisfaction in making love to her, and Flynn was almost certain he could have made her enjoy the experience, too. But there was too much risk involved. Angie was right, she wasn't a good candidate for a one-night stand. He might have been able to coax her into bed this evening, but he couldn't know what her reaction would be in the morning. She might, indeed, wake up full of recriminations, just as she had suggested.

Worse yet, she might have been so nervous around him that she would have retracted her job offer. Since he'd spent the past two days feeding her the notion that she would feel more comfortable with him along tomorrow evening, it would be a pity to scare her off now.

"Sangrey, you're a damn fool." The elevator doors slid open and Flynn stepped inside. The car was empty and he rode it up to the next floor thinking of Angie's eyes. He'd been half-consciously trying to figure out what color they were and tonight it came to him. She had eyes the color of a peacock's feathers.

Dusk shrouded the bay the next evening as the launch cut through the water with a subdued roar. Angie sat in the back, her hair shielded from the breeze by a silk scarf. At the helm a taciturn man dressed in white trousers and a white, military-style shirt guided the boat toward Cardinal's private island.

Behind her the lights of the beachfront hotel began to wink into existence. A tiny village that skirted the hotel dotted the beach with a few more lights, but there was little else to relieve the darkness. This portion of the Mexican coastline was uninhabited for long stretches. It was an area the government was just beginning to develop for tourists, and as yet there were few signs of civilization near the resort.

Angie had decided to wear a yellow-and-turquoise silk

chemise tonight. When she saw the crisply attired launch pilot, she was glad she had. Alexander Cardinal was clearly a man who valued a certain degree of formality. Beside her, Flynn was dressed in his usual fashion: an open-throated shirt and close-fitting pants. The shirt was black tonight and the pants were charcoal gray. He had on the familiar worn leather belt and moccasins. The only concession to formality was the light-colored sports jacket that lay flung over the seat in front of him. Perhaps moccasins and a sports jacket were de rigueur in the various places around the world where he went to make his living.

In that moment Angie didn't care what he wore. She was just glad he was along for the ride. None of her uneasiness was diminishing as the launch approached Cardinal's island. When she felt Flynn's hand close lightly over her fingers, she realized he was aware of her wariness. She turned her head to smile at him.

He smiled back, but didn't try to shout above the roar of the launch's motor. The balmy breeze rippled the black pelt of his hair. Angie reflected briefly that with his dark hair and eyes he might have had a Spanish ancestor somewhere on the family tree.

She felt the impact of the dark gaze as he watched her and found herself flushing a bit. Firmly she focused her attention on the small island they were approaching. Matters had been friendly, polite and casual between herself and Flynn all day today. She knew it was best to keep them that way.

But knowing that that was the wisest course had not deterred her from thinking about him for a long time before she went to sleep the night before. The memory of his large, strong hands on her body had ignited a sensual warmth in her that had taken a long time to fade. Her curiosity about what it would feel like to have him touch her had been partially satisfied, but the answers had only created more wonder and more curiosity.

She was relieved that he had been so willing to allow her to call a halt in the garden. A part of her had been uncertain of just how cooperative he would be in a situation such as that. After all, a man in his line of work undoubtedly had to take his pleasures where he could or risk losing them.

His line of work. The words echoed again in her mind as the launch pilot guided the boat into small, shallow bay on Cardinal's island. It was strange how neither Flynn nor herself ever mentioned his work directly in their conversations. He had told her about his visits to some strange, troubled places, but he hadn't actually mentioned what he did while he was there.

Angie hadn't asked. She had guessed his profession soon after meeting him. There was a toughness in him that she knew intuitively went to the bone. The sometimes cynical, often laconic, fundamentally unyielding expression in his dark eyes was not the look of a stockbroker or interior designer on vacation. Everything about Flynn Sangrey warned that he knew too much about the violent side of life.

And since Angie didn't want to think about how completely separate his world was from her own, she didn't ask him directly about his profession.

She wondered if it was hypocritical of her to have asked Flynn for his services this evening.

Before she could struggle with the ethics of the situation, the pilot had the launch tied up at the dock. Nearby rocked a gleaming white yacht that must have been in the neighborhood of fifty to sixty feet. On the hull, black letters spelled out the name: *Cardinal Rule.*

"At least the guy seems to have a sense of humor," Flynn observed as he handed Angie up out of the launch.

"Either that or an ego problem." Angie removed her

scarf and turned to smile blandly at the silent launch pilot. "Thank you," she murmured as he politely indicated the steps leading up to a formal garden. He didn't return her smile.

She stood for a moment looking at the villa that dominated the extensive gardens. A rich man's retreat in paradise, she thought, surveying the cool fountains, wide terraces and pristine white walls. Beyond the gardens palm trees swayed in the evening breeze.

"Julian's going to be sorry he missed this," Angie whispered to Flynn. "It would have been a perfect setting for a book."

"Julian writes?"

"Umm. But not under his own name. He uses the pen name Julian Taylor."

Beside her, Flynn cocked one black brow. "That sounds vaguely familiar."

Angie hid a smile. "He's the author of a series of very popular men's adventure novels featuring a character named Jake Savage. There's one out every six months or so. Translated into eight languages. I don't imagine you read that sort of thing."

Flynn frowned briefly as he walked beside her up the stone path that wound through the garden. The launch pilot was silently leading the way toward the front doors of the villa. "Some series about a guy who free-lances?"

"Free-lances?" Angie repeated.

Flynn made a cutting movement with his hand. "You know, hires himself out to people who are willing to pay for services rendered." The dark eyes flickered. "Like I'm doing tonight."

Angie took a deep breath, never having thought of Jake Savage as a mercenary. But of course that was what he was.

"I suppose you could say that. How many books have you read in the Savage series?"

Flynn shrugged. "Only one. It wasn't bad technically."

"I beg your pardon?"

"Technically. It was okay technically." He gave her an impatient glance.

"You mean grammatically and structurally it was good?" She was rather surprised that he had bothered to dissect it in those terms. Most people who read the Savage series were looking for action and adventure, not writing expertise.

"I mean," Flynn explained as if she weren't very bright, "that the technical details were good. The descriptions of the weapons and how they handled were fairly accurate."

"Oh." Yes, of course. *Technically.* The word obviously had different meanings to different people.

Before Angie could think of anything else to say, the doors of the villa swung open. Standing on the threshold was a short, powerfully built man who reminded Angie of a gorilla in evening clothes. She nearly missed her footing on the first step. Instantly Flynn's hand was under her arm, steadying her. He appeared completely unconcerned by the sight of the big man in the doorway.

"Miss Morgan and her friend," the launch pilot announced briskly. Then he turned and headed back down toward the docks.

The man in the doorway nodded formally. "Mr. Cardinal is expecting you," he said gravely to Angie. Then he looked speculatively at Flynn. "We didn't realize you were bringing a friend."

"Flynn Sangrey." Flynn announced himself easily and waited, not volunteering further explanation.

"This way, please." The gorilla stepped aside and beckoned them into the white tiled hall. "Mr. Cardinal is on the west terrace."

Angie found herself keeping close to Flynn as they followed the man ahead of them. She swept the elegantly cool interior of the villa with a fascinated gaze. Julian had a more accurate eye for such details, but she was willing to bet that the abstract art on the walls was original. The tile beneath her feet probably came from Italy, and the Oriental rugs were definitely not reproductions. More than ever she wondered what sort of business Alexander Cardinal was in. Or had once been in. The gorilla came to a halt at a point where French doors stood open onto a terrace.

"Miss Morgan and her *friend,* Mr. Sangrey."

"Thank you, Haslett." Alexander Cardinal rose from the white wicker chair in which he had been sitting and came forward.

He was rather as Angie had expected. He looked perfectly at home in the tropical fantasy surrounding him. Tall, athletically lean, Cardinal was a man in his late sixties. His features were aristocratic; the eyes piercingly blue. His hair was blazingly white, and he still had most of it. The white linen tropical suit he wore had obviously been tailor-made. Everything about him was elegantly refined and infinitely charming. Angie found herself mentally casting him in a film about a wealthy, retired and very mysterious international jewel thief. Or worse.

"It is a pleasure to have you here, Miss Morgan. I've been looking forward to your company." Cardinal took Angie's hand in his own and kissed the back of it with a natural finesse that made her eyes widen in appreciation. Then he extended his hand to Flynn. "Mr. Sangrey? We weren't expecting you but please feel welcomed."

Flynn accepted the handshake easily. "Thank you. Angie was kind enough to invite me along. I'm glad you don't mind."

"Not at all, not at all. Please be seated. Haslett will be bringing drinks out in a moment."

Angie sank down onto one of the cushioned wicker chairs and turned her head to take in the exquisite view of sea and darkening sky. "Your home is absolutely magnificent, Mr. Cardinal."

"I have been fortunate over the years. And this is my reward." Cardinal smiled genially as he seated himself.

"I didn't realize there was a reward for good fortune," Angie couldn't resist saying.

"There is when a man is directly responsible for his own luck." Cardinal looked at Flynn, who had taken the chair next to Angie. "Wouldn't you agree, Mr. Sangrey?"

"Completely, Mr. Cardinal." Flynn's eyes moved appreciatively over his surroundings. "Completely."

Angie sensed quite suddenly that Flynn and Cardinal were establishing their own lines of communication, and the knowledge was vaguely alarming. She wasn't sure she liked the subtle, assessing glances that were being exchanged between the two men. Haslett appeared with a tray of drinks before she could completely analyze what was happening.

"Margaritas, sangria, or tequila and lime?" Haslett held the tray out to Angie.

She accepted one of the salt-rimmed margaritas and nodded her thanks without quite meeting Haslett's eyes. Cardinal waited until everyone had been served before he resumed the conversation.

"I am sorry your uncle could not come with you, Miss Morgan. I had been looking forward to meeting the creator of the Jake Savage series." He glanced at Flynn. "Have you read any of the books, Mr. Sangrey?"

Flynn smiled. "Angie was just asking me the same thing. I told her I had read one or two."

"They are very good from a technical point of view, aren't they?"

"Quite accurate," Flynn agreed. He flicked a quick, amused glance at Angie.

"I have enjoyed my correspondence with Julian Torres enormously," Cardinal continued. "He seems to be a man who understands the important things in life. So few men do these days."

Angie sipped her drink. "He's very grateful to you for agreeing to sell the Torres Dagger."

"I would never have agreed to do so except to someone like your uncle who had a prior claim on the dagger. It is a fine piece of steel. Beautifully worked. I'm glad it will be going back into the family that originally owned it. As we grow older, Miss Morgan, such things as family traditions become increasingly important."

Flynn tasted the raw tequila he had accepted from Haslett. "Angie isn't interested in family traditions. She believes in living in the present."

"There is no way to avoid living in the present," Cardinal said. "But the present has so much more meaning when the past is understood and appreciated, don't you think?"

"Of course the past is important." Sitting there under the scrutiny of the two men, Angie felt as if she had to defend herself. "But it should never be allowed to dominate the present or influence decisions that must be made for the future. It also shouldn't be given undue importance. Traditions are all very well and good, but to do something simply for the sake of tradition is meaningless. The Torres Dagger is, according to Julian, very interesting and a fine example of craftsmanship. But to think that the reason two families have practically died out was because the dagger was lost a couple of generations back is ridiculous."

''Is that how your uncle feels? I would not have thought of Julian Torres as a superstitious man.'' Cardinal steepled his fingers and regarded Angie with an inquiring gaze.

She flushed, aware that she'd overstated the case. ''Naturally Julian doesn't attribute any magic to the dagger. But I think it's become symbolic to him. He's the last male of our line and it somehow represents the whole history of the family.''

''It represents the history of another family, too,'' Flynn pointed out softly. ''According to the story, Maria Isabel Torres brought that dagger with her when she married the neighboring landholder. It seems to me that the descendants of her children have more claim to the dagger than Julian Torres does.''

Angie shrugged. ''Julian doesn't think there are any descendants left.''

Cardinal considered the issue. ''Fascinating. Yet you are not overly interested, Miss Morgan.''

Angie smiled. ''I think the dagger's symbolic meaning has become far too important to Julian. He's thought of nothing else for weeks now, ever since you agreed to sell. He was very disappointed when he came down with the flu and was forced to send me in his place.''

''As I said, family traditions often become more important to us as we grow older.'' Cardinal sipped his drink. ''Those of us who reach a certain age and realize that the family will not live on after us find it…disturbing.'' His blue eyes became curiously shadowed.

Flynn leaned forward, his elbows on his knees, his drink cradled between his palms. ''Traditions are important in other ways, too, not just for nostalgic reasons. Angie says there's no magic in the dagger, but maybe there is.''

Cardinal gave him an interested glance. ''In what sense, Mr. Sangrey?''

"For two families that dagger represents history and power. It may be only a symbol, but symbols are important. Wars and revolutions have been fought over symbolic objects. Legends grow up around such objects for a reason. From what Angie tells me, there's no denying the fact that both families associated with the Torres Dagger began to die out after the thing was sold off back in the twenties. Maybe something important was lost when the dagger disappeared."

"Such as?" Angie challenged.

"Such as a unifying focus, a sense of tradition, a commitment to keeping the families strong. Who knows? All I'm saying is that you shouldn't discount the power of that dagger."

Angie sighed. "Well, it will make Julian very happy to have it back and for that reason alone, it's worth your price, Mr. Cardinal."

The older man smiled approvingly. "You appear to be quite loyal to your uncle, Miss Morgan. Loyalty is a valuable commodity in this day and age. In any day and age, for that matter. Don't you agree, Mr. Sangrey?"

Flynn looked at Angie, his expression unreadable. "Loyalty is more than merely a valuable commodity, Mr. Cardinal. It's priceless."

"You are obviously a man who has learned that lesson well." Cardinal rose to his feet and extended his arm to Angie. "If you will accompany me, I will show you my collection. The dagger is waiting to be claimed."

Angie accepted his arm, aware that Flynn was following close behind. Cardinal led the way back into the villa and on into a windowless room that had been paneled in teak. When he opened the door to reveal the collection of antique weapons, Angie thought she heard a soft exclamation from Flynn. Apparently Cardinal did, too, because he dropped

Angie's arm and turned to watch his other guest with an amused and understanding eye.

"What do you think, Mr. Sangrey?"

Flynn's gaze moved from the pike hung on one wall to a handsomely worked bowie knife housed in a glass case. "Very impressive." He walked over to another case and studied a sword that lay on black silk. The pommel was done in deeply etched silver.

"From Toledo," Cardinal murmured.

"Yes." Flynn continued to gaze at the weapon. "Eighteenth century?"

"Probably earlier."

Angie watched Flynn move on to a wall that was hung with wicked-looking two-edged swords. She remembered her own comment the previous evening when she had wondered aloud how much Flynn would have in common with Cardinal.

"My collection of rapiers is still growing," Cardinal remarked as he walked over to stand beside Flynn. He reached up, took one off the wall and examined it lovingly for a moment. Then he handed it to Flynn. "French. Sixteen hundreds."

Angie moved uneasily. The roomful of weapons was reawakening the nervousness that Alexander Cardinal had partially put to rest with his gracious hospitality. It wasn't just the sight of the instruments of war that was disturbing, it was the deep fascination they clearly held for Flynn and Cardinal. She began to hope Haslett would show up soon to announce dinner.

"Ah, Miss Morgan, are we boring you?" Cardinal looked politely concerned.

"No, of course not," she assured him quickly, not wanting to seem rude. Flynn didn't look up from the rapier he was holding. "It's quite an interesting collection," she added, aware that the words sounded weak.

Cardinal smiled understandingly. "Perhaps you would find the object of your quest more interesting." He moved soundlessly across the room to pick up a closed, black leather case. With a small bow he handed it to Angie. "The Torres Dagger."

Angie glanced down at the obviously new case and then back up to find Flynn watching her intently. Wordlessly she unfastened the catch.

The case was lined with black velvet. The dagger lay sheathed in very old leather, its handle gleaming faintly with the semiprecious stones that had been set in it. The weapon wasn't very large, Angie thought. The whole thing, handle and blade, was about a foot long. Slim, sleek, and deadly. Holding the case in one hand, she touched the handle of the dagger with her free fingers. For a few seconds she was unable to look away from the contents of the case. Without stopping to think, she closed her hand tightly around the handle and lifted the sheathed blade out of the case.

The odd sensation of possessiveness was startling. She had never seen the Torres Dagger before in her life. And she certainly didn't believe all that much about its importance to either the Torres or Challoner family.

So why did she suddenly feel as if the dagger belonged to her?

Chapter 3

The launch and its near-silent pilot delivered Angie and Flynn to the hotel dock three hours later. The boat roared off into the night as its two passengers started up the steps toward the resort. Angie didn't bother to wave goodbye.

"It seems to me, Mr. Cardinal could afford a more pleasant staff." Angie clutched the dagger case under her arm as Flynn guided her back toward the lights of the lobby. She could hear the sounds of the lounge combo drifting out over the hotel gardens.

"I have a hunch Cardinal has exactly the sort of staff he wants," Flynn said blandly. "In fact, I'd say Mr. Cardinal gets most of what he wants in life."

"He probably makes it a 'Cardinal rule.'"

"I have the feeling that maybe he hasn't got one thing, though."

"A family?" Angie hazarded.

"Yeah."

"What do you suppose his background really is, Flynn?"

"There are some people in this world you don't ask that question about."

People such as you? Angie wanted to ask but didn't. She felt a strange wistfulness settle on her as she remembered that she would be leaving Mexico the next day.

"Let's get a nightcap in the lounge."

"All right." She slanted him a smile. "Thanks for coming with me tonight, Flynn."

"No problem."

"I guess I was worrying for no reason."

"Looks like it."

"You still haven't told me how much you're charging," she ventured tentatively.

His fingers closed rather tightly around her elbow. The set of his face was grim. "You don't really think I'm going to bill you for tonight's services, do you?"

"Well, we did have an agreement. I want to keep up my end of the deal."

"Shut up, Angie."

Humor bubbled up inside her. "You're not supposed to talk to your employer that way. Didn't you notice how respectful Cardinal's employees were to him?"

"Yes," he agreed. "But since I'm not going to charge you for tonight, you're not my employer. Just a lady who's a little close to stepping out of line." He hustled her into the lounge and found a vacant table in the corner. After ordering two coffee liqueurs he leaned forward to study her face above the flickering glow of the candle. His eyes were dark and penetrating. "What are you going to do with the dagger tonight?"

Angie touched the leather case lying on the table. "Put it in the hotel safe, I think." She paused. "It's beautiful, isn't it?"

"How would I know? You've hardly let me get near it."
There was an edge to the words.

Angie chuckled. "Sorry." She opened the case for him.
The candlelight danced on the gems in the dagger's handle.
"Maria Isabel must have meant business on her wedding
night. This is no toy."

Flynn sat staring silently at the dagger for a long moment.
"No," he said at last. "It's no toy." He touched the handle
briefly and then withdrew his hands, folding his arms on the
table. "I think Maria Isabel had some very serious intentions
toward her new husband. I can imagine what he must have
thought when she pulled this beauty out of her robe."

"She was a very brave woman."

"Try arrogant, headstrong and reckless," Flynn suggested dryly.

"She was brave! It took courage to plan to defend herself
on her wedding night." More than ever she felt compelled
to champion the unknown Maria Isabel.

"You sound awfully sympathetic all of a sudden. I
thought you considered this whole business a nuisance."

Angie drummed her fingertips on the table, wondering
why she was bothering to argue Maria Isabel's side of the
story. "I don't know. Something about seeing the dagger
made me realize just how angry and frightened she must
have been to take it with her that night."

"Would you have taken it with you on your wedding
night?"

The soft question sent a ripple of tension through Angie.
She reached out abruptly and closed the leather case. "We'll
never know, will we?" She forced a smile. "Times have
changed. These days, women in the States aren't often used
as a means of sealing alliances between families. At least
not at my social level."

She'd meant it as a joke, but to her astonishment Flynn

took the comment seriously. His mouth tightened. "No, they marry for other reasons, don't they? For money or because a few hours of passion have convinced them they're in love. Sometimes they get married because all their friends are getting married. And sometimes they get married because they're bored and lonely and afraid of getting old."

"For a man who apparently doesn't spend a lot of time in the States these days, you seem to have some rather well-developed sociological theories," Angie snapped, annoyed.

"The only point I'm trying to make is that a marriage made for the sake of forming a family alliance is as good a reason as any other. Better reason than most." The hardness left Flynn's face briefly as his mouth crooked humorously. "At some point during her wedding night, Maria Isabel must have come to the same conclusion. After all, you know she didn't use the dagger."

Angie bit back a thoroughly disgusted retort. "Obviously you have your world view and I have mine," she said smoothly instead.

"Who are you going to marry, Angie? And why?"

"I have absolutely no idea *who* I'll marry, but the reason will be because I've fallen madly, passionately, wildly in love," she stated with grand conviction. "I won't give a damn about the history of his family or its future fortunes."

"Maria Isabel probably said something along those lines herself when her father told her he'd made the deal with the neighbor. Apparently her father was wise enough to ignore the dramatics."

Angie refused to let him goad her further. "You seem very interested in the tale of Maria Isabel and the two families connected with this dagger. Have you got much family of your own, Flynn?"

He shook his head, his expression suddenly remote. "Not anymore."

Instantly Angie felt contrite. She was obviously treading on forbidden ground now. "I'm sorry, Flynn. I didn't mean to pry."

He hesitated and then said, "It's all right. Your question is logical under the circumstances. I've been on my own for quite a while. A long time ago I was eighteen years old and I did what a lot of other kids do at eighteen. I enlisted. One thing led to another. After I got out of the military there were other jobs." He paused, as if memories were moving in his dark eyes. "Every year it seemed I found myself farther and farther away from anyplace I could call home."

"And now?" she asked softly.

"And now I'm pushing forty and realizing I'm still a long way from home." Flynn smiled abruptly. "What time do you leave tomorrow, Angie?"

She accepted the change of topic, knowing he had already said more than he had intended. "Not until the afternoon. My plane leaves at 3:45. The airport outside of Cancun is about an hour's drive from here. There's a shuttle bus that leaves the hotel at 2:00." Angie fell silent, realizing that she would never see this enigmatic man again after tomorrow. It was an odd sensation, far more depressing than it should have been.

"By tomorrow evening you'll be back in California." Flynn looked down at his glass of liqueur.

"Los Angeles. I'll spend the night there in an airport hotel and go on up the coast to Julian's home the next day." Angie found herself staring down at her own after-dinner drink. Quite suddenly there didn't seem to be a great deal more to say. Silence descended on the little table in the corner of the lounge.

"I don't suppose," Flynn finally said, "that you'd be interested in some company on the trip home?"

Angie's head came up abruptly, her eyes full of questions.

Flynn was watching her with more than his customary intensity. "Company?" Her mouth felt dry.

He spoke carefully, clearly feeling his way. "It's been a while since I was in California."

She licked her lips. "You're on vacation."

"True." He lifted his glass and drank from it.

"Do you...do you have the time to spare?"

"I have no, uh, pressing engagements," he murmured dryly. Flynn lowered his glass. "You haven't answered the question. Would you want my company?"

Angie took a deep breath. "I would very much enjoy having your company on the way home." She felt suddenly light-headed. The sense of depression that had been gathering around her dissipated. He was coming home with her.

They sat looking at each other for long moments, and then Flynn broke the silent tension to glance at the black metal watch on his wrist. "It's late."

"Yes, I suppose it is."

"I'd better get you up to your room. We can get up early and go swimming before breakfast."

"That sounds wonderful." She couldn't think of anything else to say.

She wasn't the only one finding herself short of conversation all of a sudden, Flynn thought. He couldn't find a great deal to say, either, now that he'd accomplished his goal. The realization that it was all working out beautifully left him with an unexpected feeling of ambivalence. Not knowing what else to do, he got to his feet and waited for Angie to pick up the dagger case. Silently he guided her out of the lounge.

As they walked into the lobby he decided he had nothing to lose by playing a long sheet. "I could keep the dagger in my room tonight if you like."

Angie's fingers tightened around the case. "That's all

right. The hotel safe is probably the best place for it." She smiled brightly. "I don't want you to feel responsible for it."

Flynn nodded, accepting the inevitable. He waited patiently at the front desk while Angie talked to the bilingual clerk. She spoke in English. A few minutes later, after seeing the dagger safely locked away, Flynn led Angie toward the elevator.

"Don't you speak Spanish?"

"Just a little California pidgin, why?"

"Well, with your family history and all, I guess I assumed you might have learned Spanish somewhere along the line."

She smiled. "I've told you before, I'm not exactly mesmerized by my past. Your Spanish is excellent, I've noticed."

He shrugged and said nothing.

"Thanks again for going with me to Cardinal's this evening," Angie said at her door.

Flynn glanced down at her fingertips, which she'd impulsively placed on his sleeve. "Thanks for asking me along." He saw the warmth in her eyes and felt the answering wave of urgency that pulsed through his own body. She seemed to trust him now. And she seemed to want him. It might be safe to let the physical attraction that flared between them take its course.

He raised his hand to let his fingers rest against the side of her throat. He could feel the excitement in her. It fueled his own desire as nothing else could have done. Flynn leaned forward and kissed her slowly, savoring the willing response he received. His fingers tightened fractionally on her throat, and his thumb moved luxuriously just under the line of her jaw. She was so soft and delicate, he thought, but with a woman's strength.

He'd seen her swimming energetically, watched her walking along the beach with a long, healthy stride. She wasn't at all fragile, and yet she made him think of fragile things. Things that should be protected.

A door opened at the end of the hall and reluctantly Flynn raised his head. Angie looked up at him with a tentative appeal. She was still uncertain of how far this should go tonight. But if he pushed a little, Flynn was sure he could push her straight into bed.

But there was so much else to consider. So much at stake. It would be better to wait a while longer, he knew. Better to let her think that he wasn't at all the type to push.

The ironic part was that it had been years since he'd felt so much like pushing a woman. God, how he wanted her tonight. He had to remember that there was a lot more involved here than one night in bed. He was no boy. He could control himself and his hormones. It would be so much more effective to keep her dangling; to ignite the flames in her and then let them blaze for a while. So much more useful. He'd learned his lesson last night. It was crucial to be the one who set the pace and called the moves.

"Good night, Angie," he whispered huskily. He stepped back, pretending to be oblivious to the flicker of disappointment in her expression. She recovered quickly with a smile.

"Good night, Flynn." She turned the key in the lock and then she was gone.

Flynn went on up to his own room with the distinct impression that he'd been ridiculously overcautious. The heavy, unsatisfied ache in his lower body reinforced that thought for the next hour.

Implementing sound strategy could be hard on a man.

Angie came awake a few hours later with the terrifying knowledge that something was very, very wrong.

The illogical fear kept her breathlessly still in the center of the wide bed. Some primitive survival instinct warned her not to open her eyes. Adrenaline surged through her veins and she thought she could hear the thudding beat of her own heart.

Perhaps she'd awakened on the heels of some nightmare, she thought, striving to understand her fear. But she couldn't remember any scenes of horror. It hadn't been a dream that had awakened her, it had been a small, almost insignificant sound.

There was someone in her room.

She'd heard the words "paralyzed with fright," but she'd never understood them until this moment. The sound came again; a faint, gliding noise such as a shoe might make on thick carpeting.

Frantically Angie strove to still the mindless fear that was threatening to take full control of her body. She had two options, she told herself. She could scream for help or keep utterly still and allow the intruder to believe she was asleep. Somewhere she had read that the latter was the safer course. If whoever was in the room was intent on robbery, he would be looking for her purse. As soon as he found it, he would be gone.

If she screamed she risked causing the thief to panic and do something crazy such as use a gun or a knife to silence her.

Where was he in the room? Lying motionless Angie struggled to control her breathing. It seemed far too loud in her own ears. She was wringing wet with fear.

She was on her side facing the balcony. The faint gliding noise came again from the vicinity of the nightstand. He must be searching the drawers. Please let him find the purse quickly.

Angie thought she detected soft sounds near the chair

where she had left her shoulder bag. *There. It's right there in front of you. Grab it. Take it and leave. Get out of here.*

What was the matter with the idiot? Couldn't he see the yellow leather bag just sitting there on the chair? She had the drapes open, and the room was not completely dark. Why didn't he take the damn purse?

The whisper of sound came again, this time from near the foot of the bed. A new fear assailed her. If the intruder had more than theft on his mind, she would have no choice but to start screaming and risk the knife or the gun. Her hand clenched silently into a fist, her nails digging into her palm.

Then, without any further warning, the door to her room opened and closed in near silence. She was alone.

The knowledge that the intruder had gone left Angie weak with an almost physically painful sense of relief. For a long moment she simply lay on her side, inhaling deeply in an attempt to steady her nerves. Her legs were trembling beneath the sheet.

She opened her eyes and stared out at the starlit balcony. The ocean gleamed in the distance as the moon painted a broad swath of silver across its surface. She wanted comfort and warmth and safety.

She wanted the feel of Flynn's strong arms around her. She wanted his protection.

Angie kicked off the sheet with a burst of energy that surprised her. She darted to the closet, yanked down her terry-cloth swim robe and belted it around her waist. Then she grabbed her room key and let herself out into the hall.

There was no sign of anyone in the corridor. Not bothering with the elevator, she headed for the stairwell and dashed up the two flights to the floor where Flynn's room was located. Panting, she halted outside the door and rapped sharply.

When it opened a moment later Angie didn't hesitate. She hurled herself into Flynn's arms.

"Angie! What the hell...?" He held her close.

"There was someone in my room. A thief. He was prowling around my room, Flynn." The words came out in short gasps. "I've never been so scared in my life. I was sure I'd locked the door. I don't understand how—" She broke off, recovered her breath and tried again. "As soon as he left I ran up here. He must have been after my purse, but he didn't take it. I guess he couldn't see it. Oh, my God, I was terrified!"

"Angie! Angie, honey, calm down. Tell me exactly what happened." Flynn's hands closed around her upper arms and he shook her gently. "Are you sure someone was in your room?"

She nodded her head sharply. "Hell, yes. I could hear him. A sort of gliding sound on the carpet. Flynn, nothing like this has ever happened to me before in my life. It's so frightening." With an effort she gathered herself together. Then she tried a shaky smile. "It's okay, I'm not going to flip out on you."

Flynn's face was hard and grim, his dark eyes glittering with controlled tension. "You're certain nothing was taken?"

"Well, no, I'm not absolutely certain. I just remember seeing my purse on the chair as I left the room a few minutes ago. I suppose he might have reached inside and taken the wallet."

"Come on."

"Where are we going?" She leaned back against the door as he released her to pick up the black shirt he'd been wearing earlier. For the first time Angie realized he was wearing only a pair of white briefs. The naked expanse of his shoulders moved sleekly as he shrugged into the shirt. He reached for a pair of jeans and quickly stepped into them. Angie glanced away from the sight of his well-muscled thighs. It was a little unsettling to encounter a nearly nude male at this hour of the night. Especially when it was a male she had gone to sleep fantasizing about a few hours earlier. She'd seen him in a swimsuit, but somehow this was different, far more intimate.

"We're going back down to your room to make certain nothing was taken. Then we're going downstairs to have a talk with the desk clerk." Flynn picked up his keys and his folded leather wallet, and then he took Angie's arm.

Obediently Angie allowed him down the stairs to her own room. She opened the door and switched on the light.

"See? There's the purse. The fool couldn't seem to see it, although it was easy enough for me to spot on my way out the door." She walked over to the chair and unfastened the catch of the shoulder bag. Her passport and billfold were still safely tucked inside.

Flynn prowled around the room, opening drawers and checking the doors that fronted the balcony. "You're sure he came and left through the hallway door?"

"Absolutely. I could hear it open and close when he left." Angie picked her bag up off the chair and sat down with it in her lap. Hands clutching the leather, she stared at Flynn as he searched the balcony. "I just don't understand how he could have missed the purse. Unless..."

Flynn walked back in from the balcony. "Unless what?"

"Unless it wasn't my purse he was after," she said starkly.

The sliding glass door closed with a vicious chunking sound. Flynn turned to face her, his gaze burning. "You're all right?"

She blinked, realizing what he was thinking. "I'm fine," she assured him. "I didn't mean that whoever it was intended rape. I meant he might be after something other than my purse. The dagger, for instance.''

''The dagger!'' Flynn sank onto the rumpled bed, frowning. ''The only one who even knows you have it is…''

''Alexander Cardinal,'' she concluded for him.

''But that doesn't make any sense, Angie. He just sold it to you a few hours ago. Why would he try to get it back?''

''You saw the size of Julian's check. That dagger wasn't cheap. And Cardinal is obviously a man who goes through a lot of money. Remember the yacht? The private island? The villa? Maybe Cardinal decided he'd take Julian's money and then take back the dagger, too. The best of both worlds.''

''I got the feeling that Cardinal, whatever else he might be, is a man of his word.'' Flynn looked thoughtful.

''A man of his word! How could you trust him? He's obviously made a fortune and no one, including Julian, seems quite sure how. He's charming, all right, but I wouldn't trust him any farther than I could throw him. What's more, I'll bet he's got everyone in the vicinity in his pocket. It would be easy enough for him to hire someone to break into my room.''

''Okay, settle down. I'm not going to argue with you about the guy. But if he's on such good terms with the hotel people, wouldn't someone have told him that you put the dagger in the safe?''

Angie shifted uneasily, thinking about it. ''Who knows? Maybe he didn't bother to ask; just assumed I'd have it in my room. Flynn, I don't know what's going on, but the fact remains that the thief didn't bother with my purse, and the only other thing of value that I have is that dagger. Cardinal is too powerful in this part of Mexico. I want to leave.''

''Angie, it's four in the morning.''

"I don't care. I want to get the dagger and leave. Right now."

"And go where?" Flynn asked patiently.

"The airport. Maybe we can get an earlier flight."

"We?"

Angie stilled. "I thought you were coming back to California with me?"

Flynn's gaze softened. "I am. I'm just not sure it's necessary to leave right this minute."

"Flynn, you once said you believed in some forms of intuition...."

"Not feminine intuition," he drawled.

"Well, I do believe in it. And I have the strongest feeling that we should get away from here." Angie looked at him pleadingly. "Please, Flynn. I'm scared. I'm responsible for getting that dagger safely back to Julian. I don't want to take any chances. As long as we hang around the resort we're just too close to Cardinal. He's too powerful."

"Angie, we don't even know if he's after the dagger," Flynn tried to say logically.

"Someone is!"

"We don't know that. The guy might have been after your purse and just missed it." Flynn got up and came across to her. "Or you might have dreamed the whole thing, honey," he added gently. "There's no sign of any forcible entry."

"I did not dream it!" She felt a rush of fury and hysteria begin to build in her. "I thought you of all people would believe me, Flynn!"

He threaded his large fingers through her tangled hair and looked down at her for a long, considering moment. "You're scared, aren't you?"

"Panicked."

He gave her a half smile. "Not quite but I can see you're

getting there. Honey, I don't even know if we can get a car at this hour of the night. This is Mexico, remember? And a rather remote part of the country to boot. People down here run on their own time, even the tourist-trade people. They're not accustomed to crazy gringos who want to rent a car at four o'clock in the morning.''

"We've got to try."

Flynn studied her a moment longer, clearly attempting to think of further arguments, but in the end he appeared to give up the effort. "Okay, Angie. I'll go downstairs and see what I can do about renting a car."

"I'll come with you."

"I had a feeling you were going to say that."

She realized with a shock that he wasn't certain yet whether he believed her tale of the intruder. His lack of faith angered her. "You don't have to humor me, Flynn. If you don't want to get involved, just go on back to your own room. I'll handle this myself." Her fingers were digging into the leather purse. Angie felt more determined than she ever had about anything in her life. "I'm not trying to force you to come with me. But I am going to get out of here tonight."

Flynn's gaze narrowed speculatively. "You know damn well I'm involved now."

"There's absolutely no need for you to go any further with this," she began defiantly. "I appreciate your help up to this point, but you certainly don't need to feel obligated to—"

"You've said enough, Angie. I'm going with you."

"Not if you're going to act patronizing or domineering, you aren't!"

He planted his palm flat against the wall behind her head and leaned over her. "You want to drive forty miles by yourself on a lonely Mexican highway at four in the morning?"

Angie flinched. The occasional tales of U.S. tourists ambushed on Mexican roads were not unknown to her. She'd researched such tales for one of Julian's books. It was relatively easy to discount those stories during the daytime, but at four in the morning they took on new meaning. But she said stubbornly, "I'd feel safer driving up the coast alone than I would staying here."

Flynn straightened away from the wall, his attitude one of resignation. "All right. I can see you're not going to be completely rational about this. Let's get going. Put some clothes on. I'm not taking you down to the front desk dressed like that."

She stood up slowly. "You don't believe me, do you?"

"I believe something scared the hell out of you tonight. But in all honesty I can't see any sign of someone having been in your room. And from what you've told me, you didn't actually see anyone, either. You just think you heard him."

Angie gritted her teeth and turned to pull a pair of jeans and a red cotton-knit pullover out of the closet. Without a word she headed toward the bathroom to change.

Ten minutes later Flynn had roused the sleeping desk clerk and explained the need to rent a car. The clerk rubbed his eyes, yawned widely and politely explained that renting a car was quite impossible at this hour of the night.

"The rental agency will not be open until nine this morning, *señor*. Surely you can understand that." The clerk smiled ingratiatingly, trying hard to be polite to the crazy *norteamericanos*. His uncle had warned him when he'd hired him that a night clerk's job was not always easy. Tourists were a strange bunch.

Flynn pulled out his wallet and peeled off several large bills. He put them down on the counter in front of the clerk. "I am prepared to pay someone for the inconvenience of renting us a car. Could you please telephone whoever is responsible for running the rental agency here in the hotel and ask if he's interested in being compensated for the extra trouble?''

The clerk looked down at the bills. Tourists were not only very strange, they were willing to pay dearly for the oddest things. Women, cigarettes made from a local product that, thanks to the vagaries of bureaucrats, could not be marketed legally; such things he could understand a man being willing to waste money on. But a rental car at four o'clock in the morning? It made no sense.

But a night desk clerk learned to be sophisticated about such matters. The clerk smiled brilliantly and put two fingers on one of the bills. ''There is no way a car can be rented at this hour, but there is a possible alternative. Where is it you wish to travel, *señor?*''

Flynn kept his hand firmly on the money. ''Cancun.''

Angie, standing behind him, waited anxiously as the clerk appeared to give considerable thought to the matter. With every passing moment she felt the need to be on her way with the dagger.

''Cancun.'' The clerk nodded. ''A long trip by car but not so long by boat. My cousin, Ramon, has a very fast boat, *señor.* He uses it to pull the tourists on water skis. I think that I might be able to convince him to take you to Cancun.''

''He'd take us down the coast in the darkness?'' Flynn looked distinctly skeptical.

The clerk shrugged. ''It is nearly four-thirty. In another half hour it will be dawn. Besides, Ramon has lived here all his life. He knows the coastline as well as he knows the faces of his six children.''

Flynn turned back to Angie. ''Are you sure you don't want to wait until the rental agency opens?''

She didn't hesitate. "I'm sure."

He studied her determined expression and gave in to the inevitable. Nothing he said was going to change her mind, he realized. "Okay. Call Cousin Ramon," Flynn said to the clerk.

The man's hand closed around the cash lying on the desk. Then, beaming, he disappeared into an office. Flynn wondered idly how much the clerk would tell his cousin he'd received from the crazy *norteamericano*. He figured Ramon would be lucky to see half the bribe.

The clerk had been right. By the time Angie and Flynn had packed, checked out of the hotel and found a cheery-looking Ramon waiting at the dock, there was a faint glow lightening the sky. The sun would be rising soon. Flynn was grateful for small favors. He hadn't been looking forward to making this little jaunt in total darkness.

"Cancun?" Ramon repeated easily when Flynn told him the destination. "No sweat." He grinned proudly at his fine English.

"That's just terrific, Ramon," Flynn said dryly as he settled himself down beside Angie. "Absolutely terrific. Let's get going." He glanced at Angie's tense face as Ramon pulled the boat away from the dock. The dagger case was resting on her lap. She didn't seem willing to trust it to the small bag that rested at her feet. When he saw the anxiety in her eyes, some of his irritation lessened. She was genuinely frightened. "Feeling better now that we're on our way?"

She nodded briefly. "Yes. Thank you for arranging everything, Flynn. I will see that you're compensated for the money you had to give the desk clerk."

"Angie, do me a favor. If you're going to insist on maintaining that insulted-employer-dealing-with-untrusting-employee attitude, keep your mouth shut, okay? I'm not in the mood for placating you right now. I've got other things on my mind.''

She glared at him. "Such as?"

"I'll think of something."

A few minutes later Flynn stopped wondering what else to think about. Something rather crucial came to mind as he glanced back over his shoulder at the lights of the resort.

"Hell."

The roar of the boat's engine masked the soft oath, but Angie must have seen his expression. She stared at his profile for a few seconds and then leaned toward him.

"What's wrong?" She held her whipping hair out of her eyes.

"I'm not sure yet." He spoke into her ear so that she could hear him above the noise of the boat and the wind. "But I think Cousin Ramon was wrong. I'm afraid we have got something to sweat about."

Angie's eyes widened in startled concern. "What are you talking about?"

But Flynn was on his feet, heading toward the front of the speeding craft, where Ramon stood at the wheel. He leaned down to tap the pilot on his shoulder.

"*Señor?*" Ramon glanced up, his face a mask of polite inquiry.

"What the hell do you think you're doing?" Flynn said, raising his voice above the engine roar. "You've been hired to take us down the coast. I didn't pay you for a sightseeing trip of the bay."

"I am very sorry, *señor*, but someone else has paid me for taking you sightseeing. And I'm also sorry to report he paid a great deal more than you did for your run to Cancun. So what can I do? I have six children to feed. We go sightseeing instead of down the coast."

Cousin Ramon raised his hand and revealed the ugly .25-caliber Star semiautomatic he had clutched in his fist.

Chapter 4

Angie couldn't hear the verbal exchange between Cousin Ramon and Flynn; the roar of the outboard blanked out the words. But moonlight glinted on the gun in Ramon's hand when he raised his arm. She froze in her seat.

She saw Flynn glance almost casually down at the weapon. In the chancy light she thought he looked more wryly disgusted than alarmed. It occurred to her that this probably wasn't the first time he had encountered a man with a gun.

He said something to the Mexican, something Ramon appeared to consider seriously for a moment. Angie guessed Flynn was following local custom and offering a bribe. It was obvious Ramon was torn, but he finally shook his head with grave regret. Evidently whoever was paying him to do this was someone he didn't want to risk offending, Angie decided. Alexander Cardinal was a local employer, after all. The gringos could only offer a one-time arrangement and then they would be gone. Mr. Cardinal undoubtedly offered the opportunity of future employment. And Cousin Ramon had all those kids to support.

Angie was aware of the trickle of dampness running down her arm. The early morning air was balmy, even a bit on the cool side, but she was perspiring as if it were already high noon. The odd part was that she didn't feel warm. She felt distinctly chilled. She sat very still, the box holding the dagger clutched on her lap.

Flynn was still talking to Ramon. Trying to bargain, perhaps. The outboard continued to roar at high speed as Ramon kept one hand casually on the wheel. Unsteadily Angie got to her feet. Instantly the eyes of both men flicked to the back of the boat. Ramon's gaze only wavered for a second, but when he saw Angie he hissed something to Flynn.

"Stay where you are, Angie." Flynn waved her back to her seat with a short, chopping movement of his hand.

She ignored him, making her way to the midpoint of the small craft. Hanging on to the dagger box, she maintained her balance with her free hand by clinging to the side of the boat.

"What does he want?" She was close enough to hear the voices of the two men now.

It was Ramon who answered in English. "Very sorry, *señorita*. But I have been told to take you to the island."

"Cardinal's island?"

Flynn shot her another glance. "Sit down, Angie."

She looked at him and then held up the dagger box. "He wants this. I knew it. He's going to try to steal it back."

Ramon glanced skeptically at the box, but his gun hand didn't waver. "I do not know why I am taking you to the island. I only do what I am told."

"This is why you're taking us to Cardinal's island. Cardinal wants this dagger back." Angrily Angie flipped open the lid of the box. She saw Ramon tense at the abrupt movement.

Then his curiosity got the better of him. He stared at the object lying on the black velvet. Caught by the moonlight, the gems in the dagger's handle gleamed richly. The steel picked up the faint yellow cast of the light and for an instant a man could have been forgiven for thinking that the object was made of gold and diamonds.

"I won't let him have it," Angie went on. She held the box out over the side of the boat. "I'll drop it into the ocean before I hand it back to Señor Cardinal."

"*Señorita!*" Ramon's eyes widened in alarm as he read the intent on her face. She stood there with the dagger box held precariously out over the foaming water. If he shot her now, the dagger would fall straight into the sea. Ramon panicked. "Tell her to stop!" he roared at Flynn.

"The lady's got a mind of her own." Flynn stood casually, one hand idly bracing himself on the top of the windshield.

"Tell her to stop or I will kill you!"

Angie's fingers tightened on the box, but she didn't bring it back to safety. Her hair whipped savagely around her face as she glared at the Mexican. "Pull that trigger, Ramon, and this thing goes into the water. Señor Cardinal will be furious, won't he?"

Ramon swore violently in Spanish, his face suddenly contorting with rage. Wildly he swung the gun away from Flynn, his intent clear.

But Flynn was in motion before the weapon could be trained on Angie. His hand came away from the windshield in a movement that resembled a striking snake. The quick, savage blow sliced into Ramon's wrist. Even as Ramon's howl of pain and rage began, Flynn was driving his other fist into the man's jaw.

A shot crashed through the night and then the semiautomatic flew into the air as Ramon sagged backward against the wheel. The boat swung crazily as his weight replaced the guidance of his hand.

"Flynn! The boat!" Hastily Angie snatched the dagger back to safety. She staggered, trying to catch her balance as the craft swerved abruptly.

Flynn yanked the half-conscious, groaning Ramon away from the wheel and tossed him down into the seat. Then he reached out to take control of the boat. A moment later the world steadied again. Flynn cut the engine.

Angie sat down abruptly as the boat came to a gliding halt in the water. It bobbed gently on the waves as Flynn released the wheel to concentrate on Ramon.

"Are you all right?"

Angie knew the harsh question was directed at her, not at the man sprawling on the seat. She huddled into herself, trying to stop shaking. Her body seemed to be going first hot and then cold. "Yes," she gasped. "Yes, I'm fine."

"Good. Then put down that damn dagger and come take the wheel."

It took a surprising amount of effort to unlock her fingers from the box, Angie discovered. But she managed it, setting the object carefully down on the rear seat. Uncertainly she got to her feet.

"You saved us, Flynn."

"No, Angie, I think I'll let you have full credit for this idiotic situation."

"What are we going to do with him?" She scrambled over Ramon's feet to get to the wheel.

"Dump him."

Her eyes widened in shock. "Overboard?"

"That would be the simplest answer. But I guess we can afford to be generous. We'll head back toward shore and leave him on the beach somewhere.'' Flynn was rapidly going through Ramon's pockets.

"What are you looking for?"

"I'd like to know who hired him."

"It's obvious who hired him. That horrible Alexander Cardinal!''

"Maybe. Maybe not.'' Flynn produced a wicked-looking switchblade knife, a wad of Mexican currency and some loose change from one pocket. The next yielded a supply of gum wrappers and a half stick of gum. There was nothing else to be found.

"Looks like he's not carrying a nice, neat, notarized contract signed by Cardinal,'' Angie observed. "But you can't have any real doubts about who hired him, Flynn. It must have been Cardinal.''

"It does look suspiciously like that, doesn't it?'' Flynn finished his task and then began rummaging around in one of the boat's storage compartments.

"Now what?'' Angie watched him intently.

"I need something to tie his hands with. Ah, here we go. Fishing line. That should do the trick.''

A few minutes later Cousin Ramon lay securely bound in the back of the boat. He groaned occasionally but other than that made no real effort to communicate. Flynn took the wheel, switched on the engine and headed toward shore. They were a couple of miles up the coast, out of sight of the resort.

"How did you know he was going to kidnap us?'' Angie sat up front, peering through the windshield as dawn warmed the horizon.

"It was no great burst of cunning logic. I simply realized, finally, that the lights of the resort were at our back as we left the dock and they didn't shift. They stayed in the same position behind us as they did the night we were taken to

Cardinal's island. They should have altered position as we turned toward Cancun. I guess good old Cousin Ramon figured that in the darkness we might not notice until it was too late.''

''That was very quick of you, Flynn,'' Angie said admiringly.

He cocked an eyebrow, slanting her an odd glance. ''Not as quick as you were when you thought of distracting him by threatening to drop the dagger overboard.''

She grinned suddenly. ''We're a pretty good team, aren't we? Maybe Julian will want to interview us for a scene in one of his books.''

''Somehow I think this might be a little tame by his standards.''

''Oh, I don't know. It's definitely got possibilities. After we drop Ramon off, are we going to use the boat to go on to Cancun?''

''That's the general idea. Unless I get struck by something more brilliant in the meantime.''

But Flynn was not struck by anything more brilliant. He guided the outboard carefully into a small cove, waded ashore with a sluggish, complaining Ramon and left his burden on the beach.

''Nice of you to leave him above the high-tide mark,'' Angie murmured as Flynn climbed, dripping, back into the boat.

''I thought so. Okay, let's get this crazy show on the road.''

''What'll we do with Cousin Ramon's boat?''

''We'll beach it somewhere outside of town and walk the rest of the way.''

''You think of everything, Flynn.''

''There was a time not too long ago when I would have modestly agreed with you. I've since changed my mind.''

The wind caught his short, dark hair, ruffling it as he guided the boat out of the cove. "What a night. You sure do know how to show a guy a good time. I'm going to be exhausted by the time we reach L.A."

Angie, who was feeling surprisingly exhilarated by the adrenaline that was still churning in her bloodstream, felt as if she could stay awake forever. She smiled to herself as she cradled the dagger box in her lap.

"Thanks, Flynn. I really mean it. I think you probably saved my life tonight. I don't even want to think about how it all would have ended if you hadn't gotten involved." Her gratitude was clear in her eyes.

Flynn looked down at her, aware once again of how much those beautiful eyes reminded him of the color of a peacock's tail. She really was grateful, he realized. He was startled at how pleased that made him feel. It must be his ego at work. Then he remembered his violent surge of rage and fear as he'd watched Ramon swing the gun toward her earlier. For an instant he felt that rage and fear again as he thought of her facing that gun alone.

What followed the episode on the boat constituted what Angie came to think of as the longest day of her entire life. The trip to Los Angeles seemed to take forever. There were delays while she and Flynn waited for a plane in Cancun and again in Mexico City. The time spent sitting nervously in airports kept Angie fretting constantly. Flynn had catnapped and thumbed through Spanish-language magazines, but Angie hadn't been able to relax. Even though she knew that they were undoubtedly far out of reach of Alexander Cardinal by the time they changed planes in Mexico City, she didn't really begin to calm down until their U.S. jet flew over the border.

She would have held on to the dagger case the entire

distance, never letting it out of her sight, if Flynn hadn't put his foot down.

"Try to get on board clutching that thing to your bosom and we're both going to spend some time explaining ourselves to the authorities. Mexico might be a little more lax about airport security regulations than the States, but I'd just as soon not take any chances. Pack the dagger into your suitcase, Angie."

Reluctantly Angie agreed. She didn't always approve of Flynn's somewhat authoritarian manner, but by now she trusted him implicitly. She still shuddered to think of what would have happened to her at the resort if she hadn't met Flynn Sangrey.

"I suppose you're right," she responded, unlocking her suitcase, "but if they lose our luggage I'm going to hold you responsible."

He'd grinned fleetingly. "I'd rather search for lost luggage than try to find you in a Mexican jail. Stay here while I check the tickets."

They'd eaten on board the flight from Mexico City to Los Angeles, but Angie couldn't even remember what she'd had. She and Flynn had been wide awake and on the move since nearly four in the morning. They'd had to take whatever flights they could get, and after the seemingly endless delays, darkness had fallen by the time Los Angeles sprawled below the plane.

"I never thought I'd by happy to see L.A." Angie glanced through the window at the maze of freeways and the endless sea of lights.

Flynn gave her a wry glance. "Goes to show you can learn to appreciate anything under the right circumstances. What now, Angie? You look exhausted."

"I am. And you don't look so perky yourself. Might as well get a hotel room for the night. We're safe now." She stifled a small yawn. "We can drive up the coast in the morning. My car's in the airport garage." She turned to him impulsively, her fingertips on his sleeve. "Thanks for coming this far with me, Flynn. Do you...do you still want to go on up the coast and meet Uncle Julian?"

"After all this you think I'm going to stop in L.A.? Not a chance." He covered her hand on his sleeve, his strong fingers enclosing hers completely.

Angie smiled tremulously. She suddenly wished she didn't look so weary and travel worn. But the truth was she felt exhausted, and she knew it probably showed. While waiting for the plane in Mexico City she had tried to brush her hair back into its normal coil but tendrils had again straggled free. The jeans and pullover she had put on in the early morning hours seemed to hang limply on her now, and she wasn't altogether certain her twenty-four-hour deodorant was living up to its advertising.

Flynn didn't look radically different than he had when they'd started out on the ill-fated trip with Cousin Ramon. His dark cotton shirt was wrinkled, but somehow on him it looked appropriate that way. Like something out of the catalog of safari gear. He looked a little travel weary but not totally exhausted. In the LAX terminal he still had plenty of strength to take charge of claiming the luggage and getting it through customs.

"Let me check the dagger," Angie said as he carried her bag out of the claim area.

Obediently he set it down and waited while she unlocked the suitcase again and examined the dagger case. "You seem to have grown rather attached to that thing," he observed dryly.

Still bent over the case, Angie smiled. "I know. I guess I feel responsible for it."

"Are you sure it doesn't amount to more than that?"

She closed the suitcase and got to her feet, pushing loose tendrils of hair back behind her ear. "Why do you say that?"

"Don't get defensive." He picked up the case again. "I was merely making a small observation."

Angie trotted a few steps in order to keep up with his long stride. She frowned as she considered his words. "You make it sound as though I'm getting obsessive about it."

"Forget it, Angie." He didn't speak again until they had finished with the formalities. Then he asked, "Where did you park the car?"

"What? Oh." Hastily she dug into her purse and found the slip of paper on which she'd jotted down the garage space. "Here it is."

Flynn studied the number on the slip. "Okay. Let's get going."

"Where's your home, Flynn?"

"I don't have one. Not yet. I keep a furnished apartment in San Diego but it's not home."

For some reason that bothered Angie. She felt a rush of sympathy for this man who had saved her life and who had stayed loyally by her side throughout the long journey to L.A. "You'll like the hacienda," she assured him gently. "And Julian's present home is quite lovely, too. I'm sure he'll want you to stay as long as you wish."

There was a moment of silence behind her as Flynn mulled over her words. Then he said quietly, "But you don't live in his house. You live in that guest cottage you mentioned."

"I like my privacy."

"Do you need a lot of privacy?"

Angie paused to study overhead corridor signs that gave directions to the parking facilities. "As much as any other woman, I imagine. What on earth do you mean, Flynn?"

Again there was a beat of silence before he answered. "Nothing. It just occurred to me that you might need privacy because there's someone important in your life. A man. We never got around to talking about that possibility, did we, Angie?"

She felt a frisson of awareness course through her. "No," she whispered, not looking at him. "We never did. I guess people don't talk about things like that when they're vacationing at exotic foreign resorts."

"Well?" There was a stark edge to the question.

"No, Flynn," she heard herself say quietly. "There's no one else. No one important the way you mean." Then, feeling that he owed her a similar response, she asked, "What about you?"

"Like I said, I've been on my own a long time. The sort of life I've been living hasn't exactly been conducive to long-term relationships. There's no one else, Angie."

She released the breath she hadn't realized she'd been holding and said brightly, "The car's just up ahead."

Flynn took charge of the driving with an easy authority that, under other circumstances, Angie might have resented. As it was, she discovered she was too tired to argue. It was a relief to let him battle the airport traffic. "There's a big chain hotel a few blocks away," she murmured after another yawn. "Why don't we stay there? I don't feel like driving any farther than absolutely necessary tonight. I can't remember when I've been this tired."

"Suits me." He pulled through the turnstile and handed the garage ticket over to the attendant.

By the time they parked the car again in a hotel parking lot and started toward the huge, brightly lit lobby, Angie could hardly keep her eyes open. The shock and the adrenaline, as well as the hours of travel, had all taken their toll. She trailed along in Flynn's wake; a small, battered little rowboat sticking close to the protection of a sleek, strong battle cruiser.

Obediently she waited to one side as Flynn registered for both of them. She patted another delicate yawn as he came back to collect her and the luggage.

"You need a hot shower and a warm bed," Flynn decided. "And so do I." He took her arm, hoisted the bags and started toward the elevators.

It was so easy to go on letting him take charge, Angie told herself. And she was so very tired.

At the door to her room she started to turn around to say good-night but he just smiled crookedly and pushed open the door, following her inside.

"I got us connecting rooms," he explained.

"Oh." She wasn't quite certain what else to say to that. The truth was she had gotten so accustomed to the idea of having him close during the day that the thought of having him nearby tonight was oddly comforting. She watched him walk through her room, turning on the lights and setting down her suitcase. Then he unlocked the door between his room and hers. Key in hand, he lounged in the doorway.

"Don't forget the hot shower, Angie."

"I won't." She didn't want him to step through that door into his own room, she realized.

"I'll be within shouting distance if you need me."

"Thank you, Flynn." She smiled fleetingly. "I seem to be saying that a lot today, don't I?" She couldn't ask him to stay. It was too soon and they had been through too much today. What was the matter with her? Her fierce awareness of him was probably just a result of the events in Mexico. She was grateful to him, that was all. She wasn't in love with the man, and it was a cinch he wasn't in love with her.

And she didn't want to go to bed with a man she didn't love. She couldn't possibly want that.

So why did she want to snuggle into bed with Flynn Sangrey tonight? Why did she long for the comfort of his arms after the trials of the day?

Gratitude. That was all it was. That was all it could be and that wasn't enough. In addition, it was entirely possible that he wasn't in the least interested in making love to her. The man must be nearly as exhausted as she was. He would probably politely decline any invitation she offered. Heaven knew the embarrassment of rejection would be exceedingly awkward to live down in the morning.

Angie ran through the complete list of all the reasons why she shouldn't ask Flynn to stay with her and when she came to the end she smiled wistfully.

"Good night," she said, her eyes soft with a longing she couldn't quite conceal, not even from herself.

For a long moment Flynn studied her forlorn, frayed figure as she stood in the middle of the hotel room. Then he nodded, turned into his own room and closed the door behind him.

Angie sighed with a deep, feminine regret that seemed to well up from that alien fissure of gold that ran through her. Tonight the part of her nature that she had never quite trusted or fully understood was close to the surface. It had threatened to take control for a moment there as she had said good-night to Flynn.

It was because she was so tired, Angie consoled herself. That was the only reason she'd come so close to surrendering to that hot-blooded streak in herself. When you were tired, all your defenses were down.

She should be grateful to Flynn for not having taken advantage of her.

That thought made her mouth curve wryly. She was already feeling enough gratitude toward Flynn Sangrey. Besides, she wasn't really certain that the small, wild streak in her nature knew anything about gratitude. She sensed it operated under its own set of rules.

The hot shower Flynn had prescribed was just what a doctor would have ordered. It released the last of the day's tension. By the time she shut off the warm spray, Angie could barely keep her eyes open. She fumbled around in her suitcase for her light cotton nightgown, checked once more to see that the dagger was where it should be and crawled wearily into bed.

Sleep claimed her just as she was wondering if it should be so hard to tell the difference between gratitude and passion. Surely gratitude didn't fill a woman with this kind of deep, abiding longing.

Angie wasn't certain just when the unfocused swirl of her dreams began to coalesce into reality. She only knew that hours after she had gone to sleep she awoke to a sense of awareness that didn't seem to belong to either the world of sleep or the state of being alert. It was some never-never land in between, a border area between night and day that allowed for all sorts of possibilities.

Slowly she turned on her side, her eyes half-closed as she slowly studied the shadowy room. The door between her bedroom and Flynn's stood open.

The knowledge ought to have jolted her into full wakefulness. Instead Angie felt only a sense of relief, as if, finally, everything was working out the way it should. In this soft, hidden area between reality and sleep, the golden fissure within her began to glow. Unstopped by logic or a woman's natural uncertainty, it leaked its potent energy into Angie's system. The open door between the two rooms meant only one thing: Flynn was here. He had come to find her.

"Angie?" There was a low rustle of movement beside

the bed. Flynn's voice was dark and deep, a little rough around the edges. The blunt tips of his fingers brushed her cheek. "If you want me to leave, I will."

Angie caught the fingers that were feathering her skin. She turned her mouth into the palm of his hand and kissed him with exquisite gentleness. "No," she whispered. "I don't want you to leave." It was the truth and in this alien borderland she was free to admit it.

"Sweet, soft Angie." Flynn lifted the light blanket and slid into the warm bed.

He was nude, Angie realized with a tingling sense of shock. What had she expected? Silk pajamas? Cautiously, but with a compelling feeling of exhilaration, she reached out to touch the muscled contours of his chest. She heard his small groan of desire and then his feet were tangling with hers.

"I've been wanting to hold you like this since the first night I met you." Flynn brought her close, one hand cradling her hips as he urged her into his own heat.

"Oh, Flynn…" She could feel the hardness of him pushing against her with unsubtle demand. Her own desire flared more fully into life, coloring the shadowy moment with gentle fire. Her body was responding to his with glorious excitement, and Angie wondered why she had ever tried to talk herself out of this union. Nothing had ever seemed so right.

She felt Flynn's strong thigh sliding up between her legs, carefully parting her own thighs so that she was open to him. His hand moved up under the hem of the cotton gown, gliding over her hip. His mouth came down on hers and Angie moaned deep in her throat. Flynn's hand continued its upward journey, pushing the nightgown out of the way until he lifted her to pull it off entirely.

"Angie, honey. I want you so much."

She believed him. The urgency in his husky words came through to her so clearly, appealing to every feminine instinct. The gold seeping into her bloodstream had turned hot under his touch, and she twisted luxuriously, straining against him.

Angie wrapped her arms around Flynn's neck, opening her mouth to let his tongue invade her intimately. His palm moved over her breast, rasping against the nipples until she cried out softly.

"Do you want me, sweetheart? Tell me you want me."

She told him in a thousand tiny ways. Her nails lightly scored his shoulders and her tongue slipped into his mouth to tease him. She trembled when he caressed her, and when he drew his hand down her stomach to find the dark tangle of hair at the apex of her thighs, she gave him the words in husky, broken little gasps.

"I do want you, Flynn. So much. I've never felt like this, never needed anyone the way I need you tonight."

He drank the words from her lips, clearly taking deep satisfaction from the tremulous confession. She felt the edge of his teeth on her earlobe just as his fingers began to discover her most intimate secrets. Angie shivered with an anticipation that was unlike anything she had ever known.

"You do want me." Flynn's lips were at her throat now. "My God, I can feel how much you need me. You're so warm, so damp and warm. Like hot gold."

How did he know? Angie wondered fleetingly. That was exactly how she felt. The hidden heat in her had surfaced, flowing through every vein, filling her with a reckless wildfire.

"Yes, Flynn. Yes, now, please!"

He groaned hoarsely, needing no further urging. Angie felt herself being pushed deeply into the bedclothes and then Flynn was looming over her, lowering himself heavily along the length of her body. His thighs pushed between hers, and his large hands closed over her shoulders.

She caught her breath as she sensed his hard, blunt manhood waiting at the gate of her softness. And in that timeless second before she gave herself up to his passion, Angie opened her eyes and found his night-darkened gaze burning down into hers.

"Angie, this is right. This is the way it's supposed to be. Trust me, sweetheart."

A part of her was alarmed by the urgency in his words. Then the demands of the moment returned, crashing over both of them in a giant wave. Flynn moved against her, suddenly, completely. Angie gasped as the thrilling shock of his possession rippled through her body. He waited for a few seconds, giving both of them time to absorb the dizzying sensations. Then, with a low, muttered groan, he began to move.

Angie's nails sank more deeply into his shoulders. Her hips lifted in response to the heavy, demanding thrusts of his body. Flynn's name was a soft litany of desire that barely escaped her throat.

The world outside the hotel room ceased to exist for an unmeasured length of time. For Angie there was only the man in whose arms she was so tightly held and the sensual claim he imposed. She could no more deny the flaming need in him than she could have stopped a sweeping brushfire. But her own need was a flame that leaped every bit as high, and the feminine demands she made were answered with a bold eagerness, a fierce, masculine desire to please and satisfy.

And when the end came in a spiral of shimmering excitement that turned on its own axis until it exploded, Angie and Flynn surrendered to it together.

As Angie lay in Flynn's arms, damp and sweetly exhausted and on the verge of sleep, she heard him whisper once more in her ear.

''This is the way it's supposed to be, Angie. I know it. I'm almost home.''

Chapter 5

Angie awoke to a smoggy Los Angeles sunrise and the certain knowledge that something fundamental had altered in her world during the night. She moved her leg, instinctively seeking Flynn's muscular calf. When she didn't find it she shifted onto her side, trying to find the warmth of his body. During the night she had discovered an enthralling comfort and sense of security in Flynn's arms. It was the sort of thing that could rapidly become addictive, Angie decided. In fact, she had a strong hunch she was already hooked.

Last night had been more than a passionate exploration of the mutual excitement she and Flynn generated in each other. If it had been only that, Angie thought she could have kept it all in some sort of perspective.

It was perfectly true that she had never before known the kind of passion she'd found during the night, but she was an adult and she thought she could have dealt with physical passion in a mature fashion. At the very least she could have convinced herself not to go off the deep end and tell herself she was in love.

But that sense of comfort and security, that feeling of *belonging* was altogether unexpected and strangely, insidiously alluring.

She tried to tell herself that her emotions were not to be trusted at this stage. The man had probably saved her life. He had most definitely saved the dagger from being stolen. Those facts alone were enough to distort a woman's judgment. Add to them the powerful physical attraction that existed between herself and Flynn, and you had a powder keg of emotions ready to be ignited.

Still, Angie thought she could have handled all those factors in an intelligent, analytical fashion now that morning had arrived. She was, after all, a woman, not a girl. But a sense of perspective remained elusive. And she thought she knew why. The unexpected feeling of rightness that she had experienced in Flynn's arms last night simply refused to be pigeonholed, cataloged or dealt with on a purely intellectual basis. She was falling in love. Perhaps she was already in so deep that fine distinctions didn't matter.

The realization both warmed her and made her uneasy. It left her feeling as though she were standing on a precipice; exposed and vulnerable in a way she had never been before in her life. She stopped seeking Flynn's strong body in the bed and slowly opened her eyes.

"You're awake."

It wasn't, Angie decided, the most loving tone of voice. She turned her head, following the sound of the low, rough words until she saw Flynn. He was fully dressed in the familiar, functional twill pants and a khaki shirt. The scarred leather belt and moccasins seemed as appropriate on him here in L.A. as they had in the exotic atmosphere of the Mexican Caribbean.

He had showered and shaved. Angie had a fleeting memory of the rough texture of his beard as he had cradled her close during the night. Flynn stood by the window, one foot propped on the low ledge shielding the air conditioner that had been installed beneath the glass. He had opened the drapes and had apparently been studying the yellowed horizon until he'd realized she was awake.

"Good morning, Flynn." This opening scene wasn't starting out quite as Angie had expected. During the night she had convinced herself that the morning after would be a time of tenderness and anticipation. But she sensed already that something was going wrong with her imagined scenario. "You're up early. After everything that happened yesterday, I thought you'd want to sleep late this morning." *With me,* she added silently. *I thought you'd want to curl up with me and perhaps make love to me while we teased each other about what to have for breakfast.* Wasn't that what lovers did the morning after?

"Angie, we have to talk."

Real anxiety set in now. Angie sat up slowly, drawing the sheet to her chin in an unconsciously defensive gesture. Her nightgown lay on the floor beside the bed, and she felt more exposed and vulnerable than ever with Flynn standing there fully dressed. She tried to think of something light and brilliant to say and ended up coughing a little to clear her throat first.

"I had no idea you were so chatty first thing in the morning. How about a cup of coffee first?" Did that sound sufficiently careless? Angie's fingers tightened on the hem of the sheet. Oh, God, she wasn't going to be any good at playing careless. She hadn't had the practice.

"We can go downstairs to breakfast later. First we have to get some things clarified between us, Angie." Flynn leaned one elbow casually on his raised knee and looked at her.

With a sickening sense of shock Angie registered the unrelenting grimness of his dark gaze. This was worse than anything she could have imagined. Her pulse began to beat more quickly. She no longer needed a cup of coffee to wake her up, Angie realized. She was suddenly, tensely alert. And her overriding instinct was to run.

Except that of course she couldn't. An image of herself dashing naked out into the hotel corridor brought her back to reality. Drawing a deep, steadying breath, Angie searched for the words that might help her regain a sense of control.

"Don't panic, Flynn. If you're, uh, worrying about last night…I mean, if you're afraid I'll make a scene or make demands or something…" She was fumbling badly and the knowledge alarmed her. "You don't have to be nervous about my reactions this morning. I know what I said down in Mexico, but I guess I didn't mean it. I'm not going to hurl a lot of accusations or…or blame you for using me. I'm perfectly well aware that what occurred last night was a…a mutual decision and I'm adult enough to—"

"Angie, please shut up." The order was almost gentle, although there was no softness in Flynn's face. "And don't make any promises about not throwing a tantrum until after you've heard what I have to say."

"Flynn, I don't—"

"My name is Flynn Sangrey Challoner, Angie."

She blinked uncertainly as the name worked its way into her brain. "Challoner?"

"That's right. Several generations back one of my ancestors married Maria Isabel Torres. And on the wedding night he discovered his bride had brought a rather unique gift to her new husband."

"The Torres Dagger." Angie couldn't hear any emotion

in her own words. They were as dull and flat as she was suddenly feeling.

"Yes." Flynn didn't take his eyes off her face. He looked like a man who has set himself a hard task; a man who won't quit until it's accomplished, regardless of how much pain is involved.

"I see." She couldn't think of anything else to say. Her mind seemed to have gone blank.

"Do you? Angie, I know this is a shock, and I know I've got a lot of explaining to do. But I *can* explain it, honey. That's what I'm trying to do this morning. I want you to understand."

"You want me to understand why you lied to me?"

His dark brows came together in a sudden, fierce frown, and Flynn's jaw hardened. "I haven't lied to you, Angie. I just didn't give you all the facts, because I didn't know how you would react. And I couldn't take a chance on losing track of that dagger again. It's taken me years to trace it this far. When I found I was one step behind someone else who wanted it, I—" He broke off abruptly.

Her chest felt tight, and her nails seemed to be trying to rip through the industrial-strength fabric of the hotel sheet. "Would you mind if I got dressed before we go any further with this?"

The unforgiving angles and planes of Flynn's face seemed to become even harder as he watched her. Angie had the impression he was genuinely torn between granting her reasonable request or making himself look slightly foolish by refusing it. She knew without being told that he wanted to refuse.

"Angie, you're going to listen to me. We're going to get this all out in the open. I know you'll probably be upset at first and I can't blame you, but after I've explained it all you'll understand. Last night you trusted me. And when I've told you all the facts, you'll trust me again."

Her chin lifted as pride twisted through her, cutting across some of the numbness. The pride seemed somehow linked to that temperamental streak of gold that had produced such passion last night. "A gentleman would not mention last night at this stage, Flynn. And a gentleman would go into his room and leave me some privacy in which to get dressed."

"Angie, I want to get this over with as quickly as possible."

"So do I," she whispered fervently. "But I am discovering that it's difficult for a woman to be told she's been a fool while she's sitting naked in bed. Hard on the morale. I'm sure you can understand that. Please leave me alone, Flynn."

He swung his foot down off the air-conditioner ledge and came toward her. "Honey, don't cry. Please don't cry. It's going to be all right. I swear it."

"Don't worry, I have no intention of crying." Her eyes felt hot and bright but she was quite certain she wouldn't cry. That pride was strong stuff. It came to her in a flash of unbidden intuition that Maria Isabel had known such pride.

Flynn hesitated a moment longer, clearly ambivalent about how to handle the situation. He stood at the side of the bed looking down at her and then he nodded abruptly. "Okay. I'll give you a few minutes to get dressed. Are you sure you're all right?"

"Oh, I'm in great shape, Flynn."

He put out a hand to stroke her cheek in a brief caress. Instantly she pulled her face away from his touch. Flynn's hand fell to his side.

"You don't have to be shy with me this morning, Angie. Not after last night."

"Are you going to leave me in peace?"

He exhaled slowly, turned and walked back into his own room. Angie waited until the door closed, and then she fled into the bathroom. She didn't cry in the shower, either. She refused to give in to the impulse, and after a while it faded.

Flynn Sangrey Challoner. The Challoner descendant about whom Uncle Julian had occasionally speculated. Angie stood beneath the steaming water and forced herself to deal with the facts. Everything fit into place so nicely now. The fortunate coincidence of her meeting Flynn in Mexico was completely explained. No wonder Flynn had been so willing to help her at every step along the way.

By the time Angie had finished showering, she only had one real question left to ask Flynn Sangrey Challoner. She coiled her hair into the familiar twist at the nape of her neck, pulled on a pair of pleated black trousers and dug out a slightly wrinkled fuchsia shirt. The strong color contrast gave her a small shot of personal strength. She had a feeling she was going to need it. Already the sense of comfort and security she had discovered during the night had faded into nothingness.

Flynn opened the door between the two rooms just as Angie was closing her suitcase. She glanced at him over her shoulder and then went back to finishing her small task.

"Feel better?" he asked quietly.

"Much. I'm starving, though. Can we have our big conversation over breakfast?" She was proud of the cool way that came out.

"If that's what you want."

"What I'd really like to know is when you intend to steal the dagger."

A shattering silence descended on the room. Angie had a few seconds in which to realize that her single question might have been exceedingly ill-timed. Then Flynn's hand clamped down on her shoulder, and he was spinning her around to face him. She found herself staring up into flint-hard eyes that seemed to burn through her. Several generations of arrogant pride crystalized in that fierce masculine gaze, and for a paralyzing instant Angie felt as if she'd stepped through a time warp and was confronting the reckless, arrogant Challoner who had married Maria Isabel. She went very still beneath the hand that was locked on her shoulder.

"If I had wanted to steal that dagger," Flynn bit out, each word a thrust of the blade, "I could have done it a dozen times since you bought it from Alexander Cardinal. I could have taken it from you and flown out of Mexico with it, and you would have been absolutely helpless to stop me. For that matter I could have taken it last night after you'd fallen asleep so trustingly in my arms. I could have disappeared with it this morning while you were in the shower. I am not a thief, Angie Morgan. My claim on that dagger is more valid than your own or your uncle's, but I will not steal it from you. Before we go a step further, you will apologize to me for your accusation."

Angie found her breath and somehow managed to keep her words under control. She would not surrender to the urge to scream at him. He might have his pride but she had her own, and it was every bit as fierce as his. At any other time that realization would have startled her. But there was no time to consider it now.

"Apologize? To a man who has been deliberately misleading, if not actually lying to me for several days now? Apologize to a man who doesn't even bother to give me his right name before taking me to bed?"

The fingers on her shoulder clenched. "The apology is for the man who saved the dagger and perhaps your life in the process. For the man who didn't steal it although he had plenty of opportunity. The apology, Angie, is for the man you gave yourself to last night. I expect anger from you, and I expect you to feel hurt this morning. You're a woman, and you've got a common ancestry with Maria Isabel. We both know about her temper. I am prepared to put up with a certain amount of temper from you, but I will not allow you to stand there and insult me by calling me a thief. Apologize, damn it!''

Angie didn't need to have it spelled out: she was walking very close to the line. Her accusation had obviously deeply offended Flynn. The logic of the situation was also suddenly inescapable. Flynn hadn't stolen the dagger. Not yet. And she couldn't deny he'd had plenty of opportunity. She drew herself up under his hand.

"My apologies, Mr. Challoner. You have not yet proven yourself a thief. Other things, perhaps, but not a thief.''

His eyes narrowed, and she knew he wanted more than that from her. But he must have realized he wouldn't get it. Flynn released her shoulder. "Let's go downstairs and get some coffee.''

"And the dagger?'' she challenged.

"You can take it with you.'' He stalked to the door and flung it open, waiting for her.

After a second's pause Angie picked up the dagger's case and followed him out into the hall. All during the long ride down in the elevator she lectured herself on maintaining her control. By the time they reached the lobby cafe Angie felt she had her emotions pushed safely back behind the wall of numbness she had discovered in herself that morning. And she still had her hands on the dagger. It seemed to give her courage.

Not quite enough courage to order a full-course breakfast, she discovered. Her appetite was nonexistent.

"I'll have coffee,'' she murmured when the waitress

came to take their order. It was the first thing Angie had said since leaving the hotel room.

"Angie, you need more than coffee." Flynn glowered at her as he looked up from his menu. "Have some eggs and toast."

"The coffee will be fine."

Flynn turned to the waitress. "We'll both have coffee. We will also each have an order of scrambled eggs and toast."

The waitress didn't wait for confirmation from Angie. She scribbled the order and disappeared in the direction of the kitchen.

Angie shook her head ruefully. "All right, Flynn, you've asserted yourself again, and I don't feel like doing battle over a couple of eggs and toast. I quit, you're the winner. Now will you please say whatever it is you feel obliged to say so we can get this whole thing over with?"

When the waitress returned with their coffee, he picked up his mug and took a deep swallow. Then he set it down with deliberation. "Angie, everything I told you in Mexico was the truth. The only thing I left out was my last name."

"Looking back, I'd say that was a rather major omission."

He sighed. "I know," he surprised her by saying bleakly. "But I didn't have much choice. Not in the beginning. Angie, I've been trying to trace that dagger for nearly eight years. I've spent a great deal of money having antique weapons specialists search gallery catalogs and private collections looking for the Torres Dagger. I didn't know your uncle was out there looking for it, too. In fact, I didn't even know your uncle existed until I finally got word that someone else had also been trying to track the dagger. By then it was too late. Julian Torres had already had more luck than I'd had. He'd located Alexander Cardinal and made an offer. Word was he'd offered a lot more than I could afford, even if I could have convinced Cardinal to deal with me instead. I learned through an antique dealer who had helped your uncle locate the dagger that Torres was going down to Mexico to collect it.''

"And you decided to follow," Angie concluded evenly.

"Yes. I'm not sure exactly what I hoped to accomplish, but I had to see the dagger for myself, so I followed and found you instead of Julian Torres. It wasn't hard making certain I'd found the right person. You talked willingly enough about why you were in Mexico."

Angie smiled without any trace of humor. "So I did. You talked a lot about why you were there, too, as I recall. You said you were on vacation."

Flynn shrugged. "I was in a sense."

"Resting between engagements," she said, reminding him of the phrase he had used.

He gave her a steady look. "It was the truth."

She picked up her coffee with an uneasy feeling. "I don't think I ever asked you exactly what kind of engagements you meant."

"No, you were afraid to ask, weren't you?"

"Perhaps I just didn't want to embarrass you," she suggested calmly.

"I don't think that was it. I think you were protecting yourself. You didn't want to know for certain if your suspicions about the way I made my living were correct. But you must have been fairly sure of your guess or you wouldn't have asked me to escort you to Cardinal's island that night."

Angie took another sip of coffee. He was right in some ways. She hadn't really wanted to hear it put into words. "I think I can handle it now. Why don't you try telling me the truth?"

He looked briefly down at his hands, which were wrapped around his coffee mug. Then he raised his eyes to meet hers. "Your guesses were all probably quite accurate."

She winced but said nothing.

"Angie, I've lived a little rough these past few years. But I'm alive, I've made some money and I haven't done anything of which I'm ashamed. There's no need to go into it in any further detail."

"I agree."

His mouth hardened. "Since you were willing to commission my services as a bodyguard that night when you went to Cardinal's island, it's a bit hypocritical of you to act as if you find my past dishonorable or disgusting."

She met his eyes. "I didn't avoid the subject of your past because I found it dishonorable or disgusting. I might not like the idea of how you make your living, but I wouldn't use words such as *dishonorable* or *disgusting* to describe it. And you're quite right. It would be hypocritical of me since I did plan to use your, uh, skills that night. In fact, your skills came in very handy when Cousin Ramon pulled that Star semiautomatic."

Curiosity flickered briefly in his eyes at her identification of the weapon, but he ignored that question to ask the more important one. "If you don't find my background repellent, why did you work so hard at avoiding the subject?"

Angie toyed with her spoon, unnecessarily stirring her coffee. "Because thinking about the way you made your living only reinforced the impossibility of our having any kind of future. I assumed that men who lived a little rough, as you put it, probably don't have much room in their lives for anything other than vacation flings."

Flynn's hand came across the short space that separated them. It closed over her restlessly moving fingers, stilling the spoon in the cup. "That assumption doesn't hold true for me, Angie. I've got plans for the future, and they don't include going back to selling myself as a bodyguard or offering my services to people who find their relatives locked up in strange jails in countries that have never heard of due process of law.''

She bit her lip. "Is that the sort of thing you did?"

He ignored the question, leaning forward intently. "Angie, I've got a past, but not the one you're thinking of. My past goes back to a time when the Challoners owned land and bred strong sons to inherit that land. It goes back to a time when a family knew its roots and knew the source of its strength. A time when a man and a woman respected that kind of strength and were willing to work hard to make it even stronger.''

She felt the intensity in him and experienced a kind of wonder. "All those things you said in Mexico about the importance of families and their ties to the land, you really believe all that, don't you?"

"I believe it. I'm going to rebuild what the Challoners once had, Angie. I'm going to make the family strong again.''

"I've got news for you, Flynn, the cattle business isn't what it used to be. If you're thinking of starting a ranch in California, you're in for a surprise. You'd probably be better off raising chickens than cattle. No glamour, I suppose, but the fact is, people eat more chicken these days. Better yet, try oil wells. Now, there's a surefire crop.''

Flynn released her hand and sat back in his chair as the plates of eggs and toast were delivered to the table. His dark eyes were gleaming with that unyielding determination she had seen earlier. It was unnerving, Angie thought. She poked idly at the scrambled eggs, thinking of the other things Flynn had said when he had discussed family history. The notion of a business marriage had seemed perfectly rational to him, she recalled. Anything that helped strengthen the family holdings. It struck her that Flynn Challoner was living in the wrong century.

Across the table Flynn picked up his fork and attacked his scrambled eggs. "I'm not going to raise cattle the way my ancestors did. And you can forget chicken farming. But the key is still the land, Angie. I'm sure of it. I feel it deep inside. But this is a new era and I understand that the land has to be handled in different ways."

Angie couldn't resist asking, "What ways?"

"You buy it and you sell it," he said with great simplicity.

She eyed him uncertainly. "I don't get it. Speculation?"

He shook his head. "It's not speculation when you know what you're doing. It's a certainty. That's the thing about land, honey. It's forever. It'll take care of the man who takes care of it. The man who knows what he's doing."

"Have you done much, uh, buying and selling?"

"I've been putting every spare cent I've had during the past few years into my first holdings. I just kept sending the money to a bank account in the States, and whenever I had enough I'd fly back and figure out where to put it. I've got a little property in the Sun Belt and some on the water in Oregon and Washington. It's not much, but it's a start. I've already sold one or two parcels in some growth areas in the Pacific Northwest and down in Arizona. Made a good return on my investment and sank the results right back into more land. I've got a long way to go and God knows right now I'm cash poor, but I've got the basis for a beginning. I can live on what the land makes now. And that's enough. I'm back in the States for good this time. Now I can really start to build."

Angie felt her stomach tighten. She put down her fork. "And the dagger?"

He paused, a bite of egg halfway to his mouth. "The dagger is part of the whole process, Angie. It's part of the past and the present and the future. Don't you see? It helps tie it all together. It's a link. A symbol."

"And you want it."

"I want it," he agreed flatly.

Angie massaged her temple with her thumb. "How on earth did I get mixed up in this?" she whispered more to herself than to him.

"You're mixed up in it because you're part of the whole thing, too, honey. I didn't realize it when I followed you to Mexico but now I do. And that's what I wanted to tell you this morning. I know that I probably should have told you last night before—"

"Before you seduced me? Yes, it might have been the polite thing to do."

"Angie, I was afraid you wouldn't understand or that you'd be so furious you wouldn't give me a chance to fully explain. I don't expect you to believe this, but after making love to you I stayed awake most of the night wondering if I'd done the right thing." Flynn's gaze didn't waver.

"Really? And what did you decide?"

"I decided that it was probably safer to have played my hand the way I did, even if it did leave me feeling guilty." His voice was suddenly harsh.

She stared at him. "Played your hand?"

"I wanted to make the bonds between us as strong as possible before I took the risk of telling you everything. Don't you see? I knew how you felt about the dagger and about your past. You'd made it very clear that none of it had much meaning to you. I couldn't risk appealing to you on that basis. But I also knew that you were attracted to me, and I had a hunch you were the kind of woman who would commit herself to a man when she let him make love to her.

You were already grateful to me for helping you get the dagger safely out of Mexico. I figured that if I could reinforce that by making you feel committed on a more intimate level..." His voice trailed off meaningfully.

Angie felt the color surge into her cheeks. "You don't need to continue. I get the point. You thought you could control me emotionally through sex."

His fork clattered on his plate, drawing a curious glance from the next table. "Damn it," Flynn snapped, "that's not it at all."

"You'll have to excuse me, I'm having a little difficulty understanding all the fine nuances of the thing."

His eyes softened for the first time that morning. "Angie, honey, do you remember what I told you last night when I came to your bed?"

She refused to answer on the grounds that she might have lost her self-control.

Flynn smiled gently. "I told you everything was going to be all right. That this was the way it was supposed to be. I'm sure of it, Angie. I trust my own instincts in this."

"That's very reassuring, naturally...."

"Don't be flippant, honey. You don't have to be defensive. I want you to know that everything *is* all right. That nothing has changed."

"Except that now you're going to take the dagger and stroll off into the sunset?"

"At this point your uncle owns that dagger."

"I'm glad we agree on something, at least."

Flynn brushed aside her brittle response, the cool determination returning to his eyes. "I intend to drive up the coast with you and meet Julian Torres. He and I will talk about the dagger and what happens next. From what you've told me, I think your uncle understands what that dagger means. And since he and I seem to be the sole surviving males on each side of the family, it's up to us to settle the matter.''

''What if he doesn't want to talk to you?'' But Angie was grasping at straws and she knew it. Julian would be utterly fascinated to meet the surviving member of the Challoner clan; doubly fascinated when he learned that Flynn Sangrey Challoner had spent a good portion of his life living the kind of adventures Jake Savage undertook within the pages of the Julian Taylor novels. Above all else, her uncle loved tales that came to life.

''Judging by what you've told me of your uncle, he'll want to talk to me.'' Flynn sounded very certain. ''As Cardinal said, he sounds like a man who understands the importance of family ties and family history.''

She was the only one who seemed to be left out in the cold, standing by while the men decided the fate of the dagger. This was probably very much how Maria Isabel had felt when she'd heard that her own fate was being decided nearly two hundred years ago. In fact, something deep inside Angie was quite certain this was how Maria Isabel had felt.

Luckily this was the twentieth century, Angie thought. The men could haggle over an antique, but they couldn't very well make decisions concerning the future of a woman.

She silently repeated the bit of wisdom several times during breakfast, but for some reason Angie didn't manage to reassure herself. Flynn had said he wanted to recreate the Challoner dynasty. The land and the dagger were a start.

The next thing on his shopping list was going to be a woman.

Chapter 6

Flynn realized that what he was feeling was an overwhelming sense of relief. She'd handled it well, he told himself as he piloted the red Toyota out of the Los Angeles area and started north along the coast. Initially she'd been a little shaken, there was no doubt about that, but it could have been a lot worse.

He'd expected tears, a tantrum, a lot of yelling and screaming. After all, as he'd learned during the night, Angie was a woman of passion. She was a Torres woman, he thought, not without a sense of pride.

But she'd been surprisingly calm when he'd finally told her the whole truth about himself. And for that, Flynn Sangrey Challoner was very, very grateful.

He hadn't lied when he'd told her that he lay awake a good portion of the night trying to decide how to reveal who he really was. He hadn't meant to let the misconception go so far. But there had been no really appropriate time to explain.

Down in Mexico he had wanted to secure her trust and friendship. If he'd announced his identity to her, she would have been immediately wary of him. He'd had no way of knowing how she would react if she suspected he might be planning to cut his own deal with Alexander Cardinal. It was a cinch she would never have let him get close to her.

He'd planned to tell her yesterday during the trip home, but there had been so much going on and they had both been so exhausted. Besides, Angie had been badly shaken by the scene with Ramon. It hadn't seemed an auspicious time for true confessions. Then last night he'd realized why he'd been putting off the hour of reckoning. On first a subconscious and then a very conscious level Flynn knew he'd wanted to strengthen the bonds between himself and Angie before telling her exactly who he was.

He'd tormented himself for hours after they'd checked into the airport hotel. Alone in his own room he'd sat in the chair by the window, the lights out, gazing at the city's night skyline. A myriad disconnected thoughts had gone through his head. He was close to the dagger at last. After working so hard and so long to trace it, victory had remained elusive, however.

It wasn't simply that the weapon technically belonged to Julian Torres. It was far more complicated than that. Somehow, Flynn wasn't quite certain why, the dagger was now inevitably connected in his mind with Angie Morgan. It had struck him there in the darkness that he no longer wanted only the cold steel with its gem-encrusted handle. He wanted the woman whose touch could warm the steel.

Angie and the dagger went together, and when he had them both he would have the real foundation for everything he planned to build in the future.

Sitting there in the darkness, Flynn could not explain to himself precisely why he was so certain that he needed both the woman and the dagger to make it all complete. Perhaps it had something to do with the fact that Angie was of the Torres clan and the dagger had originally come to the Challoners through a Torres woman. The explanation fit, he decided. It all went together to make a perfect circle. The symmetry of the whole thing pleased him on some fundamental level. Angie, the dagger and a new beginning.

It was then that he knew he would have to tell her the truth about himself in the morning. He wanted everything out in the open. The deception he'd been practicing for the past few days, however much he could justify it, disturbed him. He didn't like the feeling of guilt that was eating at him. He was an honorable man, and he wanted his association with Angie put on an honorable basis. His Challoner pride demanded it.

But she was a woman and she was part Torres. He was afraid she would not easily forgive him. After all, if the situation had been reversed, how would he behave? The thought didn't bear contemplation. Flynn knew what his own reactions would have been if he'd perceived himself the victim of this kind of deception. He would have been madder than hell.

So, he told himself determinedly, he had to expect fury; a woman's fury. Before he could risk that he had to strengthen the bonds of attraction that shimmered between them. Sitting there at two o'clock in the morning it had all seemed so entirely logical.

When he'd finally walked into her room he'd had a few more doubts, but when she'd opened her arms to him any last-minute hesitation he might have had was gone in the blaze of passion that had consumed him. This was right; the way it was supposed to be. He knew it deep inside.

As he sat behind the wheel of the Toyota, Flynn's body still reacted to the memory of Angie in the night. He felt himself tighten and had to consciously force himself to relax. She had melted in his hands last night. He had been dazed by the hot, sweet excitement, unexpectedly and totally out of control. And he had fit her the way the dagger fit its sheath.

Afterward the reality of what had to be done in the morning had returned. As if to ward off the inevitable, Flynn had pulled the sleeping Angie closer against him. And all through the sleepless night she had lain trusting in his arms.

But now as they left the smog-laden air of Los Angeles behind, Flynn allowed himself to breathe a sigh of relief. It was going to be all right. Angie had accepted the situation. He'd been right to handle it the way he had. Last night had meant something very special to her, too, and because of it she was dealing with this morning's news with more equanimity than he had expected.

Relief made him feel conversational. She hadn't talked to him a lot since they had left the hotel. She didn't seem hostile, though, just quiet. He slanted her a glance, studying her profile as she sat gazing meditatively out the window.

The fall sun was brilliant on the ocean but the warmth in the air felt temporary. It would disappear quickly after sunset when the coastal fog moved inward. With the sprawl of Los Angeles well behind them, the real California seemed to emerge. Parts of the drive cut through land that still looked very much as it had when the Torres and Challoner families began building their ranching empires. Rolling hills still met the Pacific in timeless intimacy. That was the thing about land, Flynn thought with deep satisfaction. You could plant it, ranch it, subdivide it or build cities on it. But regardless of what you did to it, it continued to exist. It would continue to take care of the man who valued it.

He wondered what Angie was thinking as she sat pensively in her seat. Her beautiful peacock eyes were shadowed with private thoughts. Not for the first time he recalled her bravery in Ramon's boat. He respected that kid of courage and quick thinking. But when he thought about Angie's actions he experienced more than respect: he knew a deep sense of pride in her. He was honest enough with himself to realize it was because he was already thinking of her as his. *His woman had courage.*

"There's something I've been meaning to ask you," Flynn said at one point. She flashed him a quick glance but said nothing. "This morning you mentioned the gun Ramon used. How did you know it was a Star?"

She hesitated. "You once told me you admired the technical side of the Jake Savage books."

He nodded, curious.

"Well," she continued, "who do you think usually gets stuck doing the technical research?"

"You?" He was startled. The Jake Savage series was high adventure with plenty of detail concerning the various lethal gadgets used by the hero.

"Me." She didn't pursue the subject. "The road to Julian's place is just a few miles outside of Ventura. We'll be there shortly."

"How far is the hacienda from your uncle's home?"

"A couple of miles. It sits on a bluff overlooking the sea. The guest house is a few hundred yards away from it."

Angie saw the interest in Flynn's eyes as he scanned the landscape. Was he imagining how this country had looked back when the Challoners and the Torreses had reigned? In many ways he seemed hard and cynical; a man who had seen nearly everything. Yet when he talked of the land and his plans for the future, there was a genuine kind of anticipation and determination in him; a sense of respect and hope for the future. She had been aware of it at breakfast when he'd explained his goals, and she could feel it emanating from him now as he drove toward his meeting with Julian Torres.

It disturbed her that she was sensitive to his feelings about the land and the future. She didn't want to be, Angie realized. She wanted to keep her distance from him emotionally. She didn't want to be seen by Flynn as a part of his plans.

Her uncle had been first astounded and then delighted when she'd phoned earlier to say that she was on her way with a genuine Challoner in tow. He'd assured her he had fully recovered from his bout with the flu and that he would be expecting them that afternoon. He would instruct Mrs. Akers, the housekeeper, to plan dinner for three.

"This is wonderful, Angie," Julian had said enthusiastically. "Absolutely wonderful. What an incredible coincidence that you should run into Challoner down in Mexico."

Looking at Flynn, who was pacing the hotel room while she made the call, Angie had murmured dryly into the phone, "Uncle Julian, you know what Jake Savage always says about coincidences."

Julian Torres had chuckled richly. "I should know, I've written it often enough." He pitched his voice low and gravelly as he muttered, "There ain't no such thing."

"Exactly. Keep it in mind. We'll see you this afternoon, Uncle Julian."

And now they were almost there. In quiet tones Angie gave directions to Flynn, who turned off the main highway to follow a narrow road that wound through a small residential area composed of secluded, expensive homes. A grove of trees protected the modern glass-and-wood structure Julian was calling home until the hacienda was finished. The house had a spectacular view of the sea. Down below it a ragged cliff descended to a quiet beach. The other homes in the area were equally secluded. Privacy was a valued commodity along this expensive strip of land, and people who could afford it were willing to pay well for the luxury. The author of the wonderfully successful Jake Savage books could afford it.

Flynn parked the Toyota in the paved drive, glancing around at the lush garden.

"Julian designed the garden a couple of years ago," Angie said politely. "He's a whiz with plants and flowers."

Flynn nodded just as the wrought-iron gates swung open and a pleasantly distinguished, middle-aged man came through to greet them. Julian still had a full head of hair, and in true California style, he kept himself trim with exercise and a healthy diet, supplemented by the medicinal properties of good Spanish sherry. He was dressed casually but expensively, and there was an air of West Coast sophistication about him.

"Angelina," Julian Torres said grandly, "you're finally here. How was the trip?" He was the only one who ever called her by her full name.

"Eventful." She hugged her uncle. "You're looking great considering you've just gotten over the flu."

"It turned out to be a fairly mild case. I dosed myself with plenty of sherry and hardly felt a thing." He looked appraisingly at Flynn. "Introduce us, Angelina."

"Julian, I'd like you to meet Flynn Sangrey… Challoner." She paused just a split second before drawing out Flynn's last name, and she saw him glance at her coolly as he shook hands with the other man.

"We've been a long while reuniting the Challoners and the Torreses, Flynn. It's about time," Julian said with satisfaction as he assessed the younger man. "Come inside. We have a lot to talk about. You can't imagine how pleased I am to meet you."

"I think I'll just play solitaire or something this eve-

ning," Angie murmured. "I don't think you're going to
need me in this discussion."

Flynn came up behind her before Julian could answer.
Angie felt his strong hand at the base of her spine, guiding
her into the house in a proprietary fashion. "Whatever we
talk about tonight will definitely involve you, Angie. You're
part of the past."

She had wanted to argue that point, but there was no real
opportunity. With typical graciousness Julian served dark,
rich coffee and small, spicy empanadas Mrs. Akers sent out
from the kitchen. Angie would have felt rude and ridiculously uncivilized if she'd made a scene at that point. Then,
his dark eyes alive with anticipation, Julian asked to see the
dagger.

"It's in my suitcase," Angie said. She rose to her feet.
"I'll get it." With a sense of relief at being able to escape
the mutual admiration society that seemed to be developing
between her uncle and Flynn, she hurried out to the car.
There she unlocked the Toyota's trunk and opened the suitcase. Reaching inside she picked up the dagger's case. For
a moment, standing there alone, she held it in her hands and
wondered again at the sense of possessiveness she felt.

This weapon had belonged to Maria Isabel. It had been
handed over to the Challoners a very long time ago, but
now it was back in the hands of a Torres woman. True,
Angie thought, her connection with Maria Isabel was vague
and quite distant, but still, she was the one who now held
the dagger Maria Isabel had once possessed.

Uneasily Angie shook off the strange sensation that
gripped her each time she touched the dagger. She was letting her imagination get the better of her. Determinedly she
stalked back into the house carrying the case. Walking up
to Julian, she opened it and displayed the object of the quest
on which he had sent her.

Silently Flynn came up beside Julian and watched as the dagger was revealed. There was a moment of silence during which Julian's face reflected the unmitigated satisfaction he was feeling.

"It's beautiful," he said at last. "And it looks exactly as it was described in the family papers." Carefully he lifted it out of the box and removed it from the old leather sheath. "Go fetch Mrs. Akers. She'll want to see it, too. It cost me a fortune, but it was worth every cent."

Angie slipped into the kitchen and made a face at the bustling, silver-haired woman who took care of her uncle's home. "Your presence has been requested, Mrs. Akers. You are to appear in the living room and make appropriately appreciative sounds."

"About that dagger?" The pleasant-faced woman chuckled, dusting the pastry flour off her hands. "Don't worry, I'll make a proper scene. Your uncle has talked of little else since you left last week. And when he heard you were returning with a genuine Challoner, well, I haven't seen him looking so satisfied since his agent negotiated that last contract with his publisher." She obediently followed Angie out into the living room, expressed the required admiration for the dagger and then excused herself on the grounds that a pie required her attention.

Julian frowned at Flynn. "Cardinal didn't give you any trouble?"

Flynn shrugged. "Not when we made the transaction, but there was a little trouble later on. It's a long story."

"From the correspondence I've had with him, I assumed the man was a gentleman," Julian said abruptly. "I never would have allowed Angie to go down there alone otherwise."

"I made the same assumption," Flynn admitted. "But someone tried to get the dagger back before we got out of

Mexico. I'm afraid we left in something of a rush. Angie's sure Cardinal was behind what happened.''

"Let's have the whole story," Julian insisted. With a serious expression on his face he set down the dagger case and picked up his coffee cup.

"It was very exciting, Uncle Julian. You would have loved it." Angie crossed her ankles and leaned back in her chair. Resting her elbows on the upholstered arms, she steepled her fingers and smiled aloofly. "Plenty of material in it for a Julian Taylor novel. Even had our own Jake Savage on the scene to handle the bad guy."

Flynn shifted restlessly in his chair by the window. "Maybe I'd better tell this story. Angie seems inclined to embellish." In a matter-of-fact way he related the incidents leading up to their hasty departure from Mexico. Before he had finished Julian was looking shocked.

"Thank God you were there with her, Flynn. It could have been disastrous if Angelina had been forced to deal with that Ramon character on her own." Julian turned to Angie. "You're quite all right?"

"Oh, I'm fine. The real excitement came later."

Across the room Flynn narrowed his gaze warningly.

Angie went on as if she hadn't gotten the hint. "I was quite surprised to find out who Flynn really was. You see, up until that point I was under the impression his name was Flynn Sangrey."

There was a moment of silence in the room, and then Julian looked questioningly at Flynn. Flynn drummed his fingers briefly on the arm of his chair and, in turn, looked at Angie.

"I didn't know who she was at first," he said quietly. "And when I found out, I wasn't at all sure how she'd react to my presence down there in Mexico. I thought she would be suspicious. Wary of me. Afraid I was after the dagger."

"Aren't you?" Angie asked. She smiled her aloof, fleeting smile.

It was Julian who answered very calmly, "Of course he is. His family has as much claim on it, if not more, than ours."

"Not any longer," Angie said. "You own it now, Julian. You've bought and paid for it."

Julian's mouth crooked slightly. "But Flynn rescued it when it was threatened by your friend Ramon and whoever he was working for. That more than restores his claim, I should think. And I believe I understand completely why he was hesitant to tell you exactly who he was. He would have risked losing track of the dagger again if you had run off in panic without him. Isn't that right, Flynn?"

"Something like that." Laconically, Flynn smiled at Angie. "But in the end she took the news very calmly. I was probably wrong to be so concerned."

Julian shook his head. "No. Not when you'd spent such a long time searching for it, Flynn. You're not wrong to tread carefully when you finally close in on the object of the hunt."

Angie watched them, withdrawing into silence as the two men began to talk freely about the dagger and its history. There were questions about Flynn's history, too, and she noticed he only provided brief answers. His responses were enough to intrigue Julian, however. Angie knew her uncle was starting to see him just as she had suspected he would see Flynn: as a real-life version of Jake Savage.

It was obvious, though, that his former method of making a living wasn't what Flynn wanted to talk about. It was when the discussion got around to his future plans that he sat forward in his chair and became very intent.

"As I was telling Angie this morning, I've got a start in land. I think the next step is to set up a sort of syndicate of investors. It takes big money to buy the best land. I've been feeling my way for a few years, and I think I'm ready to go ahead with some major investment plans. I intend to pool the cash from a few investors and make the decisions about which parcels to pick up and when to sell them off. Land is still the key to everything, Julian. Just as it was two hundred years ago. Today even the new hotshot computer firms need land and buildings. It doesn't matter how high tech a company is, it can't get very far if it isn't sitting on prime real estate. Agriculture still takes vast amounts of land. That will never change. Residential housing, shopping centers, high-rise office buildings, everything requires land. It always comes back to the land. And I think I've got a feel for it.''

Time passed as the men talked. Eventually the sun lavishly painted the western sky as it disappeared into the Pacific, and Julian genially announced that the cocktail hour had finally arrived. He poured sherry and Mrs. Akers sent out quesadillas. Angie nibbled on the cheese-filled tortillas and sipped at her drink, waiting for dinner. No one seemed concerned that she had slipped out of the conversation. She wondered when someone would ask Flynn where he intended to stay for the night.

When the subject finally arose it didn't come in the form of a question. Julian had apparently already considered the matter and come to a decision. It was announced over dinner.

''I don't know whether Angie mentioned it or not, Flynn, but the hacienda is close to completion. There's furniture in the master bedroom and the kitchen and living room areas. Also the electricity is on and the plumbing works. There's no reason someone couldn't spend a few nights there if he didn't mind stepping over some odds and ends left behind by the designer and the craftspeople. What do you say?

Would you like to stay there instead of bunking down here or finding a motel?''

"That's very generous of you," Flynn observed, not looking at Angie.

Julian looked up from his shellfish pilaf. "You'd be doing me a favor, you know. I've been uneasy about Angelina moving into the guest house all by herself. That stretch of beach is a bit isolated. It would be good to know you were nearby. I won't be ready to move in until next month. Didn't want to disrupt the book I'm working on at the moment."

Angie glanced up sharply, but she wasn't in time to halt Flynn's quietly enthusiastic response.

"I'd like that," he said. "I'd like to see what you've done with the old place. The site of the original Torres hacienda, hmm?"

"Took us a while to authenticate it," Julian told him, "but we're sure of it now. The old land records were still available. From what we can tell, the spot where the Challoner place stood was a few miles inland."

Flynn nodded. "There's nothing left of it now. I drove out there once to look for some signs of a foundation or something but I couldn't find anything. Belongs to some horse breeder. Can't complain, I guess. At least he didn't put in a subdivision. I don't mind good Arabians running over it."

"True," Julian agreed philosophically. "You know it was at the hacienda that your ancestor met Maria Isabel the first time. It was at a huge fiesta her father was giving for everyone in the territory. He even invited his enemies, the Challoners, who graciously stopped quarreling with him long enough to stuff themselves on Torres beef."

Flynn laughed. "Never let it be said that a Challoner doesn't know when to take advantage of a good thing."

Angie spoke up for the first time in half an hour. "I believe that's exactly what Maria Isabel is reputed to have told Curtis Challoner the night of the fiesta. Isn't that how the story goes, Uncle Julian?''

''Something like that,'' Julian agreed cheerfully as he poured more wine in everyone's glass. ''She apparently put it into more forceful terms, though. Walked up to Challoner while he was finishing a bottle of her father's fabulously expensive wine, which had been brought all the way from Spain, and proceeded to insult the man. Told him he was obviously nothing more than a freeloading peasant with aspirations above his station. Or words to that effect. Probably sounded much better in Spanish. Or much worse, depending on your point of view. At any rate the insult was considered outrageous since it had taken place during a time of truce when Challoner was a guest in the Torres home. Maria Isabel was reported to be a little spitfire. A real handful.''

''Spoiled rotten, no doubt,'' Flynn decided as he helped himself to another serving of asparagus.

Angie felt obliged to speak up again. ''She was a woman living in a man's world, and there were no doubt times she resented the situation. I don't blame her at all. Curtis Challoner, from all reports, was arrogant, ambitious and quite ruthless.''

''Well, whatever the rights and wrongs of the situation,'' Julian interrupted, ''that was the occasion on which Challoner informed Torres that he would be willing to take his daughter off his hands if it would resolve the land issue.''

''How generous of him,'' Angie grumbled.

A savagely amused grin crossed Flynn's face briefly. ''According to my family's side of the story, what he actually said to Maria Isabel was that the freeloading peasant was going to do her a favor. He promised to turn her from a willful little tigress into a loving wife and mother. She responded by telling him she would see him in hell first. He told her he'd heard wedding nights described in many ways but not as hell. However, he had confidence she had an original turn of mind and he looked forward to the occasion just to see what she would come up with.''

"And what she came up with was the Torres Dagger," Angie finished triumphantly.

"Cold steel and a warm woman make an interesting combination." Flynn smiled blandly and held out the bread basket. "Have some more jalapeno corn bread."

Aware that Julian was watching her with ill-concealed curiosity, Angie politely accepted the hot-pepper-flavored corn bread and sank back into silence.

"How long will you be staying in the area?" Julian inquired, looking at Flynn.

"Until I can talk you out of that dagger." Flynn took a long swallow of the wine and regarded the last male Torres. "What'll it take?"

Julian leaned back and arched one brow. A strange smile lurked deep in his eyes. "To talk me out of the dagger? I'm not sure. I'll have to think about it. I've worked very long and very hard to get it, Flynn."

"So have I."

Julian nodded complacently. "And your claim on it is as strong as my own. I realize that. It's not going to be a simple decision."

"I can't better the price you paid Alexander Cardinal for it," Flynn said with blunt honesty. "Not right now. I've got some property that I could sell to raise that kind of cash, but to tell you the truth, that land shouldn't be sold. Not yet."

"The dagger isn't something that should be bought and sold between a Torres and a Challoner anyway, is it, Flynn?"

"No," Flynn agreed. "It's not. It means too much."

Angie absorbed the implications of those words. She saw the look that was exchanged between her uncle and Flynn and she knew that with some silent, male form of communication they were arriving at a conclusion. Firmly she squashed the wave of uncertainty that assailed her. She was not Maria Isabel. She didn't have to panic. *But Maria Isabel had not only panicked, she'd been enraged.* Angie suddenly knew that as surely as if she'd been told by Maria Isabel, herself. A little shakily she put down her fork and reached for her wineglass.

Nothing more was said about the dagger at dinner that night, but by the end of the meal Angie was convinced that forces already in motion were moving toward some inevitable conclusion that involved her. She was aware of a vague sense of being trapped, and she wondered if this was how Maria Isabel had felt.

Irritably she pushed aside the bizarre question. This was ridiculous. She was a woman of the twentieth century, and she would not allow herself to be used by two men who were looking for a way to resolve ownership of an inanimate object.

Besides, she reminded herself grimly, nobody had exactly asked her to martyr herself in marriage, anyway. Talk about jumping the gun! The thought brought a reluctant smile to her lips.

"Something funny?" Flynn asked.

"A private joke."

"Going to share it?" he prodded.

"I've already shared it."

He eyed her narrowly. "With whom?"

"Maria Isabel."

Chapter 7

He hadn't planned on waking up alone.

Three days after his return to California with Angie, Flynn opened his eyes in the master bedroom of the hacienda and glared evilly at the bright morning light streaming through the window. He came alert as he always did, fully and completely, with no lazy middle ground between sleep and wakefulness. Wondering if that habit would change now that he was back in the States for good, Flynn shoved aside the quilt and sat up on the edge of the huge carved-wood bed.

Julian Torres had spared no expense in rebuilding the hacienda. Nor had he made the mistake of going overboard on authenticity. The place was intended to be a home, not a museum. Windows were larger and more plentiful than they had been in the original hacienda because twentieth-century Californians prized their views. There was air-conditioning and central heating, although the architectural focus in the living room and master suite was on the magnificent fireplaces. A beautifully landscaped courtyard was another main focus. The furniture was comfortable and in most cases new, although it had been carefully chosen to recreate the original Spanish ambience. Heavy-beamed ceilings were combined with walls that had been finished to resemble white-painted adobe. Hardwood floors and some very expensive tile work extended throughout the home.

The whole effect, although modern in many ways, called to mind the elegantly warm, uncluttered effect of the Spanish colonial style. Flynn had felt comfortably at home right from the start. He had said so to Angie that first night when he'd driven her back from Julian's.

"But it's not your home. It's a Torres home," she'd reminded him coolly as she'd shown him through the house.

"The Torres and Challoner families were linked together after the marriage between Curtis and Maria Isabel. After that the homes of each were always open to the other." He'd tried to gently emphasize that point but she hadn't seemed to be listening. Flynn had reached out to catch her wrist as she attempted to walk past him into the kitchen. Smiling slightly and pleasantly aware of the uncoiling anticipation in his body, he'd tugged her into his arms. "*Mi casa es su casa.* It's been a long day, honey. You must be exhausted."

"Not nearly as long as yesterday." She'd slipped out of his hands and walked on into the kitchen. "Mrs. Akers told Uncle Julian she didn't want a two-hundred-year-old kitchen. She insisted on all the latest appliances. But the architect did a good job of hiding everything, don't you think? And look at the tile work along the counter. That was done by a wonderful artist from Santa Barbara."

"Angie…"

"Wait until you see the view in the morning. Absolutely fabulous. There's a path down the cliff to the beach if you want to go for an early morning walk. I usually do."

"Angie, I'll build a fire in the fireplace..."

"Uncle Julian hasn't gotten around to ordering the wood yet."

"Well, maybe a glass of sherry or something."

"There aren't any supplies in the kitchen yet, either." She'd smiled politely, a hint of triumph in her eyes as she succeeded in stonewalling him. She waited for the next suggestion.

It had taken a few more attempts before Flynn realized Angie had no intention of staying with him that night. She was still a little upset over the morning's revelations, he'd decided. She needed time to accept the situation. At least she wasn't actively fighting him. She just needed time, and he was willing to be patient. After all, he'd already waited for years to gather the foundations of the next Challoner dynasty. He could wait a little longer.

When he'd eventually reconciled himself to the fact that she didn't intend to spend the night, Flynn had walked Angie to the guest cottage. It was then that he had understood Julian's concerns.

"This place really is isolated, Angie." He'd surveyed the cottage's location, noting that, while one could see the lights of the main house some distance away, there was no other place within shouting distance. The next home on the cliff was out of sight. "You shouldn't have moved in here until your uncle was ready to move into the hacienda."

"I didn't want to wait. Besides, my lease was up on the place I was renting in Ventura. The cottage was finished first, several weeks before the hacienda, so I decided to move in."

"You could have stayed at your uncle's house until the hacienda was ready." Disapprovingly Flynn had examined the small, one-bedroom arrangement from the living room door. Angie hadn't invited him any further into the cottage.

"Why would I want to live with my uncle? I'm a big girl now. I told you, I like my privacy."

That had really annoyed him. "It's not safe."

"Flynn, I'm twenty-eight years old. I've been living on my own a long time. This isn't the 1800s when single women were expected to live under the family roof until they married."

There had been a hint of a challenge in her peacock eyes, and Flynn had almost made the mistake of accepting it. Then he'd realized she was primed for a clash of wills. Telling himself that the last thing he wanted to do was provide her with an excuse for an argument, he'd backed down. The bond between them was still fragile, and he hadn't wanted to do anything to destabilize the situation.

Now, three days later, Flynn was broodingly aware that he couldn't figure out what in hell was going through Angie's head. If he pushed her too hard, the flare of defiance leaped into her eyes. But if he kept his distance emotionally, she seemed content to have him around.

It was unsettling and confusing, and it was becoming downright maddening. He didn't even know for certain if she was deliberately playing some kind of game. It had crossed his mind that she might want to punish him for the deception he had practiced in Mexico, but he'd decided he was mistaken when no screaming tirade had materialized. But if she wasn't plotting revenge, what was she doing?

Things had been much simpler in the old days, Flynn decided morosely as he got up from the bed and padded over to the window. Curtis Challoner hadn't had to deal directly with Maria Isabel while negotiating the marriage. He'd been able to hammer out the details with her father instead. It was obviously much more practical to arrange these things on a man-to-man basis.

He wasn't quite sure when the idea of marriage had crystalized in his mind. He suspected the idea had begun to take shape even before he and Angie had left Mexico. There had been no doubt about the sensual attraction between them, and he had found her intelligent and charming. He'd also come to respect her courage and fortitude. A lot of women would have had hysterics after that scene with Ramon on the boat. Her connection to the Torres Dagger had injected a sense of fate into the equation. Somewhere along the line it had all begun to seem inevitable. At least to him.

In the distance he saw Angie come out of her cottage dressed in what looked like black jeans and a full-sleeved white shirt. She had a red windbreaker hooked over her shoulder. Her hair was bound neatly at the nape of her neck, and with a little imagination he could envision her as a nineteenth-century Torres woman about to take a morning ride. Even from this distance he could see the innate grace and pride in the way she moved.

Flynn turned and hurried into the bathroom to shower and shave. He wanted to catch up with her before she finished her walk on the beach.

Angie made her way down to the sand by following the twisting narrow path that wound its way between the tumbled rocks. It wasn't a particularly treacherous walk in daylight but you had to know where the path was. It tended to be obscured by the cliff outcrop and the clutter of rocks and small boulders. She used her hands to steady herself at several points along the way, stopping once or twice to examine an interesting chunk of driftwood.

When she finally reached the beach she stood for a moment at the water's edge, staring out to sea. Instinctively she sensed that Flynn would join her soon. He had found her down here the past two mornings, and she was quite certain he would look for her today, too. In spite of her ambivalent feelings toward him, she knew a part of her was anxious to see him.

Slowly she turned to pace along the sand. It was chilly, and after a few moments she opted to slip into the windbreaker. Fingers thrust into the back pockets of her jeans, she inhaled the crisp morning scent of the ocean and waited for Flynn to materialize nearby. The man moved as silently as a ghost, she reflected. She seldom heard him until he was next to her, especially down here on the beach where the sound of the waves masked smaller noises.

The strangely cautious manner he had been using around her for the past couple of days wouldn't last much longer, she sensed. She knew he had made a decision. But apparently he wasn't certain yet how to tell her about it. She had a hunch he'd talked to Julian, however. She'd seen the speculation in her uncle's eyes yesterday when she and Flynn had returned from the drive into Ventura. Had Julian wondered whether the subject had been brought out into the open during that drive?

She had been sorely tempted to satisfy her uncle's curiosity by loudly announcing that Flynn had not asked her to marry him while going to the grocery store. But she'd resisted the brief urge to make a joke out of it. It was hardly a joking matter.

That was the whole problem, she realized. She didn't quite know what to make of the unsettling situation. It was as though she were trapped in a fog with Flynn, unable to focus clearly and unable to escape entirely. She could hardly protest an offer of marriage when none had been made. But she was far too intuitive not to know that Flynn was shaping up his ''grand destiny'' and beginning to see her as part of it. What would she do when the time came to bring it all out into the open? Angie wasn't sure she knew just how she would react. That bothered her. It kept her awake at nights, and it made her behavior a bit unpredictable during the day. The only consolation was that she had a feeling both Uncle Julian and Flynn felt as if they were walking on eggshells.

Served them right.

"Angie?"

She whirled and found Flynn not more than a couple of feet away. He hadn't bothered with a jacket over his khaki shirt, and the breeze was playing with his short, carefully combed hair. He appeared to be oblivious to the chill as he watched her with the remote, faintly appraising expression that she was learning to recognize.

"Good morning, Flynn. Sleep well?"

"So polite," he murmured. "I slept as well as could be expected under the circumstances. How about you?"

She smiled. "Fine, thank you." She turned to resume her walk, and he fell into step beside her. "Any plans for the day?"

He said slowly, "I thought you might like to take a drive."

"To where?"

"Up to that horse ranch where the Challoner home once stood. I'd like to show it to you."

She thought about it. "All right."

Her answer satisfied him. Flynn seemed to relax a bit. "You know, I've done a lot of thinking about where to build a new home, Angie."

"Have you?"

"I want it designed from scratch to my specifications. I don't want to buy one that's already built." He flicked a glance at her profile as she walked beside him. "And I don't want it built with the quick, corner-cutting construction methods so many contractors use today."

Angie's mouth curved upward gently. "I understand. You want it built to last."

He nodded and shifted his gaze toward the horizon. "Yes. It needs to be the right kind of home, you see. A place where another generation can live."

"These days new generations tend to want to go their own way. They move to new states, find different careers than those their fathers have, build their own lives. And build their own homes. People don't think in terms of building a dynasty these days, Flynn."

"I know. People these days just live for the present. But things are going to be different with my family."

For a shattering instant the simple words went through Angie like a twist of lightning. Flynn Sangrey Challoner's family. She had a mental image of little dark-haired boys and girls running freely over rolling hills; playing in a garden that surrounded a built-for-the-ages home and clustering around their father's knee at night. For some reason the children were easy enough to visualize. It was when she tried to picture their mother that her mind refused to cooperate. With a sigh she gave up the project.

"Have you always been so certain of what you wanted, Flynn?" she asked quietly.

"For as long as I can remember. Ever since I heard the stories of my past and began to think about what had been lost." He slanted her a questioning look. "Didn't the tales you heard while growing up make you think about the past, Angie? Doesn't your uncle's interest in the family legends make you want to recreate what once existed?"

The idea never crossed my mind until I met you, Angie found herself thinking wistfully. *Now I don't seem to be able to stop thinking about it.* Aloud, she said carelessly, "I told you in Mexico that I'm definitely a woman of the present."

"We all live in the present, Angie," he said impatiently, "but that doesn't mean we can't link up with our pasts and build for the future. It's the way people used to view life, you know. In a lot of places in the world, they still do. We lose something vital when we lose our connection to the past.''

"Are you hungry?"

His intent frown deepened. He obviously didn't care for the abrupt change of subject. "I suppose so. Sure. It's nearly seven thirty."

"I've got some eggs back at the cottage."

His expression cleared miraculously at the offhand invitation. It was the first time she had invited him home for breakfast after one of their morning walks.

"Sounds great."

A little disconcerted by his grateful enthusiasm, Angie led the way toward her cottage.

Two hours later Angie stood beside Flynn on the crown of a rolling sweep of ground and watched a herd of Arabians graze on the spot where the Challoner homestead had once stood. Flynn surveyed the setting with an approving eye, one fist planted on his hip, his other arm resting on Angie's shoulders.

"You still have a view of the ocean from here, but you would be above the fog. And the house would have been protected from the wind. Ah, Angie, this is such good country. You can even forget Los Angeles is down the road. No wonder our families settled here."

Angie smiled, oddly aware of the beauty of the land. "I think I've always taken it for granted."

He glanced at her. "Taken what for granted?"

"The land. You're right, Flynn. This is beautiful country. Maybe you've developed more appreciation for it because you've had to spend so much time away from it. Or maybe your kind of love for the land is something that's born in a person.''

"Maybe. I don't know. I just know that land like this should be valued.''

"Where was the disputed piece of ground? The one the Torreses and the Challoners argued over?''

He moved his hand in a wide sweep. "Over there. From what I can tell it ran from that hillside down to the sea. Had a good year-round stream on it, which was one of the reasons both families needed it so badly. See? There's some livestock grazing near the water.''

Angie nodded. "I see. And that stream was worth the price of a marriage?''

Flynn's arm tightened briefly on her shoulder, and for a moment she felt the strength in him through every fiber of her body.

"Oh, yes, Angie. It was worth the price.''

Perhaps it was, Angie found herself thinking. Standing here in the sunshine with Flynn's arm around her and the land stretched out before her, she could finally understand something of the tie that a man such as Flynn might feel for the land. A woman could feel that same connection, she realized. There was something vital, almost elemental about the sensation. For a moment Angie thought she could almost comprehend a marriage made for the reasons that first Challoner-Torres marriage had been contracted.

The realization disturbed her and she moved restlessly away from Flynn. The scent of the earth was strong today. It seemed to be affecting her reasoning processes.

"Angie?''

"Yes, Flynn?''

"I think I'd like my house to be built down there near the sea." He closed the small distance between them and pointed in the direction he wanted her to look. "Maybe somewhere around that bluff on the point. Do you like that location? I know you like to be near the water.''

"That hunk of ground would be very expensive, Flynn.''

"I know. But someday…''

She looked up at him with sudden emotion. "Someday, Flynn, I hope you get what you want.''

He regarded her in silence for a moment, his gaze unreadable. "Thank you, Angie.''

One afternoon at the end of the week, Julian walked into his study and found Angie filing some notes on handguns. He glanced around expectantly. "Here you are. Wondered where you'd disappeared. Where's Flynn?''

"He's driving into town to take some stuff to the post office.''

"And you decided not to go with him?''

"I figured he doesn't really need me to hold his hand and show him how to buy stamps. He's a big boy.''

Julian's brow lifted. "He's more than a boy, Angelina. He's a man. A good one. Aren't a lot of them around these days. Which probably explains why you haven't gotten married yet.''

She looked up from where she was sitting in front of Julian's desk. "Starting to worry I'll stay a spinster all my life, Uncle Julian?''

He shook his head, lounging against the desk. "I'm not worried about that.…''

"Good, because you're hardly in a position to talk,'' she pointed out too sweetly. "You've never married, yourself.''

His mouth crooked. "True. But you see, Angelina, dear, that only puts the entire weight of the burden on you.''

"What burden?''

"You owe it to yourself and to the families to make the

right kind of marriage, Angelina. There's a future to be considered. And a past.''

"I'm not a brood mare.''

He chuckled. ''I was thinking more in terms of the cradle of future generations. Something along those lines.''

Angie burst out laughing. ''That's very good, Uncle Julian. You may be ready to write something besides the Jake Savage stories.''

His eyes twinkled. ''Why would I want to do that when those tales pay so damn well?''

"I see your point. Well, I suppose your poetic turn of phrase will just have to go unused. It's a cinch Jake Savage doesn't talk that way.''

"And because he has a lot in common with Jake Savage, Flynn might not be able to put things so poetically, either. But, Angelina, that doesn't mean he doesn't think in those terms.''

Very slowly Angie put down the card she was filling out. ''Don't tell me,'' she said very carefully, ''that you have been delegated to broach the subject. I thought Flynn had more guts than to ask you to do it.''

Julian gave her a level stare. ''What subject?''

"Marriage.''

"To Flynn?''

"Isn't that what we're discussing?'' she demanded.

"You're right, Angelina. If and when the time comes, Flynn will take care of matters himself. He knows damn good and well we're not living in the early 1800s. I don't have any authority over you in that respect.''

"I'm so glad somebody realizes it. Lately I've had the oddest feeling I'm in the middle of a time warp.'' She tapped the card in her hand on the desk surface, her eyes on the ocean visible through the huge windows. ''But he is going to ask, isn't he, Uncle Julian?''

"He's a good man, Angelina. Rock solid."

"He's an ex-mercenary. He's arrogant, ambitious and probably quite ruthless on occasion. He's got *plans*. Big plans. And he believes in things like the dagger. He wants to find a new Challoner dynasty, and I have a feeling he'd like to do it the way it was done originally."

"With a Torres bride?"

"Do you think I'm imagining things?"

"Nope." Julian straightened away from the desk and started toward the door. "You're a woman. I expect your intuition is probably fairly accurate. When he gets good and ready, he'll probably ask."

"I'll give him the same answer Maria Isabel gave Curtis Challoner!"

Julian grinned from the door. "Well, we all know what happened to her."

Unhappily Angie watched him go. She could not possibly agree to such an arrangement. Talk about being married for all the wrong reasons!

On the other hand, she wasn't sure she could bear to let Flynn turn his back on her and walk out of her life in search of a more tractable bride. The very thought made her ache with a sense of loss that she didn't want to acknowledge.

She had fallen in love with Flynn. Angie no longer tried to fool herself on that score. It was the only explanation that made some sense out of this fog of uncertainty.

Another kind of fog rolled in that evening. This was the real kind that gathered out at sea and floated inland to shroud the coast. It had begun at sunset, and by the time Mrs. Akers had cleared the dinner dishes, it completely cloaked Julian's house.

The fire in the living room was cozy and comforting, Angie thought as she trailed in behind the men for the now-familiar sherry-hour routine. She was about to curl up in her usual position in an armchair while Julian and Flynn talked when she realized that something about tonight's routine would be different.

Flynn handed her a glass of sherry and remained standing in front of her. She looked up at him inquiringly.

"I'd like to talk to you." He was utterly calm, utterly controlled. The dark eyes were steady but unreadable.

Angie didn't need to be able to read those eyes. Her feminine intuition was screaming. The sherry in the glass she was holding slopped precariously for a moment before she managed to control it. A sudden sense of panic gripped her, and she looked helplessly across the room at Julian. Her uncle seemed totally oblivious. He'd already put on his reading glasses and was immersed in the newspaper.

"In your uncle's study, I think." Flynn reached down to take her hand.

Feeling trapped, Angie found herself letting him pull her gently to her feet. This was ridiculous. There was absolutely no reason to panic now that the moment was upon her. She was an adult, not a nineteen-year-old girl from another century. Hadn't she been expecting this for days? Now at least things would be put into words. No longer would she be forced to operate in this strange fog.

Silently she allowed herself to be towed along to Julian's study. En route she took two more sips from the sherry glass in her hand. She needed the fortification. This was it. Tonight she had to make the decision. And she still didn't know what that decision would be. *I'm not a brood mare,* she told herself on a wild little note of hysteria. *And I'm not the cradle of future generations of Challoners. I'm me, Angelina Morgan, and I've got my own plans for the future.*

Except that she didn't. Whatever plans she'd made for

herself had evaporated when Flynn Challoner walked into her life.

Before she would work it all out, Flynn was releasing her hand, turning to close the door behind them. When he glanced at her she was standing stiffly in front of the cabinet that contained the Torres Dagger.

This was how she had felt nearly two hundred years ago, Angie realized in stunned shock. This was exactly how she had felt; no, how *Maria Isabel* had felt. The same sense of panic, the same feeling of helplessness, the same outrage and the same passionate love for the man who was about to outline her future to her in no uncertain terms.

She backed another step and reached around to brace herself against the open cabinet. Her hand touched the case that contained the dagger. Damn it, she would not allow her imagination to take control like this.

"What did you want to talk about, Flynn?"

He stood in front of the door, solid and real and immovable. Well, she had wanted a solid enemy to fight, hadn't she?

"Angelina," he began in a more formal tone of voice than she had ever heard him use. "I want to discuss marriage."

"Flynn, I don't think—"

He ignored her small, breathless interruption. "I've been giving this a lot of thought, Angie."

"I was afraid of that."

"Angie, I'm serious. This is not a joke. Hear me out, please." It wasn't a request, it was an order. "You and I have more in common than most people have. We share a family history. We went through a lot together down in Mexico. That sort of experience builds a bond between people. We're attracted to each other on a physical basis, and on an intellectual basis I think we find each other interesting.

We respect each other. In Mexico we talked easily right from the beginning. That hasn't changed. I'm not wealthy yet, but I can take care of you. Someday I'll be able to give you a great deal more. I'll build you a good home. And you have my word of honor, I'll be faithful. In short, I'll make you a good husband, Angie. I swear it.''

She stared at him, her pulse racing. Behind her back her nails were digging into the dagger case. ''Isn't this a little, uh, sudden, Flynn?'' It sounded weak, even to her own ears.

His head lifted with arrogant sureness. ''I know what I want, Angie. I'm very certain about what I'm doing.''

''Yes, you are, aren't you? You're always certain about what you're doing. You've got your whole damn life mapped out and nothing is going to get in the way of your goals. Well, I'm not at all sure I want to be included in those goals, Flynn Challoner. Thank you very much for considering me as your potential wife, but as it happens I've got a few plans of my own!''

''Angie, don't get upset.'' He took a step forward and halted abruptly when she immediately moved to the side a pace.

''What in hell do you mean by telling me not to get upset? What else do you expect me to do? I'm not Maria Isabel, Flynn. I'm Angie Morgan. And I don't really have the same ambitions that you do. I have no desire to be used to fulfill some family destiny only you can visualize.''

''Will you calm down and listen to me?'' Something flickered in his eyes. It might have been impatience or it might have been concern. ''You don't have to accept my offer of marriage tonight. I'm quite willing to give you a little time to think it over.''

''How generous of you!''

''Angie—''

''Why don't you be honest, at least, Flynn? It's not me

you're offering to marry. It's the woman who can bring you the Torres Dagger. The woman you see as a link to your precious family past. The woman you think will make a good brood mare for the future. Well, I'll be damned if I'll be married for reasons such as that!''

"Stop it, Angie. You don't know what you're saying.''

"Don't I?'' She swung around and grabbed the dagger case. "You think I don't know exactly where I fit in your scheme of things? I'm one step behind this stupid dagger and I know it.''

"That's not true. Angie, you're acting like a child. I sure as hell didn't expect you to get hysterical over this!''

"Shows how little you know me!'' she shot back furiously. "You shouldn't go around offering marriage to someone you don't know very well, Flynn.'' She circled to the left, heading for the door. The dagger case was still clutched in her hand.

"Angie, come back here.''

"I'm going home to think over my fabulous offer of marriage. I plan to think it over for a very long time, Flynn. Well past my childbearing years.'' She swung around and opened the door.

"Angie, you little witch, come back here or so help me—'' He broke off, striding through the door after her.

"Leave me alone, Flynn. And stop pretending that it's me you want. I know exactly what you want.''

"You don't know what you're saying.''

"Shall I prove it? I can, you know.'' Head high, she challenged him with furious, frantic eyes.

"Angie, I'm going to lose my temper,'' he warned softly.

"I've already lost mine!'' She whirled and fled through the living room, not even glancing at Julian, who was looking startled by the unexpected scene taking place before his eyes.

"Angie!"

She paid no attention, racing through the door and out into the fog-shrouded night. Behind her she heard Flynn. He would catch up with her soon. She didn't stand a chance of outrunning him. She sucked in a breath of chilled air and dashed for the edge of the bluff overlooking the sea.

She couldn't make out the water below but she could hear it foaming and crashing against the bottom of the cliff. The tide was in, and occasionally a splash of white was visible through the fog. Frantically she opened the dagger case. Flynn was running silently. He would materialize behind her at any second.

The dagger slid easily into the wide sleeve of her yellow shirt. She snapped the case shut just as Flynn appeared. He came gliding out of the fog, his harsh face barely discernible in the swirling shadows.

"Just what the hell do you think you're doing?" he bit out.

"Proving a point!"

"What point? That I don't want you? That's idiotic and you know it. Don't you remember that night in L.A.?"

"You only care about the history around me, and I swear I won't be married for historical purposes!"

"Angie, I'm not asking you to marry me just because of the past!"

"Yes, you are and I'll prove it!" Without a second's hesitation she tossed the empty dagger case over the edge of the cliff. It sailed out into the fog and disappeared. A moment later the waves closed over it. Angie turned back to confront Flynn. "Okay, Challoner. The dagger's gone. Still want to marry me?"

Chapter 8

Time hung suspended, trapped in the light, swirling fog. For a shattering moment Angie was no longer certain of the era in which she lived. A part of her was suddenly aware that Maria Isabel had once precipitated similar confrontations with Curtis Challoner. Nothing seemed to have changed, most especially not the risks. The sea pulsed rhythmically at the base of the cliff, and the faint light from the house shone erratically through the mist. Flynn stood utterly still, staring into the foaming darkness where the dagger case had disappeared.

Angie was cold with a chill that had nothing to do with the damp night air. She was vaguely aware that her fingers were shaking. Soon her whole body would be shivering. She wished she could see Flynn's expression, but simultaneously she dreaded the moment when he would turn to face her. Instinct warned her to turn and run. Pride and a strange disorientation kept her where she was. The length of the dagger felt hard and frozen on the warmth of her skin. She should remove it from her sleeve, show it to Flynn and end this unreal scene. But she couldn't seem to move.

"Flynn?" His name was a ragged, husky sound in her throat. Angie wasn't even certain he had heard.

"Do you hate me so much, then, Angie?"

Slowly he turned to look at her and the fog-reflected glow of the house lights fell on his stark, harsh features. Angie registered the combination of shock, fury and pain in the shadows of his eyes, and she felt abruptly dizzy.

"Flynn, I don't...I didn't..." The words tripped and fell over themselves as she struggled to regain a sense of equilibrium. Unconsciously she put out a hand as if to ward him off although he had made no move to touch her.

"I knew you weren't exactly head over heels in love with me, but I didn't realize—" He broke off, shaking his head once in bleak despair. "I didn't think you would throw a couple of hundred years of our history into the sea just to make your point. What have I done to make you want this kind of revenge?"

Angie shook off the numbing disorientation. "Nothing, Flynn. Nothing at all. You saved both the dagger and me down in Mexico, and you didn't steal it when you could have done so easily. You've offered me what must seem to you a reasonable, honorable marriage alliance. You've behaved like a gentleman, and instead of returning the courtesy I lost my self-control entirely. There is absolutely no excuse for the way I acted. After all, it's not as if I'm a headstrong nineteen-year-old at the mercy of the men who ran her life. Maria Isabel had a right to fight back any way she could. She had no option."

He came forward, gliding soundlessly through the mist until he was only a step away from her.

"Angie—"

"I'm sorry, Flynn. Unlike Maria Isabel, I do have an

option. All I have to say is no.'' With fumbling fingers she extracted the dagger from her sleeve and held it out to him. "I wanted to make a point, but as you said, I wouldn't throw away a couple of hundred years of history to do it.'' *Not when that history means so much to you,* she added silently.

Flynn stared at the dagger before slowly reaching out to take it from her. She could read nothing in his face now; not even relief. That was preferable to the unmistakable fury and anguish she had seen a moment earlier. Without waiting for his response Angie turned and ran back toward the lights of her uncle's house.

At the door she changed her mind about going inside. The idea of facing Uncle Julian was sufficiently daunting to send her around to the driveway. Flynn had the keys to her car, but she kept a spare taped inside the glove compartment. Angie opened the car door, slipped into the driver's seat and dug out the extra key.

All she wanted right now was to be alone. Twisting the key in the ignition, Angie put the Toyota in gear. Gravel crunched under the wheels as she pulled out of the drive. Her startling burst of temper was firmly back under control. In fact, most of it seemed to have been replaced by a sense of shock at her own behavior.

She had known Flynn's proposal was coming. Her intuition had told her to expect it. Angie chased the car's headlights into the fog and asked herself over and over again why she had responded so violently. She wasn't Maria Isabel. She wasn't trapped the way the other woman had been.

But as often as she repeated that to herself, Angie couldn't argue with the inner conviction that she wasn't really free. To be truly free she would have to feel nothing more than casual friendship for Flynn. And heaven knew that what she felt went far beyond friendship. She was in love with the man.

Maybe that was the same trap in which Maria Isabel had found herself, Angie realized with sudden insight. Perhaps the other woman had been caught not only in the cage of the social structure in which she lived but in the snare of her growing passion for Curtis Challoner. The pressure of being forced into a marriage in which the groom was primarily interested in the settling of a land dispute would be bad enough, but to be in love with him and aware that your love was not returned would be infinitely worse. The first situation could conceivably be viewed philosophically. The second would mean anguish.

And it was the second scenario in which she found herself, Angie thought as she parked her car in front of her cottage. But her anguish had not given her the right to pull that stupid stunt with the dagger. Well, one thing was for certain. After tonight she wouldn't have to worry about dealing with a proposal of marriage from Flynn. She'd seen the expression in his eyes when he'd turned to look at her after she'd thrown the dagger case into the sea. No man who looked at a woman in that way was likely to renew his proposal.

Letting herself inside the cozy little cottage, Angie switched on the hall light and tossed the Toyota key onto a nearby table. She stood trying to decide what to do next.

Aimlessly she wandered into the living room and considered starting a fire. The chill she had felt on the cliffs still seemed to be eating at her. Building a blaze seemed to require too much effort, however, so Angie settled for turning up the thermostat and going out into the kitchen to pour herself a snifter of sherry. She was on her way back into the living room, sherry in hand, when she heard her uncle's Mercedes approaching.

It would be Flynn. Instinct told her that with nerve-shattering clarity. Angie stood riveted to the hall floor, the glass clutched in her fingers, and listened as the car's engine died. A second later the door slammed shut, and then there was a soundless interval as Flynn moved silently up the path to her front door. When the peremptory knock came she almost dropped the sherry onto the tile floor.

"Angie, open the door." Flynn didn't knock a second time. His voice was filled with command.

She could refuse to open the door, Angie thought distractedly. Would he force his way inside? "What do you want, Flynn?"

"You and I have a few things to talk about."

"I think..." She paused, moistening her lower lip. "I think it would be better if the discussion waited until morning."

"Open the door, Angie, or I'll find my own way into the house."

It wasn't a threat; simply a statement of fact. She didn't doubt for a moment that he could and would do it. Unsteadily Angie went to the door and slowly opened it. Flynn stood on the front step, harshly revealed in the light of the outside lamp. The dagger was held loosely in his left hand, the stones in its handle gleaming dully in the yellow porch light. His dark eyes moved over her and then went to her glass. He stepped purposefully into the hall.

"Why don't you pour me a glass of whatever that is. I could use it." Without waiting for her acknowledgment Flynn strode into the small living room and glanced around. Then he went over to the fireplace and picked up one of the store-bought fire logs that lay on the hearth. "I don't know why you don't buy real wood instead of this compressed sawdust."

Angie stared at his back as he set the dagger on an end table and went down on one knee to strike a match. "I buy those logs because they're so much simpler to use. Flynn, why are you complaining about my instant fire logs? No one asked you to build a fire in the first place."

"I'm aware of that. You haven't asked me for a damn thing since we got back from Mexico, have you?" He finished setting the log alight and remained crouched where he was, gazing fiercely into the flames.

"I don't understand what you're trying to say."

"Go pour me a drink, Angie." He ran his fingers wearily through his hair and got to his feet.

Nervously, feeling as if her emotions were dangling above the point of the dagger that had caused all the trouble, Angie did as she was told. When she returned to the living room with a second glass, she found Flynn sprawled in a chair. He was gazing broodingly into the fire, but he looked up briefly as she handed him the sherry.

"Thanks." He took a deep swallow. "Good Spanish sherry. Sort of fits the occasion, doesn't it?"

"What occasion?" Gingerly Angie took a seat on the other side of the fireplace. She decided she didn't want to hear the answer and rushed on to add, "Flynn, I'm sorry. I know that was a stupid trick I pulled out there on the cliffs. I don't know what got into me. I've never done anything like that before in my life."

He sighed and stretched his legs out closer to the blaze. "You're a female and you're a Torres. I should have expected the fireworks."

Some of Angie's contriteness evaporated. "That's an asinine explanation of my behavior. Oversimplified, illogical and chauvinistic."

He wasn't listening. Apparently Flynn was trying to sort something out in his mind. His brow furrowed. "It's just that for the past several days you've seemed so quiet, so reasonable, so..." He paused, searching for the word. "So amenable. I thought you understood. I was under the impression that you were feeling cooperative about the idea of rejoining the two families."

"That's how you see it, isn't it? A way of reliving the past."

His gaze flickered toward her briefly, and then he looked back at the fire. "No, Angie. That's not the way I see it. No one relives the past. You *build* on the past. Can't you understand the distinction?"

"No, but I'm beginning to think you do understand it." She took a sip of sherry. "The past means a lot to you."

"What does it mean to you, Angie? Nothing at all?"

She shook her head. "No, it's beginning to have meaning. More than I want it to have."

He frowned at her. "Why do you say that?"

"The past is starting to make me edgy, Flynn. I find it a little frightening, if you want to know the truth. Before I met you the tale of Maria Isabel Torres and Curtis Challoner was just that: a tale. Interesting on some levels, amusing on others. But essentially nothing more than a legend."

"What are you saying? That it's becoming more than a legend?"

"In some ways."

Relief flared in his gaze. "But, Angie, that's good. That's the way it should be. You should feel the past in your bones. It should be a part of you, a touchstone, a foundation. It deserves to be more than just a collection of stories."

She tilted her head to one side, studying him. "I didn't say it was becoming any of those things. I said I found it a bit frightening."

"Maybe for you that's the first step to having it become real."

"Flynn, if that's the first step, I'm not exactly anxious to take the next step. Damn it, why are you acting so pleased? I'm the person who just put you through hell by letting you think I'd thrown your precious dagger into the ocean! I should think you'd be furious.''

''It wasn't my dagger you pulled that stunt with, it was *our* dagger and I *was* furious. I couldn't believe you'd do something like that just out of spite.''

''It was hardly spite that made me do it!'' She was starting to overreact again, Angie thought wildly. What was the matter with her? A few minutes ago she was feeling apologetic and extremely guilty for having behaved in such a juvenile manner. Now the resentment was starting to flare to life again. Her emotions seesawed as they hovered over the imagined point of the dagger.

A small smile briefly edged Flynn's mouth. His eyes warmed suddenly. ''No, it wasn't spite, was it? You were enraged. There's a difference. I'll bet Maria Isabel looked a lot like you looked when she lost her temper with my ancestor. All fire and fury and passion. I really should have been expecting it. After all, I know something about the passion buried in you. But I was off guard. You'd fooled me into thinking you were going to be very twentieth century about my marriage proposal. A polite yes or no was the response I anticipated. And to tell you the truth, I was expecting a yes.''

''Flynn, I think this has gone far enough. You're obviously determined to pretend I'm another Maria Isabel. I'm not. For one thing, I'm several years older than she was when she was forced into marriage. For another I am a child of the twentieth century. You're absolutely right. All I have to give you is a simple yes or no. Frankly, though, I'm surprised the offer is still open.''

''Because of what you did back there on the cliffs?'' He looked at her quizzically. ''That doesn't change anything, Angie.''

"Really? What would you have done if I'd actually thrown that dagger into the sea?"

"Calm down," he soothed. "You didn't throw it into the ocean. Therefore we don't have to discuss alternatives."

Restlessly Angie got to her feet and put her sherry glass down on a table. She stood leaning against the mantel and stared down into the fire. "I want to know what you would have done, Flynn."

"Why?"

"I guess because I'm trying to figure out exactly how much that dagger means to you. Would you still be offering to marry me if I'd thrown that damn thing into the sea?"

"Yes."

She looked up, her eyes wide and searching. "Wouldn't you have hated me?"

"No, but I would have been a little worried that you hated me." He got to his feet and came to stand in front of her. "But you don't hate me, do you Angie?"

She caught her breath. "No."

He nodded. "Thank God for that. Your temper I can handle. Your hatred would be something else again."

"You've convinced yourself that's all my scene on the cliffs amounts to, haven't you? A display of feminine temper."

"And passion." He lifted a hand to stroke the line of her throat up to her chin. Gently he tipped her face upward. "You took me by surprise. But maybe that's because I'd let myself be lulled into believing I knew what you were thinking. The truth is I didn't know what you were really thinking. I made some assumptions that were obviously wrong. I suppose you could say I deserved that scene on the cliffs. But, Angie, you haven't been exactly communicative lately. Ever since we left L.A. you've been withdrawn."

"And you haven't quite known why, have you?" She searched his eyes.

"I thought at first it was because you were hurt by the fact that I'd kept my identity from you down in Mexico. But you seemed to get over that. You've been friendly enough this past week, just distant. This would have been so much simpler if we really were living in the past. Then I could have negotiated the marriage with Julian. I wouldn't have had to second-guess you or try to figure out what you were thinking. What have you been thinking, Angie? Why did you explode tonight?"

She watched him, feeling helpless to explain. Any man who longed for the times when a marriage alliance could be negotiated between two males was probably incapable of understanding how she had felt this evening.

"Flynn, I once told you that when I married it wouldn't be for business reasons. Do you remember?"

He inclined his head warily. "As I recall you said you would marry for love and passion."

"I haven't changed my mind."

He bent his head and brushed his mouth lightly against her own. Then, without lifting his lips from hers, he whispered, "How can you say there isn't passion between us?"

Angie shivered. She couldn't bring herself to move out of reach although Flynn held her in place with only the tip of his finger and the promise of his mouth. "I haven't said there isn't passion, Flynn. But there does seem to be a lack of love."

"Love will follow, sweetheart. Just as it followed for Maria Isabel." He kissed her again, slowly, his hand moving to cradle the nape of her neck. His fingers began toying with the pins that held her coiled hair. "Give it a chance, Angie. You want me. I've known that from the beginning. And we have so much in common, so much to build on together.

I'll take care of you, honey. I swear it. Just give me a chance.''

She closed her eyes as his lips traced a path along the line of her jaw up to her earlobe. Angie could feel the sensual tension beginning to vibrate in him, striking a chord within herself that responded eagerly.

''What about you, Flynn? Do you think that in time you'll fall in love with me?''

''Sweetheart, love is a word for women like you and Maria Isabel to use to label passion and commitment. I can use it, too, if that's what you want. But it doesn't mean much to me, not when I compare it to what I know I already feel for you.''

''And what is that, Flynn?''

He tugged free one of the pins that held her hair. It fell soundlessly to the carpet. ''Desire, for one thing. I've never wanted a woman the way I want you.'' His fingers found another pin and tugged it loose. It, too, dropped to the floor. ''A sense of protectiveness. I want to take care of you, Angie.'' A third pin followed the other two. ''A feeling of rightness. A feeling that we belong together.'' Two more pins were eased out of her dark, tawny hair. ''A sense of a shared past. And a sense of the future.'' Her hair tumbled free and spilled over his hand. He curled his fingers deeply into it and used it to gently hold her still for his kiss.

Angie's arms wound about his neck as her mouth opened for him. Her precariously balanced emotions were being pushed unmercifully in the direction Flynn wanted them to go. She knew it, recognized that she was allowing her love for him to overwhelm her logic, but in that moment she didn't want to take the necessary step back that would salvage the situation. The dagger's blade was as tempting as it was dangerous.

''Flynn...''

"I think that what happened tonight was my own fault, Angie." He whispered huskily into her mouth. "I never should have let you put so much distance between us. I should have kept you close, the way you were in Mexico. The way you were that night in the hotel in L.A. Instead I tried to give you time to adjust. That was a mistake."

"No, Flynn. It wasn't a mistake. I do need time to think."

"Come to bed with me, sweetheart, and afterward tell me where your thinking is going to lead you."

She heard the certainty in his words. "You're so sure of yourself, aren't you?"

"Angie, I know what's right for us. I can feel it, damn it!" His hands tightened on her abruptly, pulling her into the warmth of his body.

The flames from the hearth shimmered and flared as Angie surrendered to Flynn's heat. She loved him and she wanted him with all her being. The issues between them were still unresolved but she could not deny herself this chance to be with him again. All the mounting tension of the past several days seemed to be culminating tonight, first in anger and now in passion.

"Come with me, sweetheart. I'll show you that what we have is right." Flynn picked her up, cradling her in his arms as he started down the hall to her bedroom.

Angie silently abandoned herself to the smoldering flames of her love. She clung to him, head nestled on his shoulder as he carried her into the bedroom. The mounting desire in Flynn was a pulsating force that was as strong and relentless as the sea outside. It charged the atmosphere in the darkened room, and Angie was tinglingly aware of it as he let her slide slowly down the length of his body.

When she found her feet she realized that her sense of balance was off. Her fingers splayed across his shoulders as she sought to steady herself.

"Don't worry, sweetheart. I'll hold you. I'll take care of you." The words were dark, seductive caresses, every bit as effective as his touch.

"We should talk, Flynn...."

"We've talked enough. We've done too much talking. I should have been taking you to bed every night this past week instead of trying to give you time. I wasn't cut out to be a gentleman with you."

He undid the buttons of her shirt, sliding the garment off and letting it drop to the floor. Her hair flowed around her shoulders as his palms dropped to cup her bare breasts.

"Finding you at the same time I found the dagger was fate, Angie. It had to be. How can you even question it?"

She didn't try to answer that. There was, after all, no logical response to such a statement, especially not when your body was agreeing with every word. Angie shivered with impending excitement as Flynn rubbed his thumbs gently across her hardening nipples. Then she reached out with a passionate aggression of which she was only vaguely aware and began to undress him.

"Yes," he groaned hoarsely. "Show me, honey. Show me that you want me. Prove it to both of us."

She fumbled with the buttons of his shirt until, frustrated as much as she was by her ineffectual efforts, Flynn smiled a little and stepped back. He finished unfastening his clothing, discarding his moccasins, the shirt, the twill pants with quick, impatient movements. Then, standing in front of her in only his briefs, he went back to removing Angie's clothes. This task he performed with infinitely more patience than he had just exhibited with his own clothes. It was obvious he took pleasure in the process.

Angie ran her hands down his chest, an aching sensation stirring deep in her body. "You're so hard," she murmured, flexing her nails lightly into his skin.

"I know." He sounded wryly amused by the fact. "I can hardly hide it, can I?" Deliberately he cupped her buttocks in his hands and pressed his hips against her.

She flushed at the unyielding thrust of his body. "I...I didn't mean that way. I meant all over. Physically, emotionally, the way you think. You're a hard man, Flynn Challoner." She put her lips to his shoulder and tasted him with the tip of her tongue. When he responded with muttered words of desire, she let him feel the edge of her teeth.

"Little cat. I'm going to enjoy returning the favor." He released her briefly to pull back the sheet and the comforter on her bed and then he scooped her up and set her down in the middle. A moment later he followed, his body sprawling heavily along hers as he pulled her into his arms.

Angie welcomed the heat and weight of him, twining her legs with his and sinking her fingers into his hair. She sighed his name as she felt his hand gliding over her skin. He touched her with increasing intimacy while the fire between them flamed into full life. His fingers found the exquisitely sensitive skin on the inside of her thigh and then prowled closer to the dampening heart of her desire. She arced her breast against his mouth when he made good his passionate threat and trapped a nipple between his teeth.

There in the darkness Angie was able to put aside the logic and uncertainty that made her balk at the idea of marriage. There in the shadows of the bedroom she was free to glory in the passionate excitement only Flynn could arouse in her. In the morning she would deal with reality. Tonight all that mattered was losing herself in Flynn's arms.

"Angie, you don't ever have to be afraid of me. You're mine, and I'll take care of what belongs to me." He rolled onto his back, drawing her with him until she was lying on top. Then he stroked his hands down her back to the curve of her hips. "Now, honey, *now* I want to feel you all over

me. I need to be inside. You're so warm and wet and clinging inside...."

Angie gasped as he eased her down toward his waiting
hardness. The images she'd had all evening of being poised
above the dagger suddenly crystalized into an unexpected
version of reality.

She had no more time to think about it. Flynn's fingers
were digging luxuriously into her thighs, and he held her
still as he thrust upward.

"Yes, sweetheart, oh, God, *yes!*"

Angie clung to him, her body adjusting to the beloved
invasion. Flynn anchored her fiercely as he lifted his hips
against her softness. His mouth found hers, drinking deeply,
and she felt the strength of his hands as he guided her into
the rhythm he wanted.

Deep within her tendrils of delicious, aching tension spun
slowly outward and then began to coalesce. She was aware
of the slickness of perspiration on Flynn's chest, knew the
passionate firmness of him as he buried himself within her,
felt the unbreakable hold in which she was held. Suddenly
the tension broke, washing over her while she shivered in
its wake. Before she had even begun to recover she heard
Flynn's harsh cry of satisfaction and triumph and then he
was shuddering in savage release. His hold on her didn't
slacken as he followed her into the temporary oblivion.

Angie came awake slowly the next morning; calmly,
clearly aware of what she was going to do. She had known
it all along, she realized. That was why she had experienced
the frightening sensation of being trapped. She stretched and
turned on her side. The bed was empty.

Pushing back the covers, she climbed out of bed, pausing
briefly to let a few sore muscles adjust to the new position.
She listened attentively for a moment but heard no telltale

sounds from the kitchen. Intuition told her that Flynn had gone done to the beach. Either that, she thought wryly as she glanced around the room, or he had gone back to the hacienda. Either way, they were going to have to come to an understanding about this sort of behavior.

She pulled on a pair of jeans and a vivid red oversize top that fell below her waist. She belted the shirt with a wide snakeskin tie. Then Angie located a pair of shoes and her windbreaker. She didn't bother to put her hair into its usual twist. The first priority was to find Flynn.

He wasn't hard to locate. She saw him as soon as she reached the top of the cliff overlooking the beach. He was standing at the water's edge, gazing out to sea. Angie knew a wave of anguished panic. Perhaps he had changed his mind, after all. Perhaps he was down there trying to figure out how to tell her he was withdrawing his proposal of marriage.

The flash of doubt sent her hurrying forward, scrambling down the narrow path to the beach. She didn't think he could have heard her over the sound of the surf but something made him turn and watch as she walked toward him through the sand. The unreadable expression on his lean face almost caused her to lose her nerve.

"Challoner," she began, struggling to find refuge in flippancy, "there's something we have to get cleared up about your poor morning-after etiquette."

"Is there?"

He wasn't going to make this easy for her, Angie thought, dismayed. And the flippancy didn't seem to be working too well, either. "You're not supposed to just disappear from the bed the way you do. You're supposed to stick around and make warm, meaningful conversation. Or at least make coffee."

He stared at her. "I see. Did you have something warm and meaningful you wanted to say?"

She flinched but held on to her nerve. "Yes, as a matter of fact, I did."

Wariness and hope flared in his eyes. He controlled both emotions almost immediately. "And what would that be?"

"I've decided to accept your proposal of marriage." Angie took refuge now in formality. "That is, if it's still open." She held her breath.

"Why?"

The stark question was the last thing she had been expecting. Uneasily she tried to concentrate. "For all the reasons you suggested. We're compatible, we have some history in common. You're a good man, a strong man, not a playboy. I think I can trust you. And maybe there is a certain sense of fate involved. I don't know about that last part. I don't think I want to know about it." Then in silence she added the real reason, *because I love you, Flynn Sangrey Challoner.* She waited.

He studied her for a long moment, the crisp, cool wind whipping his shirt and ruffling his hair. Behind him the sea lapped almost to his moccasins. Angie felt the bite of the morning breeze. The cold seemed to go right through her.

"All right," Flynn said finally.

She smiled tremulously. "Is that all you can say? All right?"

He hesitated and then a hint of a smile touched his mouth. "How about, 'thank you and I promise not to vacate the bed in future without telling you where I'm going'?"

"That's better." She held out her hand, and after a couple of seconds he took it, his fingers closing warmly and a little fiercely around hers.

"Angie?"

"Hmm?" She caught her hair and held it out of her eyes. "I'll make it work. I'll make it all right."

Not understanding what he meant, she wrinkled her nose and smiled up at him. "I don't doubt it for a moment."

Chapter 9

Three days later Angie furtively sought refuge in her uncle's study. A quick glance around the room revealed she had the place to herself, and with a deep sigh of relief she shut the door and collapsed into the nearest chair.

She should have guessed that once Flynn had her agreement to the marriage, there would be no stopping him until the wedding had taken place. He had taken charge completely, and she had felt like a leaf caught up in a whirlwind. She had also felt quite unnecessary. Flynn was organizing everything from the flowers right down to the plane tickets for her mother.

Occasionally she was consulted, but Angie had the distinct impression it was more out of politeness than because Flynn actually wanted her opinion. Mrs. Akers was getting the brunt of Flynn's attention this morning, however, as he went over the reception menu with her. Angie had gratefully slipped out of his path, fleeing to the study on the hunch that Flynn wouldn't think to look for her there. If he missed her, he would probably assume she was taking a walk on the beach. Craftily, she had mentioned the idea earlier at breakfast.

Breakfast had been at her cottage this morning, just as it had for the past several mornings, but not because Flynn had spent the night. He hadn't. In fact, he hadn't spent any night with her since the scene with the dagger. She wasn't quite sure how to interpret that, but she suspected it had something to do with his grim determination to do things *right*.

The door opened and Angie jumped. She relaxed as Julian walked into the room. He smiled as she sank back into the chair.

"I figured you might be hiding in here. Picked up an extra cup of coffee for you from the kitchen. Mrs. Akers and Flynn never even noticed me."

"Too busy trying to decide between shrimp puffs and salmon canapes probably." Gratefully Angie accepted the coffee. She grinned wryly at her uncle as he sat down in his swivel desk chair. "Honestly, Uncle Julian, I knew he was basically a take-charge personality. I saw enough of them when I was in personnel work to recognize the type. But I never thought he'd apply his talents in quite this manner. I've always heard weddings are women's business. All the groom has to do is show up on time."

Julian shrugged. "He wants it done right."

"So he'll do it himself."

"Don't forget he also wants it done quickly. Only two weeks from today. Given the tight schedule he probably figures he'd better stay in command."

"He's like a general on a battlefield. Every time he spots me he gives me another set of orders. And Mrs. Akers appears to have been placed second in command."

"This wedding is important to him," Julian said gently.

"He's not taking charge this way because he's a natural-born social butterfly!"

In spite of herself Angie laughed at the image. "A butterfly in moccasins. I like that. No, I agree. He's about as much a social butterfly as Jake Savage is."

Julian ignored her. "You have to understand, Angelina. Rituals and traditions are bound to be important to a man who's intent on rebuilding a family. And the wedding that forms the basis of his new..."

"Dynasty?" Angie suggested dryly when her uncle stopped to fish for an appropriate word.

"Well, that's putting it a bit dramatically, I think. But your marriage is a foundation on which Flynn intends to build. He wants it started properly."

Angie smiled gently. "I understand, Uncle Julian. It's just that at times it's a little nerve-racking. Maybe I've got bridal jitters."

Julian studied her. "Are you really nervous about this marriage? There's absolutely no need, you know. Flynn will make you an excellent husband."

"The question is, will I make him the right kind of wife?" She tilted her head back against the chair cushion. "He's so set on reestablishing the Challoner-Torres line. He has an image in his head, a goal that only he can see. I'm not marrying him because I'm equally committed to founding a dynasty."

"Why are you marrying him, then?"

She closed her eyes briefly. "For the usual reasons."

"The usual reasons?" Her uncle arched one brow. "It can't be for money. Flynn's cash is tied up in land and likely to remain that way for some time to come. Every extra cent he gets for the next few years will be funneled back into property, I think. You'll have what you need and a few luxuries, but you won't be driving a Ferrari. Let's see, what other 'usual reasons' are there? How about social status? Nope, we have to assume it's not for that. Right now the Challoners and the Torreses have virtually no social status. That may change someday, but it will be a long time in the future. Desperation? You see thirty on the horizon and are starting to panic? I don't think so. You've always seemed amazingly content with yourself and your independence. So much so that I was beginning to think you never would marry. And if you had been panicking, I think you would have had some marriage candidates lined up before you went to Mexico. That leaves us with one other possibility. You're in love with him, aren't you?''

Angie looked at her uncle through eyes narrowed half in amused resignation and half in irritation. ''As I said, I'm marrying for the usual reasons.''

''He needs your love, Angelina. Any man who is as intent on his goals as Flynn is will desperately need a woman's love during the coming years. The drive and the ambition will eat him alive, otherwise.''

Angie thought about that. He seems so strong, Uncle Julian.''

''He is strong. It takes a hell of a strong man to set his kind of goals and then commit himself to the work it will take to meet them. But that kind of energy and drive can destroy even the strongest people. The effort will take a lot out of him and without a softer side in his life…well, I shouldn't have to tell you, Angelina. You're the expert in personnel work. You must have seen what can happen.''

She nodded. ''I've seen it. Strong, committed people can build their own traps. And you're right. Energy and ambition can swallow a man whole. And in Flynn's case there's the added factor of what he's already done in his life just to get to where he is now. It's strange, Uncle Julian, but

I've never thought of Flynn in the same objective terms I'm accustomed to applying to others.''

"I'd hardly call that strange." Julian smiled affectionately. "People seldom are objective about the people they love."

Angie considered where that logic led. Flynn seemed quite objective about her, she reflected. He knew exactly why he was marrying her; had all the reasons lined up in a neat, orderly row. It followed that he didn't love her, but it didn't necessarily mean he couldn't learn to love her.

With an exclamation of frustration, Angie set down her coffee cup. There was no sense tearing herself apart trying to figure out Flynn's actions. He was a law unto himself, just as Curtis Challoner and the head of the neighboring Torres family had been laws unto themselves nearly two hundred years ago. Uncle Julian was right; it took that kind of man to build a dynasty. And maybe, just maybe you could argue, as Julian had, that such a man needed love to maintain a healthy balance in his life.

But what of the woman who committed herself to giving that love? What did she need in return in order to survive emotionally? Angie stirred restlessly, drawing her legs up under her as she sat in the chair. She would receive a great deal from Flynn Challoner. He was honorable in his own way. He had his own code, but he lived by it and he could be trusted. There would be passion and honor and commitment. Why on earth was she feeling uneasy? Many women got a lot less out of the marriage contract.

Something stirred in her mind, a faint whisper of another voice from another time. It could have been Maria Isabel but of course it wasn't, Angie told herself. It was simply her own growing affinity for the woman who had married Curtis Challoner. Somehow Angie knew, though, that a lot of the thoughts going through her head lately were hardly original. Maria Isabel had given herself the same lectures; asked herself the same questions. And wound up with the same sense of frustration.

"Angie! Angie, where the hell are you?" Flynn's voice sounded loudly from the hall. A moment later the study door was flung open. "There you are. I've been looking all over for you." He nodded briefly at Julian, who smiled serenely in return, and then strode toward Angie. He had a list in his hand that was covered with his distinctive scrawl. "Do you want tomato-basil sandwiches or smoked salmon?"

"Gee, that's a tough choice, Flynn."

He frowned at her. "This is not a joke, Angie. I'm very serious. Mrs. Akers says they'll both be on the salty side and that we should probably choose one or the other. We couldn't make up our minds so I thought I'd see if you had an opinion."

"Caviar," Angie said succinctly.

"What?"

"How about caviar if you want something salty? Think how impressed the guests will be."

His face cleared. "You're absolutely right. We'll set a big bowl of caviar on an ice block and surround it with little crackers and things." He started for the door and then halted as he caught sight of Julian again. "Speaking of the guests, did you make out that list?"

"I've got it ready."

"Good. Angie can add your list to hers and address the invitations this afternoon. I want them in the mail by five o'clock. It's short enough notice as it is."

"Don't worry, Flynn," Julian advised. "Everyone on my list will show up."

Flynn nodded in satisfaction. "Good." He vanished out the door.

Angie eyed her uncle. "We're providing all the guests?"

Julian smiled wryly. "Well, Flynn doesn't have any friends in this area. And I got the feeling that the few friends he does have are scattered around the globe. By the time the invitations reached them the wedding would be over."

"I wonder if that bothers him," Angie mused.

"I doubt it. He just wants people there. I don't think he's particularly fussy about which people."

"Then why invite anyone at all? Why not keep this thing just family?"

"Angie, you don't understand. Guests are important to a wedding such as this. They're witnesses. The more witnesses the better as far as Flynn is concerned."

"Part of the foundation process, I guess." Angie levered herself to her feet. "Well, I've received my orders of the day. Fat lot of good it did trying to hide. I think I'd better go start addressing invitations. You're sure your friends will come?"

"Are you kidding? They'll be dying of curiosity. I've told them that my niece is marrying the real Jake Savage?"

"Uncle Julian!"

"That's not all. I decided Flynn was forgetting about one of the most important prewedding customs, so I took care to remedy the matter."

"What custom?"

"A surprise bachelor party for the groom. I've invited a selected handful of male friends."

"I'm not sure I want to hear the rest of this. You're planning a surprise party?"

"Yup. But it will have to be a few days before the wedding instead of the night before because your mother will be arriving the day before the ceremony. She'll be staying here, and it would be a bit awkward trying to surprise Flynn with your mother in the house."

Angie grinned. "Probably not a good idea for the mother

of the bride to see the groom in a drunken stupor the night before he marries her daughter.''

"I can't imagine Flynn in a drunken stupor."

"Neither can I. Should be interesting. One thing, though, Uncle Julian. I want you to promise me that there won't be any nude girls leaping out of cakes!''

"You're starting to sound wifely already."

A week later Flynn went down to the beach by himself to think about the expense involved in ordering the brand of champagne he wanted. When the caviar had been added to the already lengthy list of hors d'oeuvres, a considerable dent had been put into the budget.

Ah, well, he told himself. The budget was a loose one. He could worry about economizing after the wedding. He'd go ahead and order the real stuff, French champagne instead of the domestic variety.

The decision made, he halted at the water's edge and wondered why he was still feeling faintly uneasy. It couldn't be worry about the wedding, itself. Everything was going perfectly. Responses were already coming back from the invitations. Mrs. Akers seemed to have the food preparation under control. The minister had confirmed the time and day.

He scooped up a pebble and sent it skipping expertly across the waves. It did fine until an incoming breaker claimed it. No, it wasn't the wedding that was worrying him. Flynn picked up another pebble and considered how perfectly things were falling into place.

He had everything he wanted, everything he needed to lay the foundation for the future. Angie, the dagger, which he strongly suspected Julian would give him for a wedding present, and a start in land investment. The future lay before him, ready and waiting.

So why was his intuition warning him that something was missing?

The second pebble lost its rhythm on the first skip and fell into the sea without a trace. Flynn shrugged and turned to walk back toward Julian's house.

Three days before the wedding Julian sprang his surprise party. Angie, who had been warned in advance, was there to see Flynn's startled expression as he walked through the front door of Julian's home and found the partygoers assembled inside.

Angie blew her intended a kiss over the heads of the small group of men Julian had invited, and then she picked up the car keys and went outside to drive herself to the cottage. Flynn could use Julian's car when he was ready to leave this evening. Unless, of course, he was too drunk to drive home.

It would be amusing to see Flynn Challoner tipsy, Angie decided as she drove back to the cottage. She'd never seen him when he hadn't been in full control of himself. Unless she counted those two occasions when she'd lain in his arms. And his control was such that, even though she knew he desired her, he had been able to limit himself to those two occasions. Perhaps she'd feel more confident going into her marriage if she knew that in one area, at least, Flynn wasn't able to exert such control around her.

She thought about those two occasions off and on for the rest of the evening as she puttered around the cottage. In another three days she would be married. There was something unreal about the image. Flynn, himself, was as solid as granite and her own love for him was equally tangible. But the nagging wish for something more persisted.

She was as greedy as Maria Isabel had been. In the back of her mind Angie could almost see the other woman smiling in gentle commiseration. But she was also as reckless. She would take her chances with love.

At eleven o'clock Angie went to bed. A glance out the window revealed no lights on at the hacienda. Apparently the groom's party was still in full swing at Julian's. Angie pulled on her high-necked, long-sleeved flannel nightgown and turned back the bed. Before sliding under the quilt she cast a thoughtful look at the Torres Dagger, which lay on her dresser. Flynn had left it with her the night she'd pretended to toss it into the sea. When she'd mentioned its new location to her uncle, Julian had told her to keep it until the wedding.

"Why?" Angie had asked, astonished. She had been going to replace it in the cabinet in his study.

"I think you know why," Julian had said calmly. "The dagger goes with the Challoner bride."

If Flynn noticed that the dagger hadn't been returned to Julian's study, he said nothing about it.

She looked at the weapon now, moving over to the dresser to pick it up and gaze at the stones in its handle. Although she had clung to it tenaciously during the flight out of Mexico, threatened to hurl it into the sea during a moment of outrage and had it nearby for several days, she hadn't actually studied it in great detail. It was a lethal-looking thing. Could Maria Isabel have ever really intended to use it on her husband? It didn't make any sense, not now in light of what Angie was certain the other woman had been thinking on the eve of her wedding. But perhaps that was her own twentieth-century fantasies at work, Angie thought. It was risky trying to second-guess what a woman of that long-ago era had actually planned.

Setting the dagger down carefully, Angie turned out the light and climbed into bed. She had expected to lie awake, half listening for Flynn's return. She would be able to hear the car as it pulled into the hacienda drive.

An hour later it wasn't the sound of a car's engine that awakened her. It was a much smaller, far more significant sound. It was the soft noise of her living room door being opened.

A burst of excitement went through her. Flynn had returned, and instead of heading for his lonely bed at the hacienda, he had decided to spend the night with her. Wide awake, Angie pushed back the covers and climbed out of bed. Would he be very intoxicated, she wondered? She smiled to herself and went softly to the door of her bedroom.

It was as she stood there listening in the dark, trying to determine just how far gone her midnight visitor was, that a couple of things registered on Angie's brain.

The first was that she hadn't heard Flynn's car, or any car. Had he walked all the way back from Julian's? He might have if he thought he wasn't fit to drive. But the second fact hit her an instant later. If Flynn was too drunk to drive, that certainly wasn't him moving about so stealthily in her living room. She strained to hear and caught the soft, gliding sound of a foot dragging slightly on the carpet. With a flash of cold fear she remembered where she'd heard that particular gliding footstep before.

It had been the sound made by the person who had invaded her room that night in the Mexican hotel. Slowly Angie backed away from the door, horror making her almost numb for a few seconds. The gliding sound came again. Whoever it was, he was systematically going through her living room. Soon he would head down the hall to her bedroom. It was, after all, a very small cottage.

Spinning around, Angie grabbed a coat out of the closet, trying desperately not to make any noise. She knew what the intruder wanted, and she was equally certain he would not get his hands on it. She picked up a pair of sandals, not daring to take the time to put them on and then she went over to the dresser and took hold of the Torres Dagger.

There would be some noise when she went out the window, but Angie could see no alternative. Even now there was a sound from the hall. The man who had invaded her home was opening a closet door. She caught a quick stab of light and realized he must be carrying a flashlight.

Panic made her movements jerky. The window slid open with a soft, rasping sound and Angie tumbled through it, not knowing if whoever was in the hall had heard the noise.

An instant later she was on the ground, running blindly for the cliff path. In the dark a stranger might not find it. She might be able to hide down on the beach.

A light flashed behind her just as she reached the top of the path. Fear that she had been spotted sent her headlong down the unstable, pebbled surface. Her feet were already scratched and probably bleeding but she didn't dare take time to put on her sandals.

Halfway down the cliff she heard a shout in Spanish. She scrambled behind a rocky outcrop and glanced back, terrified of what she would see.

"The dagger, lady. All I want is the dagger. Give it to me and I'll go away and leave you alone."

She knew that voice but in her frozen state of mind, Angie couldn't quite place it. The light danced along the top of the cliff, sliding over the outcrop behind which she hid, and continued beyond it. He was searching for the route she had taken, she realized. If she emerged from behind her rocky cover and continued down the path he was likely to spot her. She had no choice but to stay where she was.

Trapped, Angie bent down to put on her sandals. It was hard to juggle the dagger and the jacket she had snatched from the closet. She shrugged into the jacket and shoved the blade of the dagger into an inside pocket. When the time came to run she would need both hands free.

The bobbing light paused at a point midway along the cliff, and Angie held her breath. She had a horrible premonition that whoever pursued her had found the way down the cliff.

Her breath seemed far too loud in the darkness, but she couldn't quiet it. The adrenaline pumping through her system was making her shake. Any action was preferable to none. Her scrabbling fingers found purchase on a large chunk of driftwood that had been flung high on the rocks during a storm. For some reason she found herself clinging to it as if she were caught in another kind of storm.

Then the light began to move purposefully, and Angie knew that the man had found the path. He would have trouble following it, but if he was careful and took his time, he'd probably make it down to the beach. In doing so he would pass right in front of her. Angie's fingers tightened on the length of driftwood.

As she waited, following his progress by the zigzagging motion of the flashlight, Angie prayed for loose pebbles and slippery sand. There were several curses in Spanish, a few missteps, but no major accidents. Her pursuer was going to make it down the path at least as far as her hiding point.

She would have to do something. Shrinking back against the cold rock surface, Angie clutched the driftwood and waited. She only had another few seconds.

Then time ran out. A shadowed, hulking form loomed up out of the darkness not more than a foot away. Angie swung the long stick of driftwood with all her might.

There was a muffled shout, a frantic scrabbling and then the sound of a body falling out of control down the steep path. Angie held her breath. The flashlight sailed outward,

landing soundlessly in the sand below. A moment later
something struck heavily and then there was silence.

Angie had no way of knowing how much damage she
had done. She might have knocked the man unconscious,
or she might only have unbalanced him and stunned him. It
was even possible that the man had been killed in the fall.
The thought made her sick to her stomach. In any event,
common sense told her she shouldn't stick around to find
out.

The hem of her nightgown whipped around her legs as
she darted out from behind the outcrop and started climbing
quickly up the path to the top of the cliff. Her hands were
bruised and dirty by the time she reached the top.

Breath coming painfully between her teeth, Angie ran toward the cottage. She dashed through the front door and
raced across the room to the table where she normally tossed
her car keys. They were gone. The intruder had probably
pocketed them when he'd canvased her living room. There
was no time to search. Remembering the spare key in the
glove compartment, Angie dashed back outside to the car.

Too late she realized she'd never replaced the hidden key.
It had been left on the same table as the regular set and now
it, too, was gone.

"Idiot!" Railing at herself, knowing that this sort of thing
probably never happened to Jake Savage and certainly not
to Flynn Challoner, Angie made the next decision. She
didn't dare stay around the cottage. If the man lying at the
base of the cliff revived, that would be the first place he'd
head. Picking up the skirts of her nightgown, Angie ran for
the darkened hacienda. It was a big home with lots of closets
and rooms in which to hide.

And the telephone had finally been installed earlier this
week, she recalled as she arrived, out of breath, at the back
door. The hacienda doors would all be locked, but Angie

had no hesitation about picking up a rock and using it to shatter the small bathroom window.

Scrambling awkwardly, the sheathed knife biting into the flesh of her stomach at one point, she made it through the broken window with only a couple of small nicks. Then she stopped, gasping for breath, and realized she dared not turn on any lights.

The phone. Where had Julian put it? There were two, as she recalled. One was in the master bedroom. Making her way carefully through the dark house, Angie groped her way to the bedroom Flynn had been using.

It was then that she heard the sound of her uncle's car in the drive. Flynn was home.

The wave of relief was enough to make her dizzy. If there was anyone who would know what to do in a situation such as this, it would be Flynn. Angie turned back from the bedroom and raced down the hall. Flinging open the front door she saw the lights of the car switch off. A second later the car door opened.

"Flynn! Oh, my God, Flynn, thank heavens you're here. I've never been so glad to see anyone in my life." She dashed down the front steps to where he stood beside the car. "That man, the one from Mexico, the one who was in my room that night… He's here, Flynn. He's come for the dagger. But he didn't get it. I've got it and I, oh, Flynn, I hit him with a chunk of driftwood and I—"

"Angie, honey," Flynn breathed, starting toward her. "You're here."

"Well, of course I'm here. I mean, he took my car keys and I didn't have the spare, and I couldn't think of anything else—" She broke off, her mouth falling open in shock as she realized he wasn't paying any attention to her. Instead he was advancing on her with a determination that spelled only one thing.

"Flynn," she gasped, "how drunk are you?"

"Not too drunk to take you to bed," he assured her, his voice slurred and loud as he reached for her.

"No, wait a minute. You haven't been listening. We've got to get away from here…that man…" She struggled, aware of the alcohol on his breath. And to think she had thought it would be amusing to see Flynn intoxicated.

"Angie, honey," he growled, "stop wriggling. You don't have to wait any longer. I'm gonna take care of everything." His arms came around her in a huge, clumsy hug, and he began nuzzling her with awkward passion.

"Please, Flynn, listen to me! Stop it, I'm trying to tell you, I've got the dagger and we've got to get away…"

"Why do you always have to talk so much? After we're married you're gonna have to cut out all this chitchat. Won't tolerate it."

The warning was followed by another heavy kiss on her shoulder and then, so softly Angie didn't believe her ears, she heard him whisper, "Where's the dagger?"

Stunned, she tried to pull back. "Flynn…"

"The dagger," he rasped directly into her ear.

"Inside my jacket."

And then his hand was groping heavily inside the jacket opening in what must have looked like a clumsy caress. Angie froze as she felt him pluck the dagger from its hiding place.

What happened next was almost too fast for her to follow. Angie was freed abruptly as Flynn stepped back, swung around in a smooth, tight half circle and flung the dagger.

The scream of pain that came from off to one side of the hacienda startled Angie so much she screamed in reaction.

"Flynn! What happened? How did you know he was there?"

Recovering from her shock, Angie hurried after Flynn,

who was loping toward his victim. The man lay huddled on the ground, groaning in agony. The Torres Dagger was embedded in his right shoulder. There was a gun lying beside him. He'd evidently dropped it when the dagger had struck.

"I saw him at about the same time you came running down the steps dressed in that sexy little nightie." Flynn crouched to examine the man.

Angie glanced down at her cotton flannel gown and the jacket she wore over it. "This is hardly a sexy little nightie!" And then she wondered how she could possibly be offended at a time like this.

"On you it looks good," he told her absently. "Come here and give me a hand."

Angie went closer cautiously, peering at the face revealed in the watery moonlight.

"Good grief. It's Alexander Cardinal's gorilla butler."

At that moment the phone inside the hacienda started ringing.

"You'd better answer it. Must be your uncle," Flynn instructed as he examined the wounded man's shoulder. "Maybe he's calling to see if I got home okay."

Angie raced inside, grabbed the phone and listened in amazement to Julian's terse warning.

"In Jake Savage's immortal words, you're a little late, Uncle Julian. But not to worry. Everything's under control."

Then she slammed down the receiver and dashed outside.

"Julian says he's just had the most amazing call from Alexander Cardinal. Cardinal's in L.A. at the airport. He phoned Uncle Julian to warn him that Haslett might be coming after the dagger."

"The warning's a little late, but it looks like everything's under control," Flynn said absently.

Angie blinked. "Spoken like Jake Savage."

Chapter 10

Alexander Cardinal was as refined and elegant as ever as he sat sipping Mrs. Akers's excellent coffee the next morning. He had already succeeded in charming the housekeeper by asking her in a stage whisper if she would care to move to his island home. He wasn't sure he would be able to survive now without her coffee.

He had driven up from L.A. in a rented Lincoln Continental that matched his tropical white suit, and he looked right at home on the California coast. Like something off a movie set, perhaps, but right at home.

That was the wonderful thing about California, Angie thought in amusement as she stirred cream into her own coffee. It could accommodate so many different types.

Her uncle and Cardinal had hit it off at once. Their lengthy correspondence concerning the dagger had already introduced them, and in person they found even more to discuss. As the two men solemnly considered the qualities of the steel used in such weapons as the Torres Dagger, Angie caught Flynn's eye.

It wasn't difficult to do. Flynn had barely let her out of his sight since last night. By the time the gorilla had been turned over to the authorities, it was almost two in the morning. Angie had been keyed up and exhausted. The combination had made it difficult to even think about sleeping. Flynn had hovered over her, continually demanding to know if she was really all right. He had bathed the small wounds she had acquired in her flight toward the cliff and then he had tried to fill her full of sherry.

"For your nerves," he'd said.

"My nerves are fine," she'd told him, trying to refuse the second glass.

"Then give me the sherry. Mine are shot to hell!"

There had been no question of where she would spend the night. Without bothering to discuss the subject, Flynn had tucked her into his bed at the hacienda and then slid in beside her. There had also been no question about doing anything other than sleeping. In spite of her inner tension, Angie had found the comfort of Flynn's arms was all she needed to sleep. She had gone out like a light and had not awakened until rather late. Flynn was already in the shower when she awoke. They had hurried to her uncle's house for breakfast and to await the arrival of Alexander Cardinal.

Angie was considering a second cup of coffee when the intent conversation between her uncle and Cardinal finally broke off. Cardinal smiled graciously at her.

"Julian tells me that you and Flynn will be marrying the day after tomorrow, Miss Morgan. Please accept my congratulations. And my apologies for the trouble Haslett gave you last night. Hardly an appropriate wedding gift. You're quite certain you're all right?"

"She's fine," Flynn answered for her with an edge of

aggression underlying his words. "But I've got a few questions."

Faint mockery touched Cardinal's eyes. "Somehow I suspected you might. You are not a man to leave any loose threads dangling, are you, Flynn?"

"I left one hanging down in Mexico and look what happened."

"You refer to that unpleasant incident with the owner of the boat who tried to kidnap you." Cardinal nodded. "Yes, perhaps it would have been better if you had mentioned the matter to me before you left. But I suppose that at the time you thought I might have been the one to hire the man in the first place?"

"The thought crossed our minds," Flynn agreed. "It didn't make sense that anyone else would want the dagger that badly. On the other hand," he admitted dryly, "it didn't make any sense that you'd want it back, either. After all, you had been well paid and no one had forced you to agree to the deal in the first place."

"Loose ends," Cardinal repeated thoughtfully. "You are right, Flynn. Questions should be answered before they become dangerous. Actually it was your friend Ramon who first alerted me to the fact that I had a problem with Haslett. Rumors reached me that a cousin of a certain desk clerk at the resort had taken on a small job for me. Since I had never hired this cousin to do any small jobs, I became curious. Eventually I figured out that it was Haslett who had hired him, using my name for clout. My curiosity grew when the rumors implied it might have been you who left Ramon so embarrassingly tied up in a deserted cove. There must have been an interesting scene on board the boat that night."

"Memorable," Angie put in blandly.

Cardinal chuckled. "I can imagine. Well, I learned the two of you were safe and out of the country, so I made the mistake of not being overly concerned for your future safety. I know Haslett very well, you see. He has worked for me for years. Even if he was the one responsible for trying to grab the dagger, I was sure he wouldn't be able to follow you out of Mexico. And besides, I would know at once if he left the country. All in all, I was curious to find out if he was running some small scam on the side without my knowledge, but I wasn't concerned for Miss Morgan or the dagger. Whatever attempt had been made to steal it had obviously gone awry. I wasn't expecting another.''

"But you continued to look into the possibility of Haslett having outside activities?'' It was Julian who asked, his eyes betraying his keen interest. Angie had seen that expression before. Julian was doing more than satisfying his curiosity. He was collecting material for a Jake Savage novel. Writers had one-track minds.

Cardinal nodded. ''I began making discreet inquiries and took a closer interest in Haslett's comings and goings. I learned recently that he was having clandestine meetings at the resort with a representative of a, shall we say, business conglomerate headquartered in Colombia.''

"Cocaine deals?'' Angie asked instantly.

Cardinal arched a handsome brow. ''That was a fast connection, Miss Morgan.''

"She does too much research for Julian,'' Flynn put in dryly. ''Was it cocaine?''

"To tell you the truth, I do not know. I did not ask when I arranged to meet with this businessman. A man's business is largely his own affair, after all.''

"You met with him?'' Angie was startled.

"Of course. I wanted to know exactly what was going on. He explained that Haslett owed him a certain sum of money for a deal that had gone sour. I then told this businessman that I would pay my employee's debt. In return I expected that no further business deals would be conducted with Haslett.''

"This, uh, businessman agreed?'' Julian asked.

"All he wanted was his money. I gave it to him. Then I went home to have an employer-employee chat with Haslett. Unfortunately, I discovered that he had taken advantage of my absence to leave Mexico. A check with the airline people told me he was on his way to Los Angeles. And at that point, Flynn, I began to worry that he might still have dreams of getting hold of the Torres Dagger. He would have assumed the weapon was in Julian's home but when he arrived and found the party going on he must have decided to seek out Miss Morgan and use her in some way. Or perhaps he just hoped to get lucky and find the dagger, itself, in her home. Who knows?''

Angie poured herself more coffee. "The poor guy didn't know you'd gotten him off the hook with the Colombian outfit. He must have been terrified. He was in trouble with a dangerous man. Colombian gangsters have a particularly nasty reputation.''

"Yes,'' Cardinal agreed simply. "They do. I blame myself for not having acted more swiftly in this. But I honestly did not expect Haslett to be so desperate for the dagger that he would follow it back to the States. After all, it is a beautiful weapon and has great sentimental value to a Torres or it seems, a Challoner, but, frankly, its sale on the open market would not have raised enough to pay off Haslett's debt to the Colombian group.''

"So why has he fixated on getting it back?'' Flynn got to his feet, moving restlessly toward a window. He stood staring out to sea for a moment, his expression thoughtful. "Unless he assumed it was worth more than it is?''

"I'm afraid that is precisely what he assumed. I do not discuss my financial deals with my employees. He did not realize that the dagger had more sentimental and historical value than commercial value. Haslett saw a dagger embedded with jewels and knew that I had made a deal to sell it. He assumed the weapon was very valuable. He would not know the difference between a ruby, say, and a garnet unless someone told him. All he knew was that he badly need a quick source of cash. To give Haslett his due, he would never have actually stolen the dagger from me.''

"But once you had sold it off to someone else, the dagger was fair game as far as he was concerned, right?'' Flynn looked at Cardinal.

"Exactly. Apparently poor Haslett could think of no other ready source of cash. He convinced himself he had to have that dagger. He thought it would be a simple matter at first. When the attempt to retrieve it in Mexico failed, he panicked and followed you.''

Julian's eyes lit up with an inspirational thought. "Maybe we're the ones who don't know the difference between rubies and garnets. Perhaps over the years the semiprecious stones have been switched with diamonds and rubies and emeralds!''

Cardinal laughed. "Trust a writer of adventure to come up with that possibility. I must tell you, however, that I had the weapon properly appraised when I first purchased it. I would not have sold it to you for the price I did if the stones had been more valuable. I pride myself on being a gentleman, but I'm afraid I am also a businessman.''

"Ah, well, just a thought,'' Julian said, clearly a little disappointed.

Angie spoke up again. "What happens to Haslett now?''

Cardinal looked at her. "He is in the hands of your criminal justice system. He will have to take his chances with it.''

"But you'll hire him a good lawyer?" she asked shrewdly.

"Yes. I will hire him a lawyer. The best. I am sorry if that offends you, Miss Morgan, but I really feel I have no choice."

"Of course you don't," Angie said with total understanding. "He's a longtime employee and until now he's been reliable. Apparently he got himself in over his head but if he doesn't have a history of unreliability you're right to take care of him. I approve of enlightened employers who feel some sense of obligation toward their employees." She paid no attention to Flynn's disgusted exclamation. She knew how Cardinal felt. He was from the old, paternalistic school of employers. There weren't many around these days.

"You seem to understand the situation from my point of view," Cardinal said to Angie. "Perhaps that is a legacy of your family's traditional sense of obligation to its employees?"

"It's a legacy from my years in personnel work. The only employee my family has had in recent years was the kid who cut the grass once a week! Unless you count Mrs. Akers."

"But the Torres and Challoner families must have been quite extensive. I understood their holdings took in much of this part of California. Surely there would have been many employees."

"That was a long time ago," Angie said with a smile. "The families aren't quite what they used to be in terms of money or land, let alone employees."

Flynn swung around from the window, his eyes challenging. "But Angie and I are going to combine the two families again and rebuild, aren't we, Angie?"

She looked at him. "Yes, I guess we are." She turned toward Cardinal. "You'll stay for the wedding?"

Cardinal appeared genuinely pleased. "I would enjoy that very much. I like family gatherings, and it has been a long time since I attended a wedding. Perhaps that is because people no longer seem to marry for the right reasons."

Angie changed the subject.

Two evenings later Angie slipped into the lace-trimmed peignoir her mother had bought her. She twirled in a small circle in front of the dressing room mirror and watched with pleasure as the silky material floated enticingly around her ankles. Out in the master bedroom of the hacienda she could hear Flynn moving around, preparing for bed.

The wedding had gone off beautifully, of course. With Flynn attending to every detail there was no way anything could have gone awry. The champagne had been the best, the caviar was sturgeon and had been magnificently displayed on an ice sculpture, the flowers had been huge and brilliant, and the vast quantities of food prepared by Mrs. Akers had been hailed with grand enthusiasm by the assembled guests.

Few people knew the groom personally, but everyone had been prepared by Julian to meet Jake Savage's alter ego.

"Good for book sales," Julian had confided to Angie. "Look at the guests. They love him."

"They love adventure heroes, you mean," Angie had said knowledgeably.

"With Flynn they're getting the real thing. The story of how he drove home after his groom's party the other night and wound up using the Torres Dagger on the villain chasing you has already made the rounds. It's even been embellished a bit."

"How's that?" she demanded.

Julian grinned. "They're saying he pulled off the feat

even though he'd had a considerable amount to drink at the party.''

"I wondered about that myself. How much did Flynn drink that night?"

"No more than he could handle, apparently." Julian refused to say more on the subject.

The wedding had taken place on the grounds of the hacienda, and after the solemn ceremony things had turned cheerfully boisterous. Angie had begun to wonder if people would ever leave. Flynn hadn't encouraged anyone to hurry off. He was obviously enjoying his wedding.

Her mother had been thoroughly charmed by the groom, who had made it clear he had a great sense of family feeling.

"So many men don't these days," Mrs. Morgan had observed to her daughter. "They live only for themselves and the present. Your Flynn seems to be aware of what's truly valuable in life. He'll make you a fine husband, my dear."

Angie hadn't argued. She'd simply had another glass of champagne and considered how Maria Isabel had felt at her wedding. It, too, had been a grand, boisterous affair with plenty of food and expensive wine. The guests hadn't left until three days later. Eventually, though, during the gala party following the ceremony, the groom had snagged his bride, swung her up in front of him on a huge bay stallion and taken her home. Maria Isabel had been nervous, excited and very much in love. The Torres Dagger had been secretly strapped to her arm beneath the flowing sleeve of her gown.

No one had told Angie the details of Maria Isabel's wedding. They were not part of the stories that had been handed down through the years. But as she dressed for her own wedding night, Angie knew many of those details, right down to the color of Curtis Challoner's big stallion. And she knew exactly how Maria Isabel had felt as she walked from the dressing room into Challoner's bedroom. Running a brush through her hair and checking her flushed expression in the mirror one more time, Angie prepared to make the same walk. Her fingers trembled slightly as she opened the door.

Flynn was still dressed, pacing the room like a large, restless cat. He stopped when he saw her standing in the doorway, his eyes going over her with a hunger that was shadowed with another emotion. Longing? Uncertainty? Doubt? Angie couldn't put a name to it and it alarmed her so much she couldn't move from the protection of the doorway.

"Flynn? What's wrong?"

"I wasn't sure until this afternoon," he told her starkly.

Angie felt her insides tighten with sudden anxiety. "Sure about what?"

"I've known for several days now that there was something missing from the equation. I thought I had it all put together. Everything I needed to start my family. Things should have been perfect."

"And they're not?" Her mouth felt dry.

"No," he grated, "they're not." He moved, taking a couple of the catlike, restless steps and stopped again.

"The dagger," she began desperately.

"Oh, the hell with the dagger. That's not the important thing."

Angie blinked at that. "What is the important thing, Flynn?"

"You."

"You've got me. Are…are you telling me you don't want me?"

He stared at her as if she'd lost her mind. "I want you so much it's tearing me apart."

"But, Flynn…"

He shifted abruptly, coming forward to stand only a foot away. Looking down into her wide, dismayed gaze, he shook his head slowly. "Lady with the peacock eyes. Why did you marry me?"

"I've told you," she began carefully. He didn't let her finish.

"You've told me all the reasons I gave you. Compatibility, a sense of history, mutual respect."

"Yes."

He drew a deep breath. "It's not enough."

"Not enough?" Hope flared in her, only to be followed by fear.

"That's the realization I've had this past week. It's been building in me, gnawing at me, eating me alive. This afternoon when we took our vows it all crystalized. Angie, I wanted you to marry me because you loved me. Not for any of those other reasons. I want you to love me as much as I love you."

"Do you love me, Flynn?" she asked softly.

"If I didn't I wouldn't be going through this anguish. I wouldn't have had so many doubts this past week. Honest to God, Angie, I thought I was going crazy at times. I couldn't figure out what was wrong with me and with my plans."

"Until today?"

He nodded. "I'm a slow learner, I guess. I had my head filled with all my schemes for rebuilding the family and for getting the marriage off on to a good start. I was so busy making certain everything fit together perfectly and all along there was something missing. I told myself that I had everything I needed from you, including passion. But it wasn't enough. Angie, I love you. And I won't rest until you've learned to love me, too."

She smiled tremulously. "I told you once that I'd only marry for love."

He inclined his head once in grim acceptance. "I had no right to—"

"I didn't change may mind, Flynn."

Flynn searched her face. "What are you saying?"

She pushed back the sleeve of her gown and revealed the Torres Dagger. "I love you, Flynn. I've loved you almost from the beginning. Women such as Maria Isabel and myself only marry for the right reason: love."

"Angie?" He stared at the dagger as she held it out to him, hilt first.

"Take the dagger, Flynn. I'm giving it to you the same way Maria Isabel gave it to your ancestor."

"I don't understand," he whispered, slowly taking the dagger from her hand.

"Everyone has always assumed Maria Isabel took that dagger with her on her wedding night with the intention of using it on her husband. She didn't. She took it to give to him as a symbolic act. In those days a combatant surrendered his sword to the victor of the battle. Maria Isabel had no sword, but she wanted Curtis to know that she intended to end the war. She was his wife, and she had married him because she loved him. Surrendering the dagger was her way of telling him. I'm giving it to you for the same reason: because I'm your wife and that dagger is symbolic of all that's been between us. It's yours. I'm yours. I love you."

"Angie... Oh, God, *Angie.*"

He pulled her close, cradling her against his chest, whispering his broken words of love. She clung to him, cherishing the moment of commitment, drawing the certainty of his love deep into her heart.

"This is the way it's supposed to be," Flynn said.

She lifted her head to smile mistily. "I know."

He held her fiercely for a moment longer, and then Flynn

released her abruptly. He was grinning with enthralling wickedness.

"Flynn Challoner, what are you doing?"

"Following an old family tradition!" He picked up one of the dress shoes he'd bought for the wedding, kicked a footstool over in front of the fireplace and leaped up on it, the dagger in his fist. "Hand me the sheath. Some carpenter left a couple of nails here on the mantel."

"I'm not sure we need to carry tradition this far," Angie said warily as she obediently handed him the dagger's old leather sheath.

But Flynn was already using the heel of the shoe to pound a nail into the wall. He hung the sheath, inserted the dagger and leaned back proudly to survey the results. "There's a lot to be said for tradition."

He jumped down from the footstool and scooped Angie up in his arms. Swinging her around in an abandoned whirl, he carried her over to the bed and dropped her down in the center.

Angie steadied herself and laughed up at him. "And now what, Challoner?"

"Now this upstart peasant is going to do you a favor, lady." He peeled off his shirt and unbuckled his belt. "I'm going to make you into a loving wife." The rest of his clothing fell to the floor.

"Ah, but Challoner, I already am a loving wife." Leaning back against the pillows Angie opened her arms to him.

"Show me." The laughter left his eyes, to be replaced by hungry appeal. "Please show me, Angie."

Angie had never seen him look so vulnerable. Tenderly she drew him down to her. "I love you, Flynn. I will be happy to go on demonstrating that for the rest of our lives." And then her promise was swallowed up in the depths of his kiss. Love laced with vibrant passion blazed between a

Challoner and a Torres just as it had on a similar wedding night in the long ago past.

Back at Julian's home, Alexander Cardinal poured another glass of fine Spanish sherry and toasted his host and the mother of the bride.

"I don't know when I've enjoyed myself more. I believe I'll come back for the christening."

"Christening?" Mrs. Morgan asked, startled.

"You don't think Flynn's going to waste any time founding the dynasty, do you?"

When Curtis Torres Challoner was born nine months later, Alexander Cardinal was there to celebrate. He was invited to stay at the new home Flynn Challoner had just finished building for his small family and during the tour of the house he was allowed a glance into the master bedroom.

The Torres Dagger was hung proudly over the fireplace.

* * * * *

WIZARD

Chapter 1

She preferred cowboys.

She was like a brilliantly plumed bird who had accidentally invaded his serenely black-and-white world, bringing life and color and enthusiasm. And she preferred cowboys.

Maximilian Travers swallowed a sigh along with his wine and considered the vibrant young woman sitting across from him. Sophia Athena Bennet was making it very clear that she had no real interest in professors of mathematics, with or without tenure. She was sharing dinner with him tonight in this plush Dallas restaurant purely out of a sense of duty.

Didn't she understand that even staid professors of mathematics sometimes found themselves attracted to members of the opposite sex? Or would she care, he asked himself wryly, that something about her vivid, animated presence tugged at his awareness? Probably not. She preferred cowboys.

Max eyed her over the rim of his wine glass as she went into a long and, he suspected, deliberately boring discussion of the staggering growth of Dallas, Texas. Even when she was trying to be dull, Sophy Bennet seemed to glow with barely repressed energy. He had never met anyone quite like her, he realized.

It wasn't that she was particularly beautiful; she wasn't. But she intrigued and tantalized him in a way he had never before experienced around a woman. She was the embodiment of warm, feminine energy, whereas he was accustomed to genteel, academic composure. She was slightly outrageous excitement, and he was used to well-bred civility.

"They're calling us the Third Coast, you know," Sophy said chattily in her low, faintly husky voice. "Lots of high-tech industry has moved in, and we've become a major financial center what with all the banking and brokerage firms. A real boomtown! Honestly, even those of us who live here have a hard time keeping track of the skyline. It changes so often." There was a subtle emphasis on "those of us who live here," and Max knew he was once again being delicately told that he did not belong. At least, not around her.

But he was getting accustomed to the not-so-subtle hints. He ignored this one in favor of studying Sophy's eyes. He really liked those eyes, he decided. A wonderful mixture of blue and green that kept a man guessing about the true color. Vivid. Everything about Sophy Bennet was vivid. Her amber brown hair was a mane of curls that fell to her shoulders in a frothy mass, framing strong, animated features. Actually, Max told himself, classical beauty would have been superfluous in Sophy's case. It would probably have detracted from the striking lines of her face. The expressive mouth, the firm angle of her nose, and the wide, slanting blue-green eyes somehow managed to be quite captivating all on their own. And they hinted at an inner strength.

The wild, scarcely controlled tangle of curls was a dramatic style that was more than echoed in her clothes. A blouse with a peplum and huge, puffy sleeves, done in glittering shades of vermilion and turquoise, was belted over a narrow skirt of jonquil yellow and turquoise. The belt itself was a massive affair of what appeared to be stainless steel links and red leather. It wrapped Sophy's slim waist very tightly, emphasizing the slenderness of her small figure. She wore turquoise pantyhose and high-heeled, strappy little turquoise sandals. The overall effect, combined with the wide yellow bracelet cuffs she had on each wrist, was enough to make any head turn.

"Your parents will be pleased to hear you're happily settled in Dallas," he murmured into the first conversational pause. It hadn't been easy to find the pause. Sophy had kept up a running monologue on Dallas since he had arrived at her apartment earlier that evening in his rented Ford.

She gave him a repressive glance and took a large bite of her roasted bell pepper salad. "No, they won't. Dr. Travers, my parents haven't been happy with me since I was three years old, when it became obvious that I was not going to be a little child prodigy. I am now twenty-eight and they're still hoping I'm a late bloomer." Suddenly she smiled, a ravishing, brilliant smile that seemed to contain all the mischief and promise of every woman who had ever lived. "Haven't you guessed why Mom and Dad asked you to look me up here in Dallas, Dr. Travers?"

"Please, call me Max." He had the feeling he was about to be deliberately pushed off-stride, and he wasn't at all sure how to deal with the coming taunt.

The glittering smile widened with amused warmth. "They're hoping you'll fall madly in love with me, seduce and, of course, marry me. They should know better, naturally. After all, they're both certifiable geniuses themselves, so you'd think they'd know that the chances of another genius, especially a mathematical genius, falling head over heels in love with a nongenius are pretty remote. But I imagine they're still praying for some alternative to the Disaster.''

"An alternative?'' Max heard himself ask blankly.

"Sure. They're undoubtedly hoping for another shot at a crop of little geniuses. They never got a second chance after me, you see. Mom was told she shouldn't have any more children. They were stuck with one chance at producing a wizard to follow in their footsteps, and they wound up with me. I don't think they will ever fully accept the situation, poor dears.'' She sounded affectionately regretful.

"I see.'' Did he sound as bewildered as he felt? Max wondered.

"About the only thing I can do to salvage the situation in their eyes is marry and hope their genes will combine through me with the genes of someone like you and produce the child I should have been,'' Sophy explained wryly.

"But you, uh, don't intend to carry out their wishes?'' he hazarded warily.

"Marry a brilliant mathematician like yourself?'' she scoffed. "Hardly. I spent all of my childhood and young adult years competing against geniuses. I'll be damned if I'll turn around now that I'm free and marry someone like you! No offense,'' she added quickly.

"No offense,'' he repeated slowly, thinking that the quick remorse in her eyes appeared to be genuine. "But you just happen to prefer cowboys?''

She grinned wickedly. "One particular cowboy.''

"The one you had to explain me to this afternoon?'' he pressed, remembering Sophy's dismay at having to break her date with Nick Savage.

"Nick understood. I told him you were a friend of my parents who had been asked to look me up when they learned you were going to be doing some consulting work for S & J Technology. He realized there wasn't much I could do under the circumstances except entertain you for an evening. But now you and I have discharged our duty and we can go our separate ways, hmmm? How long will you be in Dallas, Max?''

"A few weeks,'' he replied neutrally.

Sophy tilted her head to one side, her blue-green eyes narrowing in amused perception. She fully comprehended the deliberate neutrality of his tone. She'd heard her father complain about such ''consulting'' trips often enough in the past. "You're going to hate every minute of it, aren't you? The theoretical mathematician compelled to lower himself to the real world of applied mathematics. Such a boring state of affairs,'' she teased. "But don't fret. It will soon be over and you can scurry back to your ivory tower. Have you done much consulting work in the past?''

"I get out of my ivory tower a couple of times a year.''

"You mean you're pushed out by the university, which likes the prestige it gains when it occasionally lends you to industry, right?''

"I'm hardly *loaned*,'' he stressed mildly.

"No, of course not,'' Sophy chuckled. "You go for a very high price, don't you? What's the going rate now for the services of brilliant theoretical mathematicians? A thousand a day?''

"I don't get to keep the whole fee,'' he pointed out in a low voice.

"Will they let you keep enough of this particular consulting fee to enable you to buy some new clothes when you return to North Carolina?'' she asked interestedly. Then, immediately chagrined at her audacity, she flushed in sudden embarrassment and reached for her wine. "Never mind, that was very rude of me,'' she mumbled into the Burgundy.

"Besides, I know that styles among the academic elite don't change very frequently. Heavens, my father has an old tweed jacket he's worn for over twenty years. And my mother's wardrobe looks twenty years old, even if it isn't. I realize that you're quite suitably dressed for life on a university campus."

Lord, it was getting worse. Why hadn't she kept her mouth shut? She really hadn't intended to embarrass her parents' distinguished colleague, Dr. Maximilian Travers. She had set out with every intention of doing her duty tonight, even though she was well aware that both she and Max had been coerced into the untenable situation.

For just a moment she allowed herself to admit privately that under other circumstances this date wouldn't have been such a chore at all. Sophy knew she had been strangely, vitally aware of Max the moment he had entered her office to introduce himself. She had looked up from her typewriter and realized she was actually holding her breath as he approached her desk.

Then, of course, he had introduced himself and ruined everything. Yes, she should have kept her mouth shut.

"I will admit that we do tend to dress a bit more conservatively back in North Carolina," Max allowed politely. He slanted a meaningful glance around the elegant restaurant. Several of the other men were wearing obviously expensive jackets, many cut with a decidedly western flair. There was more than one pair of masculine feet clad in beautifully etched leather boots. A certain good-natured extravagance marked the attire of most people in the room, making Max's tweed jacket and white shirt seem very quiet in comparison.

It wasn't just the plain white shirt, the too-narrow tie and the old tweed jacket that marked him, Sophy thought to herself. It was also the horn-rimmed glasses that framed his serious, smoky eyes and the plastic pack of pens and pencils in his left pocket. A "nerd pack" as it was amusingly called by her co-workers at S & J Technology. Such packs were carried by engineers and mathematicians the world over and had become a symbol of their dedication to numbers. Sophy shuddered delicately. She hated numbers. Hated math of any kind.

But even if Max Travers had not arrived equipped with the accoutrements of a typical mathematician cum university professor, she would have recognized him anywhere. After all, she had spent her formative years surrounded by his type.

Perhaps it was the intense, undeniable intelligence that flared in those smoke-colored eyes that identified him. Or it might have been the quiet, analytical air that was so much a part of him. Sophy had the feeling that Max Travers never did anything on impulse. He would carefully weigh all options, analyze all data and catalog every scrap of information before acting. He looked out of place here in this flashy restaurant, and he certainly looked out of place as her date. Max should have been sipping sherry at a faculty party and discussing his latest treatise on math with someone who could understand.

Too bad he had that faintly disapproving, wet-blanket attitude, Sophy found herself thinking. Too bad he was brilliant. Too bad he was from that other world, which she had avoided so carefully for the past few years. Too bad about a lot of things because there had been that breathless moment just before he had introduced himself. It was a moment that existed only in her imagination, she sternly told herself.

But all the same Sophy found herself wondering what it would be like to see passion in that remote, smoky gaze. Instantly she stifled the dangerous question. She had to admit, however, that there was something about the fiercely carved masculine features that subtly invited her awareness. Almost absently Sophy pegged his age at thirty-five or thirty-six. For a man who had spent his entire life in the rarefied atmosphere of academia, he didn't appear soft or weak. But then, who knew better than she that there was nothing particularly soft about genius?

Maximilian Travers wasn't conventionally attractive. The austere line of his nose and the aggressive planes of cheek and jaw left little room for good looks. Instead his features revealed an inner power that wasn't diminished even by the severe white shirt, old-fashioned tie and well-worn jacket. Sophy decided she didn't care for the implication of masculine strength. Oh, she liked strong men well enough; she just didn't like strength allied to brilliance. It didn't seem fair.

It would have been reassuring to discover a paunch beneath the old jacket, but there was none. The narrow, scuffed leather belt Max wore clasped a lean waist, and Sophy had to admit that she had seen no other signs of physical weakness in him either. Very unfair, really.

"Your parents said you just recently moved to Dallas?"

"That's right. A few months ago," Sophy agreed easily as she buttered a chunk of French bread. "It took me a while to find a new job. I'm afraid Mom and Dad are still shuddering over the one I did find." She lowered the butter knife and leaned forward melodramatically. "I'm only a secretary, you know," she confided in a stage whisper. "The horror of it all. A Bennet working as a mere secretary." Then she sat back and smiled blandly. "But it's better than selling clothes in a department store, which is what I was doing in Los Angeles, don't you think?"

"I wouldn't know," Max mumbled a bit uneasily.

Sophy's smiled broadened. "Of course you wouldn't. I'll bet you've never had to do anything so mundane in your whole life, have you? Shall I take a stab at outlining your past?''

''You don't know me at all,'' he protested quietly.

''The hell I don't.'' She grinned. ''I know your kind. How's this? Declared academically gifted at an early age, perhaps even before first grade. Immediately placed in advanced preschools, advanced kindergarten and then into classes for the mentally gifted. Probably skipped a couple of grades here and there. Finished high school a few years ahead of the rest of the plodders and entered college at a tender age. Zipped through college and went directly into a doctoral program. From there it was merely a hop, skip and a jump to the faculty of a fine university where your talents are appreciated and duly rewarded with a corner office and a light teaching load. Right so far?''

''Do you read tea leaves as a hobby?'' There was a dry note to his voice, and his smoky eyes narrowed fractionally. It occurred to Sophy that there might be more than academic temperament buried in this man. There might be genuine male temper. And that implied passion. Sophy brushed the thought aside. Mathematicians were rarely passionate about anything except math.

''No tea leaves,'' she responded airily. ''It's just that, as I said, I know your kind. I spent too many years desperately trying to keep up with your type and failing. I'm lucky I wasn't traumatized for life. Or perhaps I was,'' she added thoughtfully. She reached for her wine glass and smiled again.

''You don't appear terribly traumatized.''

''Just ask my parents. They think I'm on the verge of going off the deep end. Twenty-eight years old and still changing jobs regularly. And what terrible jobs! Cocktail waitress, department store clerk, secretary. So demeaning for someone who should have inherited brains." Sophy shuddered delicately.

"You don't appear any more demeaned than you do trau-matized." Max paused while the waiter served the entrée, lamb with apricot sauce.

"Well, to tell you the truth," Sophy confided cheerfully, "I really don't suffer from either of those two conditions. Not anymore. Not since I discovered the real world. I do very well in the real world, Max."

"What did you mean, you spent a lot of years trying to keep up with 'my kind'?" Max frowned down at his lamb chop. He was accustomed to mint sauce, not apricot sauce, on lamb. Sophy had recommended the apricot but now he wasn't so sure.

"I'm afraid my parents were never reconciled to the fact that they had produced an ordinary little girl, not a brilliant little prodigy," Sophy explained equably. "It was very hard on them. Go ahead. Try the apricot sauce. It's delicious on lamb. Live a little, Max." She ignored his frown. "Where was I? Oh, yes. As I said, my not being brilliant was hard on my parents. They had been so sure that the mating of two highly intelligent people would produce intelligent off-spring. They refused to believe otherwise and, of course, no one dared to tell them differently."

Max looked up, still frowning. "What do you mean?"

"Well, before he went into semiretirement, Dad was one of the leading mathematicians in the country—"

"He still is," Max interrupted.

"Yes, I know, but in those days he was wildly sought after by just about every university in the nation. They all wanted him as a shining ornament for their math depart-ments. The last thing anyone wanted to do was risk offend-ing him. My mother, being such a prominent physicist, was also considered a prize. The pair of them wrote their own tickets as far as their careers were concerned. Naturally I was pushed into advanced, avant-garde classes, the kind they have on campuses for the children of the faculty. Everyone knew who I was and none of the teachers wanted the responsibility of informing my parents that I wasn't exactly a genius. Mom and Dad kept thinking that I was just late in developing my talent, whatever it was.'' She leaned forward expectantly. ''How's the lamb?''

''It's all right,'' Max allowed cautiously.

She sat back, smiling. ''Of course it is. Geniuses tend to be much too unadventurous. Back to my traumatic childhood. Well, Mom and Dad kept shoving me into the most advanced classes they could find. Classrooms that were filled with little boys and girls who, like you, really did grow up to be geniuses. I consider my school years the worst years of my life.''

''Because you always found yourself competing with people like me?''

''Exactly. Oh, I had my role in the grand scheme of things, I suppose. I mean, with me around, the rest of you always looked positively brilliant. I helped maintain the class curve, as it were. The low end of the curve was my slot. The *very* low end. Do you have any idea what it was like to always be the dumbest kid in class?'' Sophy shook her head once, answering her own question. The mane of amber curls bounced in a lively manner and her eyes brimmed with laughter. ''No, of course you don't. What a silly question. You were always the one bringing up the class average to levels that were impossible for people like me to even approach.''

''Did you drop out of school?''

''Oh, no, I stuck it out through high school, and, although my grades were terrible, my father managed to convince a small college in the Midwest to accept me. College, I discovered, wasn't really bad at all. It was chock-full of real people, not just you gifted types. I held my own very nicely in college, but I was so soured on formal education by that time that I still disliked the work. To please my parents, though, I made it to graduation. Then I pronounced myself free, informed Mom and Dad that there was no help for it, I was doomed to be average, and went out to make my way in the world. It's a world they know very little about, however, so they worry constantly. They would feel far more content if I would just get married to a proper math wiz such as yourself and settle down to producing a bunch of little wizards.''

"Something you have no intention of doing?" Max eyed her questioningly.

"Not on your Ph.D.! Don't worry, Dr. Travers," Sophy chuckled, "you're safe. I guarantee I have absolutely no matrimonial designs on your person."

"Only on the person of a certain cowboy?"

"Nick's not just any cowboy," Sophy drawled. "He's an ex-rodeo star with a sizable ranch outside of Dallas."

"Are you going to marry him?" Max persisted.

"We're considering the matter," she allowed loftily. "Nick and I lead very full lives and we're content to let our relationship develop naturally."

"And after things develop *naturally,* will you settle down and raise lots of little cowboys? I should think Texas already had enough of those," Max commented with a hint of irritation.

"Spoken with the true disdain of the intellectual elite for the rest of us lowly mortals," she shot back, some of her amusement fading.

To her surprise, Max had the grace to redden slightly. "Sophy, I didn't mean to sound elitist about it."

"No, I expect it comes naturally. Don't worry, Max, I

understand. Far better than you will ever know. When you go back to North Carolina, feel free to tell my parents that I am alive and thriving in Dallas and that I have no intention of becoming a broodmare for geniuses.''

"I think you misunderstood their motives in asking me to look you up," Max said repressively.

"Dr. Travers," Sophy countered with rueful humor, "I may not understand differential equations or vector analysis, but I do understand my mother and father. Furthermore, I think it's safe to say that I understand people in general a good deal better than Mom and Dad and you ever will.''

"Sophy," Max began in a severely pedantic tone, "when your parents learned that I was being sent to S & J Technology for a consulting trip, it was quite reasonable that they should ask me to introduce myself to their daughter. There was no ulterior motive.''

Sophy shook her head. "Take it from me," she said with a grin. "There was. You've been tagged as good breeding stock, as we say here in Texas. They'd be absolutely thrilled if you got me pregnant.''

"Sophy, I think you're being deliberately outrageous.'' The high bones of Max's cheeks were stained a dull red beneath the natural tan of his skin.

"We underachievers sometimes resort to such tactics to hold our own against people like you," Sophy admitted pleasantly. "But in this case, I'm only trying to give you fair warning. Not that you're in any genuine danger.''

"Because you prefer cowboys," he concluded flatly.

"I prefer just about anyone to a genius. And if you're honest, you'll admit that you would be horrified at the idea of being tied to someone who wasn't as intelligent as yourself. No one likes to be mismatched. It's extraordinarily painful, believe me.''

"People like me intimidate you?" he asked quietly.

"Not anymore! But your type did a hell of a good job of it all during my school years. It wasn't your fault. I was the misfit sparrow thrust in among the mental peacocks."

Max suddenly, unexpectedly, smiled. "I would have said it was just the opposite."

"What?" Sophy eyed him uncertainly.

"I would have said you were the peacock tossed in with us rather dull sparrows," he explained gently.

Sophy blinked, taken aback at the quiet sureness of his words. Hastily she recovered. "Well, that's all over now. I'm free and I intend to remain free. As much as I love my parents, I'm not going to live my life for them. They will just have to accept the Disaster."

"When did you start calling yourself their Disaster?" he queried.

"So long ago I can't even remember. I realized very early in life that I wasn't going to be the daughter they had dreamed of producing. I'll bet your parents were absolutely delighted with you, though, weren't they?" she asked.

He glanced down at his plate as if doing a quick mathematical analysis of the position of the lamb in relation to the peas. "They seem satisfied, yes."

"Where do they live?"

"In California. They're both retired now."

Sophy sensed the shutters coming down and wondered why. Instinctively she pressed a bit further, finding herself suddenly very curious about Dr. Maximilian Travers. "Are they both from the academic world?"

"Yes."

"Mathematicians?"

"My father is a mathematician. My mother is a biologist. They were both on the faculty of a West Coast university until they elected to retire a couple of years ago."

There was a stilted inflection in his words, but Sophy

couldn't quite put her finger on what was wrong. Oh, well, she told herself firmly, it wasn't her problem. Geniuses didn't need someone ordinary like herself worrying about them. "Well, I'm sure they're very pleased at your success," she said bracingly. "Have they urged you to marry and carry on the tradition of academic excellence?"

"They, uh, mention marriage occasionally. I imagine they'd like a grandchild."

"Sound just like my parents." Sophy nodded wisely.

"Sophy, it's considered natural for parents to want grandchildren."

"Ah, but in our case they wouldn't want just any sort of grandchildren, would they? They'd want little wizards. Are you going to have dessert? They make a fabulous margarita pie here."

"That sounds awful." He looked genuinely appalled.

"Be daring. After all, you'll have to go back to your ivory tower in a couple of weeks, and you may never get another chance to sample margarita pie."

"I don't know. Maybe a slice of cheesecake...."

But Sophy was already signaling the waiter. There was something amusingly pleasant about pushing a wizard around a bit, even if it was only over something as trivial as margarita pie. "We'll have two margarita pies," she announced as the waiter hurried over to their table.

The man swept off with the order before Max could change it. Accepting the failure with good grace, he gave Sophy a rather hard smile. "It will be an experience, I suppose."

"You'll love it, Max. Where are you staying while you're in Dallas?"

"One of the downtown hotels." He told her the name and she raised her expressive brows.

"My, my. Nothing but the best for visiting genius mathematicians, hmmm? That's a very posh place."

"Perhaps you'd like to drop by for an afterdinner drink in the lounge before I take you home?" he suggested politely.

"Oh, I don't think so, thank you. It's getting rather late and I'm sure you've got better things to do than entertain your colleagues' daughter. Besides, I told Nick I'd meet him for a drink around ten. He's spending the evening with some fellow ranchers at one of the local clubs. When I told him I wasn't going to be free tonight, he decided to join his friends for a few hours and wait for me."

Max abruptly became aware that his fingers were curling very tightly around his knife as he set it down beside his plate. She'd set up another date for the evening. After she left him, Sophia Athena Bennet was planning on going straight to another man. The knowledge was strangely annoying.

"Your cowboy didn't mind your coming out with me this evening?" he asked deliberately as he finished the lamb and waited in resignation for the margarita pie.

"Oh, he wasn't thrilled, but he understood. After all, he's got family, too, and he knows they can make demands."

"It's not your family that made the demand, it was me," Max felt obliged to point out in a very even tone.

"Only because my family asked you to look me up."

"It doesn't occur to you that I might have wanted to have dinner with you?"

"In a word, no," she said, grinning.

He winced inwardly because in a sense she was absolutely right. He *had* looked her up as a favor to her parents. But the moment he'd seen her, he'd been grateful he'd had the excuse of knowing Paul and Anna Bennet. Without that he wouldn't have been at all certain how to approach such an alien creature. In the natural order of things, he simply didn't encounter women like Sophy very often. Dealing with her was going to be like dealing with a new and exotic math frontier.

"Sophy…"

"Oh, I realize you might be a bit lonely here in Dallas," she said quickly. "Maybe having dinner with me was better than sitting alone in a hotel room."

"It was," he agreed dryly.

"But not much, hmmm? You're probably bored already. We haven't even touched on the theory of relativity or Boolean logic."

"Believe it or not, I do find other things in life interesting besides mathematics!" he growled.

"I'm sure you do," she soothed in a condescending tone that irritated him even further. "But I don't know any more about those things than I do about math, so I'd make pretty poor company."

"I wasn't talking about academic interests," Max gritted as the margarita pie arrived. He eyed the dessert apprehensively.

"Really? What other things were you referring to, then?" Sophy asked idly, digging into her pie with obvious relish.

He seriously considered telling her that professors of mathematics were just as capable as anyone else of being interested in sex, but almost immediately dismissed the idea. If he said anything that blunt, she'd probably fling the pie in his face and get up on the table to declare once and for all that she was not a broodmare for wizards. Seeing no acceptable alternative and mindful, as always, of his role as a gentleman and a scholar, Max shook his head. "Never mind. Where is your cowboy going to meet you? Should I drop you somewhere downtown?"

"No, you can take me home. He'll be meeting me there."

"I see. Will he be staying the night?" What the hell had made him ask that? Max wondered savagely.

Instantly the mischievous smile in her eyes disappeared. "That's really none of your business, is it, Dr. Travers?"

He was learning, Max thought. When she called him Dr. Travers, she was annoyed. "No," he admitted, "it isn't. I'm sorry I asked."

The smile reappeared. "I'm sure my parents are just as curious."

"Have they met him?"

"No," Sophy said carelessly. "How's the pie?"

"Not nearly as bad as I had feared."

"You shouldn't be so shy about new experiences, Max."

"In your own way, you can be quite condescending, did you know that?" he asked coolly.

She chuckled. "This is turning into a pretty horrible evening, isn't it? Sorry about that, but I could have warned you. People like you and me don't mix very well together. Don't fret about it. You've done your duty and you can report back to my parents that you did, indeed, look me up while you were in Dallas. That's all they can reasonably ask of you."

"Meaning they won't demand that I perform stud services, too?" The words were out before he could stop them, and Max was shocked at his lack of control. What the hell was the matter with him? He never talked like this! Especially not to women. It was all wrapped up with the fact that Sophy was going straight home to that damned cowboy.

"I think you can rest assured that they won't embarrass everyone concerned by asking whether or not you managed to sleep with me while you were here in Dallas," she shot back. "Now if you don't mind, Max, I would like to leave. Nick will be expecting me."

Max nodded, not trusting himself to speak for a few seconds while he recovered his equilibrium. Mutely he pulled out his worn leather wallet and found his credit card. Then he signed the slip the waiter had prepared. He was getting up from the table, his mind on taking Sophy home to her cowboy, when she abruptly put a restraining hand on his arm and smiled pointedly.

"You forgot your copy of the credit slip."

"What? Oh." Unaccountably embarrassed at the small oversight, Max hastily reached out to tear off the slip.

"Don't worry, my father does that all the time. So does Mom, for that matter."

Max winced at the unspoken implications concerning absentminded professors. He had the sinking feeling the cowboy never had such lapses.

"Are you sure you don't want to stop by my hotel for a nightcap?" It was a halfhearted attempt that Max knew was doomed to failure. He had always been a little socially awkward simply because socializing had seemed relatively unimportant in the grand scheme of his life. But tonight he would have given a lot for some suave social polish. Tonight it would have been very pleasant to be the kind of man capable of sweeping a woman like Sophy off her feet.

"No, thanks," Sophy said predictably as she slipped into the front seat of the rented Ford. "It's almost ten."

"And you wouldn't want to keep the cowboy waiting, would you?" Max muttered under his breath as she shut the door. He wasn't sure whether or not she had heard him. If she had, she chose to ignore the hint of masculine disgust. Or worse, perhaps she found it amusing.

The drive into the north side of Dallas was accompanied by another running monologue on the city's growth and prospects. At several points along the way Max was sorely tempted to clamp a hand over Sophia Athena Bennet's sweet mouth to halt the flow of deliberately boring words.

And then what? Stop the car and drag her into the back seat? Hardly the sort of behavior expected of a tenured professor of mathematics. Also hardly the sort of behavior he was accustomed to indulging in around women. Max realized with a start of surprise that he'd never met a woman he wanted to treat in such an elementary fashion. Christ! If her father only knew what he was thinking at the moment. Dr. Paul Bennet was a gentleman and a scholar and assumed that Max was in the same league.

"Well, Max, thank you very much for dinner." Sophy sounded relieved as the Ford pulled into the driveway of her garden apartment complex. "I suppose I'll see you around the office off and on for the next few weeks."

"You don't sound terribly thrilled at the prospect."

Instantly an expression of genuine contrition swept over her face, and she lightly patted his arm with five carmine-tipped nails. In the shadowed interior of the car, her eyes seemed very wide and deep.

"I'm sorry if I've offended you, Max. Please believe me, I didn't intend to. I know this evening was just a duty date for both of us. But now we've met our obligations, so there's no need to worry about the matter further. You can go back to North Carolina in a few weeks and assure my parents I'm alive and well out here. I'm going to be seeing them myself weekend after next when I go back to Chapel Hill for an award ceremony honoring Mom. I'll give you some good press when I see them. We'll both be off the hook."

She was already sliding along the seat, her hand leaving his arm as she opened the car door. A sudden glare of headlights in the rearview mirror caught Max's attention, and he turned to glance out the back window in time to see a long white Lincoln purring to a halt behind the Ford.

The cowboy had arrived to claim his lady. As Max

watched the vivid creature he had just taken to dinner fly into the arms of the tall man with the Stetson who had just alighted from the depths of the Lincoln, he felt a wave of grim resentment.

It was a resentment that had no logical basis, he told himself roughly, and put the Ford in gear.

No logical basis unless you counted the very primitive logic that Max wanted to be the man who spent the night in Sophia Athena's bed.

Damned cowboy.

Chapter 2

She had told Max Travers that her relationship with Nick Savage was developing naturally, and Sophy was positive that was true. Even as she hurried from the Ford to meet Nick, Sophy told herself that it was a great relief to end the evening with Max.

But the relief she experienced was not precisely the right sort, she realized vaguely. She ought to feel as though she had just escaped a dull, boring evening with a man in whom she could never be even remotely interested, even as a friend.

Instead the feeling welling up inside was one of relief at having escaped a potentially dangerous situation. And there was absolutely no reason for the sensation. Deliberately she pushed the thought out of her mind as she lifted her face for Nick's kiss. Tall and rugged, with black, wavy hair and bedroom eyes, Nick Savage was the perfect antidote to an evening spent with a wizard.

"What are you smilin' at, darlin'?" Nick asked as he took her hand and walked toward the apartment door.

Sophy told herself that his Texas drawl was sensual and sexy. She wasn't about to admit that occasionally it got on her nerves. The good-ole-boy twang was as much a part of Nick as his Lincoln, she reminded herself.

"I was thinking how good an ex-rodeo cowboy looks after an evening spent with a professor of math," Sophy teased, digging her key out of the tiny leather purse that was clipped to her wide belt. "Honestly, Nick, I thought the evening would never end."

"I can't say I'm sorry to hear your visitin' genius was a little dull." Nick took the key from her hand and used it on the front door. "Just don't expect me to give up any more evenings so that you can do your duty," he warned as he stepped into the hall behind her.

"Never again." With a happy sigh, Sophy turned and put her arms around his neck, standing on tiptoe to kiss him.

Nick wrapped one arm around her waist and used his free hand to remove the gray Stetson. With practiced skill he sent it sailing across the room to land on the coffee table. There it struck a pile of magazines and sent them slithering to the floor.

"You're getting awfully good at that," Sophy marveled, ignoring her scattered magazines.

"I intend to get a whole lot better, darlin'. Pretty soon I'm gonna make that hat land on the bedpost in your bedroom."

His meaning was clear and Sophy didn't demur. Surely it was only a matter of time before she went to bed with Nick Savage. After all, they were falling in love and they were both mature adults. If the truth were known, Sophy had already wondered silently at Nick's willingness to be put off this long. But he seemed to respect her desire to be sure of their emotions. It was one of the many things she liked about him.

The only thing that secretly bothered her on occasion was why she, herself, kept hesitating.

"I'll get the brandy," Sophy said after a moment, slipping from his arms to head for the kitchen. "I don't know about you, but I need something."

"Don't mind if I do a little celebratin' myself. Won a fair piece of change off Cal Henderson this evening."

"So that's what you spent the evening doing—playing poker. Shame on you." She sent him a laughingly reproachful glance across the counter that divided the living room from the sleek, modern kitchen.

"Honey, any Texan worth his salt plays poker on occasion. Be downright suspiciously unpatriotic and unneighborly to refuse a friendly game." With a satisfied grin, Nick threw himself down onto the melon-colored sofa and propped his booted feet on the Lucite coffee table.

Sophy smiled at the sight of him sprawled in her living room. Nick Savage was everything that had traditionally attracted women to cowboys. He had a handsome, suntanned face that was attractively open and rugged, and he was over six feet tall. He had the casual western manners that thrived in Texas, and he wore the local style of clothing well. The feet on her coffee table were encased in hand-tooled gray leather, and the gray, western-cut suit he wore was perfectly detailed from the yoked shoulders to the flare-legged pants.

As usual, Nick wore the huge, inlaid-silver belt buckle that proclaimed his past championship status as a rodeo star. It was a trifle unfortunate that a small paunch was beginning to appear over the edge of the buckle, but there was still enough masculine, western-style arrogance about him to pique any woman's interest. Sophy felt quite lucky that he had taken to her at the party where they met.

Cradling a brandy glass in each palm, she walked out of the starkly done black-and-white kitchen and into the colorful living room. Sophy's love of exotic, eye-catching hues was evident not only in her apparel but throughout her home.

The melon-colored couch on which Nick lounged was set off by vanilla walls and a jade green carpet. The rainbow-hued easy chair by the fireplace had a mate on the opposite side of the room, and here and there dramatic touches of black underscored the vivid effect. It was a room that fit her personality and her lifestyle.

"Ah missed you this evenin', darlin'." Nick draped a casual arm around Sophy's shoulders as she sank down beside him and curled her feet under her. He smiled, fingering one of the huge sleeves of the blouse she wore. "This new?"

"Umm." Sophy swallowed a sip of brandy. "Just finished it yesterday. Like it?"

"Oh, I like it well enough. Just don't fancy you wearin' it for the first time with that visitin' nerd." Nick moved his fingers absently on her shoulder.

For some reason his use of the term "nerd" to describe Max bothered Sophy, although she admitted she might easily have used it herself. With a touch of restlessness, she put down her brandy glass and sat forward to restack the magazines that had been pushed onto the rug by the flying Stetson.

"You sure do subscribe to a lot of those business magazines," Nick observed, watching her idly.

"A woman who has plans to start her own business has to do a lot of groundwork." Sophy smiled, piling a government pamphlet profiling successful entrepreneurial women on top of a magazine describing women in business.

"All your plans still goin' along fine?"

"Oh, yes. In a few more months I should have the financial backing I need."

"Won't be no need for my woman to work, you know," Nick said softly.

Sophy ignored the comment about not needing to work and told herself that the possessive sound of "my woman" was very nice to hear. She gracefully yielded the brandy glass when he reached out to remove it from her hand, and then she allowed herself to be drawn close.

Nick's kiss was warm and pleasurable, his mouth moving on hers with undeniable expertise. Sophy gave herself up to it, wondering what it would be like when she and Nick finally went to bed together. Soon. The time would soon arrive. Nick had been so considerate, so patient, so respectful of her desire to be certain....

"I wish to hell I didn't have to get up at five tomorrow mornin'," Nick groaned a few minutes later.

"That trip to Phoenix?"

"Yeah. You'll be a good girl while I'm gone?" Nick nuzzled her neck.

"Of course."

"You'd better." He got reluctantly to his feet, collecting the Stetson. "Much as I hate to leave, I reckon I'll have to get goin'. Long drive back out to the ranch."

"When will you be back?" Sophy asked conversationally as she walked beside him to the Lincoln. There was very little of the long, white luxury automobile that wasn't decorated with chrome. The license plate was personalized with the brand of Nick's ranch, the Diamond S.

"Wednesday," Nick said as he stopped beside the car to light one of his long, dark cigarettes. He cupped his palm around the flame from the gold lighter, which was also embossed with a diamond and an S, and bent his head to light the cigarette. It was a delightfully masculine gesture that made Sophy smile. Too bad she didn't approve of smoking, she thought. It could be so damn sexy. She'd bet her new electronic sewing machine that Max Travers had never touched a cigarette in his life. He would have decided long ago that it was foolish to take the health risk.

"I'll be back in time to take you to the Everet shindig," Nick went on as he exhaled. He wrapped his arm around her shoulders and leaned back against the car.

"I'm looking forward to it. A real Texas barbecue, hmmm?"

"They pull out all the stops once a year. We'll have a good time. Bring your swimsuit. There's a pool that folks will be using." He took the cigarette out of his mouth and bent his head to kiss her goodbye.

Sophy steadfastly ignored the taste of smoke in his mouth, but she couldn't quite ignore the sudden jab of pain in her midsection.

"Ummph!"

"What's wrong, honey?"

"Nothing," she assured him quickly, adjusting her position. "I just came close to committing hari-kari on your belt buckle."

He chuckled, glancing down at the huge silver championship buckle with evident satisfaction. "A good year. Had some wild times on the circuit."

"Miss the rodeo?"

He shrugged. "It's a young man's game. Best to get out while you're on top. And after Dad died, the ranch needed attention, anyway. It's time I settled down." He smiled meaningfully. "With the right woman."

Sophy smiled up at him brilliantly and stood on tiptoe to

brush his mouth with her own. "Good night, Nick. Drive carefully."

"I will. I'll call you on Wednesday when I get back from Phoenix."

Sophy stood in her doorway for a minute after Nick left, watching the big white barge of a car slip silently down the street and out of sight. At least she'd managed to spend a little time with Nick tonight. The duty date hadn't spoiled the entire evening.

Back inside she shook her head wryly as she began to undress for bed. If ever there were two men who were diametrical opposites, they were Nick Savage and Max Travers. One was exciting, the other quite dull. One was unintimidating intellectually; the other came from another world, the totally intimidating world of higher math. Nick would surely be a sexy, experienced lover. Max probably made love by the numbers. One would make a dynamic, successful husband, and the other would probably spend hours at a time so wrapped up in his math that he would forget he was married altogether. Sophy knew which man was right for her.

Didn't she?

"Getting married isn't like buying a bull," she advised herself as she climbed into bed wearing the plum-covered nightgown she had made the previous week. "I'm not looking for good breeding stock! I'm looking for love and passion and compatibility."

Tongue absently touching her lower lip, Sophy found herself wondering what would have happened if she'd accepted Max's offer of a drink at his hotel. Nothing, probably. Men like Max didn't lower themselves to making passes at women. Men like Max were gentlemen and scholars.

But if he had made a pass, attempted to take her in his arms, how would she have reacted? Why was she even asking herself the question? It was ridiculous! Annoyed, Sophy twisted onto her side and fluffed her pillow. Perhaps there had been too much tequila in that margarita pie. Something was making her imagination take some bizarre turns tonight!

She smiled wryly to herself in the darkness. Her parents would be disappointed that she and Max hadn't instantly fallen for each other. But they'd had twenty-eight years to adjust to the continuing disappointment of their only child. They'd handle this current matchmaking failure just as they'd handled all the other failures: with stoic bravery.

Deep down, in their own way, Sophy knew, they loved her, just as she loved them; but communication between parents and child had always been difficult. When she was younger, Sophy had felt as badly about the Disaster as Paul and Anna had. Guilt over her own lack of genius had kept her doggedly plodding her way through all those endless accelerated classes designed for the intellectually gifted.

As one despairing teacher after another had failed to find the courage to tell the Bennets that their daughter simply was not a genius, Sophy had begun to hate the role into which she had been cast.

"She simply doesn't apply herself," her fourth-grade teacher had explained to the Bennets at a conference. "I'm sure she has the ability, but she seems perpetually bored in class. It's like that sometimes with the truly gifted. It's hard to engage their attention, even in advanced classes such as this one, because they're so far ahead mentally."

"She'll come into her own in high school," the seventh-grade instructor had assured the Bennets. "In the meantime, all we can do is keep exposing her to as much intellectual stimulation as possible."

"She'll blossom in college," the high school teachers had insisted. "Some bright teenagers simply don't do well in high school, even in these academically accelerated classes.''

And all along, the only one who had admitted the truth was Sophy. She wasn't bored in class; she was usually totally lost, desperately trying to comprehend what her fellow students picked up so easily. She wasn't failing to apply herself. She worked hard, driven by guilt and the fear of disappointing her parents.

But always there had been the wizards surrounding her. From the day she had been sent off to the carefully selected preschool for precocious children, Sophy had been trapped in the midst of the truly brilliant.

Sophy's only satisfaction during those formative years had been pursuits that involved color and fabric. In kindergarten she had latched on to the discovery of crayons with a vengeance, going through one coloring book after another until she was designing her own coloring books. Unfortunately, the rest of the class was working on the rudiments of mathematical set theory.

In grade school, art had been taught in the accelerated classes, usually in relation to mathematical perspective and the properties of light. Sophy hadn't been overly interested in the scientific side of the matter, but she'd happily played with the watercolor paints until they were gently but firmly taken from her.

Her parents had briefly considered the possibility that her true genius might lie in the realm of art, but when she showed no great interest in drawing anything other than doll clothes, they abandoned the idea.

When she discovered dressmaking, Paul and Anna Bennet steadfastly decided to treat it as a hobby. They were still treating it that way. In all honesty, they weren't the only ones who looked on her skills as a hobby. There were times when she suspected that Nick Savage did, too. That realization was vaguely annoying, but she told herself that in time he would realize how important her budding career as a designer was to her. Firmly she dismissed the concern. Nick would learn.

Someone like Max Travers would probably never understand, though. His academic elitism would always get in the way. Not that it mattered. She could care less what Max Travers thought of her future career. But why had she felt so wary around the man tonight? Hadn't she left those old feelings of intimidation behind for good? Of course she had. So why that primitive wariness? Why had she practically run from his car tonight? It made no sense.

Sophy had put the restless questions out of her head by the next morning when she walked into the downtown highrise building that housed S & J Technology. She had a large box under one arm, and as soon as she stepped off the elevator on the fifteenth floor and into the section where most of the clerks and secretaries worked, a murmur of anticipation went up from the group standing around the coffee machine. A half dozen people came hurrying across the room.

"Is it finished?" Marcie Fremont, who had joined the staff shortly before Sophy and who had the desk next to hers, glanced expectantly at the box.

Sophy smiled at her and began unwrapping it. Marcie had paid well for what was inside, but Sophy was satisfied that she had delivered a dress worth the money.

Co-workers privately thought the two women offered an interesting contrast. Where Sophy was vivid and colorful and slightly outrageous at times, Marcie was cool and sophisticated. Her blond hair was always confined in a sleek, businesslike twist, and her beautiful, patrician features were always made up in subdued, refined tones.

Marcie Fremont dressed for success, as she herself put it, firmly convinced that the route out of the secretarial pool was going to be easier in the right clothes. Slim, tailored suits, silk blouses and restrained jewelry comprised her professional wardrobe. The overall effect was poised, efficient and rather distant. Sophy had kept that image in mind when she'd designed the after-hours dress.

"Remember, if you don't like it, you don't have to pay for it." Sophy smiled as she lifted the lid. Marcie smiled back quickly and Sophy was pleased to see the genuine anticipation in her eyes. Lately she had sensed a kind of quiet desperation about her new friend. Secretarial work was strictly a temporary situation for Sophy, but for Marcie it could prove to be a dead end.

"If Marcie doesn't want it, I'll take it, sight unseen," Karen Gibson announced. The others standing around nearby agreed.

"I'm sure I'll like it," Marcie said firmly. The gown came fluidly out of the box to murmured gasps of appreciation. A long, body-hugging line of black crepe with the dramatic impact of a swirling white organdy collar, it was obviously perfect for Marcie Fremont. It dipped low in the back to reveal an elegant length of spine, and it was slit up one side to the knee.

Marcie reached for it with real delight. "It's stunning, Sophy. Absolutely stunning! You're a genius." She held it to her while everyone else admired the effect.

"No doubt about it," Karen remarked, "it's absolutely right for you, Marcie."

The outer door opened at that moment and everyone swung around to see Max Travers standing just inside the room. There was a faint frown of curiosity on his face. He took in the sight of the women grouped around the sleek black gown and looked as if he were about to back out of the room. He held a sheaf of papers clutched in one hand as his eyes sought out Sophy.

Look at her, he thought as he found her instantly, so full of warmth and life and enthusiasm. She'd make any man happy. Any man who could hold her, that was. And she only let cowboys hold her. Damn it to hell, what's the matter with me? Grimly he took a grip on himself, unaware that his frown had intensified.

"Excuse me," Max began aloofly. "I was told I could get someone down here to type up these notes for me."

Feeling mildly chagrined at having been the one to create the decidedly unbusinesslike scene, Sophy stepped forward. "I'll take those, Dr. Travers."

Max's smoky eyes darkened behind the horn-rimmed glasses as he thrust the papers into her hand with an abrupt gesture. "What's all the fuss about over that dress?" he asked gruffly, nodding his head at the small group still hovering over the black gown.

"I just finished designing it for Marcie." Absently Sophy flipped through the sheaf of papers.

"Oh." Max glanced at the dress with more curiosity. "I didn't know you sewed."

"My parents have tried to keep it a deep, dark secret. We all pretend it's just a hobby." She nodded at the papers. "Anything unusual about these notes? Want them done in a standard format?"

Max brought his attention back to the papers. "It's company proprietary stuff, so don't make any copies. Your management probably would just as soon not have any duplicates floating around."

"Max, you can trust everyone here." Sophy smiled blandly. "We all work for the company. We wouldn't spill its little secrets. Besides, who here could understand all this complicated stuff about a mathematical model for a chemical processing system?''

Max cocked an eyebrow. ''You apparently understand it enough to tell what it is just by glancing through a few notes.''

Sophy shook her head indulgently. ''I have a good mathematical and scientific vocabulary, thanks to all those years spent among wizards. I can translate what you're saying, but that doesn't mean I can comprehend it. It's like being a medical secretary. She might have the vocabulary for writing up the doctor's notes, but she couldn't perform the surgery. Get it?''

Max looked vaguely uncomfortable and his mouth firmed. ''Was your cowboy glad to have you back safe and sound last night?''

''He seemed happy enough to see me.''

''I'll bet. What would he have done if I'd been a little late getting you home?'' There was a surprisingly belligerent tone to Max's query.

''Beaten you to a pulp, probably. Now aren't you grateful I didn't stop off to have that drink at your hotel?'' Sophy asked sweetly.

''I would have been willing to take my chances,'' Max told her softly.

Sophy blinked, startled by the quiet conviction in his voice. For a split second their eyes met in complete understanding. In Max's smoky gaze Sophy saw the answer to the question she had asked herself the night before. Max Travers would most definitely have made a pass at her if she'd gone to his hotel with him. That question answered, she was faced with the remaining one. What would she have done in response?

In that moment of frighteningly honest communication, Sophy had a terrifying premonition about the answer to that question, too. And she didn't like the way her nerves seemed to thrill to it. What on earth was wrong with her? It was impossible for her to be interested in Maximilian Travers. Desperately she tried to regain her composure, breaking off the intense eye contact.

"You might have been willing to take your chances, but I certainly wouldn't have been so willing," she said staunchly. "My parents would be furious if I sent you back to North Carolina in a pulped condition. They're already convinced I don't have enough respect for higher math as it is!"

"Maybe I could teach you a little respect for it," Max suggested whimsically. "Will you have dinner with me tonight?"

"Max, please..." Sophy felt suddenly very nervous, and it made her angry.

"The cowboy?"

"Nick is out of town. And I'd appreciate it if you'd stop calling him the cowboy!"

"You call me the wizard."

"So I do," she sighed. "Your logic is impeccable. Only to be expected from a professor of mathematics." Sophy waved the papers in her hand. "I'll see that these are ready by noon."

"Wednesday night?"

Sophy bit her lip. "Is that hotel room really so bad, Max?" Good heavens! Now what was she doing? Was she actually making excuses to see him again? Trying to convince herself that she felt sorry for him?

"Yes. The hotel room really is that bad."

"I'm busy Wednesday night," she heard herself say hesitantly. "But I might be able to make it for lunch sometime this week. Or...or a drink after work, perhaps." She must be feeling sorry for him. That was the only reason she could think of for agreeing to go out with him again now that her duty was done. But even as she made the uncertain suggestion, Sophy knew she was kidding herself.

"Thank you, Sophy, I'll look forward to lunch and a drink. Thursday for the lunch?" he asked calmly.

"Yes, well, I suppose…"

"Friday after work for the drink?"

"Max, I'm…" She broke off in annoyance. "Nick will be in town by then and we'll probably have plans for Friday evening."

"We'll discuss it Thursday at lunch," Max compromised smoothly. Then he turned around and walked out of the office without another word.

Sophy watched him go with a sense of foreboding. Then she slowly made her way back to her desk.

"You're going to type up Dr. Travers's notes, Sophy?" Marcie Fremont glanced at her co-worker. The dress was back in its box, safely stowed under Marcie's desk.

"Yes," Sophy mumbled, sitting down and arranging the work.

"Maybe you can learn something from them," Marcie observed. Marcie, in her efforts to climb the corporate ladder, was the kind of secretary who didn't just type up data, she studied what she typed. As a result she had an excellent working knowledge of the technical side of the company's business. So far, though, that knowledge hadn't done her much good in securing advancement.

"I doubt it," Sophy said. "It's very complicated. A lot of higher math. I'll be lucky to translate it. By the way, have you heard anything from Personnel yet?"

Marcie's mouth curved wryly. "Not a word. They're sure taking their time selecting someone for that position in Quality Control. I get the feeling they think it's a man's job."

"When the truth is, you could do it better than anyone else who's applied!"

"Thanks." Marcie smiled. "I needed that. What's with you and Dr. Travers, though? Did I hear you agreeing to have lunch with him?"

"He's a friend of my parents'. They all live back in North Carolina." Sophy busied herself with Max's notes.

"But he seems personally interested in you," Marcie persisted.

"He's just lonely. He's spending a few weeks here in Dallas, and I guess the hotel walls are closing in on him." And that was all it amounted to, she assured herself silently. That was all it could amount to. So why was she so damned aware of the man? Why was she anticipating, and yet nervous about, having lunch with him?

During the next two days Max seemed to be nearby every time Sophy turned around. He dropped by to check on the progress of his notes. He made a point of being in the building lobby when Sophy was leaving work. He somehow managed to go through the cafeteria line behind her when she was on morning break.

And when he wasn't around, Sophy realized she was unconsciously watching for him. A hundred times she lectured herself about the dangers of letting Dr. Max Travers get too close, and a hundred times she assured herself that she was only treating him like a family friend.

Late Wednesday afternoon, however, Sophy had cause to wish she had heeded her own lecture. She glanced up at a quarter to five as Max came toward her desk with a stack of papers and an intense, preoccupied air.

"Sophy, I hate to ask this, but I've got to have these done by eight tomorrow morning." He wasn't looking at her, rather at the notes in his hand, so he missed Sophy's horrified expression.

"Max! It's almost five o'clock! I can't possibly get those typed up today!"

"It's okay," he assured her absently as he arranged the papers on her desk. "I'm allowed to authorize overtime for you."

Sophy felt a wave of panic. "Max, I don't want any overtime. Not tonight. I've got a date with Nick. You know that. Maybe someone else…"

Max met her eyes very steadily across the width of the desk, and Sophy was startled by the cool, calculating expression in the depths of his smoky gaze. "Sophy, you know none of the other secretaries can handle this tonight. You're the only one with the vocabulary and the scientific background to get through this in an evening. Besides, you're the one who's been working on this project all along. It will take any of the others a couple of days to get up to speed, and I haven't got that much time." He tapped the folder on her desk with a pen he had removed from the pack in his shirt pocket.

"Max, I'm going out tonight. I just don't have the time. Maybe I could come in early tomorrow," she tried desperately. She was feeling trapped. For some reason it seemed absolutely imperative that she see Nick tonight. She needed to reassure herself about her relationship with him.

Sophy realized in a blinding flash of perception that she badly needed Nick Savage tonight as an antidote to Dr. Maximilian Travers.

Max shook his head at her suggestion. "I need the report typed up first thing in the morning for a meeting with S & J management. Don't make me pull rank, Sophy."

Rage swept through her. Sophy's chin came up and her

eyes flashed with warning. "Rank, Dr. Travers? Exactly what kind of threat are you making?" Damn him!

Max leaned forward with an aggressiveness Sophy had not yet seen in him. His palms were spread flat on the desk, and it struck her that he had rather large, strong hands for an academician. Dangerous hands.

"Miss Bennet, may I remind you of what it's costing your company per day to engage my services? Your boss would not be pleased to have to pay for even one unnecessary day. When he discovered that that delay had been caused by the intransigence of one of his secretaries, I think he would be downright furious, don't you?"

Sophy went very still, watching him with bitter eyes. Max was absolutely right about her boss's reaction. Frank Williams would be thoroughly angered if he thought her stubbornness had cost an extra day of Max's expensive time. He'd catch hell from his boss, and she'd probably wind up being the scapegoat.

And right at the moment, Sophy knew, she couldn't afford to lose her job. Too many of her future plans depended on the income.

But there was more involved here than her personal plans for the dress boutique and her association with Nick. Max was making it abundantly clear that on this level, at least, she was more or less in his power. And that thought alarmed her more than any other aspect of the situation. Instinctively she knew she should be putting as much distance between herself and Max as possible, not allowing herself to slip into such untenable situations as this one. But for the life of her, she couldn't see a way out. She took refuge in sarcasm.

"Ah, Dr. Travers, how quickly the facade of the gentle professor disappears. Give me your precious report. You'll have it by eight tomorrow."

Max's mouth twisted. "Sophy..."

"If that's an apology hovering on your lips, let's just forget about it, shall we, Dr. Travers? I'm not really all that surprised at the use of the threat, you know. I've known all my life that, in the pursuit of their goals, wizards have a way of not letting anyone or anything stand in their path. They have some notion that they are the elite and the rest of us should be only too happy to serve. My parents could be absolute tyrants when the occasion demanded."

"Sophy," Max tried again, "I'm sorry the occasion demanded I play the tyrant."

"I understand, Dr. Travers. And I'm sure you'll understand when I say that something has arisen which will make it impossible for me to have lunch with you tomorrow." It was a poor retaliation, but it was all she could manage on such short notice.

"What has arisen?" he shot back, eyes narrowing.

"Your academic arrogance. Excuse me, I'd better get started on these notes right away."

Damn it to hell, Sophy seethed as she began to work. Now she had to call Nick. He wasn't going to appreciate this. And she didn't want him mad at her. Not now. It was so important that he provide her with some reassuring evidence that she couldn't possibly have begun to fall for anyone as arrogant and as out of her world as Dr. Max Travers.

Chapter 3

He *had* been arrogant, Max admitted to himself an hour later as he carried a paper sack full of hamburgers and french fries and coffee up in the elevator to Sophy's floor.

Incredibly arrogant.

Sophy herself didn't even appreciate the full extent of his arrogance! He had deliberately set out to sabotage her date with the cowboy, and if she ever learned the truth there would be hell to pay. Much better to have her thinking he was simply pulling rank in order to get his project done.

For all the good it had done him.

Look at the price he was paying, Max chided himself. She'd canceled their lunch date tomorrow! But the convenient necessity of needing those notes typed up into a full-fledged report had seemed too good an opportunity to pass up.

Would she condescend to share the hamburgers with him? Since he was out to lunch tomorrow, and since she had flatly refused to consider a break for dinner tonight, Max hadn't been able to think of any way to get a meal with her other than to bring in the fast food.

This evening was his once chance with Sophy, and he couldn't afford not to take advantage of it. He hoped the damned cowboy was frustrated as hell.

As he opened the door into the office, which was empty except for Sophy, Max braced himself for more of the ice treatment. He took a deep breath as she swung coldly accusing eyes on him for a fraction of a second and then returned to her work. She had been working with single-minded determination since she'd surrendered to his threat. Max's mouth hardened at the memory of how he had forced her to spend the evening with him. Then, for a moment, he simply drank in the sight of her, letting the pleasure of seeing her push out the uncertainties and feelings of guilt. What was it about Sophy that had attracted him from the first?

As usual, she made a vibrant splash of color against the subdued, neutral shades of the office decor. The curling mass of her hair was pulled back above her ears with wide yellow combs. Her outfit was a racy little yellow coatdress with lapels and cuffs in royal blue. Her narrow waist was cinched with a wide belt of blue leather trimmed with silver. As vivid as she was, Max was all too well aware that the attraction she held for him went far deeper than her appearance.

He was trained to see beneath the surface of things, but always before he had used that training in the realm of mathematics. With Sophy he wanted to use those skills in a new way. He wanted to know her completely. He wanted to secure her inner warmth and captivating *aliveness* for himself. Seeing her safely stuck behind the desk instead of dashing off to meet her cowboy gave him a feeling of untold satisfaction. Let tomorrow take care of itself. Tonight he had hours ahead with Sophy.

"I brought some hamburgers," he said on a determined note. She had to eat something, didn't she? "Since you insist on working through dinner, I feel obliged to make sure you get fed."

"Your consideration leaves me positively breathless, Dr. Travers." But she paused long enough to glance inside the sack. Then, to Max's relief, she withdrew a packet of french fries and began munching. Cautiously he sat down on the other side of her desk and reached for a burger.

"You can proofread the first section in a minute," she remarked shortly.

There was a long silence. "Was your cowboy very angry?" It was stupid to bring Nick Savage into the discussion, but Max suddenly had to know what the other man's reaction had been to the broken date.

"He wasn't thrilled."

Good, thought Max. Aloud he said, "I imagine he understands about the demands of your work."

There was another painful silence. When she failed to respond to the remark, Max decided to take the offensive. "Sophy, about our lunch date tomorrow..."

Her swivel chair swung around and she fixed him with a frozen glare. "Max, if you want this report done on time, you'll have to shut up and let me work. That was the whole point of the enforced overtime, wasn't it? To get this damn report out?"

He stifled a sigh and glanced down at what she had accomplished so far. "It looks like you're making good progress."

"I am." She swung the chair back around and returned to work.

"Well, in that case, we'll be able to knock off early and have a drink."

"My intention is to finish early and try to get to the party you forced me to miss this evening!"

Max froze. Damn it to hell. "Is your cowboy expecting you?"

"I'm going to surprise him. He said he was going to go anyway."

"I see. Sophy—"

"Shut up, Max, or you can damn well type this up yourself!"

"I don't know how to type," he retorted.

"Figures. I always thought they overlooked a few useful items in the education of wizards. I didn't get anything as useful as typing until I went off to college! Probably never let you waste much time playing with crayons, either, did they?"

"Well, no," Max replied bemusedly, "they didn't. I wasn't much interested in crayons, to tell you the truth. Why do you ask?"

"Never mind. Let me work."

Max hesitated a few minutes longer and then made his decision. It was time he met Nick Savage. "When you're done I'll drive you to the party," he stated gruffly. In that moment he couldn't have said exactly what made him want to see Sophy's lover. Max only knew that he had to find out what the other man was like. What did it take to attract Sophia Athena Bennet?

"That's not necessary, thank you," she said briskly.

"I don't want you taking the bus so late at night."

She glanced up in momentary surprise. "How did you know I took the bus this morning?"

"I, uh, just happened to see you come into work," he muttered, not meeting her eyes. Not for the world would he admit that when she came to work he was always standing at his office window, like a kid with his nose pressed to the candy store window.

"Well, don't worry. I've ridden the bus before at night," she assured him coolly.

"Sophy, I said I'll drive you to the party and that's final!" Was that him losing his temper? Good God!

She narrowed her eyes as if assessing his temper. "Oh, all right, if it will make you happy. Anything to keep the expensive consultant in a good mood."

Max found himself torn between wanting to beat her and wanting to drag her down onto the floor and cover her body with his own. It was a bewildering and unfair tangle of emotions, and it clouded his normally very logical mind in an unfamiliar fashion.

By ten o'clock he could think of no further excuse to delay the inevitable. The report had been completed and proofed. It was perfect, and he knew Sophy was well aware of that fact. Time to meet the cowboy.

"I'll just freshen up in the ladies' room and then I'll be ready to go," Sophy said as she started for the door.

Max nodded bleakly behind her, watching as she disappeared down the hall. He did not want to turn her over to Nick Savage tonight, he realized. He wanted to take Sophy Bennet back to his hotel room and keep her there with him.

Max's mood became increasingly grim as he followed Sophy's chatty directions to one of the exclusive homes in the northern area of Dallas. Her mood was lightening in an inverse ratio to his own heavy frame of mind, he realized in disgust. She was looking forward to being with her cowboy.

"I'd like to come in with you and meet this guy," Max announced as he parked the Ford at the end of a long line of Lincolns, Cadillacs and Mercedeses.

"I don't see why you should want to meet Nick," Sophy began as she stepped out of the car.

"Curiosity," he told her flatly. "Put it down to sheer curiosity. Besides, if I like him I can always mention that to your parents. It might help them adjust to the shock of having a cowboy for a son-in-law." There was no way on earth he was going to like Nick Savage, of course, but Max saw no reason to mention that fact to Sophy, who was already watching him a bit warily.

"Well, I suppose there's no harm, but Max, there must be nearly two hundred people at this party tonight. It's going to take a while to find him in the crowd."

"I'll help you look," Max said smoothly, resisting the urge to say that the search might be difficult for him due to the fact that all cowboys looked alike.

"Oh, all right, if you insist," she muttered, too eager to find Nick to waste time arguing.

The party had clearly progressed beyond dinner to the steady drinking stage. Max and Sophy were virtually ignored as they came through the door. Max glanced around uneasily. Stetson hats, flared trousers and leather boots were everywhere. The crowd was lively, raucous and well on its way to a hangover.

"He said he was going to be here," Sophy muttered above the din. "The Everets are good friends of his."

Max watch her expressive profile as she searched the room. It would be nice to have Sophy search that earnestly for him, he thought grimly. That fantasy led to other, more fundamental fantasies, and he found himself disliking all cowboys intensely.

"A lot of people seem to have drifted out onto the back patio," Sophy said abruptly. "Let's try there."

With a sense of mounting irritation, Max followed as she cut a bright swath through the crowd. By the time he caught up with her again she had reached the flagstoned area at the rear of the house. The soft glow of lights from artfully styled lanterns illuminated a scene that seemed as crowded as the living room had been. Sophy singled out an elderly-looking man and got his polite attention at once.

"Nick Savage?" Max heard him say. "Thought I saw him a while ago with…" The elderly cowboy frowned and broke off hurriedly. "Uh, he was heading toward the pool, little lady. Yes, I do believe he was heading toward the pool." The man glanced up and sent Max a straight look. "You with this little lady here?"

"Yes I am," Max said firmly, ignoring Sophy's irritation.

"Well, then, I reckon that's okay, isn't it?" the other man said, clearly relaxing. "Yup, I think you might find Nick out by the pool." He winked at Max. "Might be a good idea to let him have a bit more time to himself, if you catch my drift."

Max heard the hint of warning in the stranger's voice, but Sophy appeared oblivious. She was already dragging him off toward the shadowy area round the huge, curving pool.

"Sophy…" Max started, and then stopped abruptly. A part of him instinctively wanted to urge caution, but another, more aggressive side wanted Sophy to push ahead and discover the possibly appalling truth. If he had understood what the older man had been trying to say, Max had a strong suspicion as to what Nick Savage was doing out by the pool. With a little luck the damn cowboy might obligingly condemn himself in Sophy's eyes.

"I don't see anyone," she complained as she hurried around the edge of the pool toward a row of shadowed cabanas. Then she stopped so suddenly Max nearly collided with her. An instant later he heard the soft sound. It was the unmistakable voice of a woman followed by the husky laughter of a man, and it emanated from the nearest cabana.

Before either of them could respond, the door of the cabana opened and Max looked up to see a man emerge, the
same man who had emerged from the Lincoln the night he
had taken Sophy home. Nick Savage had a pleased grin on
his face, and he was just fastening his pants. In the moonlight the huge silver buckle of his belt gleamed obscenely.

"Nick." Sophy looked absolutely stricken. She stood
staring at the man, who appeared nearly as startled. As they
faced each other, a woman emerged from the cabana. She
was blond and beautiful and still getting dressed.

The four people involved in the dramatic tableau simply
stared at each other for an endless moment. Max knew a
shattering, wholly elemental satisfaction as the full ramifi-
cations of the scene came home to him. Nick Savage had
been making love to the blond.

But even as he realized just how thoroughly the cowboy
had compromised himself, Max was aware of a fierce desire
to protect Sophy. He caught her wrist and pulled her back
toward him. "Let's get out of here, Sophy," he growled.

"No!"

He heard the feminine shock and fury that underlined the
single word.

"You bastard, Nick! You lying, cheating *bastard!* How
could you do this to me? How dare you?"

Nick finally moved, disengaging himself from the blond,
who had caught hold of his arm with a possessive grip.
"Sophy, wait!"

"Friends of yours, Nicky dear?" the blond inquired with
commendable aplomb as she adjusted her blouse. She ran a
hand through her long hair. "I thought this was a private
party. Just you and me." Deliberately she smiled.

Nick swore furiously, striding forward as if he would
catch hold of Sophy. Max moved, yanking Sophy out of

reach. She turned to him with a pleading, desperate look on her face.

"Max, please," she whispered raggedly. "Please take me home."

He didn't hesitate. "This way, Sophy." With sudden decision he tugged her around the pool, leaving the cowboy and his friend behind. Sophy followed mutely, seemingly grateful to have him take charge. She was still in shock, Max thought worriedly. Gently he helped her into the front seat of the Ford and then he slid in beside her, switching on the ignition. Was she all right? She looked so pale and frozen in the moonlight.

He guided the car down the winding drive to the road and started back toward downtown Dallas. If Sophy noticed she wasn't being driven home, she didn't seem to care. Max glanced at her stark, set profile. Was she furious or overwhelmed with grief? He hoped to God it was fury she was feeling.

"Sophy, I'm sorry you had to go through that scene back there."

"I thought he loved me, Max." She sounded so stricken; so listless. Max decided he could cheerfully strangle the cowboy. And then he thought about how Nick Savage had just ruined himself in Sophy's eyes.

"Maybe he does love you, Sophy. In his own way. Some men aren't very good at being faithful." What a bunch of bull that was, he told himself wryly. But he felt obliged to say something.

Her small hand doubled into a fist in her lap. "I could kill him."

"That makes two of us," Max muttered half under his breath.

"I trusted him, Max. I believed him when he said there

was no one else. He's been making a complete fool out of me. What a stupid little idiot I've been.''

Max didn't know what to say to that. In a way, he decided, she was absolutely right. Damned cowboy. ''You need a drink,'' he stated.

''Several of them, I think. Oh, God, Max, this has got to be one of the most humiliating moments of my entire life!''

She said nothing more as he completed the drive to the hotel. He saw her blank, uncaring glance take in the fact that he was taking her to a lounge and not to her own home, and then she seemed to lose interest completely in her surroundings. Max was torn. On the one hand, he wanted to comfort her, but on the other he found himself aching to seize the opportunity! *The cowboy was no longer in the way.*

The cowboy was no longer in the way, he repeated to himself as he gently guided Sophy into the darkened lounge and seated her in a private corner. There he ordered drinks and watched as Sophy took great gulps of her Manhattan.

Never again, he told himself, would he be given the chance of getting this close to Sophia Athena Bennet. When she recovered her normal poise, she would once again put leagues of distance between them. But tonight she seemed to need him. Max sipped his drink patiently and waited.

''I don't understand it,'' Sophy finally mumbled sadly. ''How could he do that to me? I thought we were building something. Something important. Oh, Max, I thought he was falling in love with me. I thought he wanted me.''

Careful, Max told himself, don't come on too strong, or she'll turn the anger on you. Just be supportive. ''I don't know why he would do it, Sophy. He doesn't deserve you, that's obvious. Probably thought he could have his cake and eat it, too.''

She took another swallow of the Manhattan and stared at him over the rim, blue-green eyes huge and vulnerable. Max wanted to pull her into his arms to comfort her but didn't quite dare. Not yet.

"I could kill him," she repeated a bit violently.

"The thing to do," Max found the daring to advise, "is not waste another thought on him. There are other men, Sophy. Men who will appreciate you."

"All men are probably alike," she sniffed wretchedly.

"Sophy, you're smart enough to know that's not true."

"I don't feel smart at all at the moment. I feel as dumb as I used to feel back in school!"

"Feeling sorry for yourself?" he chided carefully.

"Yes, dammit!"

"Okay, okay," he soothed at once. "You're entitled, God knows. I hate to see you wasting any more emotion on that creep. You're too good for him. You deserve someone who appreciates you!"

"Such as?" she challenged morosely.

Max sucked in his breath, watching her intently. "Such as me, Sophy."

"You!" She drew back, eyes widening. For a moment Max could have sworn he saw genuine, feminine panic in that bottomless gaze. Panic? Over him?

"I think you're the most fascinating woman I've ever met, Sophy." And that was no less than the truth, he realized.

She eyed him across the table, her expressive face revealing an indefinable emotion. What the hell was she thinking? He shouldn't have pushed so fast, Max admonished himself.

"It's very kind of you to try to make me feel better," she finally said in a small voice.

"Sophy, I'm not..."

"Could I have another drink, please?" she inquired with what sounded suspiciously like a sniffle.

He ordered, and they sat in silence while she sipped the second Manhattan a little more slowly than the first.

"It's sweet of you to be concerned, Max," she said at last in a polite little voice, "but I'll be all right, really I will. I feel like a fool at the moment, but I'm quite capable of looking after myself."

"Are you?"

"Oh, yes. We average types are really much better at handling the day-to-day shocks of life than you sheltered, ivory-tower geniuses. It's because you spend all your time wrapped up in your intellectual pursuits. People like you never learn about the emotional side of life." She paused. "Maybe you're lucky."

"Because the emotional side of life can be painful?" he queried softly.

Her eyes glistened with unshed tears, and Max wanted to put his arms around her and let her cry out the pain she was clearly feeling.

"Yes," she whispered tightly. "Very painful. Oh, *Max…*"

He got to his feet at once and pulled her gently up beside him, holding her close with one arm while he signed the tab. "It's okay, Sophy," he murmured as he led her through the lobby. "It's okay, honey. Go ahead and cry. Get it out of your system. Then maybe you can start to forget him."

He kept up the soft monologue all during the ride in the elevator and the walk down the hall to his room. She clung to him and he took a strange, unfamiliar satisfaction in that. Sophy said nothing until he was turning the key in the door. Then she sniffed and moved restlessly within the curve of his arm.

"I should be getting home," she whispered a little dazedly, dashing the back of her hand across her eyes. "It's very nice of you to spend so much time with me, but…"

The words trailed off on a small sob. "Maybe if I could wash my face?" She glanced up at him pleadingly.

"Right through there," Max said, inclining his head toward the bathroom door. God help him, his fingers were trembling. This was the first time he'd ever held her close, he thought. He watched her walk slowly across the room toward the bath. His hands were actually shaking!

She was here, right here in his hotel room. Now what?

Was she aware of where she was? Did she care? She couldn't be drunk, not after only two drinks. But she was, perhaps, a bit drunk on her own humiliation and anger, he told himself.

It wouldn't be fair to take advantage of her under the present circumstances.

Not fair at all. Not the act of a gentleman and a scholar.

She was feeling lost and hurt and miserable and she was very, very vulnerable, Max told himself grimly. Damn it to hell, what was he thinking of doing? Taking advantage of Sophia Athena? Daughter of Paul and Anna Bennet? God forbid.

He'd probably get no further than trying to kiss her, he told himself angrily as he stalked across the room to find the bottle of complimentary champagne that the hotel had sent up when he'd arrived. It was where he had stuck it, safely stored in the small refrigerator. Moodily he removed it and began to open it.

She'd probably turn all her fury and pain on him if he even so much as tried to take her in his arms and kiss her. He poured the champagne.

But she was so weak and vulnerable right now. She might not realize his intentions until it was far too late. The champagne tasted strange. He glared down at the bubbling stuff in the glass in his hand. Simultaneously he heard the sound of running water from the bath. How long would she be in there? Max wondered. He tried another sip of the drink and stared at his reflection in the mirror.

He didn't look anything like a cowboy, and Sophia preferred cowboys. Or she had until tonight, he reminded himself savagely. Then Max groaned. He wasn't likely ever to get another chance with Sophy Bennet and he knew it. Never again would he have her all to himself in a hotel room. Never again was he likely to find himself cast in the role of comforter.

What if he abused the unique position in which he found himself tonight? What if he actually managed to get her into bed? His palms went abruptly damp.

"She'd hate my guts in the morning," he told his reflection with grim certainty. *God help him, he wanted her.*

Max winced and turned away from the too-revealing mirror. She'd hate him even more than she hated that cowboy.

But he'd never get another chance like this. Max was so certain of that. If he didn't take advantage of the situation, he'd never know what it was like to make love to the most intriguing woman he'd ever met. He'd never wanted a woman so badly in his life. What in hell was the matter with him?

His fingers tightened around the stem of the champagne glass. How could he make himself walk away now from the glittering temptation that had been put in his path? God help him, he was only a man, regardless of how often she called him a wizard.

Was having Sophy tonight worth the risks of incurring her fury in the morning?

Damn it, the answer was yes. He downed the last of the champagne, staring out the window with unseeing eyes. What if he could make it so good for her that she wouldn't remember their time together with rage? What if he managed to show her just how much he needed her? There was a streak of compassion in her, a gentleness that might temper her anger. If she realized how much he needed her, perhaps she would be kind to him in the morning. Perhaps she would stay with him....

The door to the bathroom opened on that dangerously tantalizing thought. He turned abruptly to find Sophy framed in the doorway. She looked so miserable and bleak. And it was all that stupid cowboy's fault.

"I could kill him."

"What?" She glanced at him in confusion, and Max realized he'd spoken aloud. He shook his head and walked stiffly across the room to put a glass of champagne in her hand.

"I said I could kill him. Except that he's not worth the trouble. Sophy, you're better off without him. You'll realize that eventually."

"I suppose you're right." Wistfully she took the champagne and sat down on the edge of the bed, smiling wanly. "It's just so hard to admit how stupid I've been. I *trusted* him, Max."

"You weren't stupid." He sat down carefully beside her and put his arm around her. She accepted the proffered comfort, leaning her head against his shoulder. "You thought you were in love and you thought he loved you."

"It could have been worse," Sophy mumbled, sipping the champagne.

"Worse?"

"I think I would have felt even worse if...if Nick and I had been lovers," she mumbled into the glass.

Max stifled a surge of satisfaction, barely managing to keep his tone neutral. "You mean you weren't sleeping with him?"

She shook her head. "Maybe that's why he turned to that

blond," she chastised herself. "Maybe I shouldn't have kept him waiting."

"Sophy, you mustn't blame yourself."

"But I…"

Max cut off the self-castigating flow of words with his fingers on her lips. "No. Sophy, he's the one who cheated on you. None of this is your fault. You're the wronged party in this mess. Remember that."

Her wide blue-green eyes stared at him as he continued to press her mouth gently with his hand. Was that a flicker of awareness he saw in her gaze? Was it possible she might want him just a little?

"Oh, God, Sophy…"

On a low groan of barely controlled need, he removed the glass from her hand.

"Max? Max, I'm not sure…"

"Hush, Sophy. Don't think about anything. Just relax and let me comfort you. Please, honey. It's all I want to do." It was the truth and it was a lie and Max didn't know how to explain it.

Slowly, half-afraid she might disappear in his grasp if he moved too quickly, Max lowered his mouth to feather her parted lips with his own. She didn't move as he made exquisitely exciting contact. He felt the tiny tremor that went through her, however, and somehow it fueled his own carefully contained desire. At least she wasn't totally indifferent to him, he thought exultantly.

"Relax, Sophy, just relax. Let me hold you until you forget him." He didn't know where the soothing words were coming from. They seemed half-instinctive, the calming, gentling words men had used from the beginning of time to tame nervous women.

She tensed as he drew her slowly backward onto the quilted bedspread. He sensed she was about to resist and he didn't know what else to do except chain her with another kiss. His mouth closed more deliberately over hers and he heard a faint moan from far back in her throat. The sound made the urgent longing in him all the more insistent. A part of her did want him, damn it!

"Max, no, I don't..." Her head shifted restlessly on the quilt as she freed her mouth.

"I always seem to find myself looking for ways to shut you up," he muttered hoarsely, yanking off his glasses and tossing them heedlessly onto the nightstand. For a second he stared down at her, glorying in the knowledge that there was a tiny, faltering flame in her now. She trembled again as she met his gaze, and with a rasping exclamation Max lowered his head to plunge his tongue deeply into her mouth.

Instinctively he used his weight to pin her more securely to the quilt. Her slender body was still stiff and uncertain beneath him, but he could feel the thrusting softness of her breasts. She felt so good lying there under him. He pushed his lower body strongly against her thighs, seeking to let her know the extent of his own arousal.

"Max!" It was a soft cry, torn from her when he freed her mouth temporarily to explore the sensitive place behind her ear.

"Hush, Sophy. Just relax and trust me tonight. I'll take care of you. I'll make you forget him. By morning you'll only think of me, I swear it."

Chapter 4

Sophy's senses seemed to be spinning. Not in a mad, frightening whirl, but in a deliciously intriguing manner. Everything was suddenly right. The moment Max had taken her in his arms, everything had become right.

The restless uncertainty, the attraction she had been experiencing, the indefinable aura about Max that made her so totally aware of him were suddenly explained. Fully explained.

She wanted him.

The realization was too startling to deal with on an intellectual level tonight. Sophy wanted only to give herself up to the sweeping feelings of the moment. Her emotions felt raw, and Max's arms promised soothing safety. There would be time enough in the morning to consider what she was doing.

With a sigh of longing that had been suppressed since she had first set eyes on Max Travers, Sophy pushed aside all thoughts of the future and surrendered to the wonder of the moment.

This was what had been missing all along in her relationship with Nick Savage: this marvelous *rightness,* this sensation of need and the promise of shared satisfaction. This soft, sweet longing was a totally new and unexplored element in her life, and it was all bound up with Max Travers. In that moment Sophy was absolutely certain the emotions she was experiencing could not exist without Max as their focus.

It made no sense and yet it made all the sense in the world.

Sophy sighed against Max's mouth, a sensation of thrilling languor flowing through her. Her leg moved slightly on the bedspread, and Max's thigh covered it, pressing down firmly, trapping it.

"I want to be your lover tonight, Sophy. I want to hold you and make you forget that damned cowboy," Max growled against the skin of her throat.

"I don't want to think about him," she agreed fervently, sinking her fingertips into the dark brown depths of his hair. "You're the only one I seem to be able to think about at the moment." She heard him draw in his breath quite sharply and knew a distinct sense of satisfaction. He wanted her. Max wanted her as much as she wanted him.

"That cowboy is a fool!"

"Oh, Max…"

"Any man who would risk losing you just for the sake of a quickie at a party has got to be a fool."

"Please, Max. I don't want to talk about him."

Max cradled her in one arm as he stretched out slowly beside her on the bed. His other hand began to move with sureness and wonder on her body. The soothing words he murmured contained a tense urgency, a sense of demand that was at once wholly masculine and completely enthralling.

"Let me touch you, darling. Sophy, honey, you feel so good under my hands. So very good."

Sophy shifted restlessly, closing her eyes as her body warmed under his touch. When Max buried his lips in her throat, letting her feel the edge of his teeth, she shivered.

"Sophy! Sophy, I want you. I need you tonight. I have to keep you here with me." He shaped her breast with exploring fingers and she whispered his name.

"Max…I feel so strange. I've never felt like this before. Oh, Max, what have you done to me?" Sophy asked wonderingly. Her arms went around him almost convulsively.

"Ah, sweetheart, you're so warm and soft and vibrant. You're all the colors of the rainbow. Did you know that? All the colors that have been missing in my life. I want to see you shimmer in my arms. I want to make you even more alive than you already are!" Max groaned again, his voice raw and husky. He found the buckle of the wide blue leather belt and undid it with deliberate movements.

Sophy could feel his body straining against hers as he slowly, carefully undressed her. The full, waiting male power of him was electrifying. As the yellow dress fell aside, he curved his hand around her buttocks and pulled her tightly against him. Sophy shuddered in helpless response.

"Feel how much I want you," he grated.

Her nails dug into the strongly contoured muscles of his back, and she found herself pressing closer, inhaling the satisfying scent of his body. The yellow dress seemed to have disappeared of its own accord, and a moment later the lacy little bra went the same route. All she wore now was a small triangle of satin.

"You're so incredibly exciting," Max growled in wonder

as he bent his head to kiss her breast. "Just looking at you across a room is exciting. But having you here in my bed is almost unbelievable."

"Oh!" Sophy flinched in thrilling reaction as he drew her sensitized nipple into his mouth. Tiny shivers of pleasure pulsated through her, and she began to murmur his name over and over again. The nipple hardened at once beneath the compelling touch of his rasping tongue.

"So responsive," he breathed. "You must want me, Sophy. Please say you want me."

"Yes, Max," she whispered obediently. "I want you."

His palm was gliding down the warm skin of her stomach, and she writhed under the touch with the uninhibited pleasure of a cat being stroked. The prowling, tantalizing fingers slid down her thigh and up along the silken inside to the point where the satin underpanties barred his path. Sophy's knee flexed convulsively, her toes curling tightly.

"You're safe here with me, sweetheart," he murmured as he slipped his finger under the elasticized edge of the panties and began to touch her in the most thrilling manner. The patterns he wove at the center of her softness made her cry out in wonder and delight.

"Please, Max. Please…"

The urge to touch him more intimately came upon her in a rush, and suddenly Sophy was pulling at the knot of his narrow tie, yanking at the buttons of his shirt and fumbling with the buckle of his belt.

"Yes, darling, yes," he muttered, shrugging out of the shirt. He caught her fluttering hands when she would have paused to explore the expanse of his hair-roughened chest. "Finish undressing me, honey."

Sophy did as he demanded and a moment later he lay beside her, totally nude. She gasped with pleasure and flexed her fingers like tiny claws against the bronzed skin of his sleek body.

"God, Sophy, I feel like I'm burning up."

"Oh, Max, you're so...so..." She couldn't take her eyes off his aroused, utterly masculine body.

"So what?" he taunted softly with a shaky laugh. "So desperate for you? So full of aching desire that I hurt? I am, darling. Only you can give me any relief tonight. I've been wanting you since the first moment I saw you. I've never known such a hunger for a woman. You've got to satisfy me or I'll go out of my head. I can't wait any longer for you."

He sprawled suddenly across her with undeniable intent, forcing her thighs apart with his own. His hands closed over her shoulders, anchoring her firmly beneath him, and he lay looking down at her with a fire blazing in his eyes.

"Max, wait..." Too late Sophy realized it had all gone too far. Everything was spinning out of control. Her body was filled with sensual longing and her head was filled only with the desire to respond to Max's urgent demands.

"No, darling, I can't wait," he gritted with unexpected savagery as he covered her. "If I wait, I'll lose you." He blocked the words in her mouth with his lips and then he moved aggressively against her.

He was so heavy, Sophy thought. Heavy and hard and irresistible. God, how she wanted him. Her own body was shivering with reaction and desire.

"Put your arms around me and hold on to me," he ordered thickly. "I'll keep you safe, Sophy. Just hold on to me."

Blindly she obeyed, clinging to him as if he were her only source of security, even as a part of her dimly recognized that he was really the source of a threat unlike any she had ever known. Then he forged into her damp, heated softness, bringing a breathless cry of surrender into her throat. Greedily he swallowed the small sound. For a moment they both lay locked together in a kind of shock at the completeness of the union. Then slowly, powerfully, Max began to move.

Sophy was utterly lost. Never had she known such exquisite, almost terrifying passion. It captivated and compelled and controlled. She could no more have escaped it now than she could have stopped the earth in its orbit. Max held her, taking everything she had to give and rewarding her with the gift of himself. It was unbelievably primitive, an act of fire and passion, and it came to an end in a shivering culmination that had Sophy's nails leaving small wounds on Max's back. Her whole body tightened with the exploding release, and even as she gave herself up to it, Sophy heard Max's shout of heady satisfaction as he followed her over the edge.

For long, endless moments Sophy allowed herself to drift on the outgoing tide of passion. Vaguely aware of the warmth of Max's perspiration-damp body, she listened to the sound of his breathing as it settled back into a normal pattern. His thigh still sprawled across her legs, holding her immobile.

She didn't want to open her eyes, she realized. She wanted only to go on drifting forever in this pleasant, safe realm where reality could not reach her.

"Go to sleep, Sophy," Max drawled in her ear. "Just relax and go to sleep. We can talk it all out in the morning."

The command fit in very well with her own desire to avoid the reality of what had happened. Sophy closed her eyes and obeyed.

It was a faint sound in the hall outside the room that awakened her several hours later. For a moment Sophy lay perfectly still, trying to orient herself, and then she became violently aware of Max's hard thigh lying alongside her own soft one. Her head turned on the pillow to stare at his shadowed face. He was sound asleep.

The sound outside in the hallway registered. It was merely the scraping of a key in the lock of the room next door.

My God, Sophy thought, sitting up slowly. *What have I done?*

She stared down at herself as the sheet fell aside, and she knew a sense of shock at her own nakedness. How could she have been so weak? Nervously she looked down at Max's bare chest as he lay sprawled on his back.

He lay beside her like some ancient conquering hero. There was an arrogance in the lean, sleek lines of his body that she had never noticed before. But that was because she had always seen him in the camouflage of his academic uniform, Sophy thought on a note of hysteria. He had used the old-fashioned white shirt, the little nerd pack, the glasses and the corduroy trousers to get close to her the way a hunter stalks his prey in camouflaged clothing.

Maximilian Travers had promised comfort and given her passion instead.

Even with Nick Savage, Sophy thought grimly, she hadn't been so stupid.

But she had always lost out to wizards. All her life she had been unable to hold her own against them. This time was no different, except that a part of her had always felt that this was an area of life in which wizards would never be a threat.

Sophy's hands clenched in small fists as she continued to stare down at Max. She had to get out of there. Max was everything he had no right to be: strong, virile, dominant. And brilliant. She must get away from him as quickly as possible.

The damned wizard had deliberately taken advantage of her, Sophy told herself ruthlessly as she pushed aside the sheet and slid off the bed. Yes, that was what had happened. He had used her. Taken advantage of her emotional vulnerability last night. She was torn between a fierce desire to pound him with her hands and the equally strong desire to flee.

She elected flight.

With painful caution Sophy searched for her clothing, scrambling awkwardly into her underwear and the yellow coatdress. She found her shoes under the bed. In the end she couldn't find her belt, however, and she didn't want to waste any more time searching for it. She dressed hurriedly, her only goal to escape from the scene of her stupidity. No, damn it! Not stupidity. *Vulnerability.* It was her own vulnerability that had gotten her into this situation.

After running a hand through her heavy, tangled curls, Sophy checked for her small purse and then headed for the door. It was almost five o'clock according to the digital clock beside the bed. To her great relief, Max didn't stir as she let herself out into the hall. Cautiously, knowing she couldn't bear to face him at that moment, she shut the door behind her and hurried downstairs to find a cab.

Max watched her leave through slitted eyes. There was no point in calling out to her. She was running away from him.

"Hell," he muttered in the darkness as the door closed softly behind her. "Damn it to hell." She hadn't even waited until morning to leave him. She probably hated him.

With a groan, he sat up in bed and switched on the bedside lamp. Almost instantly his eyes fell on the familiar outline of her wide leather belt. Reaching down, he picked it up and then pushed his glasses onto his nose. For a long moment he simply sat staring at it. Cinderella had left her calling card, but he didn't need to be told that she didn't view him as a prince.

Such a slender little waist, he thought, fingering the belt. And such beautiful, flaring thighs below that tiny waist. Darn it, his body was hardening just at the memory!

Max stood up with a muttered groan. He had about as much chance of getting Sophy Bennet back in his bed as he did of flying to the moon. Less. Then his hand tightened on the belt. Hadn't he been just as pessimistic about his chances with Sophy before that cowboy had been so obligingly dumb?

And she *had* responded to him last night, Max reminded himself resolutely as he headed toward the bathroom. Responded, hell. That was putting it mildly. She had been like molten gold in his arms. Would she try to deny it if he confronted her with that fact this morning? Probably. Reminding her of how she had surrendered in his arms would not be a gentlemanly thing to do. But he had to convince her that there was something between them, and he could think of no other way.

On the opposite side of town, Sophy dressed for work with equally grim intent. In her mind she planned wildly different strategies for dealing with Max Travers. No sense pretending she could avoid him. The company wasn't that large and he would probably seek her out, anyway. Would he gloat about her surrender?

A part of her wanted to rail at him like a wronged woman, but another part wanted to maintain some sense of dignity. After all, she was twenty-eight years old. Dignity was crucial. It was about all she had left.

Half an hour early, she made her way into the office wearing a pinstriped dress trimmed with white collar and cuffs. It was the most severely styled dress in her wardrobe, designed primarily for weddings and funerals. It gave her a sense of aloof arrogance, however, and she badly needed that this morning. There was no one else around, so she occupied herself with brewing coffee. She was watching it drip into the pot when the door opened and Max walked into the room.

For an instant Sophy just stared at him, terribly unprepared for the confrontation. It was too soon. She needed more time, she thought nervously. Max was back in his familiar clothing but it didn't help. Sophy knew she would never forget the man underneath those unthreatening garments. All the camouflage in the world wouldn't serve to hide Max Travers from her eyes now.

"Good morning, Max. Come for a cup of coffee?" Sophy forced a breezy little smile from out of nowhere. Damn it, she would not let herself be intimidated. She had stopped being intimidated by wizards years ago, and Sophy told herself she had no intention of going back to those feelings of intimidation now.

He walked steadily across the room until he was standing beside her. His smoky eyes watched her intently behind the shield of his glasses. "I could use a cup, yes, thank you."

"Here you go," she said briskly, pouring out two cups and handing him one. "All set to discuss your preliminary report with management?"

He blinked warily. "What report?"

"Oh, you remember, Max," she said very sweetly. "The one you kept me working on until nearly ten last night."

A slow stain of red spread across his cheeks. "Uh, yes. I'm ready."

"Good. I wouldn't want to think the *entire* evening had been a waste. Heaven knows a good chunk of it certainly was. Nice to know something was salvaged." Darn it! She would not allow him to revel in her reactions to him last night. She would make him think it meant nothing. Absolutely nothing.

"Sophy…"

"Yes, Max?"

"Sophy, about last night," he began decisively.

"Max, you're supposed to be a very bright man. I should think you'd have enough intelligence not to discuss last night." Her tone was one of mild amusement, and Sophy was proud of it. But her blue-green eyes were swirling with chilled fury.

Max's face hardened. "You know as well as I do that we can't ignore last night."

"Why not? It seems like an excellent idea to me!"

"Damn it, Sophy. Stop acting like a brittle little creature whose emotions don't run any deeper than icing on a cake!"

"How do you know that's not exactly how deep my emotions run?" she challenged tightly.

"Because you showed me how deep the passion runs in you last night. And if the passion is that deep, so are the rest of your emotions!" he suddenly blazed.

"Your degrees are in mathematics! Not amateur psychology!" she stormed. "All you saw in me last night was desire!"

"The hell I did," he ground out coldly. "You gave yourself completely last night, Sophy Bennet. You gave yourself to me. Surrendered to me. I know the difference between temporary desire and real passion."

"How could you? You're only a mathematician!"

His mouth crooked in a strange little smile that faded almost instantly. "You taught me the difference, Sophy. You have only yourself to blame."

"Don't you dare blame last night on me!" she cried. "You took advantage of me! I was feeling emotionally weak and vulnerable. I'd had a great shock. You were supposed to be a friend. You said you wanted to comfort me. I trusted you.''

''Sophy, all of that may have been true up to a point...''

''Nice of you to take a little responsibility for what happened!''

''I take fully responsibility for what happened,'' he returned gently. ''But that doesn't change the basic fact that you surrendered last night, sweetheart. You came to me with no reservations and you gave yourself completely. I've never had a woman give herself to me like that. And now that I've had you, you can't expect me to let you just walk away saying it was only a case of temporary attraction.''

''That's all it was! And you had no right to take advantage of me! Hardly the action of a gentleman and a scholar!'' she seethed, grasping at the only insult available.

''I know.'' He offered no excuses, no explanations. He just admitted it.

''Damn you!'' Sophy lost her frail temper completely and flung the rapidly cooling contents of her coffee cup all over his white shirt and narrow nerd tie.

For an instant they stared at each other in ominous, shocked silence, and into that frozen setting walked Marcie Fremont. Her blue eyes widened briefly in surprise as she took in the highly charged scene.

''I'm sorry. Excuse me, please.'' Politely she turned to walk back out the door through which she had just entered, but Sophy reached it ahead of her, flinging it open and racing madly down the hall towards the ladies' room.

She was vaguely aware of Marcie staring after her in concerned astonishment and she thought she heard Max angrily calling her name, but Sophy didn't stop until she was safely behind the door of one of the few refuges allowed modern woman.

Instantly she began to regret her lack of self-control. Hastily she dabbed at her eyes with a damp paper towel. How could she have made such a fool of herself in front of Marcie? Marcie was always so perfectly controlled. The scene would undoubtedly be all over the office within an hour.

No, perhaps not. Marcie Fremont was not a gossip. She was too conscious of her professional image to lower herself to common office gossip. Thank heavens it had been Marcie who had walked in on that horrible confrontation with Max. If it had been Karen or Sandy or Steve or Peter, the rumor mill would already be humming.

The door to the rest room opened and Sophy glanced up.

"Are you all right?" Marcie Fremont asked seriously.

"Yes. Yes, I'm fine."

"I'm awfully sorry about walking in on you and Dr. Travers like that."

"You could hardly have known what was going on." Sophy smiled shakily.

"Dr. Travers said you were a little upset about something that happened last night. Anything I can do? Does it involve you and your friend Nick Savage?"

"It's all tied up in one big mess, but no, there's nothing you can do, Marcie." Sophy sighed.

"Dr. Travers seemed very concerned."

"He should be! It's all his fault!"

"I see." Marcie hesitated a moment, watching as Sophy finished dabbing at her eyes. "Look, you don't have to worry about my saying anything, Sophy."

Sophy smiled her gratitude. "Thank you, Marcie. It's very kind of you to be so discreet."

"Dr. Travers asked me to have you call him when you've, uh, recovered," Marcie added gently.

"Dr. Travers can wait until the sixth dimension freezes over before I call him about anything," Sophy hissed, her temper flaring. "The bastard. I thought Nick was a bastard.

He could take lessons from Dr. Maximilian Travers. God, Marcie, right now I don't care if I never date another man again!'' Taking a deep breath, Sophy shook back her curling mane and fixed a grim little smile on her face. "I guess I'd better get back to work. Thanks,'' she mumbled again in helpless gratitude for the other woman's support and discretion.

"If you're sure you're all right?''

"I'm madder than hell, but I'm all right.''

Marcie relaxed with a faint smile. "I guess today is going to be a traumatic day for both of us, one way or another.''

Sophy arched an eyebrow inquiringly. "Personnel is going to make the decision?''

Marcie nodded, her excitement barely suppressed. "I heard they were going to announce the name of the person who's going to get that job in Quality Control. Oh, Sophy, I'm so nervous...''

"Marcie, you know you're the most qualified person for that job. You've got your business administration degree, and you've been assisting Quality Control on all those special tasks since you arrived. You've got a real working knowledge of what they're doing down there in QC!''

"Well, we'll find out today if Personnel sees things that way!''

Both women walked back to the office with determined resolve. Max had had the sense to depart.

When he made the mistake of calling at ten o'clock, Sophy didn't even bother to return his cautious greeting.

"Sorry, wrong number,'' she said sweetly, and replaced the receiver. "Arrogant wizard,'' she muttered as she hung up.

Max called again at eleven and she repeated the action. When he tried again at twelve it was Marcie who answered the phone, and as soon as she made eye contact with Sophy, the blond said, ''I'm sorry, Dr. Travers, she just stepped out for a few minutes. I'll tell her you called.''

Max showed up in person, however, right after lunch, advancing on Sophy's desk with a determined expression and a file of notes in his hand.

''Some revisions to that report you did for me last night,'' he stated without giving her a chance to react verbally to his unwanted presence. ''They came out of this morning's meeting.''

''Nice of you not to bring them by at five and order me to stay late to finish them,'' Sophy observed coldly.

''I had a feeling you might not be interested in working overtime this evening,'' he admitted dryly.

''You're quite right. I worked far too much of it last night.''

He frowned and leaned forward, apparently conscious of Marcie sitting nearby where she could overhear the conversation. ''I'd like to talk to you. Privately.''

''Go to hell, Dr. Travers,'' Sophy gritted with an artificial smile.

''I'll take you out to dinner tonight,'' he continued roughly.

''I'm afraid that's impossible. I have other plans.''

''Don't give me that. I know damn well you don't have a date tonight.''

''You're wrong, Dr. Travers,'' Sophy retorted as inspiration struck. ''I'm having a drink with Marcie after work. Aren't I, Marcie? We're going to celebrate Marcie's new promotion.'' She turned in her swivel chair and looked at her co-worker, eyes pleading for support.

''If the promotion comes through, we'll be celebrating it,'' Marcie said quickly. ''If not we'll be having a consolation drink.''

Max glared at Sophy and then at Marcie. Both women

met his look with bland smiles. He was beaten for the moment and he was wise enough to know it. He turned on his heel and stalked out of the office without another word. A long, charged silence hovered in his wake. Then Marcie spoke.

"I'd really be quite happy to have a drink with you, Sophy."

"Thank you. I have a hunch we'll both need it."

"Yes."

The news about the promotion arrived just before five o'clock. It came in the form of a brief call from Personnel to Marcie. Even as Sophy watched her friend's face become closed and withdrawn, she knew what the verdict was. Marcie thanked the caller with distant politeness and hung up the phone, her eyes glacier cold and filled with anger and disappointment.

"Oh, Marcie..." Sophy began sympathetically, knowing how much the job had meant to the other woman.

"They gave it to Steve Cameron," Marcie whispered. "Steve Cameron. He doesn't even have a business degree. He hasn't had the experience I've had working on QC projects. His only recommendation for that job is that he's a man."

"They're fools to give it to him. That man is all self-hype and no genuine ability!" Sophy said with sudden, fierce loyalty to Marcie. "God, if there's one thing I learned to recognize at a tender age, it's real ability. Believe me, Cameron doesn't have it. Idiots!"

"Oh, God, Sophy. I was counting on that job. When I took this position in the secretarial pool they more or less promised me that it would only be temporary. It was understood it was only to last until something better came up for which I was qualified! And I was qualified for that promotion, damn it!'' Marcie's hand curled into a small fist.

Sophy bit her lip and then started shoving her unfinished work into drawers. ''Come on, Marcie. Let's get out of here. Both of us have had enough for one day.''

''It's not quite five,'' Marcie said automatically.

''Who the hell cares!''

The cocktail lounge they found nearby was just beginning to fill up with an after-work crowd. The hum of conversation provided a pleasant cover for Sophy and Marcie's grim discussion. Secluded at a small booth toward the back, they ordered margaritas and considered the circumstances in which they found themselves.

Under the influence of the bond cemented between them that day, Sophy found herself telling Marcie the whole sordid story of her night with Max. She explained the humiliating scene with Nick, the way Max had offered comfort and the way he had taken advantage of her emotional vulnerability.

Marcie listened compassionately, and then she poured out her own frustrations with trying to make it up the corporate ladder in what was still essentially a man's world.

''There are times when old-fashioned words like *revenge* sound very sweet,'' Sophy finally announced over the second margarita. ''I've been having daydreams of revenge all day.''

''I've been having them off and on for five years,'' Marcie admitted wryly. ''Every time I got my fingers stepped on whenever I tried to climb the ladder. Damn it, I think this time I've had enough....''

She let the words trail off and Sophy looked at her curiously. ''What are you talking about, Marcie?''

The other woman hesitated, and Sophy had the feeling she was carefully assessing her next words. Then she gave

Sophy a very level glance. "Would you honestly like a chance at punishing Dr. Maximilian Travers?"

"I'd give anything to be able to teach him a lesson for what he did to me last night," Sophy heard herself whisper savagely. "But I don't see how that's possible. What could I possibly do to Max to repay him for what he did to me last night?"

"You could join me in what I have planned for S & J Technology," Marcie said simply. Setting aside her drink, she leaned forward and told Sophy exactly what revenge could mean and how it could be taken.

Chapter 5

The following evening Sophy stood in the corridor outside Max's hotel room, her hand lifted to knock. At the last moment she almost changed her mind. In an agony of suspense she let her knuckles hover just above the door panel.

It would be simple to turn around and forget the whole thing. But deep down she knew what she had to do. With a sigh, she rapped her hand gently against the door.

"Who is it?" Max called impatiently from within.

"Room service," she muttered, not feeling like yelling out her name. There was the sound of a phone being dropped into its cradle, and a few seconds later the door was swung inward.

"I didn't order any...Sophy!" Max stared at her, his eyes narrowing in wary surprise. His tie was hanging loose and his dark hair looked as though he'd been running his fingers through it. "What the hell are you doing here? I've been trying to call you all evening!"

"Would you rather I turned around and went home to wait for your call?" she murmured sullenly.

"Don't be ridiculous. Come in." Max reached out to grasp her by the shoulder, tugging her into the room and slamming the door shut behind her as if afraid she might escape. Then he released her and leaned back against the door. His eyes roved hungrily over the narrow white skirt and safari-style shirt she wore, and Sophy could guess the memories he was recalling. She edged away from him, moving across the room toward a chair. She refused to glance at the bed.

"You must be wondering why I'm here," she began, feeling a wave of unease as she realized she was back at the scene of her debacle. Max must have seen the expression on her face, because he levered himself away from the door and motioned to the chair near the window.

"Please sit down," he invited gruffly. "I'll order something from room service." He picked up the phone.

"Make mine tea," she drawled, sinking into the chair with what she hoped was nonchalance. "I had a little problem handling my liquor the last time I was here, so I'd just as soon not take any chances."

One of Max's dark brows lifted tauntingly. "Going to blame everything on the fact that you had too much to drink? You weren't really drunk and you know it, Sophy."

"Tea," she repeated, disdaining to argue with him.

Max's mouth hardened but he ordered a pot of tea for two. Then he came slowly toward her to take the chair on the other side of the small oval table. "You've been ignoring my call all day. When I came to see you at lunch you claimed you were eating with your friend Marcie. When I asked you to have dinner with me last night you said you had plans with Marcie. When I tried to contact you this afternoon you had someone say you'd been sent across town on an errand. All that avoidance and now you show up on my doorstep." He ran a hand through his hair. "Why, Sophy?"

"Why have you been trying so hard to see me?" she countered coolly.

"You know damn well why."

"You're feeling guilty?"

"Guilt doesn't enter into it," he gritted. "I want you."

"You've had me," she reminded him gently.

"Stop trying to be so darn blasé about the whole thing."

"What exactly do you want from me, Max? Another toss in the hay? A few evenings in bed to help relieve the boredom while you're in Dallas?"

"Sophy, you're trying to twist everything."

"Shall I put a more sophisticated label on it? Do you want an *affair* with me, Max?"

"Yes, damn it, I do!" he exploded.

"Ah." She nodded. "Marcie was right." Sophy leaned back into her chair while Max eyed her warily.

"Marcie?" he finally asked cautiously.

"Ummm. She told me she thought you wanted a full-scale affair. Said she could tell by the way you watched me run out of the office the other morning when she walked in on us. Marcie, you'll be interested to know, is a very shrewd woman. Has her eye on the highest levels of corporate management. And she knows a lot about what motivates people. Probably going to be very successful someday."

"Stop playing with me, Sophy. Are you here because Marcie said I wanted to go on sleeping with you? Believe me, that analysis didn't take any great intelligence on her part. Any moron could tell I want you."

Sophy flushed in spite of her determination to remain serenely cool. "You weren't the only one Marcie Fremont analyzed. She had the astuteness to also realize that I was thirsting for revenge.'' Max looked startled at the matter-of-fact way Sophy announced the information. ''But, then, she's a woman,'' Sophy continued coolly. ''Probably only another woman could understand the wish for revenge in a situation such as this.''

''Sophy…'' Max began dangerously.

''Which brings us to my reason for being here tonight,'' she interrupted evenly.

''Revenge?'' His smoky eyes were chilled.

''She suggested an interesting method, Max. Marcie proposed I continue with the affair. She thought I should show up on your doorstep tonight and admit that I simply couldn't stay away from your bed. She said I should imply I had been so overwhelmed by your virility and prowess in bed that I simply had no other choice but to surrender completely.''

''Your friend Marcie seems to know her way around the male ego,'' Max drawled.

''Oh, yes. She's under the impression that as a staid, shy, humble professor of mathematics who's unaccustomed to dealing with situations such as this, you'd fall for it hook, line and sinker.''

''May I ask what the point would be of leading on the staid, shy, humble professor?'' Max's expression was one of unyielding granite.

''Now we come to the real beauty of Marcie's plan,'' Sophy said rather wearily. She had been up most of the previous night agonizing over Marcie's idea for revenge. The weariness she felt now was physical as well as mental. ''While your male ego is thriving on my physical surrender, I am utilizing the opportunity to get close to you on every level.''

''Marcie suggested some weird scheme whereby you allow me to think you're mine and then you betray me with another man, right?'' he gritted.

"Nothing so primitive. Marcie Fremont is not a primitive sort of person. No, the idea was far more sophisticated than that. I'm to have my revenge on you by gaining access to the final version of the mathematical model you're doing for S & J Technology's new processing system. Once I have a copy of the model, I turn it over to Marcie.''

Max looked blank. "Who will do what with it?"

"Who will then use it to exact her own revenge on S & J. She will use it to buy her way into a management position at a rival company. Marcie Fremont has given up waiting to have her abilities discovered and appreciated. She's going to find her own way to the top.'' Sophy closed her eyes and leaned her head back in the chair, remembering the incredible conversation with her friend. When she lifted her lashes again, she found Max staring at her in amazement.

"Oh, my God," he growled.

"Don't look so disgusted," Sophy advised. "Frankly, I think it might have worked."

"You're not making any of this up, are you?" he demanded incredulously.

"Nope. I have to admit my imagination is not that good."

There was a knock on the door, and with an irritated movement Max went to get the tray of tea. "Thanks," he muttered gruffly, hurriedly signing the tab and adding a tip. When he closed the door and turned back into the room, Sophy was reaching for her purse.

"Hold on, Sophy. You're not going anywhere just yet. Sit down." There was a new element of command in his voice, causing Sophy to blink warily. She hadn't heard that tone from him before.

"I've told you everything I know, Max."

"Why?"

"Why what?"

"Why did you tell me about Marcie's scheme? Why not simply go through with it?" He sat down again and watched her as if she were some infinitely complex formula he was trying to solve.

Sophy hesitated, unwilling to put into words the real reason she had been driven into coming to see Max. He was not to know that in the long hours of the preceding night she had battled with her own inability to exact a fitting revenge in such a manner. He was not to know that she had finally acknowledged at three o'clock in the morning that she could not bring herself to harm Max Travers in such a manner. If she stole the math model, he was bound to be implicated. He would be immediately suspect for having sold his work to a higher bidder. She had known with frightening clarity that she could not do that to Max Travers.

Her first loyalty had been to Max. But never would she admit that she was here tonight because she had discovered she felt strangely bound to this man.

"My parents might not have succeeded in drumming the principles of Einstein's theory of relativity into my head, but they did manage to teach me something about honorable conduct." It was as good an excuse as any.

"I see." Max appeared to be working out a problem. There was a preoccupied gleam in his eyes now.

"Look, Dr. Travers, I think this has gone far enough. I came here tonight to warn you because, frankly, I'm not sure I'm going to be able to stop Marcie. She's dead set on getting even with S & J Technology. To tell you the truth, I think she has a right to do exactly that. They treated her pretty shabbily. I think I can make her see reason eventually. She just needs a few days to cool down. In the meantime, I was afraid...I mean I thought she might..."

"You thought she might go through with the plan on her

own somehow, right? So you decided to warn me, just in case." Max nodded, still looking thoughtful. "You're not interested in having your revenge, Sophy?" he finally asked.

She stiffened. "I'm not foolish enough to think there's much chance of real revenge in a situation like this. This sort of thing has been happening to women since the dawn of time, and the victims rarely get a crack at getting even. Not if the victims, unlike the victors, have a sense of honor!"

She knew she'd gone too far with that last sentence. Sophy saw the grim fury in Max's eyes as she voiced the insult, and she badly wished she could recall the appalling words. In the tense moment that followed she fully expected to reap a whirlwind in retaliation. Her fingers clenched on the arms of her chair and her chin lifted in unconscious pride and defiance.

The effort Max made to control his anger was visible. What astonished Sophy was that he managed the feat. But when he spoke again his words were measured. "If the corporate-espionage bit was a little too extreme for you, I'm surprised you didn't consider the other alternative."

"What alternative?" she asked cautiously.

"The one I suggested. That of having an affair with me—leading me on and then betraying me with another man."

"And thoroughly cheapen myself in the process!"

"Having an affair with me would make you feel cheap?" Slowly Max got to his feet.

"Yes." Sophy eyed him uncertainly. It was time to leave, she realized, getting to her feet as well. The atmosphere in this hotel room had gone several points above the danger level.

But even as the realization struck her, Max's hands were coming down on her shoulders. "You're determined to play the wronged woman in all this, aren't you?'' he bit out, giving her a small shake.

''I was wronged!''

''The hell with it. Since I'm already a condemned man in your eyes, I haven't anything left to lose, have I?'' He dragged her against him, forcing her head back over his arm as he lowered his mouth to plunder her lips.

Sophy struggled wildly as his kiss claimed her. It was the other night all over again, but she didn't have the excuse this time of being in a state of emotional shock or even of having had too much to drink. How can it be like this? she raged helplessly as she felt her body leap to life. *It isn't fair!*

She hadn't realized she'd spoken her last thoughts aloud until Max muttered his response against her mouth.

''What you do to me isn't fair either. Sophy, Sophy, please don't fight me. Just let me have you. I need you.'' His hands moved down her back to her hips, shaping the full curve with hungry familiarity. ''You can't walk away from what we had the other night. You can't expect me to walk away from it either.''

Sophy wrenched her head to one side, trying to avoid his seeking mouth. ''Max, you don't understand. I don't want this. I don't want a relationship based on physical attraction. I want a whole lot more than that. Why do you think I wouldn't go to bed with Nick?''

''For God's sake, don't talk to me about that damned cowboy! Not now!''

''I'm trying to make a point, darn you! I didn't go to bed with Nick because I was trying to build a relationship with him first. I have no intention of leading a life full of one-night stands!''

''The other night wasn't a one-night stand and you know

it,'' he gritted, and then fastened his mouth on hers so that her next words were caught in her throat.

"Max, no…" she gasped when he finally pulled away.

"If you want a relationship, build one with me!"

"In the few days you'll be here in Dallas?" she mocked furiously. "That's hardly likely, is it? You can't build a meaningful relationship in a few days, and even if it were possible, you and I couldn't do it in a lifetime!"

"Why not?" he demanded flatly, holding her still as he lifted his head to stare down at her taut features.

"Because a relationship has to be based on such things as mutual respect, and there's no way on earth a man of your intellectual caliber is ever going to be able to respect my abilities. The most I'd ever be for you, Max, is a toy," she snapped. "And I won't play that role for any man."

His mouth curved into a faint hint of amusement for the first time. "Are you trying to tell me you want to be loved for your mind?"

The humor in him pushed her over the edge. It severed the careful rein she had on her temper. How dare he laugh at her on top of everything else? "Even the thought of such a thing makes you laugh, doesn't it?" she blazed at him. "You insult me and then you have the nerve to wonder why I won't have an affair with you. Maybe you're not quite as bright as your academic achievements would indicate, Dr. Travers. Let me go!"

She stepped backward abruptly and his hands fell away, along with the amusement that had been edging his mouth. His eyes hardened.

"Sophy, stop it. You're behaving irrationally."

"Sometimes those of us at the lower end of the intelligence scale tend to function more on our emotions than on reason!"

"Then why don't you listen to your emotions?" he

charged. "The way you did the other night when you gave yourself to me!"

"I'm not that big a fool!" she flung back harshly. Darn it, if she wasn't very careful she was going to burst into tears, and that must not be allowed to happen!

Yanking at the door handle, Sophy fled out into the hall. All she wanted to do now was escape. She needed to be free of the compelling influence this man had over her; needed to be free of the torment of her own emotions.

"Sophy, come back here. You can't go on running away from me!" He came after her, catching up to her at the elevators, his strong hands reaching out to halt her flight. She whirled angrily to face him.

"Let me go!"

"Not until you calm down."

"Someone's going to come along any minute and see you manhandling me in the hallway," she pointed out tautly. "Is that what you want?"

"What I want is a rational conversation!"

"Then you'll have to contact one of your academic colleagues. I don't have much talent in that area. Or any other area you're likely to be interested in either!"

At that his eyes became abruptly darker. "Now, that is an outright lie," he drawled. "You have a great deal of natural talent in bed."

She stared him for an instant, utterly shattered by his wicked teasing, and then she lost her temper completely. Sophy slapped him. Not a ladylike tap on the cheek but a full-blown, arcing blow that had enough force behind it to snap his head to one side.

He didn't release her. When he looked back down at her there was warning in his gaze and his words were clipped. "I find your fiery temperament rather fascinating at times, but there are limits to how much of it I'll tolerate. Don't hit me again, Sophy.''

''Or you'll hit me back?'' she challenged. ''I always said you were a real gentleman!''

Satisfied with the frustrated anger that leaped into his eyes, Sophy wrenched herself out of his grasp and stepped into the elevator as it arrived. Without a word she stared straight ahead as the doors closed. Only when she was safely out of sight and she realized she was alone in the elevator did Sophy relax her internal hold on her emotions. The tears began to trickle slowly down her cheeks.

Oh, God, what was the matter with her? How could she let him affect her this way? Half-blinded by the gleaming moisture in her eyes, she found her way through the huge lobby of the hotel and out into the parking lot. There, in the safety of her car, she gave way completely to the emotional storm that seemed to be raging inside her.

Eventually she managed to control the bout of tears and make her way home. It was Friday night. A week ago she would have looked forward to spending the evening with Nick Savage. Now every time she tried to think of Nick, the image of Max got in the way. She realized vaguely that she couldn't even summon up any anger toward Nick Savage now. All her emotions seemed to be focused on Max Travers.

Why a wizard? Why a man who lived in another world, an unreal world? A man who could never share her life, only her bed? Why did it have to be Max Travers who had succeeded in tapping the emotion that had lain dormant within her?

Sophy asked herself that question over and over again during the long drive home. She asked it as she morosely poured herself a glass of Chenin Blanc and settled down in her rainbow-hued chair to consider her life. She was still asking it an hour later when the telephone rang.

"Sophy? Don't hang up, this is important." Max's voice came across the wire with clipped command. "I've just been in touch with Graham Younger about what you told me this evening."

"Max! You didn't! I never meant for you to go to the president of the company!" Shocked, Sophy pulled herself out of her dismal reverie, her anxiety taking a sudden new twist. "I told you I'd handle Marcie."

"Sophy, have you told Marcie you aren't interested in her little scheme?"

"Well, no, not yet…" No sense trying to explain that she had been reluctant to confess to Marcie that she couldn't go through with it. "But I will!"

"No you won't."

"Says who?" she shot back angrily.

"Says your upper management. They've got plans."

"The hell they have!"

"We're to be in conference room number eighteen-oh-nine at eight o'clock tomorrow morning. S & J Security will be there to discuss the situation."

"Max! What have you done? I only warned you to be on the safe side. I never meant for you to drag management and Security into this!"

"You could hardly expect me to let a thing like this ride on your assumption that you can talk Marcie out of it! From what you told me and from what I've seen of her, she seems quite likely to go through with some sort of corporate espionage on her own, whether or not you get involved. She has to be stopped. S & J wants her neutralized."

"Neutralized! For God's sake! You don't know her the way I do. There is no need to take this kind of action. Max, why didn't you call me before you contacted Graham

Younger? Why are *you* getting involved? Neutralizing would-be corporate espionage types is hardly your line of work. As long as you were warned, you could have taken a few precautions…"

"Just show up in the conference room on time, all right?" he asked wearily.

"Wait a minute. Tomorrow is Saturday!" Desperately Sophy tried to think. She could hardly refuse to show up. Not if she wanted to keep her own job at S & J secure.

"Exactly. Security figures there won't be too many people around."

She needed time to work this out. And she couldn't afford to jeopardize her job. Sophy chewed on her lip. "All right, Max. It doesn't look like I have much choice. I'll be in tomorrow at eight."

"I'll see you there." Max hung up the phone before she had a chance to beat him to it.

Sophy sat glaring at the instrument for a long time before she roused herself to fix something for dinner. She had gotten so wrapped up in her own dangerously emotional response to Max that she had neglected to think about the implications of this whole mess for poor Marcie. Somehow warning Max had taken precedence. She hadn't stopped to consider what might happen if he dragged S & J management into it.

Not wanting to annoy the highest levels of corporate management, most of whom she had never met in person, Sophy arrived a little before eight the next morning and walked through the silent halls to the conference room. Though she was early, everyone else, it seemed, was there ahead of her.

Apparently S & J Technology had chosen to take the matter of Marcie Fremont very seriously. Sophy sighed and wondered what she'd unleashed as she greeted the president

and his assistant very formally. Then she smiled at Sam
Edison, the rather harried-looking man in the polyester suit
who was in charge of S & J Security. She inclined her head
very aloofly to Max, who had risen politely when she entered the room. Flustered by seeing someone in their midst
rise to greet a mere secretary, the other males in the room
had awkwardly done the same. Everyone sat down with relief.

"Miss Bennet," Graham Younger began pedantically,
"we certainly appreciate your willingness to cooperate with
us in this matter."

As if I had any choice, Sophy thought, sliding a glance
at Max's impassive face.

"It was very good of you to go straight to Dr. Travers
with a report of the Fremont incident," he went on pom-
pously. "You have brought to our attention a serious threat
to this firm, Miss Bennet. Industrial and corporate espionage
are major problems these days. As a company involved in
high technology we are especially vulnerable. Therefore we
are most anxious to nip Marcie Fremont's larcenous ten-
dencies in the bud. We intend to make an example of her."

Sophy stared at the older man's implacable face, feeling
suddenly chilled. Poor Marcie.

"Miss Fremont is only a secretary, of course," the president's assistant put in mildly, "but we feel we must make
it clear that this sort of thing will not be dealt with lightly."

Only a secretary. The words were vastly annoying. "If
you'll excuse me, sir," Sophy said coolly, "I think too
much is being made of all this. I seriously doubt that any
corporate espionage attempt will actually be made. Miss
Fremont is not the sort to involve herself in that kind of
thing. Miss Fremont is very professional."

"I'm afraid we can't take the chance," Sam Edison put

in quickly. "We don't know who she might be working for."

"That's right, Miss Bennet," Younger said evenly. "Frankly, we don't believe Miss Fremont is working alone. This sort of sophisticated plot requires planning at much higher levels. We don't just want to stop her. We want to find out who she's working with and stop the entire espionage ring."

"Espionage ring! I don't think…" Sophy began earnestly.

"We're not asking for your opinion, Miss Bennet," Younger interrupted coolly. "You will be expected to give your full cooperation to our plan."

Sophy bit back her annoyance. "What plan?"

"As I understand it, Marcie Fremont seems to feel you, ah, have reason to be rather upset with Dr. Travers. A lovers' quarrel or something. You're supposedly motivated by revenge," Edison said quickly, obviously uncomfortable with the delicate matter.

Sophy's mouth fell open in amazement. Then her head swung around and she pinned Max with an infuriated glare. "You told him about…about…" Words dried up in her throat. The tide of her fury threatened to stifle her. Max had told S & J management that she wanted revenge because of a lovers' quarrel? She'd kill him! She'd slice him apart with her pinking shears!

"Calm down, Sophy," Max cut in sharply. "I explained that Marcie apparently misunderstood the situation between us and is trying to capitalize on it."

She stared at him. Everyone else in the room was looking distinctly uncomfortable, including Graham Younger. *They know,* she thought. *Max is going to answer for this!* Exerting her willpower to the utmost, she managed to bring her shaking fingers under control and bury them in her lap.

"What, exactly, do you want me to do, Mr. Edison?" she asked far too softly.

"Well, we, er, that is, if you'd pretend to go through with Miss Fremont's plan, we might be able to trace the flow of information. Dr. Travers will supply you with a phony version of the math model he's working on. You will pass it along to Miss Fremont and we'll be watching to see who she gives it to."

"Pretend to go through with Marcie's plan?" Sophy's eyes went to Max. He met her glare unflinchingly, but she could read nothing in his expression.

"Sophy," he said coolly, "I have explained to everyone in this room that you and I are not, uh, romantically involved and that Marcie simply misunderstood the situation. What Sam is asking is that you pretend to be involved with me and that you tell Marcie you're going through with the espionage scheme."

"There will, of course, be a bonus in it for you if the plan works," Graham Younger put in.

"I see." So, on top of everything else, they intended to buy her cooperation. Sophy had never felt so disgusted in her whole life. They were trying to trap her just as they intended to trap Marcie. And with the unlimited ego of the ruling elite of the business world, they assumed it would be a snap to manipulate two dumb little secretaries. Sophy let the heavy silence reign for a few minutes, refusing to surrender to the pressure. All of these males needed a lesson.

"I suppose you won't believe me if I tell you that you're all overreacting?" she finally murmured quietly.

"I think we're the best judges of the sort of reaction required in this instance, Miss Bennet," the president's assistant declared politely. "If you just concentrate on the bonus and on your duty to S & J Technology, we'll do the rest."

The bonus. Sophy smiled coldly. Let them think she was going to do it for the money. Let them think they could push Marcie and herself around. "Very well," she finally agreed. "I'll cooperate." There was a collective sigh of relief from everyone except Max, who eyed her warily but said nothing.

Sam Edison leaned forward, his elbows planted on the table, and intently began to explain their plan. The more he talked, the less she thought of it, but she let him babble on because she was busy making a few plans of her own.

An hour later she and Max both left the offices of S & J Technology, but they left separately.

"Meet me at the hotel," he ordered brusquely as he said goodbye.

"No more orders, Max." She faced him in the building lobby. "Is that very clear? We're supposed to pretend to be lovers, but I won't go a step farther unless you agree to treat me as an equal partner in this stupid scheme."

"Sophy, I don't like this charade any better than you do, believe me!"

"I suppose there's nothing to do but make the best of it."

"Agreed. Now, how about lunch?" He sounded relieved.

"Lunch?"

"We are supposed to be spending the weekend together, remember? Part of the charade," he reminded her patiently. "I was wondering what plans you would like to make for lunch."

"Oh." She considered the matter and then said, "Actually, I did have some things to do today at home. Maybe dinner—"

"I'll bring some papers along and work on them while you're doing the things you wanted to do around your apartment," he interrupted. "We can have a sandwich or something for lunch. Doesn't have to be fancy."

For an instant Sophy thought she saw the jaws of a very lethal trap closing around her, and then she dismissed the image. She could handle Max Travers. As well as the management of S & J Technology.

Actually things might be easier if Max was busy working. She knew how totally involved people like him became when they were in the middle of a problem. She'd seen her parents disappear into their study for endless hours often enough. "All right, if that's what you would prefer."

"I'll get my briefcase from the hotel," he said before she could change her mind.

An hour later Sophy found that having Max in her kitchen was a strangely unsettling experience. He immediately adopted the kitchen table for a desk, appearing quite satisfied with the surroundings although they must have been much different from those in which he normally worked.

"What are you going to be doing this afternoon?" he asked as she opened the refrigerator to prepare sandwiches.

"I'm making a dress for one of the women at the office." Sophy found some cheese and a tomato and placed them on the counter. "Whole wheat bread or rye?"

"Rye please." He waited a moment and then said carefully, "That black dress you brought into the office the other morning looked rather nice."

She smiled cynically. "Thank you."

"Do you make your own clothes too?"

"Max, I know you're not really interested in discussing my sewing. Mustard or mayonnaise?"

"Both. What makes you say I'm not interested in your sewing?"

"Let me see if I can remember all the reasons why someone shouldn't take a hobby like sewing too seriously," she drawled, recalling her parents' lecture on the subject. "It's frivolous, takes up time that could better be spent on studying, and doesn't really engage the brain to any important extent."

"Whom are you quoting?" He half smiled, looking up from the table to watch her make the sandwiches.

"My mother and father. They were horrified when it became apparent that dress design wasn't going to be just a hobby for me but my main interest in life. They're going to be even more shocked when they find out I intend to open a design boutique here in Dallas." She slapped the cheese on the bread and sliced the tomatoes. When she turned to carry the sandwiches over to the table, she found Max smiling at her.

"It was hard on you, wasn't it, Sophy?" he asked quietly. "Growing up with two academically brilliant parents…?"

"Who couldn't bring themselves to admit that they hadn't produced an equally brilliant child. Yeah, it was a little tough at times." She smiled wryly. "But I survived. And so did they."

"They love you."

"I know."

"You're lucky," he murmured.

She glanced up, frowning. "What do you mean?"

"Only that through all the trauma and the frustration, at least you knew you were loved."

"Meaning you weren't?"

"My parents were a lot like yours, Sophy. They wanted a child in their own image. But they were far too involved in their own careers to waste any time on loving me. They simply saw to it that I was given the best possible education. They apparently thought that was all that was necessarily to raise a child."

She watched him uneasily. "You don't love your parents? They don't love you?"

"We can discuss higher math until three in the morning, and that's generally what we talk about when I visit. But that's about all we do together. When I was a kid I remember several Christmases when we didn't even have a tree because my parents were so busy with their studies and their research that they just forgot to get one. When they remembered presents they were always the educational variety."

"No crayons?" she asked with a smile.

"No crayons. Or anything else that was just plain fun."

Sophy felt a tide of compassion for the little boy who had been programmed to be a genius and who was never allowed to deviate from the program. Firmly she squelched the sensation. Damn it, she was not going to allow this man to play on her sympathy.

"You don't trust me, do you, Sophy?" he asked.

"Would you in my place?" she countered.

Unexpectedly he smiled. "You could try seducing me and we could find out what my reaction would be. I think I'd trust you afterward."

"Forget it." She got to her feet and picked up her dish. "Do you want ribs or a steak tonight? I'd better get them out of the freezer now so they'll be ready to barbecue later."

"A steak sounds fine."

"Okay." She reached into the freezer and dragged out a package. "I'll look forward to seeing you earn your keep tonight."

"What's that mean?"

She glanced up ingenuously. "I'll look forward to watching you grill the steak tonight," she clarified politely.

Max's mouth lifted wryly. "Sorry, you're out of luck. My domestic skills are limited to opening cans and sticking frozen dinners in microwave ovens."

Sophy's sense of humor rose to the surface. Exactly as she had suspected. "Another gap in your education. You can't type and you can't barbecue. Well, Max, prepare yourself. You're in Texas now, and here in Texas every real man knows how to grill a steak."

"Now, wait a minute, Sophy…"

"No excuses are necessary. Tonight, Max, you're going to cook a steak. Consider it an extension of your education."

Chapter 6

When she emerged from her elaborately outfitted sewing room later that afternoon, Sophy smelled smoke. Curious, she followed the scent through the kitchen, where Max's paper work was neatly stacked on the table, and out onto the patio. There she found Max, white shirt smudged with charcoal, eyeing the small flame he had produced in the pit of the barbecue grill.

"You look as if you're going to be forced to walk across the coals in your bare feet," she teased as he continued to stare at the charcoal with deep suspicion.

"Sophy, I told you I don't know much about this sort of thing," he growled.

"What good is a man who can't barbecue a steak?" she asked flippantly. "I'll go see about the salad. Women's work, you know." With a small sense of triumph that she knew was really very childish, Sophy went back inside the kitchen. He was going to ruin the steak, of course. It was a small thing, but he was going to make a fool out of himself in front of her and the thought brought some satisfaction. Well worth the price she had paid for the meat.

From time to time as she went about the business of preparing the salad and warming crusty rolls, she glanced surreptitiously out the window to watch Max. He was deep in concentration, intently studying the few instructions printed on the back of the package of charcoal briquettes. Sophy laughed to herself, relishing the moment when he would actually have to put the meat on the fire. She just hoped he realized that he was supposed to put it on the grill and not directly in the flames!

He was getting anxious, she thought as she came and went on the patio, setting the small, glass-topped wicker table and arranging the salad dishes.

"About ready for the steak?" she asked brightly.

Max looked up from his intent contemplation of the coals and started to say something. Whatever it was, he changed his mind at the last moment and nodded brusquely. Sophy smiled serenely and went back inside to get the meat.

"A pity to sacrifice a good piece of steak," she muttered to herself as she hoisted the tray and carried it out to Max with a flourish. "But it is going to be interesting to see just how burnt the offering is before he elects to serve it to me."

Max's gaze narrowed as he watched her approach with the meat. "Sophy, are you sure you don't want to take over?"

"Nonsense. Any man can grill a steak. It's an instinct, I believe. Every man I've ever known could handle a barbecue. Except my father, of course," she added blandly. "And I guess, now that I think about it, there were a few other exceptions. Mostly academic exceptions. Let me rephrase my original statement. Every man I've ever *dated* could handle a barbecue and a steak."

"In other words, you don't date men who can't project

the machismo image, is that it?'' he gritted, practically yanking the glass tray out of her hands. ''Should I buy a horse and start wearing a six-gun?''

''I wouldn't bother going to the expense, if I were you. After all, you'll only be in town a short while, remember? I'll fix you a drink. Men usually sip a whiskey or something while they're grilling a steak.''

''Actually,'' he retorted, carefully unwrapping the steak from its plastic covering, ''that sounds like one of your better ideas.''

Sophy grinned again and went back inside to fix the drinks. After handing him his, she sank down onto the nearest patio chair, propped up her feet and prepared to witness the debacle. Max had already thrown the meat on the grill. Much too soon, she thought critically. It was going to be charred on the outside and raw on the inside.

''I'll tell Marcie that I'm going along with her big plan on Monday morning,'' Sophy said conversationally. ''How long shall we wait before I turn over the fake information?'' No sense telling Max she had other plans for S & J.

Max didn't look up from the burning steak. ''A week, maybe. We can't rush it any more than that or she'll be suspicious.''

''If she's as smart as I think she is she'll be suspicious anyway. Honestly, this has got to be the craziest scheme I've ever heard. Hard to believe it came from a man of Graham Younger's stature.''

''Don't forget that the head of Security thinks it will work too.''

Sophy shook her head in disgust. ''Let's drop it, Max.''

''What would you like to talk about?'' he asked evenly.

She lifted one shoulder negligently. ''Anything but higher mathematics.''

"How about your plans to open a design boutique?" he surprised her by suggesting.

She watched him through half-concealing lashes. "Are you sure you're interested in my plans?"

"Sophy, anything that you're involved in interests me," he said simply.

She hesitated. "Okay, but don't blame me if you get bored quickly."

"The one thing I never am around you is bored." He gave her a fleeting smile. "I think you're my missing crayons."

"Your what?"

"The crayons I never had a chance to play with as a child. Life has always been rather black-and-white for me, Sophy. You're like a rainbow in it."

Sophy stared at him, uncertain how to take the gentle confession. He was doing it again, she thought, making her feel sorry for him, eliciting her compassion. She was going to have to be extremely careful around this man. He was proving to be dangerous in ways she would never have expected.

"Well, pay attention," she ordered gruffly. "My folks will want to know all the shocking details of my decision to make my dress designing into a career." And while he finished massacring the steak, she told him about her plans for the future.

"Designing and sewing for people has been a sideline for me since college, but it's only been during the past year that I've actually considered making a full-time career out of it," she concluded. "Dallas, with its optimistic, adventurous, anybody-can-get-rich-here atmosphere, seemed like a good place to try my luck. That bonus Younger promised me this morning might make the difference between my being able to take the plunge a few months from now or a year from now." Except that she never intended to collect that bonus!

"Is that the real reason you agreed to go along with the plan? The bonus?" Clearly he was remembering her comment about Marcie's threat to his career.

"Let's just say it was an excellent incentive," she murmured, not wanting to discuss the issue. The truth was, she realized unhappily, if Max hadn't been threatened along with S & J, she might have been tempted to let the company take its chances. It might teach management a good lesson if it got ripped off by a "mere" secretary! Now she had to concoct a more involved scheme to show Graham Younger the error of his ways.

Max stared down at the incinerated steak, and she sensed the wary anxiety he was feeling about the meat's condition. "I guess if we're ever going to eat, it might as well be now," he said.

"Lovely," she drawled smoothly, rising to her feet. "I'll get the wine."

The steak was charred almost beyond recognition. In a land where everyone preferred his meat rare, it was a total disaster. Oh, there was a rare, almost raw section left in the center, Sophy noted as she cut into her piece, but it looked quite unappetizing surrounded by the overdone part. There was little if any natural juice left in the meat. Max had stabbed the poor thing so many times with his cooking fork that it had all drained out. Dry, charred and tough, the steak was as thoroughly ruined as it was possible for a piece of meat to be. Sophy should have been feeling a sense of triumph.

After all, Max was clearly feeling as nervous and awkward about his failure at the barbecue as she would have felt trying to work a problem in one of his math classes. It was a small thing, but Sophy told herself she was giving him a taste of being a failure. Served him right. As she took the first bite she considered exactly how she would show her disdain for his inability to cope with such an elementary task.

Then she glanced up and found him watching her with nervous dread apparent in his gray eyes. He was waiting for the axe to fall, she realized abruptly. He knew as well as she did that the meat was terrible, and he undoubtedly knew exactly what she was going to say. There was a grim, stoically resigned expression on his hard features. He hadn't held his own against the men he was being measured against and he knew it. He'd probably known from the beginning that he didn't stand a chance. What hope did he have, never having grilled a steak before in his life?

Sophy read the reaction in him and told herself it was all she could have wished. Now was the time for a cold, cutting remark and a few choice, derogatory comments on his failure as a chef. It wasn't much, but it might be all the revenge she ever got. In some small way she had a chance to show Max Travers that as far as she was concerned, he was a nonstarter in her world.

"It's delicious," she heard herself say as she chewed with polite greed. "Exactly the way I like it. Honestly, everyone here in Texas insists on serving it so raw that it bleeds all over the plate. I've been too embarrassed to tell anyone that I like my meat well-done."

He stared at her, plainly astonished. He wasn't the only one, Sophy decided ruefully; she was equally startled at her words. But she knew she wasn't going to retract them. Instead she gave him a genuine smile and passed the glass salad bowl. What in the world was the matter with her?

Taking it automatically from her hands, Max continued to survey her intently. "You like it?" he finally managed.

"Ummm. I guess you have a natural talent for the barbecue, after all. Would you like some steak sauce?'' She was pouring a lot over her own meat. It might help.

"Yes, thank you," he murmured humbly. Then he visibly began to relax. "I was a little uncertain about the timing," he confessed, picking up his own knife and fork. "You're sure you like it well-done?"

"My favorite way," Sophy assured him cheerfully.

He took his first bite and chewed steadily for a long moment. "Don't you think it's a little tough?" he asked diffidently.

"That's the fault of the meat, not you." She smiled. "It was a cheap cut. They usually turn out tough on the grill." Actually, she'd paid a fortune for it.

"Oh." He nodded wisely, apparently relieved.

"I probably should have served the ribs, but I wanted to use up this beef. It's been in the freezer quite a while." Another lie. Why?

"It's not very juicy," he said tentatively, obviously appealing for more reassurance.

"That's because it spent so long in the freezer," she lied gamely. "Have a little more steak sauce on it."

Max appeared to relax even further. "Maybe we should have marinated this steak beforehand," he said very knowledgeably.

Sophy stifled a laugh. All the marinating in the world would not have compensated for the way it was treated on the grill. "You're probably right. Next time I have an old, cheap cut of beef, I'll try marinating it first. You did an excellent job with what you had to work with, Max. Delicious."

Why, she asked herself anxiously, was she bothering to pretend Max had acquitted himself well at the barbecue? Why hadn't she seized her small moment of triumph? What on earth had made her compliment him on the ruined meat just as though he were a man she really cared about, a male whose ego she wanted to soothe?

Damn it! This was the man who had deliberately taken advantage of her, and here she was comforting and reassuring him! She must be out of her mind.

By the end of the meal, Max was showing signs of reacting to his success at the barbecue the way men always react to their triumphs. He was pleased with himself, jovial, willing to talk about anything and everything. A man on top of the world. Sophy didn't know whether to laugh or cry. It occurred to her that she might have created a monster.

"Next time I think I'll experiment a bit with the coals," he informed her seriously. "I think it might be a good idea to let them die down a little first before putting on the meat. What do you think?"

"Possibly," she agreed cautiously. "I'm really not much of an expert on barbecues."

"Because you always leave that side of things to the men in your life?" He smiled wryly. "Well, now that I'm the only man in your life, you won't have to worry about whether or not your next date can grill a steak, will you?"

Sophy looked at him helplessly. She *had* created a monster. "Are you as good at washing dishes as you are at barbecuing?"

"Better. I've had more practice in that department. Been a bachelor for thirty-six years, you know. I've washed a lot of dishes in my time."

"That may be more of an asset in the long run than being accomplished at the barbecue," she said lightly, rising to begin clearing the table. "A lot of women would value that talent more than barbecuing skill!"

"How about you, Sophy?"

"I've got a dishwasher," she informed him sweetly.

"Good thing I passed the test at the barbecue grill, then,

isn't it?'' he drawled softly behind her. "Since my other skills don't count with you?''

"Would you like some dessert, Max?'' Determinedly, she started toward the kitchen with a stack of dishes. Damned if she was going to let him drag her any deeper into the quagmire that seemed to be stretching at her feet.

"Sure. What have you got?''

"Ice cream?''

"I can prepare ice cream even better than I can grill a steak,'' he confided cheerfully, opening the freezer and searching out the carton of chocolate ice cream she had inside.

What was she going to do with him this evening? Sophy wondered a little nervously. He was settling in very thoroughly. Very soon now she was going to have to make it quite clear that she had no intention of playing out Graham Younger's charade to the extent of allowing him to spend the night. Sophy began to feel trapped by the complex web of circumstances. She must perform this balancing act very carefully or face disaster.

She was lecturing herself on that point when the doorbell rang imperiously. "Now what? One more problem is all I need.''

Max glanced up from his task of shoveling out huge scoops of chocolate ice cream. "What did you say?''

"I said, there's the doorbell,'' she lied politely, wiping her hands on a towel and walking into the living room to answer it. Who could it be on Saturday night? If it was Sam Edison or someone from S & J Technology checking up on her, she would be furious. On the other hand, what if it was Marcie Fremont?

Sophy opened the door with a frown and found all six feet, three inches of Nick Savage standing there. She stared at his handsome face in utter shock.

"You were the last person I expected to see here to-night," she informed him starkly. "What the hell do you want?"

"You," he said with devastating simplicity. He pushed the Stetson back on his head and his eyes gleamed down at her. "I figured I'd given you long enough to get over your little temper tantrum. I've missed you, darlin'."

Sophy was incredulous. "You've *missed* me! What an idiotic thing to say! The last time I saw you, you had plenty of company, as I recall. Go visit your blond girlfriend if you're lonely this evening."

Nick put out a hand and tousled her curls in the old, familiar manner. "You know, you're kinda cute when you're mad, honey. Now stop glaring at me and I'll explain all about Trisha."

"If Trisha is the blond, I'd just as soon not hear all the details."

"Honey," he drawled, "Trisha was just a way of fillin' time until you were willing to let me into your bed. She means nothin' to me. She's just a good-time girl."

"Well, go have a good time with her. You're not going to have one with me, I guarantee!" she hissed.

"Now, you don't mean that and you know it." He smiled confidently. "You're just a little upset because you caught me foolin' around with Trisha. I wouldn't have been, you know, if you'd kept our date that night."

"How dare you make it sound as if it were all my fault! You've probably been playing around with her all the time I've known you!"

"Like I said, honey, I was just fillin' in time—"

"Oh, shut up, Nick, and leave. I'm really not interested in discussing this further."

"Now, that's where you're wrong, darlin'. We both know you're very interested in discussing this. You're in love with me, remember?'' His voice was smooth and assured. Nick was very sure of himself, Sophy realized.

"You really believe you can just walk back in like this and everything will be all right?'' she whispered scathingly.

"I know you're a little upset about Trisha...''

Sophy shook her head. "Oh, Nick, you don't even have an inkling, do you?''

"I've got more than an inkling of how you feel about me,'' he murmured, stepping through the door. "You might be mad as hell about that little scene by the pool, but you'll get over it. With some help.''

On the last words, he hauled her into his arms and lowered his head to find her mouth. Sophy stood perfectly still, deciding that the quickest way to discourage him was to show him that he couldn't influence her now with his casually expert lovemaking.

Even though she had no intention of betraying any reaction, it still came as something of a surprise to Sophy to find she *had* no reaction. Where was the pleasant warmth she had once experienced in Nick's arms? Why wasn't she responding even a little to the sensuous expertise he wielded so well?

Sophy was still working that one out when Max Travers's voice cut through the air like an uncoiling whip.

"Take your hands off her, Savage, or I'll stuff that Stetson hat down your throat!''

Sophy jumped, as much from the shock of hearing such violence in Max's tone as from his unexpected interruption. "Max!'' She tried to push herself away from a grim-faced Nick, but he reached out to hold her, his arm gripping her shoulders. They both stared at Max, who was standing in the kitchen doorway with the carton of ice cream still in one hand.

"Who the hell is this?'' Nick asked in astonishment,

clearly not seeing any threat in the man who was challenging him.

"I'm the man who took her to bed the night you had your private little poolside party with the blond. Remember me? I was standing right behind Sophy when you came out of the cabana. I took her to my hotel after the show."

"Max! Please!" Sophy felt anger and fear rising up and twisting together in her stomach. She was angry at Max for his blatant claim on her, and she was afraid for him—afraid that Nick Savage would tear him apart. Already she could feel the fighting tension in Nick's body. The arm locked around her shoulders tightened.

"I don't believe you," Nick said dangerously. He sent a disdainful glance over Max. "You're not exactly her type."

"Maybe not," Max agreed easily. "But she's my type. Ask her. Ask her if she didn't spend the night with me. Ask her if she didn't give herself to me completely that night. *Go ahead! Ask her!*"

"What the hell's he talkin' about, Sophy?" Nick didn't look down at her, his whole attention on Max, whom he clearly couldn't imagine as real competition.

"He's just trying to be protective," Sophy said hurriedly, pulling free of Nick's grip. "He saw you that night by the pool and he's trying to protect me from you!" It was all she could think of at the moment. Damned if she was going to stand there and admit Max was telling the truth! The bastard! When this was over she'd give him a piece of her mind.

"I see," Nick said coolly. "Well, there's no call to play Sir Galahad. The little lady and I can work this out for ourselves. We don't need your interference. Why don't you run along and finish eating your ice cream? On second thought, why don't you just leave altogether? I don't much like the idea of Sophy here entertaining other men in the evening, even if they do let her cry on their shoulders.''

Sophy caught her breath as Max slowly put down the carton of ice cream and removed his glasses. Automatically he began polishing them on his shirt. "I'm not going anywhere, Savage. You're the one who will have to leave." He held the frames up to the light, squinting to check the polishing job. "Tell him, Sophy."

"Tell him what?" she snapped, enraged and genuinely frightened now. If Max didn't stop goading Nick there would be hell to pay. On the other hand, she told herself a little violently, maybe Max deserved to find himself flat on the floor.

"Tell him you're mine now. That you've spent a night in my bed and that you'll probably spend tonight with me too." He replaced the glasses with great care.

"Not tonight, too!" she shouted, and realized too late it was the wrong thing to deny. She should have denied spending the first night with him. Nick's narrowed eyes swung to her instantly.

"Sophy?" he began with soft menace, and for the first time Sophy realized just how dangerous the situation really was. She summoned her poise and faced him as coolly as possible.

"I think you'd better leave, Nick."

"Why, you little bitch!" he snarled. "It's true, isn't it? You actually went to bed with this little nerd, didn't you? Of all the cheatin', lyin', little bitches!" His hand came around so fast, so unexpectedly, that Sophy didn't even have a chance to avoid it. Nick struck the side of her face in a flat, vicious slap that sent her sprawling to the floor. She was too stunned even to cry out.

Before she could gather her senses, the room seemed to explode around her. She saw Max's nearly silent rush across the jade green carpet and cried out. "Max, no! He'll kill you!"

But neither man paid her the slightest attention. The atmosphere in the room had gone very primitive in a hurry, Sophy realized, terrified. She struggled to a sitting position, her palm on her sore cheek, and watched in horror as Nick closed with Max.

The police! If she could just get to the phone... Sophy tried to rise to her knees and succeeded in doing so just as Nick landed with a thud on the carpet beside her. Eyes wide with shock, she knelt, looking down at him. Then she glanced up at Max, who was calmly brushing off his sleeve.

"Are you ready to leave yet, Savage?" Max asked quietly.

"I'm gonna kill you, you bastard!" Nick gritted, getting to his feet and launching himself at Max in a low, powerful rush.

The results were the same as before. Max did something very economical and smooth with his hands and Nick landed once again flat on his back. This time he didn't get up quite so quickly. Max stood calmly waiting for him.

"You think 'cause you got lucky a couple of times I can't take you?" Nick muttered furiously. "Well, you're wrong. I'm gonna take you apart limb from limb!"

Max easily sidestepped the next bull-like rush, slicing down with his hand as Nick flew past. Like a matador in a ring, he toppled the other man with a seemingly casual display of skill. This time Nick didn't rise at all. He simply lay groaning on the floor. Sophy watched, half-numb with shock, as Max went over to his fallen victim and crouched beside him.

"Come near her again, Savage, and I'll do a lot more damage. She's mine now and she stays mine. You don't want her, anyway, remember? You threw away your chances with Sophy the night you screwed that little blond by the pool. You're a fool, but that's not my problem. Go find yourself another little blond.''

Nick glowered up at him, massaging his arm. ''I'll get you for this!''

Max raised one eyebrow. ''Why bother? Would you really want her back? Knowing she gave herself to me so easily after refusing you for months?''

Nick's angry glare swung back to where Sophy still knelt on the carpet. ''Cheatin' little bitch. Nah, I don't want her,'' he spat. ''You can have her!'' He rolled to his feet and lurched furiously for the door. Max rose slowly, his eyes never leaving his opponent. On the threshold, Nick turned to stare briefly at him. ''I guess you won her fair and square, nerd, but take some advice. Don't let her string you along the way she did me. Made a damn fool out of me, puttin' me off while she decided how she really felt! Led me a real dance, she did.''

''While you were busy dancing with someone else?'' Max half smiled.

''Man's got a right to some action on the side,'' Nick grunted huffily.

''Goodbye, Savage.'' Max waited for the other man to leave. Neither male glanced at Sophy, who was beginning to feel like a doe during mating season. Never in her life had she had a fight conducted over her, and the experience was the most primitive and unpleasant she had ever been through.

Without another word Nick slammed the door behind him and stalked down the path toward the waiting Lincoln. It wasn't until they heard the muted roar of the powerful engine that Max turned slowly to confront Sophy.

In absolute silence they regarded each other across the room. Sophy felt a combination of wariness and relief that left her trembling. Slowly she staggered to her feet, clutching at the nearest chair for support. She didn't like the glinting, fundamentally male expression in Max's smoky gray eyes.

"Max?" she began uneasily.

"I think," Max said slowly, "that the dumb cowboy may have had a point." He started toward her with an even, purposeful pace. "I did win you fair and square, didn't I? And I would be a fool to let you string me along, wouldn't I? You belong to me now."

"Max, stop it!" she whispered, backing away carefully as he approached. "I mean it. Stop it."

"I just fought a knock-down, drag-out battle for you, lady. I've never fought over a woman in my life."

"Max, this has gone far enough. I won't have any more violence in this house!" She backed away another step, chilled at the implacable look on his face.

"No," he agreed. "No violence."

"I'll call the police!"

"Not just now." He spoke almost absently as he came to a halt a foot away from her and lifted a hand to touch the cheek Nick had struck. "If he ever tries to hit you again I'll kill him."

Sophy shivered as he possessively smoothed her cheek. Her eyes never left his face. She could feel the male aggression flowing from him, a by-product of the fight, no doubt. And she knew before he said another word that she was going to be the target of that aggression.

"You belong to me," he repeated in a soft, rasping voice. "I just won you fair and square." He pulled her into his arms.

Chapter 7

The unfathomable, unnerving, incomprehensible part was that a part of Sophy agreed with him. She was shaken, overwhelmed by the violence that had just taken place. She was equally unsettled by the knowledge that, having lain once in Max Travers's arms, she no longer felt anything when Nick Savage kissed her. What had this wizard done to her?

She couldn't seem to think logically as his mouth descended to claim hers. Sophy tried to tell herself that she shouldn't be responding so unreservedly to Max's compelling hold, but her lips parted in surrender beneath his and she knew the truth. She was deeply attracted to this man and she wanted him. In some distant corner of her mind she even acknowledged that the attraction went far beyond anything she had ever known—perilously close to love. Oh, no! She must not be in love with him!

He was all wrong for her! But even as the lecture rang through her brain, Sophy heard a soft moan and knew it came from her own throat.

"I want you, sweetheart," Max grated as he teased her mouth with his own.

"Oh, Max…"

"I'm going to take you tonight," he muttered, pulling away to look down at her flushed face with burning eyes. His hands moved compellingly along the length of her spine, finding the nerves at the bottom of it and kneading sensually. "I'm going to strip all these bright clothes from your beautiful body and find the rainbow underneath. And then I'm going to make love to the rainbow. Oh, God, Sophy, don't try to stop me. Nothing could stop me now. I need you too much."

She trembled in his embrace, knowing that she wouldn't stop him even if she could. "Wizard," she whispered, burying her face against his shoulder.

She knew he sensed the surrender in her. She could feel the triumph and satisfaction in him, yet at the same time his hands on her were tender. Locked against the length of his body by one of his arms, Sophy felt him fumbling with the fastenings of her clothes. His fingers trembled slightly with the force of his desire, but they didn't hesitate. The colorful cotton knit skirt and top were lying in a pool at her feet before Sophy was fully aware of what had happened.

"You have skin like silk." Max brushed his lips along her shoulder while he undid the clasp of her small bra. When the garment fell away, he groaned and curved his palms wonderingly around her breasts. "I love the feel of your nipples when they get hard under my hands. Like small, ripe berries."

His hands slid to her waist, lifting her up with an easy strength. When her breasts were level with his mouth, he nipped erotically at both before lowering her down along the length of his body. Sophy shivered and whispered his name.

"Put your arms around my neck and hold on to me while I get undressed," he ordered thickly. Obediently she did as she was told, twining her arms around him. She met his steady, fiercely glowing gaze as he unbuttoned his shirt and unfastened his belt buckle. A moment later his clothes, too, lay on the floor, and he stood fully naked in front of her.

Deliberately he reached up to catch hold of her wrists, drawing her hands down over his shoulders, across his chest and along the firm, taut line of his stomach. Then he bent his head and plunged his tongue deeply into her mouth as he pushed her hands down further to the throbbing evidence of his desire.

Sophy gasped at the bold demand, but the masculine aggression in him brooked no denial. With delicate fingers she found the waiting hardness and gently caressed.

"Sophy," he groaned into her mouth, "Sophy, your touch is enough to send me out of my mind!" He deepened the kiss and slid his hand around to clench the curve of her buttocks. When Sophy gasped again, he slipped his palms inside the nylon panties she still wore and found the secret hidden in the triangle of tightly curling hair. Impatiently he pushed the panties off altogether.

"Oh, Max!"

"I can feel the heat in you, sweetheart," he groaned as he began to stroke magic patterns on the heart of her desire. "So warm and welcoming. Put your arms back around my neck."

"But, Max..." She wanted to go on touching him, exciting him. Arousing a wizard was heady business.

"Do as I say, my sweet love," he urged. When she once again had her hands locked around his neck, he pushed his bare foot between her legs, gently forcing her to stand with her feet apart.

Sophy was suddenly aware of feeling incredibly, sensuously vulnerable. Too vulnerable. Instinctively she started to lower her hands, but he stopped her with a muttered word and a reassuring kiss. She trembled as he began to caress her more intimately, his fingers boldly invading her body.

"I want to know I can make you want me," he growled huskily as his hand stroked the fire in her. "I want to feel you trembling and hear the soft sounds you make when you're aroused. I want you to know just how much you want me, too. Tell me, Sophy. Tell me with words as well as with your body!"

Her head fell back as she looked up into his passion-carved face. How could she deny this wizard anything he asked tonight? She belonged to him. He had fought for her and now he seemed to have every right to seduce her. God help her, she was feeling every bit as primitive as he was.

"Max, I want you. You must know I want you," she got out in a throaty little voice.

"Did you ever want that damn cowboy this much? Did your body become hot and damp and did you tremble when he touched you?"

"No," she gasped as he did something unbelievable to the center of her. "No, never like this. It was never like this with him.... It's never been like this with anyone," she added helplessly as she moved against his hand. "Please, Max, please make love to me...."

"I am making love to you," he drawled gently.

"You know what I mean." Urgently she writhed, forcing her hips closer to his.

"What do you mean, Sophy?" he growled. "Tell me exactly what you mean."

"Take me," she begged. "Here. Now. Please take me." She used her hands on his neck, trying to make him sink to the carpet with her. Slowly he followed her as she went down to her knees.

"You're sure this is what you want?" he taunted.

"Don't tease me, Max!" Sophy went down onto her back, pulling him urgently across her body.

"I only take what's mine," he warned deeply.

"I am yours," she cried, opening her thighs for him. "Oh, Max, I *am* yours. I belong to you."

"Fair and square," he murmured hoarsely, and then he was completing the union with a rush of power and strength that momentarily deprived her of breath.

Sophy gave herself up joyously to the passionate wizardry of the man who was claiming her body so completely. There might be a price to pay later, but tonight everything seemed right. There was no alternative tonight other than to succumb to this thrilling torture.

The overwhelming excitement seemed to twist tighter and tighter within her until Sophy thought she would break apart into a thousand glittering pieces. Max seemed to understand every nuance of the sensations that assaulted her, and he capitalized on each one. His body drove relentlessly into hers, mastering, taking, leading and guiding. She could do nothing but cling to him, her legs wrapped around his waist, her arms clutching at his shoulders.

Higher and higher they raced until the final twisting convulsion claimed Sophy completely.

"Oh, my God, *Max!*"

"Yes, darling, yes," he ground in her ear, nipping savagely. "Hold on to me and let yourself go."

Her throat arched and her eyes were tightly shut as Sophy let the tide of passion sweep through her. She was dimly aware of an exultant masculine cry and felt Max's body go rigid in the final response. Then she was drifting, catching her breath and marveling at the utter relaxation of her body.

When she gradually surfaced a long time later it was to find Max still lying along the length of her, his legs tangled with her own. She opened her eyes to find him balanced on his elbows, looking down into her face. For a moment they stared at each other.

It was Max who broke the spell of bemusement. "If someone had told me two weeks ago that I would take advantage of a woman and seduce her and then fight some cigarette-ad cowboy for her and follow that up with another seduction, I would have told him to go play with an abacus. Sophy, you bring out a side of me I never knew existed." He looked dazzled and stunned by his own actions.

She lifted a hand to play with the hair at the back of his damp neck. "And if anyone had told me I'd be seduced by a wizard, I would have said he was crazy. Max, what have you done to me?" she whispered, dazed.

"Made you mine." He dipped his head and feathered a kiss along the top of her breast. Then he licked the glistening perspiration that had collected in the hollow between the two soft globes. "And I'm going to go on making you mine again and again until you finally believe it yourself. I want you to know it for a fact, not just when I've got you lying under me like this, but every waking moment of your life."

She didn't know what to say—didn't really want to say anything. It was all too frightening and dangerous to consider closely. Her instincts bid her flee and her body said that was impossible. When she stayed silent, her blue-green eyes wide and eloquent, his mouth kicked upward in wry amusement and he kissed her gently. "Don't fight me, Sophy. I want you so, and I can't resist reaching out to take you."

Her lashes lowered as Sophy realized she couldn't maintain direct contact with his eyes. She licked her lips tentatively, aware of the swollen feel of them. Her whole body felt the vivid aftermath of passion. "Max, why didn't Nick beat you to a pulp?"

"You thought he was going to, didn't you?" he retorted whimsically. "You were afraid for me, weren't you?"

"Yes." It was the truth. She had been terrified that Nick would hurt him badly.

"I like having you worried about me," Max decided.

"But how did you handle him so easily? It was like watching a matador and a rather awkward bull. You didn't even get your shirt rumpled."

He grinned, a wicked, utterly masculine grin that told her just how pleased he was with himself. The triumphant male. "Right," he stated categorically, "was on my side."

"Uh-huh. Along with a little scientific judo?"

"Hapkido," he corrected. "I work out with a colleague of mine who's an expert." He lost interest in the matter, beginning to toy with the crown of her breast. "You make me feel so unbelievably fantastic, Sophy. I would have fought ten clones of that cowboy tonight for the right to possess you." Before she could say anything he suddenly came alert.

"What's wrong?"

"The ice cream! I just remembered I left it sitting on the table over there. It's going to be melting all over the place." He got to his feet in a lithe movement and strode across the room to collect the rapidly softening ice cream. At the doorway into the kitchen he turned and glared at her. "Don't move. I'll be right back."

Sophy stayed where she was, not at all certain she could move. Her body felt boneless, utterly satiated. Her mind was in a shifting, dreamy state that was new to her. She had no will to look beyond the present. It was far easier to focus only on this moment. Sophy was still telling herself that when she realized Max was standing beside her.

"Now you can get up," he murmured, reaching down to lift her to her feet.

She opened her eyes and drew in her breath at the arrogant maleness of him. Every inch of his body seemed to tug at her senses. The musky scent of him was intoxicating. When she came to her feet in front of him, she stumbled as her legs refused to function properly.

"Poor Sophy," he whispered, sounding quite satisfied with her unsteady condition. "You're not sure yet what's happened to you, are you?" He bent and lifted her easily into his arms and smiled as the curling mane of her hair tumbled across his shoulder.

"Where...where are we going?" Not that she would be able to protest if she didn't like the destination, Sophy decided with an inner smile. She was too enthralled by Max's wizardry tonight to do anything else except stay with him.

"To bed."

She leaned her head against his shoulder, her fingers playing idly with the fascinating cloud of hair on his chest, and let herself be carried down the hall to the bedroom. There in the darkness he settled her gently onto turned-down sheets. Then he stood for a moment, drinking in the sight of her lying in the center of the bed, waiting for him. Sophy could read the exultant arousal that was beginning anew in his eyes. Wordlessly she opened her arms.

"Sophy, you make my blood sing." Then he was lowering himself to her once more, gathering her close. All through the endless night Sophy stayed safely locked in the wizard's possessive embrace. She refused to think about the coming dawn.

Ultimately, it wasn't the dawn that awakened her the next morning. It was the ringing of the telephone. Sophy came drowsily to her senses, aware that the bed was empty beside her and aware, too, of the fragrance of freshly made coffee.

The phone rang again. There was something about the phone in the mornings, she reminded herself vaguely. Something about the phone ringing on Sunday mornings. Was it Sunday? Her mother always called on Sunday mornings. With a start, Sophy struggled to a sitting position and reached for the extension beside the bed.

Before she could pick it up she heard Max answer on the living room extension. Helplessly Sophy listened to his greeting. She prayed that it was not her mother.

"Hello? No, you've got the right number. This is Sophy Bennet's apartment. What? Who's this? This is Max Travers speaking. Why, hello, Dr. Bennet. Good to talk to you again. How's the weather back there? Hotter 'n' hell down here in Texas. You were right about Dallas, by the way, all chrome and glass and western atmosphere. Did you know they've still got real live cowboys left down here? Not as tough as they used to be. Then again, maybe they never really were all that tough to begin with. Maybe we've all just been fed a romanticized image of the western folk hero."

Her worst fears confirmed, Sophy quickly lifted the bedside receiver. "Max, wait. Mother? This is Sophy. That's Max on the other extension. He, uh, came by early this morning. I'm taking him to see some of the local sights." Frantically Sophy rushed into the conversation, desperate to correct the impression her mother must have gotten when Max answered her daughter's phone so early in the morning.

"I see," Anna Bennet began, only to be interrupted by Max again.

"Sophy's been very gracious to me, Dr. Bennet," he drawled easily. Where the hell had he picked up that faint Texas drawl? "She and I grilled steaks last night and this morning we're going to have breakfast together. Then we'll have to see about making some plans for the rest of the day."

"You're having breakfast together?" Anna Bennet inquired with a mother's deep interest. "It's rather early for Sophy."

"You can say that again. She's still in bed. I was just about to take her some coffee, in fact, to help her get her eyes open," Max chuckled fondly.

"Max just arrived, mother," Sophy put in abruptly. "He caught me a bit unprepared." Shut up, Max, she begged silently. For God's sake, just shut up!

"How's your husband?" Max was saying cheerfully. "Good. Tell him I got a chance to read that paper he gave me on Jordan curves. Fascinating."

"He'll be looking forward to discussing it with you when you get back to Chapel Hill," Anna Bennet said. "And I'm so glad you and Sophy are hitting it off well. You know, Sophy was hanging around with some cowboy, last we heard, and her father and I were a trifle nervous about the relationship, to say the least."

"Mother!"

"No need to worry about the cowboy," Max assured Dr. Bennet a little too smoothly. "He's not in the picture any longer. Rode his horse off into the sunset."

"Max!"

"Well, that's reassuring," Dr. Bennet said happily. "Sophy, dear, you know how I felt about that cowboy. When you lived in California I used to dread your getting involved with some long-haired surfer type. Then when you moved to Texas I had to worry about cowboys. Such a relief to know you're seeing a nice young man like Max. Why don't you talk Max into coming back to Chapel Hill with you next weekend?"

"Excellent idea," Max put in swiftly before Sophy could hedge.

"I'm sure he's much too busy…" Sophy tried valiantly.

"I can manage the time."

Sophy could practically see her mother's beaming smile. "Fine. What times does the flight arrive at the Releigh-Durham airport, Sophy dear? Your father and I will meet the plane."

"The flight gets in at ten-thirty," Sophy sighed, knowing she was beaten.

"Wonderful. We'll be there. Can't wait to see both of you. Oh, and Max, thank you so much for looking Sophy up down there in Dallas."

"Believe me," Max drawled, "it's been my pleasure. You don't have to worry about Sophy anymore, Dr. Bennet. I'll be looking after her here in Dallas."

"Well, of course, Max," Dr. Bennet said, sounding vaguely surprised he should even bother to mention the subject. "Paul and I both know you're a gentleman as well as an outstanding scholar. See you next weekend!"

"With pleasure," Max laughed. "I could use a couple of days back in an academic environment. You know what a thrill it is to get out into the real world and lend industry a hand," he added derisively. "Actually, the only thing that has made this trip worthwhile is Sophy."

"Goodbye, mother!" Sophy tried to infuse a certain amount of command into her voice, and fortunately the other two seemed to sense it.

"Goodbye, Sophy, dear. And goodbye to you, Max. See you soon."

Max and Sophy put down their separate extensions simultaneously, but Sophy's came down a good deal harder. "Damn it! Max, how could you!" she shouted.

He appeared in the doorway of her bedroom, coffee in hand, a charmingly bland expression of inquiry on his face. "How could I what?"

Hastily Sophy yanked the sheet up to her throat, blushing

at the possessive gleam in his eyes as he surveyed her in bed. "What on earth were you thinking of, answering the phone at this hour? Do you have any notion at all of what my mother must be thinking? She'll be weaving all sorts of marriage plans around the two of us, if I know her. She's probably already planning on enrolling him at Harvard!"

"Enrolling who?" Max looked at her blankly.

"Their grandchild!"

"Oh, him. I was thinking of Princeton, myself. That's where I went to school. Best math department in the country…" He broke off to dodge the pillow Sophy hurled at him and managed the feat without spilling the coffee.

For some reason the casual masculine grace of the movement stirred memories of his lovemaking during the night, and Sophy grabbed another pillow in blind self-defense.

"Sophy, honey, wait a minute." Max grinned, coming forward with the coffee in a gesture of appeasement. "Just listen to me."

She ignored him but dropped the pillow back on the bed as she got to her feet and grabbed for her robe. "No, you listen to me, Dr. Travers. You can play all the male games you want and my parents can dream all the dreams they want, but I am not going to be the ball you big cats bat around for fun, is that clear? I'm going to live my own life. I will not be your mistress, in spite of what happened last night. I will not settle down to producing little wizards for my parents to educate. I am going to open my own business here in Dallas and I'm going to date all the cowboys I want to date. And if and when I ever decide to marry, I'll send you all an invitation."

"Sophy!" As Max set down the coffee cup, his voice lost its teasing tone. Suddenly it held ice and steel. "To begin with, I don't recall mentioning marriage."

"Then you shouldn't have answered that telephone and

implied to my mother that we're sleeping together!'' she stormed, inexplicably hurt by the way he brushed off the word *marriage*. What was the matter with her, anyway? Of course she had no intention of marrying him. Why should she want him to be thinking of it?

"But now that the subject of marriage has arisen," Max put in deliberately, "I think it should be discussed."

That made her even angrier. "It sounds like much too academic a subject for me. I'm going to take a shower!" She whirled. How dare he treat it so deliberately and...and *academically?*

"Now hold on just one damn minute, Sophy Bennet." Max reached for her and yanked her around to face him. His gray eyes glittered with sudden male dominance. It occurred to Sophy that Max had undergone a dangerous transformation in the few days she had known him. That first night, when he had taken her out to dinner, he had been far more diffident and unassertive. She would never have guessed that in such a short time she would find herself not only seduced by him but intimidated on something other than an intellectual level.

"Let me go, Dr. Travers!"

"In a moment, Miss Bennet. There are a few things we should get settled first. What happened last night doesn't just get wiped out by a phone call from your mother, or because you're having second thoughts this morning. You're mine now. I told you that last night, and what's more important, you admitted it."

"I was...was caught up in an emotional, highly charged situation and I...I..."

"Are you going to claim I took advantage of you again? That you were emotionally vulnerable and I pushed you into bed? Don't bother, Sophy. It won't wash. You and I are definitely, undeniably *involved*, whether you like it or not. We're having an affair—''

"Two nights in bed together doesn't constitute an affair!"

"It does in our case," he retorted coldly. "Furthermore, I have some surprisingly primitive feelings on the subject of fidelity. Don't threaten me with cowboys ever again, because if I ever catch you with another cowboy or any other man, I'll beat you so thoroughly you'll think studying differential calculus was a treat by comparison!"

Sophy couldn't believe her ears. "And to think I once considered possessiveness in a man rather quaintly attractive, a sign of affection. But it's nothing but the basic male ego at work, isn't it? You think that because you've made love to me a couple of times you can set down all kinds of rules!"

"I haven't just made love to you a couple of times, Sophy Bennet," he gritted. "I have also fought another man for you and I have had you surrender completely in my arms. That gives me all kinds of rights, and I'm sorry if you don't like the possessiveness. It's a little new to me, too. I haven't ever felt quite this way about a woman before. But I'm damn well not going to go back to the stage where you walk all over me."

"I never tried to walk all over you! I simply tried to put as much distance as possible between us!" she cried wretchedly.

"Well, we're not going back to that stage either," he vowed, hauling her against his half-nude body. "I've worked too hard to get close to you!" He crushed her mouth under his, ignoring Sophy's impotent attempts at freeing herself.

She was terribly vulnerable, trying to battle him while she stood nearly naked in his arms, Sophy realized hysterically. All the memories of last night's passion were still too strong, especially in these surroundings—the rumpled bed; the memory of the way his shoulders had blocked out the moonlight when he'd lowered himself to her in the middle of the night. Even the scent of their lovemaking seemed to hover in the air. And they all contrived to leave her without any weapons when he forced his kiss on her lips.

God help her, Sophy thought agonizingly as she felt her body's reaction to Max's embrace, she was falling in love with the man. This wasn't mere sexual attraction, and it wasn't anything like what she had known with Nick Savage. She would be fooling herself terribly if she pretended she wasn't falling in love with Max Travers. And it was all so hopeless. He was so very wrong for her. Just as wrong as she would be for him. She would not be his crayons!

"Sophy," Max groaned huskily, "don't be afraid of me or of what we have together."

She shivered in his grasp, but whatever she would have said was lost in his deep kiss. When he lifted his head, they both knew the fight had gone out of her. Wordlessly she freed herself and headed for the shower.

Over breakfast forty minutes later she tried the rational approach. Pouring herself another cup of coffee, she took a deep breath and plunged in. "Max, have you given any real thought at all to what everyone's going to think if you go back to Chapel Hill with me next weekend?"

"Sure. They'll think we're passionately in love." His smile was very bland and very dangerous.

She must never forget for one moment that the intelligence behind those smoky eyes was formidable, Sophy reminded herself. Men like this had always been intimidating, but since she had left the academic world behind they had never posed a real threat to her. Now this man had moved into a sphere in which she should have been more than able to hold her own. And he was outmaneuvering her. He was ably assisted by her own traitorous emotions.

She had to fight or go under the tidal wave that threatened to engulf her.

"Well, we'll just have to make very sure that folks back in North Carolina don't accidentally get the wrong impression, won't we?" she said with a smile every bit as bland as his own. But she could still hear the satisfaction in her mother's voice.

And I'll have to make damn sure I learn how to stay out of Max Travers's bed, she added with grim conviction.

Chapter 8

On Monday morning Sophy walked into the offices of S & J Technology with a briefcase full of business-oriented magazines lifted off her coffee table and a profound thankfulness that Max had displayed a certain forbearance the night before. He had allowed himself to be sent home after dinner, much to Sophy's astonishment.

She hadn't questioned her luck, but she did question the emptiness of her apartment after he'd gone. Briskly she thrust aside the thought and walked toward Marcie's desk with firm purpose.

The blond looked up expectantly, a bit surprised.

"Marcie, we need to talk."

Warily Marcie bit her lip. "I know. It was a stupid idea, wasn't it? Of course you don't want to go through with it. And now that I've had the weekend to think it over, I don't either." She sighed. "I want to make it to the top, and I'm willing to be a little ruthless to get there, but I guess the truth is I'm not willing to compromise myself."

Sophy smiled. "I had a hunch you'd feel this way. But there's something else we need to talk about. Let's go down to the cafeteria and get some coffee."

"But it's too early to take a break," Marcie noted uneasily.

"Believe me, taking an early break is the last thing we should spend time worrying about. Marcie, this is important."

"All right."

Fifteen minutes later they secluded themselves at a corner table with two cups of hot coffee. A few members of junior management cast displeased glances at the pair of secretaries who had dared to take an unofficial break, but nothing was said.

"I don't know what got into me on Thursday," Marcie began unhappily. "I was so damned furious over being rejected for that promotion. I let my temper get the better of me."

"And I was just as angry over the fool I made of myself with Max Travers." Sophy couldn't bring herself to explain about the manner in which she'd run to Max to warn him and how everything had blown up in her face. There was no point, she told herself. This was a time for action. "Both of us let our anger get the best of us for a while. But when all is said and done, we really were rather justified, don't you think?"

Marcie smiled wryly. "Oh, yes. I think we both had justification."

"When dealing with a large corporation, a certain amount of subtlety is necessary," Sophy murmured thoughtfully as she stirred cream into her coffee. "And that applies to the fine art of teaching a lesson."

Marcie stared at her. "What are you talking about, Sophy?"

"I think the management of S & J needs a lesson."

"What kind of lesson?"

"It needs to learn that mere secretaries should be taken a bit more seriously in the future."

"Sophy, you look very dangerous right at this moment," Marcie observed.

"I'm feeling a little dangerous. And a little reckless. We're going to find you a job, Marcie."

"A job!"

"Ummm. Oh, not here at S & J. We're just going to make sure that S & J appreciates what it lost when it loses you."

Marcie grinned. "A pleasant thought, but I don't see how we can manage that."

Sophy opened her briefcase and drew out a handful of booklets. Automatically Marcie leaned over to read the titles. "*Women in Business? Successful Women? Profiles of Successful Women and their Corporations?* Sophy, what are you going to do?"

"Find you a job at management level in one of the female-run technology firms profiled in these pamphlets. Oh, there aren't a lot of them because most such firms are run by men. But there are a couple, and all we need is one good one." She fanned out the pamphlets and grinned. "Pick a company, Marcie. Any company."

"And then what?"

"Then we convince that company they can't survive without you," Sophy said simply.

"What if the company doesn't happen to have any job openings?"

"It will. A good company always has openings for brilliant managers."

"And how are we going to make me look brilliant? The only jobs I have on my résumé are secretarial positions!"

"We start by rewriting your résumé," Sophy said. "And we go from there."

"Sophy, I get the feeling I'm seeing a new side of you."

"Not really. I just haven't had much chance to display this side before now," Sophy laughed.

Throughout the rest of the day Marcie snatched every spare moment to study the magazines and pamphlets Sophy had given her. While she did so, Sophy concealed a copy of her friend's résumé among the pile of papers on her desk and surreptitiously made notes.

"It's too bad no one realizes just how much a good secretary really learns in the process of her work," Sophy noted at one point.

"I'm tired of waiting for recognition. You know the first thing I'm going to do when I get a high-level position, Sophy? Hire a male secretary."

"One with good legs?"

"Go ahead and laugh. I'm going to do it. It will be a symbolic action."

"I'd rather like to see Max Travers working as someone's secretary," Sophy decided wistfully. "The man can't even type."

As if the thought of him had conjured him up, the phone on Sophy's desk rang. Before she even said hello, she had an instinctive knowledge of who would be on the other end of the line.

"Sophy? I'm going to have to stay late with the programmer and work on this processing model this evening. I was planning to take you out to dinner tonight, but it looks like we'll have to postpone it. I'll call you later this evening."

Sophy heard the preoccupied note in his voice and almost found it endearing. The wizard at work. It was amazing, actually, that he'd even remembered to call. She knew a sense of relief mixed with a very real disappointment at the information that she would be spending the evening alone. "That will be fine, Max."

Her sense of disappointment had become anxiety by that evening, when she analyzed the situation. She was aware of feeling pressured, trapped and terrified at the prospect of being in love with a man who was totally wrong for her.

How could Dr. Maximilian Travers ever really love and respect a woman who wasn't his intellectual equal? And how could she love a man who was destined to spend his life in an ivory tower?

"What I want is a man who can laugh with me as well as make love to me," she muttered aloud as she lay stretched out under the kitchen sink, preparing to fix the leaking fitting. "I want a man who lives life down here on my ordinary, humdrum level, not in the rarefied atmosphere of an academic tower. Damn sink. I want a man who can respect my abilities. A man who really thinks I'm his equal, not a toy he can play with. I'm not a pack of crayons, for crying out loud!"

The doorbell cut into the monologue.

"Oh, for pity's sake!" she exclaimed, as a box of soap nearby fell over when she scrambled out from under the sink. Sophy glared at it and at the evidence of the leak she had set out to fix. Then, grumbling, she headed for the door. Max Travers was on the threshold.

"What I really want," she gritted, waving the wrench at him, "is a man who knows how to fix a sink, unclog a toilet and grill a steak!"

Max's gaze went from the menacing wrench to the yellow tee shirt and orange trousers Sophy was wearing. Then his eyes went to the smudge on her nose and he smiled. "You want a plumber who can cook?"

"This is not funny!" She glared at him and then thrust the wrench into his hand. "Here. Show me you can do something useful in the world. We don't need more people who can think in five dimensions at the same time; we need people who can fix leaky plumbing. Cheap. What good is a man who can't fix a faucet?''

His eyes slitted as he looked down at the wrench. ''You're in a swell mood, aren't you?''

''I mean it, Max. If you can't fix my faucet, just get in your car and go back to your hotel!''

''Sophy, I came here tonight to talk to you, not to fix your sink,'' he began reasonably, stepping inside the door and shutting it firmly behind him.

''Well, I don't have time to talk.''

''Listen, honey, why don't you just call a plumber? Or the apartment manager?''

''At this hour of the night? It's nearly ten o'clock,'' she exploded. ''One doesn't call managers or plumbers at ten o'clock at night unless it's a real emergency!''

He frowned. ''Well, isn't it?''

''Max, all that is necessary is to use this wrench to tighten up a loose fitting on the pipe under the sink,'' Sophy retorted with exaggerated patience. She spun around on her heel and stalked back to the kitchen. ''I realize that someone with a Ph.D. in mathematics might find such simple household repairs beyond his ability, but the rest of us have learned to take care of the little problems in life.''

''Sophy…''

She heard the incipient irritation in his voice and ignored it. ''Go away, Max. Tonight I need a man who knows and understands the real world, not a mathematician.''

''Damn it, Sophy, give me the wrench!'' He yanked it out of her hand just as she was about to lower herself back under the sink.

Sophy looked at him in astonishment. He was scowling

rather fiercely. "Forget it, Max. I don't want a bigger leak than the one I've already got."

"I'll fix your damned sink!"

"You don't know how to fix a sink!"

"I learned how to grill a steak, didn't I? You said yourself there are some things men are supposed to know instinctively. Well, I'm a man and I've got instincts like every other man. I'll put my instincts up against those of any dumb cowboy you can find in Texas! Now, get out of my way, woman. I'm going to fix the plumbing."

Sophy blinked and found herself stepping aside. She thought about telling him he'd cooked a lousy steak, but for some reason she couldn't do it. He looked so determined to fix the sink that she didn't have the courage to refuse him the opportunity. He was already examining the unique shape of the wrench in his hand. The next thing she knew he was crouching under the sink, eyeing the shape of the fittings. She watched him check the position of the leak, and then his hand tentatively went to the fitting above it.

"That's the one," she grudgingly admitted, kneeling beside him and peering at the piping.

"Geometry," he muttered. "Simple geometry."

"You fix plumbing your way and I'll fix it mine. I don't use geometry!"

He leaned down and turned over on his back, sliding under the curved pipe. "This," he said in satisfaction, "is going to be a snap compared to grilling a steak."

Sophy got to her feet with a muffled groan. What was she going to do if he succeeded in actually fixing the damn fitting? "As long as you're down there…" she began.

"If you're going to make me spend the whole evening working on your plumbing, you can darn well think again. One fitting is all I'm going to do tonight."

"What I was going to say," she shot back far too sweetly,

"is that as long as you're down there, I thought I could give you some advice."

"Wonderful."

"Don't waste any more time working up a fake computer math model of that processing system. I can tell you right now that Marcie isn't going to steal it."

He paused and she wondered at the sudden stillness in him. "You're sure?"

"I'm sure."

Another pause. "What about, uh, Younger's big charade?" he finally asked carefully. "Our posing as lovers and all."

"Oh, that can stand as it is," Sophy said airily.

Another pause. Longer this time. "Mind telling me why?"

"I've got plans of my own. Besides, we'll never be able to convince Younger that his scheme won't work. For the time being I want to act as though I'm still following orders."

"Sophy..." He sounded abruptly worried.

"Don't fret, Max. I'll explain everything when it's all over. I'm just telling you a bit now so you won't waste your time dummying up a fake printout. You can let Younger think you're still working on it, though."

"Sophy, I don't know what you're up to, but I don't like it."

"Don't worry about it, Max. This is my world. I know what I'm doing."

"I do not want you getting into any trouble," he began adamantly.

"The only trouble I have at the moment is a leaking faucet. How are you doing down there?"

"I don't know yet."

"There was one other thing I wanted to mention."

"I knew it," he groaned. "What is it?"

Sophy took hold of all the fortitude she possessed. "Max, I am not going to sleep with you again. Is that very, very clear?"

There was a sudden loud clang as something metallic scraped harshly along something else that was also metallic and then fell on the floor of the cupboard.

"Max! Are you all right?"

"Damn it to hell," Max growled.

"What's wrong?" she asked anxiously, going down on her knees to glance inside the cupboard.

"Nothing." The single word came out sounding like a curse. It was followed by another four-letter word that was definitely out of the "expletive deleted" variety. "I'm just fixing the darned sink."

Sophy climbed back to her feet, frowning worriedly. "Oh. Well, did you hear what I said, Max?" Somehow it was easier having this very necessary conversation with him trapped under the sink. Sophy realized that the last thing she wanted to do was to have to look him in the eye while she told him she wouldn't go to bed with him.

"I heard you. Would you please hand me a rag?" One strong arm extended itself from the confines of the cupboard. Wordlessly Sophy stuffed a rag into the waiting fingers. "Thank you," Max said very politely, and went back to work. Several moments passed. Sophy began to grow restless.

"Max?"

"Hmmm?"

She cleared her throat. "Max, I mean it. I know I haven't given you any reason to think I have willpower, but I assure you—"

"What I'd really like at the moment, Sophy, is a drink. I think the fitting is going to stay tight now." He began to inch his way out of the cupboard. Then he was crouching in front, surveying his handiwork while he wiped his hands on the rag. He looked rather pleased with himself, Sophy thought, and squelched an inner groan of dismay. "You know," he announced, "that wasn't really too hard. It's just a matter of analyzing the situation and then applying the wrench in the proper manner. Take a look."

Sophy slanted him a long glance and then obediently bent down to check his workmanship. "It looks like it's stopped leaking," she agreed cautiously, and realized almost at once that wasn't enough. He was hovering beside her like a proud artist showing off his masterpiece. Max wanted some genuine applause, and for some damn fool reason she couldn't resist giving his ego the stroking it wanted. "You did a terrific job." She could have kicked herself for saying the words he wanted to hear. "It's definitely stopped leaking." What else could one say about a fixed pipe? She leaned into the cabinet and tested the once-loose fitting. "Oh, that's on a lot more securely than I could have managed," she added brightly. Idiot. What was the matter with her? But Sophy couldn't bring herself to denigrate his first attempt at fixing plumbing. "You're very useful around the house, Max. I really appreciate your help tonight. That leak has been pestering me for days."

"No problem," he declared smoothly, getting to his feet. "Now, about that drink?"

"Actually," she said carefully, "I was going to pop some popcorn and watch an old movie on television this evening." Best to scare him out of the house before things got dangerous, Sophy told herself firmly. And she *had* been planning to watch the film.

He looked closely at her. "What old movie?"

"Nothing you'd be interested in, I'm sure," she said quickly. "It's one of those old science-fiction thrillers from the early fifties. You know, *The Eggplant That Ate Seattle* or something. You wouldn't like it at all.''

"Why are you going to watch it?" he asked, leaning back against the counter.

"Because those old science-fiction flicks are hilarious," she said without thinking.

"I could use a good laugh after working on that damn program all evening and coming home to fix broken plumbing." Max rubbed the back of his neck in a gesture of weariness.

Sophy flinched at his use of the word "home" and narrowed her eyes. "It will keep you up rather late, Max. If you're tired, you should go back to the hotel and get some rest."

"I can rest sitting on your couch watching the film. Where's the popcorn? I haven't had popcorn in ages." He glanced around the kitchen in anticipation.

"Max..."

"There's the corn popper. Up on top of your refrigerator. I'll get it down for you." He reached up to lift the machine down before she could find any words of protest. "Now, where's the oil?"

She grimaced. "It *has* been a long time since you had popcorn, hasn't it? That's one of the new air poppers. It doesn't use oil."

"Oh, yeah?" He glanced down at the machine in his hands. "How does it work?"

"You mean the physics of it?" she drawled, rummaging around in the small pantry for the popcorn. "I wouldn't have the vaguest idea. All I know is that you dump the corn in here and turn the sucker on. Presto! Popcorn."

"Fascinating."

"Uh-huh. Something tells me you're not going to be equally fascinated by this movie, Max," Sophy warned above the roar of the popping machine. "Are you sure you shouldn't be heading back to the hotel? You must be tired."

He gave her a level glance. "I'll survive."

She sucked in her breath. "I meant it, you know. You can't spend the night here, Max." She studied the growing pile of fluffy popcorn in the bowl on the counter.

"Are you afraid of me, Sophy?" His voice was low and gentle.

"I've behaved like a fool with you. I suppose we're all a little afraid of people who can make fools out of us."

"Look at me, honey."

Her head lifted warily. There was a curiously earnest gleam in his smoky eyes. It made her even more uneasy. "Max, please, I..."

"Don't be afraid of me, Sophy. Just relax. Treat me like a man, not a mathematician," he said with a faint edge of humor curving his mouth. "Give me a chance, honey. I told you I've got all the normal instincts."

"I've already encountered your normal instincts!" she snapped, switching off the popper. "On at least two different occasions. And as far as I'm concerned, that's twice too often. I meant what I said, Max. There will be no more sex between us! Now, if you're going to stay and watch this movie and eat my popcorn, you'll have to give me your word of honor as a gentleman that you won't force yourself on me."

He sighed, folding his arms across his chest. "Sophy, listen to me."

"Your word, Max."

"All right, all right. My word as a gentleman and a scholar. You can eat your popcorn in peace."

She chewed her lip and then nodded, accepting his promise. "Okay. You can stay. But you won't like it."

"Not being able to make love to you? I know I won't like it, but I'll live."

"I meant the film! You won't like the film!" she corrected waspishly as she carried the popcorn out into the living room and set the bowl down on the coffee table. Then she switched on the television.

"How can you be so sure of what I'll like and not like?" he demanded, following her into the front room.

"Believe me, this is not going to be your kind of film. The science in it is shoddy in the extreme. Mostly, it's completely lacking. Lots of bug-eyed monsters and mad scientists."

"I know a few of those, myself," he retorted equably.

"Monsters or mad scientists?"

"Mad scientists. Hey, the film's in black-and-white."

"I told you it was old. These were pretty low-budget flicks." She sat down beside him on the couch and reached for the popcorn. "Just let me know when you get bored and want to leave."

"I'll let you know," he promised sardonically.

But he didn't get bored. Much to Sophy's surprise, he joined with her in cheering for the monster and booing the newspaper reporter and the good scientist who were trying to stop him. The corny dialogue and ridiculously old-fashioned special effects sent Sophy off into gales of laughter, and Max was not far behind. Together they wolfed down the entire bowl of popcorn and gave the monster a lot of advice on how to survive. But at last the creature went down, drawn under the sea in a whirlpool created by the scientist.

"Gone but not forgotten," Sophy pronounced. "He'll return, mark my words. You can't keep a good monster down."

"I hope not. I'd like to see him return. He was a fairly

decent sort of monster. Not his fault the humans kept getting in his way. All he wanted was to feed off the energy in those bombs.'' Max leaned his head back against the couch, his legs stretched out in front of him. He glanced at Sophy. ''Thanks.''

''For what? The popcorn?'' she asked lightly.

''And the film. I've never seen anything quite like it.''

''Obviously you had a deprived childhood.'' She smiled. ''Personally, I would have had a deprived one, too, if I hadn't snuck downstairs late at night to watch television. I also nourished myself during my formative years with a pile of super-hero comics I kept stashed under my mattress. I read them with a flashlight under the covers.''

''I didn't get to read a comic until I was in college,'' Max said quietly. ''Not even the funny pages from the newspaper. My parents thought they were silly and frivolous. To tell you the truth, I agreed with them.''

''They are silly and frivolous. That's why they're good for you.''

Max smiled. ''You're good for me,'' he said softly, reaching out to gather her into his arms.

Instantly Sophy was on her feet, scooping up the empty bowl of popcorn. ''I think it's time you went home, Max.'' Turning her back on him, she headed for the kitchen. Behind her she heard him slowly get to his feet.

''It's a long drive back downtown…''

''Then you should have left earlier.''

''Before I found out whether the monster or the scientist won?'' he protested, ambling into the kitchen behind her.

She swung around, her chin lifted proudly. ''I meant what I said, Max. You're not staying the night.'' There was almost a pleading note in her words.

He looked down at her for a long moment, and she could read nothing in the depths of his eyes. Then he lifted his hand to toy with the curls that fell on her shoulders. "Such wonderful hair," he breathed, leaning forward to inhale the scent of it.

"Good night, Max," she whispered huskily. Already she could feel the flickering sensual tension beginning to flare between them. But this time she would not succumb.

"Sophy, at least let me kiss you," he murmured in that low, persuasive voice that he always seemed to use when he got close to her. It played havoc with her senses. Sophy's fingernails bit into the softness of her palm, but she held fast to her resolve.

"No, Max."

"I want you, sweetheart."

"No, Max."

He groaned and abruptly hauled her into his arms, the flash of desire in his eyes burning strongly for a moment. "You can keep me out of your bed tonight, but you owe me this kiss, damn it!"

"Why?" she challenged, bringing up her hands to push against his chest.

"Because I fixed your leaky plumbing!" Then he was drinking his fill from her lips as if he anticipated dying of thirst in the near future. His mouth moved on hers with the sensual, plundering provocation she had already learned was her nemesis. But before she could summon the will to resist, he freed her, stepping away with an annoyed, frustrated and dangerously male expression on his hard features. "If you'll excuse me, I'll get my coat and be on my way," he drawled far too politely.

Sophy waited restlessly in the kitchen for him to collect the old tweed jacket from the hall closet. She heard the closet door open and close, and then she heard nothing more. There was no sound of his footsteps coming back down the hall. Damn that man! If he thought he could get away with forcing his way into her bedroom, he had a few things to learn about her!

"Max?" she called menacingly as she went down the hall. There was no answer. "Max, where are you?" The light was off in the bedroom. If that man was playing games with her, she would be furious!

"I'm in here, Sophy," his answer finally came, sounding distant and vague, as if he were only half-aware of her call. The sound of his voice was emanating from her sewing room.

"Max? What in the world are you doing in here?" she demanded, pushing open the door.

"Just looking." He was bent over the large worktable, examining the pattern pieces lying on top of a length of material. He seemed as intent and curious as if he were looking at an oversized math problem. "How does all this work, Sophy?" he asked, glancing up briefly as she came into the room. "These lines on the pattern—they're very precise."

"Well, of course they're precise. Start out with a sloppy pattern and you'd wind up with a sloppy garment," she muttered, moving to stand on the opposite side of the table.

"The angles here—"

"Those are called darts. You use them to create shape in a piece of flat fabric, to help shape material to the human body. People have a lot of odd curves and angles on them, you know." A touch of humor laced her voice. "The wider the angle of the dart—"

"The greater the curving shape that will be created." He nodded at once, looking very serious.

"Well, yes," she agreed, momentarily surprised.

"What are these parallel lines for?"

"Pleats. They give fullness where I want it but with a sense of control."

He traced another line with the tip of his finger. "And this?"

"Just a seam line."

"And this curved section?"

"A collar. I want it to roll a bit, so I'm adding extra width at the outside edge." She leaned across the table to show the point where she had adjusted the outer curve of the pattern piece. "The more the neckline curve flattens, the greater the roll I'll get in the finished collar."

Max nodded again, looking surprisingly intrigued. Then he walked across the room and stood before a large sketch of a deceptively simple dress. "I think I can visualize how you get from the pattern to the finished garment," he said after a moment. "But there's no way on earth I could do it. And I can't even begin to figure out how you get from the sketch to the basic pattern. The original design is art. The pattern is a mathematical procedure. The final construction is art again. Amazing."

Sophy stood staring at him, equally amazed. No one from Max's world, not even her parents, had ever shown any interest in her work. The designing and construction of a garment were loosely labeled "sewing" and relegated to a pile of topics deemed mundane or frivolous. For a moment Sophy experienced a bond of communication, an understanding, that she rarely knew when dealing with someone from Max's world. He understood enough of her work to appreciate it. Her heart warmed.

She was still staring when Max turned around, swung his coat over his shoulder and walked back across the room to brush her mouth gently with his. "I'll go now, Sophy. But there's one other thing..."

"Yes, Max?" What was she hoping for. That he might insist on staying?

"I think you should call off whatever little scheme you've

got going with Marcie Fremont. The woman suggested corporate espionage to you once. No telling what she might involve you in now.''

The warmth that had crept into her began to fade. ''I know what I'm doing, Max. And the scheme isn't Marcie's idea. It's all mine.''

He frowned. ''Sophy...''

''Don't worry. This won't affect you. All I'm going to do is find Marcie another job,'' she said too easily.

''Sophy, I...'' He broke off on a sigh of resignation. ''You're not going to tell me what's going on, are you?''

''Last time I did that, you ran straight to Graham Younger.''

He winced. ''I thought it was for the best.''

''And look what you got us involved in.''

''I can see this conversation is going nowhere. Good night, Sophy. I'll see you at work.''

And then he was gone, leaving her with a new uncertainty and a new sense of ambivalence to add to her already unmanageable list of problems concerning Dr. Max Travers.

Chapter 9

The following morning Sophy put the next step of her plan into action. Marcie had selected her ideal company, a California firm run by a woman. It was a high-technology company competing in many of the same areas as S & J.

"I could really make a contribution there," Marcie said earnestly over coffee. "And there seems to be a fairly equal spread of men and women in management. It's an aggressive young firm, but it seems well founded financially. From what I can tell, though, the staff seem to be pretty heavy on technological skills and rather light on business experience. Maybe they could use someone like me who has a slightly different background."

"If that's the one you want, that's the one we'll go for," Sophy said firmly. "Oh, by the way, here's your new résumé." She handed the paper to Marcie.

"But, Sophy, this doesn't even sound like me," Marcie gasped after a moment's close concentration. "This makes

me sound...well, fabulous. Like I've been practically running S & J since I got here!''

"What we're going to do next," Sophy announced
smugly, "is get some letters from S & J management tes-
tifying to that."

"What?" Marcie looked startled.

"Let's go back to work, Marcie. I have some letters to
write."

The letters eulogizing the contributions of one Marcie
Fremont to S & J Technology went out to be signed by
appropriate members of management that afternoon. Sophy
judged it wise not to allow Marcie to see them before they
went out. The blond was liable to be somewhat appalled by
the liberties Sophy had taken.

"Actually, it's just a bit of creative writing," Sophy had
explained when Marcie anxiously tried to read one. "Now
go back to work. You've got your hands full doing my tasks
as well as your own today."

The first letter was slipped into a pile of correspondence
waiting to be signed by the vice-president in charge of planning. It graphically detailed Marcie's expertise in that area.
The second letter went into a stack sitting on the desk of
the president's assistant. In each case Sophy waited until the
executive's personal secretary was out of the office. Then
she waylaid the secretaries and chatted with them while their
bosses signed the letters while hurriedly pausing by the secretaries' desks. It was an easy matter to remove the letters
from the piles of legitimate correspondence when the secretaries turned their backs.

A few more such letters from important people in the
company joined the first two. And then Sophy wrote the
cover letter that was to accompany Marcie's résumé and
letters of recommendation. This she let Marcie see.

"But, Sophy, it says here I'm sending this packet of information at the request of their manager in charge of executive recruiting! I didn't get any such request.''

''Details.''

''Sophy, you're sending the letter to the vice-president instead of Personnel.''

''The first rule in dealing with a corporation is to ignore Personnel,'' Sophy assured her blithely, stuffing the packet into a large envelope. ''No one ever got a really high-level position by going through Personnel.''

Marcie stared at her in wondering admiration. ''You seem to know your way around corporations.''

Sophy grinned. ''I should. I've been studying them very carefully for several years. When I start my own business, I want to know as much as possible. Believe me, the vice-president who receives this packet will never figure out that his recruiting officer knows nothing about it.''

''I'm fascinated. What's next?''

''A phone call later on in the week after we know this envelope has had a chance to reach its destination.''

''Phone call? From whom?''

''From Graham Younger's office, of course, complaining loudly that the other firm is attempting to pirate you away. A few threats and requests to please not tempt you. That sort of thing.''

''From Younger's office?'' Marcie gasped.

''That's what the other company will think.''

''Who's really going to make the call, Sophy?'' Marcie demanded with an arched brow.

''Me.''

''Oh, my.''

''Believe me, hype is everything. Once they learn that S & J is frantic not to let you go, nothing will keep that California company from hiring you.''

"Sophy, something tells me I should stick around here a little longer and learn from you!"

Sophy laughed. "I won't be here much longer myself."

The phone call went as planned. By the time Sophy hung up the receiver she was feeling very pleased with herself. Now it was all a matter of time.

"But something tells me they won't take long beating a path to your door, Wonder Woman," she told Marcie with a laughing smile.

Max was aware of an oddly possessive sense of pride as he escorted Sophy off the plane and into the waiting lounge of the Raleigh-Durham airport. She was as vivid and colorful as ever today, he thought. Her expressive face was full of anticipation and pleasure at the prospect of seeing her parents. Even without the added effect of the racy turquoise jumpsuit she was wearing and the tumble of thick curls cascading down to her shoulders, that face caught and held one's attention. It held his at any rate, he amended wryly. She certainly wasn't trying to hold him with sex!

He still had no clear idea of what she was up to with Marcie Fremont, but he had made a conscious decision not to question his luck. She was still playing out the charade demanded of her by Graham Younger and his associates. Right now that seemed to be all that mattered. He'd keep an eye on her and make sure she didn't get into any real trouble. In the meantime, he'd told Younger's assistant that the plan was going well. They had agreed to let him manage things by himself until the crucial juncture.

The fact that there wasn't going to be a "crucial juncture" didn't particularly worry him. All he cared about was keeping Sophy within reach.

Until this past week Dr. Max Travers hadn't realized that he could actually lie alone in bed and hunger physically for a particular woman. The knowledge left him unsettled and restless, but it didn't affect him as badly as knowing that what he felt was not just a craving of the body. He found himself making every excuse imaginable just to be around Sophy. The time that he wasted running back and forth to her office to check up on the various reports she typed for him was appalling!

"Mom! Dad!" Sophy was running ahead, leaving Max to bring her small under-the-seat bag. He had a momentary wish that the obviously feminine case weren't such an eye-catching shade of magenta. Then he grinned to himself. If a man was going to hang around Sophy Bennet very long, he would have to get used to being seen amid a lot of color.

Max watched a little wistfully as Sophy threw herself into her parents' arms. Then he took a firm grip on himself. One of these days, he vowed, Sophy would learn to greet him that enthusiastically.

"Sophy, dear, it's so good to see you again." Anna Bennet smiled warmly as she hugged her daughter. The older woman was something of a contrast to Sophy, and Max had to look closely to see the faint traces of resemblance. They were there in the curling hair that Anna Bennet kept severely trimmed, and in the gentle shape of the nose, but they weren't startlingly obvious. Dr. Bennet wore a conservatively cut tweed skirt, a sweater and a pair of sensible shoes.

Sophy's eyes, Max decided, came from her father, although his blue-green gaze seemed slightly faded compared to his daughter's vivid one. Paul Bennet was taller than his wife and daughter, his gray hair cut much like Max's. The realization made Max wince. Maybe he should think about getting his dark hair trimmed in a slightly less conservative style. Sophy might like it better. Paul Bennet was still a handsome man, his strong features revealing the intelligence and character that had shaped his career. He was dressed in a slightly rumpled tweed jacket, and in his shirt pocket there was a plastic pack of pencils and implements. The horn-rimmed glasses reminded Max uncomfortably of his own pair.

Watching Sophy flutter energetically among the three of them as greetings were accomplished, Max realized just how different she was from himself and her parents. She was colorful and outrageous, whereas the other three were bland and conservative. She was lively and full of laughter while he and the Bennets were reserved and far quieter in their demeanor. Watching the Bennets interact with their daughter, Max had a flash of insight into just how difficult things must have been for Sophy at times. It had undoubtedly worked both ways, he decided. Paul and Anna Bennet must have had moments when they wondered whether or not their daughter had been a changeling, a mischievous elf substituted at birth for the quiet, serenely brilliant daughter who should have been theirs.

But there was love in the family, even if the three people concerned sometimes wondered how Paul and Anna Bennet had managed to produce such an unexpected sort of daughter. Max's sense of wistfulness grew. He had been everything his parents had wanted and more, and yet he'd never known this kind of family affection.

"Max! Glad you could make it," Paul Bennet said genially, extending his hand. There was genuine pleasure in the eyes that so resembled Sophy's, and Max relaxed. Sophy might not appreciate his interest in her, but her parents were quite content with him, he thought on a note of humor.

"Thank you, sir. To tell you the truth, I was glad of the excuse to take a break from Dallas." *And I'd have followed your daughter to the North Pole.*

"Miss North Carolina, do you?" Paul chuckled as he shepherded everyone to the baggage claim area.

Max cast an appreciative glance out at the rich green countryside. "Let's just say Dallas is a little different," he murmured dryly.

"Poor Max has been suffering greatly," Sophy informed everyone melodramatically. "Nearly three weeks of the real world and he's about to pine away."

"Sophy has done a great deal to cheer me up during the course of my exile," Max shot back smoothly, catching her eye and daring her to push the topic further. He received a speculative glance in return and then, much to his surprise, she moved on to another subject.

"What time is the ceremony and reception, Mom?" she asked brightly.

"Seven o'clock tonight. Did you bring something to wear?"

"What a silly question," Paul Bennet murmured as three huge magenta suitcases came trundling around the baggage belt.

Max grinned at the older man. "Sophy claims she likes to travel prepared."

Paul shook his head in wry affection. "She always did have a thing about clothes."

"I'll have you know that at least one of those suitcases is full of presents," Sophy tossed out indignantly as the two men picked up the colorful baggage. "After all, one can't go visiting an award-winning physicist without a few gifts!"

Max slid her a sidelong glance as he picked up the two heaviest cases and led the way out to the parking lot. She really was quite proud of her mother, he thought, in spite of her comments about academicians.

"Sophy's presents are always interesting, to say the least," Ann Bennet said with a knowing smile. She glanced at Max as the magenta cases were stowed in the back of the Bennets' car. "Has she had occasion to give you anything yet, Max?"

Max smiled as he slammed the trunk lid. "Yes, Sophy's given me some very special gifts," he said softly. He saw the sudden wariness in Sophy's eyes, and his smile broadened as he took her arm and guided her into the back seat of the car. "But I'm having a hard time finding out what she wants in return. Would you like me to drive, Dr. Bennet?"

"Thank you, Max." He handed over the keys. "It will give me a chance to talk to Sophy." He assisted his wife onto the seat alongside Sophy and then climbed into the front seat as Max started the car. "I understand the two of you have been seeing a lot of each other lately. Any surprises in the offing?"

There was a moment of electric silence during which Max considered a hundred different ways of saying he wanted Paul Bennet's daughter. But it was Sophy who rushed in to fill the breach.

"How did you know?" she demanded cheerfully. Max glanced quickly into the rearview mirror and caught the look of determination on her face. One thing was certain, she wasn't going to announce any engagement. "I've decided to open my own design boutique down in Dallas. I'm really very excited about it, aren't I, Max? Of course, I'll have to take out a loan, but I think I can get that. I made a dress for the woman who manages the loan department of my bank, and I'm sure she'll back me now that she's seen my work."

Another tense silence followed the exuberant announcement. It was Anna Bennet who broke it this time. "Oh, Sophy, dear, are you sure that's what you want to do? Have you given any more thought to going back for your master's degree? You know your father and I would love to have you get at least one more degree and we'd be more than happy to finance your educational costs.''

Sophy took a deep breath. ''Mom, I don't care if I never set foot on a campus again. Wasting time getting another degree is just about the last thing in the world I want to do. I'm going to open the boutique.''

Her father coughed meaningfully. ''But what about you and Max? I understood the two of you were hitting it off rather well. If the two of you decide to…that is, why would you want to open a little clothing shop if you're going to be getting—''

''Dad, I think this is an appropriate moment to say quite clearly that Max and I have absolutely no plans for marriage, do we, Max?'' Sophy challenged him from the back seat.

Max heard the defiant taunting in her voice and simultaneously sensed the questioning glances he was getting from both of the Doctors Bennet. Trust Sophy to find a way of putting him on the spot. Maybe the Bennets should have spent more time applying their palms to Sophy's sweet backside rather than force-feeding her quadratic equations.

''Your daughter, sir,'' he said coolly to Paul Bennet, ''seems to have a certain aversion to marrying anyone with a Ph.D. after his name.''

''Oh, is that the problem?'' Anna Bennet chuckled from the back seat, patting Sophy's hand affectionately. ''I'm sure you'll overcome her prejudice, Max. She always claimed she'd never marry a professor, but we've told her time and time again that when the right man comes along, she'll change her mind.''

''Well, since I haven't changed my mind,'' Sophy muttered forcefully, ''we have to conclude that the right man hasn't yet come along.''

There was a painful pause as everyone in the car absorbed the full implications of her words. There was no doubt but that her statement hovered on being an outright insult. Sophy, herself, bit her lip in sudden anxiety, wishing she'd kept her mouth shut. But, damn it, she wasn't going to be pushed into anything, regardless of what her parents wanted! Max had created this mess by answering the phone last Sunday morning. Let him figure a way out of it.

Guiding the car along the stretch of freeway leading toward the town of Chapel Hill, Max could almost read her thoughts. She was feeling pressured again and she was gong to fight the pressure, just as she had been doing for so many years.

"I get the feeling that Sophy would rather, er, live in sin than compromise her principles where professors are concerned," he drawled.

"I think it should be noted at this juncture," Sophy began dryly, "that I haven't been given a choice where Max is concerned."

Paul Bennet turned in the seat to stare quizzically at his daughter. "What are you talking about, Sophy? For heaven's sake, girl, make sense!"

"Okay, I'll lay it on the line," Sophy retorted with obvious relish. "Max has not asked me to marry him. Therefore, this whole discussion is absolutely pointless, isn't it, Max?"

He flicked another glance in the rearview mirror, and this time it was Anna Bennet's questioning gaze he found there. His hands tightened on the wheel.

"I have learned," Max said evenly, in response to the uncomfortable silence in the car, "that if one wants the best results from Sophy, one doesn't *ask* her anything. One tells her."

Suddenly Paul Bennet laughed out loud and a moment

later his wife joined him. "I think you may have the right approach, Travers. She's an independent little thing, isn't she?"

"Probably gets it from her parents," Max said gently.

Anna Bennet smiled contentedly. "Oh, we tried to make a proper daughter out of her, Max. Don't think we didn't try. But Sophy always went off on her own tangents. She brought home stray kittens instead of straight A's on her report cards. She read Nancy Drew stories when she should have been reading her Boolean algebra, and she was forever playing with scraps of fabric when she should have been playing with physics. Every time I turned around, the child had a crayon in her hand instead of a pencil and a calculator. When she was five, my entire kitchen was decorated with designs for doll clothes."

And your house was filled with color and the unexpected, Max added silently.

"Mind you," Paul Bennet inserted quickly, "she has the basic ability; it's just that her interests have never been, well, properly focused. That's why we keep hoping she'll go back to school."

"Dad, you don't have to sell me to Max," Sophy drawled from the back seat. "He knows perfectly well that I'm not a wizard. No point trying to fool him."

Paul shifted uncomfortably in the front seat, and suddenly Max found himself grinning conspiratorially at the older man. "Sassy, rebellious and undisciplined," Max said, "but I would say that the genes are undoubtedly quite sound. Couldn't be anything else coming from you and Anna."

"Max Travers!" Sophy nearly choked on her outrage, but everyone else was laughing and a moment later she succumbed to the humor of the situation. Max was getting a little too fast on his feet, she decided wryly. He was starting to hold his own in areas that had been exclusively hers, like taunting wizards.

By seven o'clock that evening equilibrium had been restored to the Bennet household. Max had walked from the Bennets' to his own home a few tree-shaded blocks away, saying he would return in time to walk with them to the campus where the ceremonies were being held.

"I'm going to see if I can dig out a new nerd pack for the occasion," he'd murmured to Sophy on the way out.

"Good idea," she retorted. "Why don't you fill it with crayons instead of pens and pencils? Might set a whole new style on campus." She smiled saucily as he gave her a strange glance.

When he returned at seven, wearing his best tweed jacket and his newest tie—which was still about an inch too narrow—Sophy and her parents were ready to go.

"You look very charming tonight, Anna," Max said politely, meaning it. She was dressed more fashionably than usual in a striking black and white suit that complemented her refined, academic air.

"Sophy made this for me." Anna smiled, gesturing at the skirt and jacket. "It was one of the presents in the suitcase."

Max looked at Sophy. "I've heard people say she's a genius with clothing design," he said softly. Sophy herself was wearing one of her typically flashy outfits, a tiny, pencil-slim suit with a nipped-in jacket trimmed with broad lapels. The suit was white, the lapels shocking pink. "What was your present, Dr. Bennet?" he asked, nodding at Paul.

"A smoking jacket." Paul Bennet chuckled. "Never had one before. Sophy says it will go nicely with the image. I'm supposed to sit in front of the fire and smoke my pipe in it. Really, my boy, I think it's time you started calling me

Paul," he added firmly as he pulled his wife's coat out of the closet.

"Thank you," Max murmured politely, his eyes on Sophy. "Are we ready?"

"Not quite," Sophy said abruptly, turning away to head down the hall toward the bedrooms. Her impossibly high heels made tantalizingly tapping sounds on the parquet floor, and Max watched until she disappeared.

In the bedroom she used whenever she visited her parents, Sophy opened one of the magenta suitcases and removed the last gift. Up until now she had been of two minds about whether or not to give it, but for some reason the decision had been made. Clutching it firmly in her left hand, she went back into the paneled living room where Max and her parents waited.

"Here," she said brusquely. "This one's for you, Max."

Behind the lenses of his glasses Max's smoky eyes flared for an instant before he lowered his gaze to the long, narrow box in her hand. "For me?" He looked as if he didn't know what to do with it, and Sophy found herself remembering all the Christmases and birthdays when his parents had forgotten to give him presents or had given him "learning" toys.

"Don't worry," Sophy murmured, "it's not an educational toy."

He grinned suddenly, taking the box with an eagerness that left her nonplussed. Wasting no time on the outer wrapping, Max tore off the paper and the small strip of ribbon and yanked open the box.

"A tie!" He lifted the length of silk fabric out of the tissue paper. For a long moment he simply stared at it, and then he looked at Sophy. "You made this?"

"Ummm." She nodded, feeling a little uncertain about her decision to give it to him. It wasn't really Max's style at all. Then again, could anyone truthfully say that Max had a style? "If you don't like it, I can always palm it off on Dad, here." The words were defensive and she knew it. Was she afraid of his rejecting the gift? What nonsense. How could it matter one way or the other? But it did. It mattered terribly.

"Sophy, it's beautiful. I've never seen anything like it." Max was turning it over in his hand, examining the delicate handwork on the other side, noting the way it had been cut on the bias. The silk was not a loud pattern, rather an unusually refined and conservative one, considering Sophy's basic tastes. It looked rich and elegant.

"You can make me one like that any time," Paul Bennet said to his daughter.

Anna Bennet looked bemusedly at the new clothes and the tie, and then at her daughter. "You really do have a certain talent, don't you, darling?"

Paul Bennet nodded agreement. "I hadn't quite realized…" He broke off as he peered over Max's shoulder. "Going to wear it tonight, Max?"

"You bet I am!" Max was already tearing free the old-fashioned narrow tie he was wearing, tossing it carelessly on a nearby chair. Then, collar flipped up, he stood in front of the living room mirror and knotted the new tie with careful precision. When the task was done, he stepped back and eyed his reflection with obvious satisfaction. "Thank you, Sophy. Thank you very much."

Before she realized his intention, he strode the three paces that separated them and kissed her soundly. As she stood there, blinking in wide-eyed surprise over her own actions, Max took her arm and guided her out the door. "Shall we go?" he asked. "Dr. Anna Bennet's fans will be waiting."

Anna Bennet laughed gently, her pleased eyes on the way Max was holding her daughter's arm. With her own arm linked in that of her husband, she traded a knowing glance with her mate. Then the four of them walked through the brisk evening toward the university campus.

Sophy watched the award ceremony with deep pride. Anna Bennet's accomplishments in the field of physics were known by many in the academic world, and the honors she received that evening were well deserved. No one knew that better than Sophy, and no one could have been prouder, unless it was Anna's husband, who glowed with pride and happiness.

The reception that followed the short ceremony was crowded with friends and colleagues of the Bennets' and of Max's. In fact, most of the academic community had turned out for the event. Sophy felt as if she had been plunged back into the world she had fought so long to escape. If it hadn't been for the fact that it was her mother who was being honored, she told herself as she hovered near the small hors d'oeuvre table, she would leave immediately. She'd always dreaded academic receptions. Lousy food and pompous people.

"Are you Sophy Bennet?" A somewhat rumpled-looking young man with wire-rimmed glasses, a corduroy jacket and curling hair that badly needed a cut smiled tentatively from the other side of the table.

Sophy smiled back, labeling him instantly and accurately as a graduate student. "Yes, I am."

The young man nodded in quick relief and adjusted his tie—a tie that was too narrow. "I'm Hal Anderson. A student of your mother's. She suggested I might like to meet you." His eyes darted curiously over her outrageously stylish appearance.

"I'm pleased to know you, Hal," Sophy said easily, helping herself to a pile of little cucumber sandwiches. "Was there some special reason you wanted to meet me?"

He turned a dull red. "Oh, no, well…that is, I, er, saw you standing over here and I sort of wondered aloud who you were, and your mother heard me and said you were her daughter and why didn't I come over and say hello."

Sophy nearly choked on her bite of cucumber sandwich and then recovered nicely. An academic pickup! She seemed to be rather popular with the academic community these days. Still, this was a student of her mother's and he really was rather sweet. "I'm glad you came on over, Hal." The young man relaxed slightly and smiled faintly. "What area are you specializing in?"

That was all the opening Hal Anderson needed. He plunged into a rousing discussion of solid-state physics that enabled Sophy to smile encouragingly a lot and munch cucumber sandwiches to her heart's content.

"Don't let Hal bore you to death," another man warned, wandering over to join in the discussion. "I'm Dick Santini. I'm in the math department."

"Oh, I'm quite fascinated with Hal's area of expertise. I'm sure he's going to make some outstanding contributions to his field," Sophy said smoothly. "And what about you, Dr. Santini? What area of research are you engaged in?"

Santini was well into a discussion of his work in spherical trigonometry, and Hal Anderson was putting in several more comments on physics, when two or three other graduate students and faculty members wandered up to join the discussion. Sophy found herself surrounded by earnest academicians, each eager to tell her about his line of work.

Across the room she briefly caught Max's eye and saw that he was beginning to frown as the group around Sophy grew. Cheerfully she smiled back, silently assuring him that she was quite content, and then she went back to orchestrating the discussion.

They followed her lead readily enough, and somehow her

pile of cucumber sandwiches grew rather than shrank as eager hands sought to make her comfortable. Somewhere along the line Sophy realized just how well she was doing juggling all the different academic disciplines. Where had she picked up this marvelous social skill? Heretofore at such receptions, she'd always wound up standing alone, unable to maintain any kind of conversation.

It came from juggling members of corporate management, she decided in a flash of perception. The thought made her smile broaden. Some skills were useful in both worlds.

"Excuse me, gentlemen." Max's deep voice cut through the lively discussion like a hot knife through Jell-O. Sophy glanced up at him and found that there was a certain amount of fire behind the smoke of his eyes. Max was looking a bit dangerous. "Sophy, I came to take you outside for a breath of fresh air," he began determinedly, moving to stand possessively close.

"Oh, I'm doing fine, Max. Dr. Mortenson here has been keeping my glass full of sherry and I don't feel the heat at all. We were just having the most interesting discussion on the applications of probability theory in various disciplines. Dr. Santini has done some fascinating work on the subject of—"

"I'm aware of Dr. Santini's work," Max drawled dryly.

Good grief, Sophy thought in astonishment, Max *was* starting to exhibit a certain southwestern accent. Strangely enough, although it had annoyed her faintly in Nick Savage, it seemed rather attractive in Max.

Dr. Santini was looking vaguely uncomfortable under Max's assessing glance and hastened to fill in the conversational lapse. "Miss Bennet is very interested in quite a variety of topics, Max."

"Is she?"

Sophy moved to intercept. "Oh, yes, Max! After all, occasionally one should check up on investments, don't you think?"

Everyone in the group, including Max, stared at her blankly. "Investments?" Dr. Mortenson asked.

"Well, of course," Sophy laughed gently. "You, all of you"—she waved a graceful hand to include the entire academic campus—"represent a considerable investment on the part of the business world. Sizable investments should occasionally be monitored."

"I'm not quite sure what you mean," Hal Anderson said carefully.

Sophy grinned. "Gentlemen, where do you think the money for research and education comes from? It comes from business. Funding universities and colleges represents a long-range investment in the future. The corporate world, the *working* world, has its faults, but you have to admit that it has the guts to put its money where its mouth is, even when it isn't always sure of what the final outcome will be. If there's one thing the business world believes in, it's the future."

There was a pause while the group digested that. Finally Hal Anderson chuckled. "Not the most flattering way of looking at the matter, but I suppose it contains a good deal of truth. I guess academic elitism sometimes sets in around a campus."

Sophy nodded wisely. "And corporate elitism sometimes sets in around a large company. People are people. But the reality is that the academic world and the business world are interdependent. We need the education and skills and research done on campuses to further practical development in the business world. And you need the continuing financial investment and support of the business world to continue your education and research. We all benefit in the end."

In her own way, perhaps, Sophy realized, she had been just as guilty of elitism as any academician. With that realization came another: She was no longer intimidated by the academic world.

"I just hope," Dr. Santini said wistfully, "that you'll continue to check up on your investments occasionally. A bit of interaction between the academic and business worlds is always useful..."

"Definitely," Hal Anderson declared. "Would you like some more cucumber sandwiches, Sophy?"

"Or some more sherry, Miss Bennet?" Dr. Mortenson asked anxiously.

Max made a firm bid for Sophy's arm, wrapping it protectively around his own. "I promised Anna Bennet I would rescue her daughter and return her to her parents," he said smoothly. "Come along, Sophy. You've done enough investment counseling for the evening."

Sophy slid him a sidelong glance as he coolly led her away. Her lips curved with inner laughter. "I think you may have spent too much time in Texas, Max. I'm seeing glimpses of lean, mean cowboy in you lately. Complete with accent."

He arched one brow over the rim of his glasses and there was a faintly sardonic twist to his mouth. "A good academician is always willing to learn, honey. I intend to get as good at handling you as you've gotten at handling members of a university faculty."

Sophy thought about that. "I did all right tonight, didn't I?"

"Sophy, honey, I've never seen you when you didn't do all right. Sometimes you scare the hell out of me!"

"You sound serious!"

"Professors of mathematics are always serious," he informed her. "And I will seriously consider beating you if I find you doing too many impromptu lectures on the inter-dependence of the academic world and the business world in front of an all-male audience!''

''Yes, Max, I do believe you've been a little too long in Texas.'' But in her heart Sophy was thinking about serious professors of mathematics. Was it possible she could be more to Dr. Max Travers than a pack of crayons? Would a serious academician like Max waste time pursuing a mere pack of crayons?

Together with that question came a pleasant feeling of having held her own very comfortably in a world that had always been distinctly uncomfortable.

Perhaps, as she had just lectured several members of the university faculty and staff, the two worlds were inter-twined. More than she had realized, herself.

Chapter 10

Max found himself unable to take his eyes off Sophy's profile as she sat beside him, staring out the jet's window. In another hour they would be back in Dallas. Back to where they started? The time in Chapel Hill seemed like a kind of truce that could be shattered again at any moment now that they were on their way back to Texas. There were so many questions. What was she up to with Marcie? How much longer would she be willing to play out the charade of having an affair with him for Graham Younger's benefit? How much time did he have?

Does she need me at all? Max wondered. *The way I need her?* Damn it to hell. What did you do with a woman who melted in your arms in bed but who kept you at arm's length outside it?

"I haven't thanked you for defending my boutique plans to my parents," Sophy said quietly, interrupting his thoughts. "It was very gracious of you to tell them you

thought the idea was a good idea and that you believe I
have real talent in business as well as design.''

Max leaned his head back against his seat. ''I meant it,
Sophy. Every word. You do have real talents as a designer
and a businesswoman. Even I can tell that.'' He fingered
the tie she had made. He was wearing it again today. ''I
think your parents appreciate your abilities. They just don't
understand the business world enough to see how you could
ever make a career out of what they've always considered
a hobby.''

''The academic world is their whole life,'' Sophy sighed.
''It's the only meaningful sort of career they can imagine.
Your defense of my plans gave me some credibility because
you have credibility in their eyes. Knowing you respected
my ideas made them think twice.''

''Sophy...''

''I'm rather grateful, Max.''

''I don't want your gratitude,'' he half snarled.

''I didn't think I'd ever have reason to be grateful to a
professor of mathematics, but it just goes to show, you never
can tell,'' she went on, sounding vaguely surprised.

''Consider it a dividend on your investment!''

Something told Sophy it might be time to shut up. Max's
temper these days had grown somewhat unpredictable. A
woman in love learned to read the signs, she told herself
wisely.

And then she realized exactly what she'd said. A woman
in love.

She was in love with Max Travers. In love with a wizard.
How could it have happened? Two hours later, as she threw
her magenta suitcases onto the bed and began to unpack,
Sophy was still turning the question over in her mind.

Could she really be more than a pack of crayons for Max
Travers? Maybe the urge to play with them was simply a

momentary diversion for him. But people like Max Travers, she reminded herself, rarely allowed themselves momentary diversions. They were too intent on the important things in life, like mathematics.

Max had been very silent tonight when he'd dropped her off at her apartment after the flight. He hadn't even attempted to kiss her good night. All he'd said as she got out of the car was that he'd see her at work in the morning. What had he been thinking? That he was tired of pursuing a pack of crayons who continually made life difficult for him? With a groan of apprehension and gloom, Sophy got undressed and went to bed.

For someone who had prided herself on her ability to deal with the real world, she seemed to have gotten herself into one heck of a mess.

It wasn't Max whom she saw first at work the next morning, however, it was Marcie Fremont. The other woman was already at work when Sophy entered the office. Marcie was always hard at work, Sophy thought with a rueful smile.

"How was the weekend?" Marcie poured coffee for both of them, eyeing Sophy curiously.

"Confusing. Interesting. Strange. I'm not sure how the weekend was, Marcie. My major accomplishment was surviving an academic reception without finding myself all alone in a corner."

"I can't imagine you ever finding yourself all alone in a corner at a party."

"I used to. Regularly. At least at academic parties. But it was different this time. It's been a while. I didn't realize how much I'd changed."

"A good feeling?"

"Yes." Sophy considered that further. "Yes, it was. I

actually felt relaxed. Definitely a change for the better,'' she concluded firmly.

Two hours later the phone on Marcie's desk rang imperiously. Sophy, who had been just about to leave with her friend for coffee, paused and waited as Marcie picked up the receiver. And then intuition made her lunge forward to grab the instrument from her friend's hand before she had even spoken a greeting.

"S & J Technology, Miss Bennet speaking," Sophy said crisply, waving off Marcie. "Yes, this is Miss Fremont's office. She's busy at the moment. May I take a message?... Oh, I see. Well, perhaps I could slip a message into the conference room where she's conducting the meeting. Would you care to hold?" Regally Sophy put the call on hold and turned to an astonished Marcie.

"It's them! It's that company in California. The vice-president we contacted!"

Marcie's eyes widened as she reached for the phone. Sophy saw that her fingers trembled slightly.

"Oh, Sophy. This is it!"

"Not yet. You mustn't sound to eager. You're an executive they're trying to pirate away, remember? You're only vaguely interested in the position."

"Vaguely interested!" But Marcie dropped her hand and smiled reluctantly. "What now?"

"We let them wait on hold for a few minutes, and then you come to the phone, a bit irritable but aloofly polite."

"Oh, my God!"

"You can do it."

And Marcie did do it. Beautifully. When they finally rescued the unfortunate caller from several minutes on hold, Marcie was in perfect command of herself. Cool, in charge, full of executive presence. And when she eventually hung up the phone, she stared at Sophy with eyes that shone.

"They're begging me to come to work for them. I've been offered my choice of two management positions. One reports directly to the president!"

"That's the one you'll take." Sophy grinned decisively. "We'll let them stew a couple of days and then you'll accept."

"And in the meantime?"

"In the meantime, we'll go have that coffee we were heading for when we were so rudely interrupted."

The two women walked to the elevators, drawing stares, as usual, because of the contrast they presented. They were unaware of the attention, however. Coffee break this morning was going to be a celebration.

Two days later Marcie made her phone call to California, and the excited, grateful company in California promised everything including a first-class airplane seat for the interview, which would be "merely a formality."

"You'll do beautifully," Sophy assured her, and then she reached for the phone on her own desk.

Max answered a bit brusquely and she knew she'd caught him in the middle of something. He softened immediately when he realized who was on the other end.

"I have to talk to you, Max," Sophy told him without preamble.

He didn't hesitate. "I'll be right down. The cafeteria?"

"Fine." She'd been spending a lot of time discussing business in the cafeteria lately, Sophy thought wryly.

Five minutes later she walked into the nearly empty room and found that Max had already obtained two cups of coffee and a private table. He looked up a bit warily as she came striding briskly toward him, and then his expression became impassive.

"It's over, Max." Sophy sat down and reached for her coffee. There was a deadly silence from the other side of the table. When she raised her eyes from her cup, she found Max looking at her with such intensity that she swallowed awkwardly and nearly choked.

"No."

That was all he said. She blinked in confusion. "But, Max, it is. There's nothing you can do. It's over."

"The hell it is!" He leaned forward, his palms flat on the table, eyes glittering icily behind the lenses of his glasses. "You're not going to just calmly phone me up and invite me for coffee and then tell me it's over. Not after all I've been through!"

Sophy edged back in her seat, shocked by the rough vehemence in his words. "Max, I'm sorry I started this whole thing by telling you what Marcie had planned, but at the time I sort of...well, panicked. I never wanted you to go to management with the information. But now everything's changed. Marcie has a new job and she'll be leaving the company soon. There's no way Graham Younger can ever implicate her in corporate espionage. You never even completed the phony model. There was no espionage."

"Marcie!" Max looked dumbfounded. "We're talking about Marcie? About your mysterious plans?"

"Well, of course. My plans to get Marcie a job in management. What did you think we were talking about?"

"You and me."

"Oh." Nonplussed, Sophy eyed him cautiously. He looked vastly relieved and at the same time thoroughly annoyed. "Well, uh, we're not. We're talking about the end of Younger's idiotic little scheme to trap Marcie and her 'web of conspirators.' Now we're going to have to tell Younger his brilliant plan didn't work, and I'm going to take great pleasure in doing so, if you want the truth."

She stood decisively and Max followed more reluctantly. "Uh...Sophy, there's something I have to tell you. You know this brilliant plan you've been criticizing from the beginning?'' He ushered her into the elevator.

"What about it?"

"Well, it wasn't exactly Graham Younger's idea."

"Edison's? The head of Security?"

"Nope. It was all mine," he sighed.

"Yours!" Sophy stared up at him, her mouth falling open in astonishment. "It was *your* idea to play out this silly farce just for the sake of trapping poor Marcie Fremont? But, Max…!"

"I'm afraid so. Younger and Edison and I agreed before the meeting with you that you'd be more likely to go along with it if you thought it was a request from your boss. Besides, Younger thought it was a pretty good scheme. One that would work. He was willing enough to take credit for it."

"But, Max…!" She swallowed. "Why?"

"Not because I give a damn about Marcie Fremont and her potential as a corporate espionage agent, that's for sure!" The elevator doors slid open on the executive suite floor. "You can bet I normally don't get involved in such mundane things as corporate security," he growled.

"So why did you become involved?"

"The single merit of this asinine scheme was that it ensured that you had to keep seeing me. Think about it."

"But, Max," Sophy couldn't help but say, "it was such a silly idea."

"I know. You'd think I'd have enough sense to stick to mathematics, wouldn't you?"

Chapter 11

"**Y**ou were marvelously arrogant with Younger and Edison, Max." Sophy gave him a mischievous smile as she sat across from him at dinner that night. "Thanks."

The scene in Graham Younger's office had not been pleasant, Max reflected as he munched the taco salad Sophy had insisted he sample. Younger and Edison were both angry at having had their potential prey snatched from their grasp.

They had been even more furious to learn they'd been outmaneuvered by a mere secretary. And word of Marcie's new management position had made Younger positively livid, especially when Sophy explained just how much Marcie's undervalued knowledge of S & J's Quality Control would benefit her new employer.

Sophy had seemed rather unconcerned about her boss's attempt to make mincemeat out of her, although Max had caught a flash of appreciative gratitude in her eyes when he'd stepped in and restored a certain civility to the proceedings.

And now she was thanking him. No, she wasn't actually *thanking* him, Max decided unhappily, she was merely complimenting him on having put the other two men in their place. She hadn't really needed him to defend her, he realized. Sophy didn't seem to *need* him for anything.

Therein lay the crux of his whole problem.

Max picked up his wine. "You were a little arrogant yourself."

She shrugged, the frilly, flounced sleeve of her red dinner dress shifting intriguingly. "I can afford to be a bit uppity." She grinned. "I'll be quitting soon."

"To open your boutique?"

"Ummm. How do you like the taco salad, Max?"

"I'm not sure I like hamburger and corn chips in my salads."

"You'll get used to it."

"I doubt it. I'm going back to North Carolina on Wednesday." He delivered the statement with a deliberate lack of intonation. How would she react? Probably be thrilled.

There was a beat of hesitation, and for the life of him he couldn't begin to imagine what she was thinking. "Where you can eat hush puppies all day long and work on math equations? Are you sure you can readapt? What about that Texas drawl you're working on?"

Max was suddenly tired of the flippancy. "Why don't you come back with me and find out what happens to it?"

Sophy flushed. "Sorry. I keep my visits to Chapel Hill to a minimum. I love my parents, but I knew a long time ago I couldn't live too close to them or spend too much time with them. I don't have to be in their company five minutes before they're giving such useful advice as telling me to go back for my master's."

"They aren't fighting your boutique idea," he pointed out carefully. She was avoiding the point, but he let her for the moment.

"Only because you defended it. People back down when you come to the rescue. Have you noticed that, Max? Younger, Edison, my parents, poor Nick. They all either respect your opinion or are intimidated by you now. Quite a track record."

"Except you."

"Except me. Would you like me to be intimidated by you, Max?"

"No. I'd like you to need me," he said flatly. She went very still. "The way I need you."

"Max," Sophy said. "You don't need me. Not really. I don't fit in your world. I never have. You'd be bored with me in two months!"

"Come back with me for two months and find out."

"No!"

"I think the truth of the matter is that you're the one who's afraid she'll be bored. Bored with a staid, sober, dull professor of mathematics." He looked straight into her eyes. "Sophy, I've given this a lot of thought. The only way things will ever really work between us is if you discover on some level that you need me. You have to decide that you really need me in your life." He spoke slowly, setting everything out in the open. He had nothing left to lose. "And there may come a time when you do decide that, Sophy."

"Max, I don't know what you're trying to say, but..."

"But I think you need a little time. You're basically a very bright young woman, just as your parents have claimed all along," he noted whimsically. "And now I believe you need some time to think."

"About what, Dr. Travers?"

"About such matters as why I kept wanting to see you, be with you, whenever possible, even though you had sworn you wouldn't go to bed with me again. About why I stepped outside my area of expertise to concoct that ridiculous scheme and then convinced Graham Younger to involve you in it. About a lot of things."

"Oh, Max…!" she wailed softly. "I don't know. I can't seem to think. It's all so confusing."

"That's why I'm going back to North Carolina on Wednesday. Sophy, when you've thought it all out and made your decision, I'll be waiting." He leaned forward to catch her agitated fingers and squeeze them gently. "Come back to Chapel Hill anytime, sweetheart. You'll find me there, waiting for you."

Max sat in his third-floor corner office, oblivious to the lush green grounds of the campus outside his window, and wondered if he was going out of his mind.

He hadn't been able to concentrate on anything since he had returned from Dallas. Oh, he'd gotten through the work on his desk and occasionally he'd picked up an article in one of the many esoteric journals he read. But the intense concentration that had always characterized him seemed to have disappeared. He had to struggle to think of anything at all except Sophy.

It had only been five days since he'd left Dallas. Monday morning. He had a graduate seminar in half an hour. He hoped he could fake his way through it. Shouldn't be too difficult. The students were studying the work of Evariste Galois, the brilliant French mathematician who, because of his fiery temper, had managed to get himself killed in a duel at the age of twenty. People had wondered for years just how much Galois might have gone on to contribute to the world of mathematics if his temper hadn't been quite so passionate. Before his death he had already established himself as one of the most original thinkers who ever lived.

For the first time in his life Max thought he understood Evariste Galois. Never before had he been able to comprehend a man as brilliant as Galois letting himself get sidetracked from his real work long enough to become involved in such an idiotic thing as a duel over a woman. Now he could.

He'd skip the graduate seminar altogether if it meant he could fight another cowboy for Sophy. Some things were more important than math.

He *must* be going out of his mind to think that!

Max crumpled the piece of paper he'd idly been twisting into a Möbius strip, a shape with the curious property of having only one side, and listened to the staccato tap of a pair of high heels out in the hall.

The sound reminded him of Sophy. Bright, energetic, alive. He wondered who on the third floor had worn high heels today. Usually the women in his department wore more sensible shoes.

The aggressive tap of the heels came to a halt outside his door and he glanced up automatically, aware that his body was tense with anticipation, just because of the sound of a pair of high heels that reminded him of Sophy. Things were getting worse. He really was going to go slowly out of his mind if he didn't do something drastic.

The knock on the door made him frown. "Come in." Simultaneously he realized that the sound of the high heels in the corridor had stopped. Whoever was knocking on his door was wearing the shoes. It was going to be painful to have the door open and find another woman besides Sophy standing there.

But the door opened and it wasn't another woman.

"Sophy!" Max surged to his feet. He felt dazed. "Sophy,'' he repeated far more softly. He realized he was staring, but he couldn't help himself. It was almost impossible to believe she was here in his office, bringing light and color and confusion to his orderly surroundings. Her mane of curls seemed more delightfully frizzy than ever. The high heels he had heard tapping out the exciting rhythm in the hall were purple. Max thought vaguely that he'd never seen purple shoes. They went wonderfully with the purple and red dress she was wearing. Nobody else he knew could successfully wear purple and red. But the best color of all was the strange blue-green shade of her eyes. And right now those eyes were smiling at him.

"Hello, Max,'' she said softly. "I brought you something.'' She came toward him, carrying a small package in her right hand.

Feeling as if he were moving under the force of a spell, Max extended his hand for the gift. It wasn't what he wanted to do. What he really wanted to do was grab Sophy and hold her close to make certain she was real and not a bright illusion. She put the package in his fingers and he looked down at it.

"Sophy.'' He wasn't certain what to say next, so he tried to concentrate on unwrapping the package. The paper fell away beneath his unusually clumsy attempts, and he stared at the box of crayons, a slow smile edging the corner of his mouth. "Thank you.'' Damn it, couldn't he think of anything more intelligent?

"Do you still want me, Max?''

He heard the uncertainty and the wistful hope in her voice and groaned, dropping the crayons on his desk to walk around the front and pull her into his arms. "Sophy, honey, I've been sitting here for five days thinking about what I was going to do if you didn't come to me.'' He buried his face in the cascading curls and inhaled deeply. "My God, Sophy, I can't believe you're really here."

He held her close, and when her arms went around his waist he muttered her name again and searched out her mouth. For a long moment they clung together, mouths joined in heated dampness, their bodies touching intimately. Max let the tension seep out of his body, felt the happiness welling up inside. She was here. He couldn't believe his luck.

"Sophy, honey, I know I'm no macho cowboy..."

"No," she laughed into his shirt, "you're a macho university professor. Until you came along, I didn't know they existed. You've got a foot in both worlds now."

"So do you. How can you doubt it after the way you handled yourself at that faculty reception? And the way you handle yourself in the corporate world is a bit frightening! Someday I want to hear the whole story of how you got Marcie Fremont that job in California."

"Someday I'll tell you. You'll probably be shocked, though."

"Nothing you can do would shock me anymore," he murmured.

"Then maybe you really have come out of your ivory tower!" She lifted her head abruptly. "What would you have done, Max, if I hadn't come to Chapel Hill?" she asked, her eyes wide and inviting.

"I told myself I'd give you a month or so and then I'd find some excuse to fly back to Dallas. I was making lists of reasons I could give S & J Technology for having to update that math model I did for them."

"Your creativity outside the realm of math leaves me breathless," Sophy laughed gently.

"Don't worry. When creativity fails me I can always fall back on my new macho mentality."

"The direct approach?"

"Umm. Like carrying you off over my shoulder."

"Max, you wouldn't! Imagine what your colleagues would think."

"That's their problem. I learned a few things down in Texas."

"Yes, I know." Sophy grinned ruefully. "Like how to fix plumbing, and grill steaks, and wear stylish ties." She let her hand trail lightly down his shoulder to the tie he was wearing. She smoothed it affectionately. "You're going to wear out your new tie, Max."

"You can make me another one."

"I will."

"A wedding gift?" he suggested tenderly.

"You want to marry me?" He saw the flutter of hope and joy in her eyes and gathered her close again.

"That's the logical conclusion when two people are in love."

"Love? You love me, Max? Are you sure?"

"I'm very, very sure." He wrapped her close, his voice husky and low. "Only love could have made me go crazy that night after you discovered that dumb cowboy was cheating on you. I've never taken advantage of a woman before in my life! A whole lifetime of being a gentleman went up in smoke. And the worst part was that I didn't regret it afterward. That was just the beginning. When I found myself concocting ridiculous schemes so that I could have an excuse to go on seeing you, I knew I was in over my head."

"Oh, Max, I've always been so careful to steer clear of people in your world. I was intimidated by wizards for so long. I couldn't bear the thought of loving a man who couldn't possibly respect me as an equal."

"Sophy, you have your own kind of wizardry. You're an

artist and a businesswoman. Do you realize what a rare combination that is? Few people have the ability to be both. I have a tremendous respect for your abilities.''

''But my parents always thought—''

''Darling, I'm very fond of your parents. They've been wonderful to me. But I'm aware they're a little blind where you're concerned. They love you deeply, but they don't quite understand you. That's why they've always tried to push you back into their world—a world they do understand.''

Sophy slanted a wondering glance at his loving eyes. ''You're a bridge between my world and theirs, aren't you Max?''

He gave her a strange half smile and shook his head. ''No, you're the bridge, Sophy. For all of us. If it wasn't for you in their lives, occasionally turning it upside down and filling it with confusion, your mother and father undoubtedly would have turned out a lot like my parents. Cold and unemotional and completely secluded in their academic world. I probably would have wound up like my parents too, if it hadn't been for you. I was well on my way! But I looked out of my ivory tower one day and saw what I'd been missing.''

''The fun of brawling with cowboys?'' she taunted gently.

''And the joy of eating popcorn while watching old sci fi flicks, and of seducing you. Most of all seducing you. I need you. You make my life complete. But I can't help wondering why you love me, although I'm not about to question my luck!''

She saw the anxious hope in his eyes and lifted her finger to smooth the harsh brackets around his mouth. ''Much to my astonishment, I found myself loving you for some of the same reasons you say you love me,'' she admitted softly.

''When you left Dallas all the color went out of my life. But it's so much more than that. I realized I had to take the chance of going to you. Our worlds may be different, but they complement each other. You make me feel complete. I love you.''

He was watching her face with raw hunger now in his eyes. There was a longing in him that was a combination of love and desire and need, and Sophy felt herself responding to the potent mixture.

''I never thought wizards were capable of real passion for anything except their work until I met you,'' she breathed.

''You bring out the passionate side of me, along with a few other sides I didn't know existed.''

''And you bring out some sides of me I didn't know existed, either. I've taken risks with you I've never even thought of taking with any other man. I can't imagine being willing to come back to Chapel Hill for any other man. But with you I was willing to take the chance. And I can't imagine letting myself get seduced by a man I hardly even knew the way I did with you. Oh, Max, we've both done some crazy things around each other, haven't we?''

''We should have realized it was love right from the beginning,'' he drawled.

''But I thought I had nothing worthwhile to give a wizard,'' she said wistfully.

''And I thought I had nothing worthwhile to offer someone like you, who seemed to have everything and who seemed to prefer cowboys. Sophy, will you marry me and live with me for the rest of our lives?''

She linked her arms around his neck and smiled dreamily. ''Yes,'' she whispered, touching her lips to his. ''Yes, yes, yes.'' A teasing light came into her eyes. ''But do you suppose North Carolina is ready for my style of clothing design?''

She felt Max's warm chuckle as it moved through his chest. "Possibly not. But even if it is, I'm rather inclined to agree with your feeling that you should live some distance from your parents. It's true that you now have me to run interference with them when they start worrying overmuch about your lifestyle, but I think, all things considered, we'd be better off in Texas."

"Texas!" Startled, she stared up at him. He ruffled the curling halo of her hair and smiled.

"Umm. I hate to sound arrogant about this, knowing as I do how you feel about arrogant math wizards, but frankly, I can write my own ticket to any school in the country. How does Austin sound? I know it's not Dallas, but…"

"Austin. You're going to get a job at the University of Texas?"

"Why not? I had an offer from them last year, which I put on ice as I usually do. But if I were to change my mind, I don't think there would be any problem."

"But, Max, you've got tenure here."

"Tenure isn't particularly important to me. Your career is a lot more important. And I think you could pursue it better in a wide-open state like Texas than you could in North Carolina. And in Texas you won't have to worry about your charming parents gazing over your shoulder all the time."

"You really mean that, don't you? You're willing to take another position in another state for my sake? Max, I don't know what to say. I'm stunned."

"The expression is very becoming on you. Don't worry, honey, it's all going to work out perfectly."

"But will you be happy in Texas?"

"Sweetheart, I've begun to think lately that I was born in Texas," he drawled in his new accent. "I fit right in down there. Didn't you notice? I spent all my spare time brawling and grilling steaks and taking you to bed. A classic Texan. First thing I'm going to do when we get there is buy a pair of hand-tooled cowboy boots suitable for squashing rattle-snakes.''

"Max, I love you."

"I love you." He feathered her mouth lightly with his own and then suddenly remembered something.

"Sweetheart, I'm supposed to be teaching a graduate seminar in about two minutes..."

She noticed that he didn't sound too concerned. "Really?"

"But I think my students will understand that mathematics can't always come first," he murmured, reaching behind him to punch an intercom button. Quickly, he arranged for an associate to take his place, then beckoned her. "Right now I've got other things on my mind besides teaching class. We Texans keep our priorities straight, you know."

"Ah, the marvelous, multidimensional, eminently logical mind of a wizard," she murmured, going back into his arms. "As a matter of fact, I was thinking about keeping the same priorities straight."

"Must be a case of great minds traveling on the same path."

"Could be. You know, I've come to the conclusion you're going to be very useful around the house, Max. I've got this checkbook that hasn't been balanced in six months, for starters."

"It's so nice to feel needed." He grinned wickedly. "Honey, I will be happy to barbecue your meals, fix your plumbing, fight off cowboys and balance your checkbook. But there is a price for a wizard's services. I believe I once pointed out that I don't come cheap."

"What's the price?"

"Let me show you." His mouth came down on hers, and Sophy gave herself up to the wizardry of love.

*   *   *   *   *

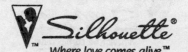

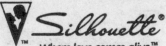